WISH ME LUCK

Fleur Bosley didn't believe in love at first sight, until she bumped into Robbie Rodwell in the blackout. Posted to a Lincolnshire airfield, Robbie as a wireless operator on bombers and Fleur as a radio telephone operator, their only escape is the little cottage Fleur shares with another WAAF, Ruth. Hurt by the loss of one of the pilots, Ruth disapproves of wartime romances, and she is not the only one. When Fleur's mother hears Robbie's surname she becomes hysterical. While secrets from the past threaten their future, Fleur must keep watch, praying that Robbie's plane will come back...

WISH ME LUCK

WISH ME LUCK

by

Margaret Dickinson

Magna Large Print Books
Long Preston, North Yorkshire,
BD23 4ND, England.

British Library Cataloguing in Publication Data.

Dickinson, Margaret
    Wish me luck.

    A catalogue record of this book is
    available from the British Library

    ISBN   978-0-7505-2833-7

First published in Great Britain in 2007 by Macmillan
an imprint of Macmillan Publishers Ltd.

Published in Large Print 2008 by arrangement with
Pan Macmillan Publishers Limited

Magna Large Print is an imprint of Library Magna Books Ltd.

Printed and bound in Great Britain by
T.J. (International) Ltd., Cornwall, PL28 8RW

ACKNOWLEDGEMENTS

Many people have helped me in my research for this novel. I am especially grateful to Mick Richardson for his generosity in lending me the private papers and flying log book of his father, Sergeant W.J. Proffitt, the wireless operator of a Lancaster bomber, who was killed whilst on a bombing mission in March 1944.

My thanks also for his help to my brother-in-law Peter Harrison, who flew thirty missions as a wireless operator during the Second World War; to Mrs Lillian Streets and Mrs Barbara Brooke-Taylor for sharing with me their memories of their time in the WAAF; to Mike Smith, Curator of the Newark Air Museum, for answering my questions; to Fred and Harold Panton at the Lincolnshire Aviation Heritage Centre at East Kirkby for all the marvellous displays and wealth of information that have helped me so much, and to Michael Simpson, head of exhibitions at the Imperial War Museum North, Trafford Park, Manchester, for his advice and help.

I have also consulted numerous books in the course of my research, but special mention should be made of *A WAAF in Bomber Command* by Pip Beck (Goodall, 1989) and *Square-Bashing by the Sea (RAF Skegness, 1941–1944)* by Jack Loveday

(J. Loveday, 2003).

Very special thanks to the members of my family who read and commented on the script: Robena and Fred Hill, and David and Alan Dickinson. As always, my love and thanks to all my family and friends whose support and encouragement means more than I can say. And not forgetting Darley and his Angels at the Darley Anderson Literary Agency and Imogen Taylor, my editor at Macmillan. To all of you – you're always there when I need you – thank you!

One

APRIL 1941

Fleur Bosley stepped down from the train, hitching her kitbag onto her back. The platform was in darkness, the blackout complete. She moved forward carefully. It was like stepping into the unknown. Behind her someone else jumped down from the train and cannoned into her, knocking her forward onto her knees. She let out a cry, startled rather than injured. At once, a man's voice came out of the darkness. 'Oh, I'm sorry, miss. I didn't see you.'

His hands were reaching out, feeling for her to help her up, but she pushed him away. 'I'm all right,' she said, feeling foolish.

A thin beam of torchlight shone in her face. She blinked and put up her hand to shield her eyes. 'D'you have to do that?' she asked testily, but the only answer coming out of the darkness was a low chuckle. 'I just wanted to see if whoever I knocked over was worth picking up.' A young man's voice, deep with a jovial, teasing note in it.

'Well, you needn't bother trying to pick me up.' She emphasized the words, making sure he knew she understood his double meaning.

His only answer was to laugh out loud. 'Come on, the least I can do is buy you a nice cuppa. Let's see if there's a cafe or a canteen open somewhere nearby.'

'Shouldn't think so at this time of night,' she said, slightly mollified by his offer as she bent to feel around for her kitbag. Fleur hadn't had anything to eat or drink since midday and her throat was parched. Travelling from the south of the country had taken all day. There'd been delays all along the line because of air raid warnings and now she was stranded in Nottingham with no promise of further transport for the last leg of her journey. Fleur was hungry, thirsty – and cross!

'Here, let me...' The man shone his torch and picked up her bag, then ran the beam of light up and down her.

'Snap!'

'What?'

'You're a WAAF.' He turned the light on himself and she saw he was wearing RAF uniform. 'Come on, you can't refuse a cup of tea with me now, can you?'

In the darkness, she smiled. 'Oh, go on then.'

Minutes later, as she was sitting at a table whilst he went to the counter to fetch two teas, she was able to study him. Tall, with fair, curly hair; bright, mischievous blue eyes; a firm, square jaw and the cheekiest grin she'd ever seen. As he came back, set the tea on the table and sat down opposite her, she knew that he, in turn, was appraising her.

She took off her cap and laid it on the chair beside her. Shaking out her soft brown curls, she returned his gaze steadily with a saucy sparkle in her dark brown eyes. 'Will I do then?'

He took in her smooth skin, her small, neat nose and perfectly shaped mouth that was delicately enhanced with just a touch of pale pink lipstick. 'Oh, you'll do very well, miss. It's usually little grey-haired old ladies I knock over, not pretty young ones. My luck must be changing.' He held out his hand across the table. 'Robert Rodwell, at your service. But my friends call me Robbie.'

She was about to answer tartly, 'How do you do, Mr Rodwell.' But something in his open face made her put her hand into his warm grasp and say instead, 'Fleur Bosley. Pleased to meet you – Robbie.'

As they drank their tea, he asked, 'So, where are you heading? Here in Nottingham?'

'No. South Monkford. It's a small town not far from Newark.'

Robbie nodded. 'Yes, I know it.' A slight frown line deepened between his eyebrows. 'I think we used to live there years ago, but my mother never talks about it much and we came to live in the city when I was little. But I seem to think my father – he died before I was born – ran a tailor's shop there.'

Fleur wrinkled her forehead. 'Can't think of a tailor's shop there now. There's old Miss Pinkerton's; she's a dressmaker and–'

'That's it. That'll be the one. Mother said once that a woman who was a dressmaker had taken it over.'

'Her and her sister run it. They sell women's clothes.' She giggled. 'They call it "Pinkertons' Emporium", would you believe? They're sweet old dears, but they're both a bit doddery now. And their shop is so old-fashioned. It's like stepping back in time when you walk in.'

13

'All corsets, wool vests and big knickers, eh?'

Fleur laughed and pretended to be coy. 'Really, sir, saying such things to a lady. And when we've only just met too. I do declare!'

They laughed together, feeling already as if they had known each other far longer than a few minutes.

'So – were you hoping to get to South Monkford tonight?' Robbie asked.

Fleur pulled a face. 'I was, but it's doubtful – there won't be a train out of here now. I could ring up and get my dad to fetch me, but I don't like to ask him to come all this way at this time of night. And using his precious petrol.'

'You've got a car? *And* a telephone?'

Fleur grinned. 'Yes. The car's called Bertha. It's a 1923 Ford and it's seen more "active service" down dirt tracks and across fields than many a tank. As for the phone – we live on a farm in the middle of nowhere. My mum insisted it was essential.' Her brown eyes twinkled. 'But I think it's just so that we've no excuse for not letting her know exactly where we are and what we're doing.'

'And do you?'

'What?'

'Let her know exactly where you are and what you're doing?'

Fleur laughed. 'Not likely!'

Trying to sound casual, but failing, Robbie asked, 'Er – who's "we"?'

'My brother, Kenny, and me. And Dad too. She likes to keep us all close.' There was an edge of resentment in her tone as she added, '"Tied to her apron strings" is the phrase, I think.' Her face

14

clouded and a small frown puckered her smooth forehead. She didn't know why, but for some reason she felt she could confide in him. The words were out before she'd even thought to stop them. 'She ... she didn't want me to volunteer. It ... it's caused a lot of rows at home.'

'That's a shame,' he said gently. 'How long have you been in?'

'Oh, right from the start. I volunteered as soon as I could.'

His blue eyes twinkled. 'Me too. The day after Mr Chamberlain's "we are at war" broadcast.'

They stared at each other and then smiled, amazed that they'd both felt the same.

'Are they calling up women yet?'

'Don't know,' Fleur replied cheerfully. 'I didn't wait to find out.'

'And you live on a farm? You could've applied to be classed as a reserved occupation, couldn't you?'

Fleur grimaced. 'I know. That's why my mother was so put out. I could quite legitimately have stayed at home for one reason or another, but I didn't want to. I ... I wanted to "do my bit" as they say.'

'But you're not regretting it, are you?'

'Not for a minute.' Her reply was swift and genuine. 'But it's still – well – difficult when I go home.' She sighed. 'But I'll have to go. I've just been posted and I've got three days' leave before I have to report there. It might be a while before I get any more.'

'Where are you going?'

She opened her mouth to reply and then

15

hesitated, her smile causing two deep dimples in her cheeks as she said impishly, 'I'm not sure I should be telling you. Careless talk and all that.'

'Well, I'll be terribly careless and tell you exactly where I'm going. Wickerton Wood just south of Lincoln. It's a new airfield. Parts of it are still being built, so they say, but it's ready enough to start flying.'

Fleur's eyes widened and she couldn't prevent a little gasp of surprise. Chuckling, he leant forward to say softly, 'Don't ever volunteer for special operations, will you? Your face gives you away. That's where you're headed too, isn't it? Wickerton?'

Feeling reprimanded, she nodded and murmured, 'Oh dear.'

'Don't worry,' he said cheerfully. 'Your secret's safe with me.'

'Is ... is that where you're going now?'

'Yes, the day after tomorrow, but first I'm going home to see Ma.'

'What are you going to do at Wickerton Wood?'

'Ah, now that *would* be telling.'

'You're right. I'm sorry,' she said at once.

He laughed with a deep chuckle that was infectious and somehow endearing too. Don't be silly, Fleur, she told herself firmly, you've only just met him. He could be anybody. But already, she realized he wasn't just anybody. He was someone she'd like to get to know so much better. The thought surprised and shocked her.

Fleur regarded herself as a no-nonsense type of girl: down to earth and with no foolish romantic notions, especially now that they were plunged into war and all its uncertainties.

'I was only teasing.' The sound of his voice brought her back and she saw that his eyes were suddenly serious. 'You know,' he went on and now there was a note of surprise in his tone. 'It might sound daft, but I feel I could tell you anything.' Then, as if fearing he was sounding soppy, the mischievous twinkle was back and he leant towards her again. 'You're not a spy, are you?'

Now Fleur laughed. 'No. Like you say, I'd give the game away all too easily. Too honest for my own good, that's me.'

'Mm, me too.'

She hesitated, but then asked, 'Where've you been up till now?'

His face clouded. 'Down south. It's been pretty rough for the past few months, especially between July and October last year. The Battle of Britain, as Churchill called it.'

'Is that what you are?' she asked, filled with a sudden dread. 'A fighter pilot?' She knew all too well the average number of ops a fighter pilot was expected to survive and then...

But Robbie was shaking his head. 'No – no. I'm on bombers.' His smile crinkled his eyes. 'I'm a wireless operator.'

But Fleur wasn't comforted. She shuddered. 'Don't ... don't wireless operators have to – have to fill in for other crewmembers if...' Her voice trailed away.

He was looking at her keenly. 'If one of them gets injured?'

Wordlessly, she nodded.

'I'm trained as an air gunner too. And yes, sometimes it happens, but not often.' He paused

17

and then asked, 'How do you know so much?'

She took a deep breath. He'd know soon anyway if they were both going to be working on the same station. 'I've just finished training as an R/T operator. That's what I'm coming to Wickerton to do.'

'Ah,' he said, understanding. 'A radio telephone operator? Yes, I'd heard a lot of WAAFs are being trained for that. One of the chaps was saying he thinks it's because a woman's voice is more high-pitched. Comes across the airwaves better.'

Fleur pulled a comical face. 'At least you know what we do. Most people just look blank when I tell them.'

'Will you be in Control?'

'I ... I don't know yet. Maybe.'

He smiled. 'It'll make a nice change to have a lovely girl to talk us down when we come back from a raid...' He paused a moment and then added softly, 'Or who waits up all night for us if ... if we're late?'

A lump came into her throat as she remembered how they'd all been warned during their training that that was exactly what they'd be expected to do. Wait and wait into the small hours until there was no more hope. 'Are you fixed up with a crew?'

'Oh yes. We met up at Operational Training Unit. They put us all together in a huge briefing room and left us to sort ourselves out. It's a very informal way, but it seems to work.' He laughed. 'That way, it's unlikely you end up flying with a chap you can't stand the sight of.'

Fleur nodded. 'I'd heard that's what happens at OTU, but ... but doesn't it make it more difficult?

18

Flying with people who become your friends?'

Robbie's face sobered as he shook his head. 'Strangely, no. I expect it's a bit like the "pals' regiments" they had in the last war. There's just something about going into battle with a "brother" at your side.' He paused and then added, 'I've been lucky. Tommy Laughton, the skipper, is a great bloke. You can't help but like him and the rest of the crew – well – I'll soon be getting to know them a lot better. But they seemed OK. We'll be flying Hampdens, we've been told. With a crew of four.' Robbie grinned, trying to lift the mood that was getting all too serious for his liking. 'We shouldn't be talking like this.'

'No.' She forced herself to return his smile. 'There's more than likely a policeman hiding behind the counter over there ready to spring out and arrest us for careless talk.'

As the cafe was now otherwise deserted – even the girl behind the counter had disappeared – they laughed together at the likelihood of anyone overhearing them. That they perhaps should not trust each other never occurred to either of them for a moment.

'What did you do? Before the war, I mean.'

'Worked in a bank.'

'Oh, very posh!' she teased.

He grimaced. 'It was a good job, I have to admit, but it was a bit too staid for me. I was always getting told off for cracking jokes or laughing with the customers. We're supposed to be very polite and formal. I agree with the polite bit, but–' He cast his eyes to the ceiling in mock despair. 'The formality got to me in the end. I couldn't wait to get out.'

'But there's lots of rules and regulations in the RAF surely. It can be very "formal". All that saluting officers and calling them "sir".'

'True, but most of them have earned the right to be treated with that degree of respect.' He leant forward. 'And there's always the compensation of nights out with the lads, *and* – best of all – flirting with a pretty WAAF.'

Fleur arched her eyebrows sardonically, but smiled nonetheless.

'So? What are you doing for the night then?' he asked.

'Bed down in the station waiting room,' she replied promptly. 'It won't be the first time I've done it.'

'Oh no, I won't hear of it. You're coming home with me. You can have my bed. I'll sleep on the sofa.'

Fleur suddenly remembered just how short a time she had known this rather nice young man. Her face sobered, but he read her thoughts at once. 'Of course, I've got an ulterior motive.' He pretended to leer at her, but then added, 'But there's not much a chap can do with his mother in the next bedroom. And my grandfather lives with us too. We'll be well chaperoned.' He pulled a comical expression, displaying mock disappointment. 'More's the pity.'

'But it's an awful imposition on your mother. Bringing a strange girl home in the middle of the night.' Impishly, she added, 'Or is she used to it?'

'Sort of. One or two of the lads have bunked down at our place when they've been stranded, but this'll be the first time I've taken a *girl* home. She'll not mind a bit, though. She helps out at the WVS and she's always picking up waifs and strays from the forces, taking them home and feeding them.'

'Well, if you're sure...'

'I am,' he said firmly as he got up and picked up her kitbag as well as his own. 'We've got a bit of a walk, though. Hope you're up for it?'

'Now if my drill sergeant could hear you even asking me that – I'd be on a charge!'

Laughing together, they stepped into the blacked-out street.

Two

'Let's get inside quickly,' Robbie said as he unlocked the front door of the terraced house. 'Our warden has got eyes like a hawk and if he sees the tiniest chink of light, he's down on us like a ton of bricks.'

Fleur giggled. 'That's an unfortunate turn of phrase, isn't it?'

Through the darkness, she heard his chuckle. 'Yes, I see what you mean. We might get a ton of bricks on top of us literally if Jerry sees a light when he's flying over.'

They were still laughing, his hand cupping her elbow as he guided her into the strange house in the darkness. 'This is Ma's best front room.' The door from the street had opened directly into it.

'Be careful, because she–' he began when the inner door opened and a light streamed in.

'Robbie? Is that you?'

'Hope so, Ma,' he called out cheerily, 'else you've got burglars.'

'Oh, you rogue! Come on in and let me see who you've brought home this time.'

Fleur drew in breath sharply and was about to kick his shins for having lied to her, but as he led her into the light of the next room, she saw the surprise on his mother's face and knew it was genuine.

'Oh! A WAAF!' The woman smiled a welcome and held out her hands. 'And what a pretty one too.'

'I bumped into her in the blackout, Ma. Knocked her over getting off the train as a matter of fact.' He put his arm about Fleur's shoulders with an easy familiarity that she was amazed to realize she didn't mind. 'You could say she fell for me there and then.'

Now Fleur did retort, muttering beneath her breath so that only he could hear, 'You should be so lucky!'

She heard – and felt – his laughter rising from deep within his chest. She glanced up to find him looking down at her, his face so close that she could feel his warm breath on her cheek. In just that brief moment she noticed the way his eyes crinkled at the corners when he laughed and the tiny, stray hairs at the end of his eyebrows. And his smile – oh, his smile – such white, even teeth with tiny spaces between them. She'd only to stretch just a tiny bit and she could've kissed his mouth... At the unbidden thought, she felt the blush rise in her face.

'The least I could do was bring her home,' Robbie went on smoothly as she felt him squeeze her shoulder. For one foolish moment she wondered if he could read what was in her mind. 'She can't get transport tonight to where she wants to be,' he went on, explaining to his mother. 'I couldn't let her sleep in the station waiting room, now could I?'

'Dear, dear,' Meg Rodwell tutted. 'Certainly not. Come in, love, and make yourself at home. You're very welcome.'

Now that Fleur's eyes were becoming used to the bright light after the darkness, she saw that Robbie's mother was slim and youthful looking. Her shoulder-length red hair, showing not a trace of grey, was swept back over her ears in curls and waves. Her green eyes smiled a welcome. She was wearing a fashionable patterned cotton dress with short sleeves and padded shoulders, its hem only just covering the knees of her shapely legs. Fleur couldn't help smiling at the contrast between this woman and her own mother, who, as a busy farmer's wife, had little time for 'titivating', as she would have called it. Fleur's mother wore her greying hair drawn back into a bun at the nape of her neck and dressed in plain blouses and skirts that were usually covered with a paisley overall. And sensible shoes were a must about the farm. At the thought, Fleur looked down at Mrs Rodwell's dainty feet. It was no surprise to see the high-heeled shoes with a ribbon bow at the front.

But the woman was smiling so kindly at her, drawing her further into the room and towards a chair beside the warm fire burning in the grate of the old-fashioned kitchen range. Fleur gave a start as she suddenly noticed a bent old man with a crocheted shawl around his shoulders sitting on the opposite side of the hearth.

Robbie let his arm slip from about her and moved towards him, putting his hand on his shoulder. 'Now, Pops. How are you?'

The old man looked up and reached out with a hand that was misshapen with arthritis, the knuckles swollen and painful. 'Mustn't grumble, lad, mustn't grumble.'

'You never do, Pops.'

To Fleur's surprise, the old man's eyes watered as his fond gaze followed Robbie's mother while she bustled between kitchen and the back scullery, setting food on the table. 'No,' he said in a quavering voice. 'Because I know how lucky I am.'

Meg came into the room carrying two laden plates. 'Come and eat. You must be starving. I'll just go and change the sheets on your bed, Robbie...'

Fleur roused herself. The warm fire was already making her drowsy. 'Oh, please, don't go to any trouble on my account. I can sleep on the sofa–'

'I wouldn't hear of it–'

'Certainly not–'

Robbie and his mother spoke together and the old man laughed wheezily. 'There you are, lass, outnumbered.' He tapped the side of his nose. 'And if you take my advice, you won't argue with m'lady here. Rules the roost, she does.'

'Now, Dad.' Mrs Rodwell stepped towards the old man, tucked the shawl cosily around him and planted a kiss on his white hair. 'You'll have this nice young lady thinking I'm a regular tartar.'

Robbie pulled a comical face. 'Well, you are.' He winked at Fleur. 'We'd better do as she says before I get my legs smacked.'

As Robbie towered over his mother by at least eight or ten inches, Fleur could not suppress a giggle at the picture that sprang into her mind of the grown-up young man hopping from one foot to another to avoid the chastising hand. They were all laughing now.

'Come and eat.' Robbie urged her to take a seat at the table. 'And then it's night-nights for you. You look as if you might fall asleep in the gravy.'

'What did you say her name was?' Meg Rodwell asked her son the following morning as she cooked breakfast.

'Fleur,' Robbie replied, his mouth full of fried bread. They had both been so tired the previous evening that, once they had eaten, Meg had shown Fleur to Robbie's bedroom and he had headed for the sofa set against the wall in the cluttered front room which his mother used, working from her home as a dressmaker. Despite the austerity of the war – or more likely because of it – there were still many calls on Meg's talents with her sewing machine. 'Make do and mend' was the order of the day. Whilst much of her work was now altering and re-styling second-hand clothes, it was a matter of pride to Meg that she was still able to support her family. And now that Robbie contributed some of his RAF pay whenever he came home on leave, she didn't have to work long into the night these days. Though she would gladly have worked around the clock if it meant keeping her boy safe.

Smiling brightly as she determined not to spoil their few precious hours together with her darkest fears, Meg turned to greet the young WAAF her son had brought home as the girl appeared in the kitchen. She looked rested this morning, but still a little self-conscious and perhaps feeling awkward now at having allowed herself to be taken home by a complete stranger.

'Come and sit down, love,' Meg greeted her warmly. 'What would you like to eat? I'm sorry I've no eggs–'

'Please, don't apologize. I don't want you to go to any trouble. I feel very embarrassed, descending on you like that in the middle of the night and eating your rations.'

'Don't mention it. We were glad to help. Sit down, do.'

'What about the old gentleman?'

Meg laughed. 'Oh, he doesn't get up until later. You're not taking his place or his breakfast – I promise.' She returned to the stove in the scullery, but left the door open so that she could talk to them as they sat at the table. Dropping a single rasher of bacon into the frying pan, she said, 'Now, have your breakfast and then Robbie will walk you back to the station. Where is it you're going?'

Fleur sat down at the table. 'South Monkford.'

Meg was suddenly very still, staring at the girl.

'South Monkford,' she murmured, her eyes misting over. 'Fancy.'

'Robbie mentioned that you used to live there.'

Meg nodded slowly. 'A long time ago,' she whispered. 'A long time ago now.'

'My father had a tailoring business there, didn't he?' Robbie put in. 'And didn't you say someone called Pinkerton took the shop over from you? Well, Fleur says they're still there. Two old dears – sisters – running it.'

'Fancy,' Meg murmured again, prodding absent-mindedly at the sizzling bacon.

'Maybe you know Fleur's family. Her surname's Bosley–' Robbie began, but he got no further as his mother turned sharply, catching the handle of the frying pan. It clattered to the floor, spilling hot fat and the precious piece of bacon over the tiles and splashing her legs. Meg's hands flew to her face and her eyes were wide, staring at Fleur. She swayed as if she might fall.

'Ma? Ma, what is it?' Robbie was on his feet and moving swiftly to catch hold of her. He helped her to a chair, whilst Fleur hurried to the tap in the scullery to get a glass of water.

'Here,' Fleur said gently. 'Drink this.'

Meg took the glass with shaking hands and sipped it. 'I'm sorry. How stupid of me.'

The young couple glanced at each other and then, concern on both their faces, looked back at Meg, but neither asked the questions that were racing around their minds. It had been Fleur's name – her surname – that had startled Meg so.

'I'm sorry,' Meg said, placing the glass of water on the table and taking a deep breath. 'It was just

27

hearing your name.' She looked up into the open face of the lovely girl standing in front of her, so smart, so confident in her WAAF uniform.

And now she looked more carefully she could see the likeness. The rich, brown hair and deep, dark brown eyes, watching her at this moment, with such concern.

'How is he?' Meg asked softly. 'How's Jake?'

Now it was Fleur who sank into a chair, staring at Robbie's mother. 'My dad? You ... you know my dad?'

Meg nodded.

'He ... he's fine.' Fleur waited a moment but Meg volunteered no more. 'How d'you know him?'

'I–' Meg hesitated. It was an ironic and cruel fate that had conspired against her to bring these two young people together. The past that she wanted to keep buried was doing its best to catch up with her. She must say nothing. It was not her place to be telling this girl things that perhaps her parents had never told her and most likely didn't want her to know. After all, she hadn't told her own son, had she?

Meg shuddered, and Robbie sat down beside his mother too, chafing her hand that was suddenly cold between his warm ones. He was willing Fleur not to ask any more questions that were obviously upsetting his mother. 'Are you all right, Ma?'

Absently, as if she had only just become aware of the pain, Meg rubbed her leg. 'The fat splashed, but it's nothing.'

'You ought to put something on it.'

'Don't fuss, Robbie,' she said sharply, her spirit

returning, the colour coming back into her face. 'I'm all right.' Now she turned to Fleur. 'I'm sorry, my dear. How silly of me.' She was back in control of her feelings now and of the situation. But inside she was still quaking. I must be careful what I say, what I ask, she was thinking. Forcing a brightness into her tone, she said, 'It was just hearing the name after all these years. Of course I knew your father when we lived there. Both your parents.'

The two young people were aware that there was much more to it than just that. They glanced at each other, wanting to ask more, but afraid of distressing Robbie's mother again.

But in her turn and despite her desire to let secrets stay hidden, Meg could not stop herself asking, 'Are they still at Middleditch Farm? Still working for the Smallwoods?'

Fleur hesitated but, seeing Robbie's slight nod, she answered, 'Dad owns the farm now. The Smallwoods both died about eight years ago and they left the farm to my father and mother.'

Meg gasped and before she could stop herself, she blurted out, 'Not – not to their daughter?'

Fleur was puzzled. 'I didn't know they had a daughter.'

Meg closed her eyes and shook her head. 'I'm sorry, I shouldn't have said anything.'

Again Fleur and Robbie exchanged a glance, but their attention was brought back to his mother as she asked one last question. Was it Fleur's imagination or was there a slight hardening of her tone as Meg asked, 'And your mother? How is Betsy?'

Three

'So – what do you make of all that then?' Robbie said as he pulled the front door shut behind them and shouldered Fleur's kitbag. They began to walk side by side along the street towards the station.

Fleur frowned. 'I honestly don't know.'

'There's more to it than she's letting on,' Robbie said.

'Well yes, I thought so too, but I didn't like to say. I mean, it's none of our business, is it? Certainly not mine.'

He touched her arm. 'I'd like it to be. I'd like to see you again. We're going to be on the same camp. It shouldn't be too difficult. I mean – that is if ... if you...?' He was suddenly boyishly unsure.

She smiled up at him, surprised that he even needed to ask. 'Of course I want to see you again. That's if you want to be seen with a lowly ACW, Flight Sergeant Rodwell?'

'Mm,' he murmured absently as if the matter of rank was the very last thing on his mind at this precise moment. He squeezed her elbow. 'It's strange, but I feel as if I've known you years.'

'I know,' she said simply and without being conscious of what she was doing, she slipped her arm through his and they walked closely side by side, matching their strides.

They didn't speak again until they were standing on the platform. Robbie had put her kitbag in the carriage and now they stood facing each other. He put his hands on her shoulders, smiling down at her. 'I'll see you soon then?'

She nodded and now she did what she'd been wanting to do almost since they'd first met. She stood on tiptoe and kissed him. Not a chaste kiss on the cheek, but on his wide, generous mouth.

As she drew back, he laughed softly and murmured, 'You hussy...' Then his arms were tightly around her, his warm mouth on hers. Her arms wound themselves around his neck, her body pressed to his.

A whistle sounded and a merry, gruff voice said, 'Break it up, now. Train's leaving if you're catching it.'

They broke apart and turned to see the guard with the whistle in his hand, grinning at them. 'Sorry, folks, but the train can't wait.' The man's craggy face softened. 'Not even for you.' In his job he saw so many partings, so many tears. He often wondered what happened to all those youngsters whose poignant goodbyes he witnessed. Did they meet again or did those tears of 'sweet sorrow' become a deluge of grief?

But these two were laughing and blushing, and the older man guessed their love was new and young, just on the threshold... But his train couldn't wait – not even for love.

Fleur scrambled aboard and leant out of the window, clasping his hands. 'Come out to the farm later,' she invited rashly, 'and bring your mother.'

'I'll be there. Can't vouch for Ma, but I'll be there,' he vowed.

He stood watching the train out of sight, marvelling that in the space of a few hours he had found the girl he wanted to spend the rest of his life with. However long or short, he thought soberly, that life might be.

'I wish you'd've let me know you were coming. I could've come to fetch you from Nottingham last night.' Jake Bosley frowned worriedly. 'I don't like the idea of you going home with a complete stranger. Even if he is in the RAF, he could be anyone.'

Fleur grinned as she dropped her kitbag to the floor, returned her father's bear hug and then dutifully kissed her mother's cheek.

Betsy sniffed. 'It's nice of you to remember you have a home.' There was a pause before she added, 'When are you going back?'

Deciding to ignore the barbed remark, Fleur responded gaily, 'Good old Mum. You always say the same thing. It sounds as if you can't wait to get rid of me again.'

Betsy's mouth tightened. 'You know very well that's not the case. We never wanted you to go in the first place. But you had to have your own way, didn't you? Couldn't wait to get away. Anyone would think—'

'Now, now, Betsy love. Don't spoil the precious time we've got with her,' Jake said, trying as he always did to quench the sparks that so easily flared between mother and daughter.

'I'm sorry, Mum. I was only teasing.' Fleur kicked herself mentally. She ought to know by now that her mother rarely took teasing from anyone – unless, of course, it was Fleur's younger

32

brother, Kenny, doing the tormenting.

Fleur turned back to her father. He was still frowning anxiously. He was a good-looking man and middle age was being kind to him, for there were only a few flecks of grey in his thick, brown hair. His build was stocky and strong from years of farm work even though he walked with a stiff leg – the result of a wound in the Great War that everyone had believed would 'end all wars'. How wrong they had all been! But she saw now that the laughter lines on his face were deepening into anxiety and the look in his dark brown eyes troubled her, for she knew she was the cause.

He hadn't wanted her to join up. Neither of them had. Her mother had cried and stormed and demanded that she stay at home, whilst her father had gone about his work on the farm with a worried frown permanently on his face.

'You don't have to go. You're doing important work here on the farm,' he'd tried to insist.

'You'll be killed,' Betsy had wailed dramatically. 'I know you will.'

'Oh, Mum, girls don't fly. I'll just be on an aerodrome. In the offices or the canteen or – or something.'

'Airfields get bombed,' Betsy had persisted. She'd got Fleur dead and buried already before she'd even signed up. But for once Fleur had stood her ground. She wanted to do her bit, wanted to see something of life away from the farm, though of course she didn't tell them that.

'Kenny's still here.' She'd tried to soften the blow. 'He's too young to go.'

'That depends on how long this wretched war

33

goes on,' her mother had said bitterly. 'He's seventeen now.'

'Only just,' Fleur said.

'What if it lasts another two years?' her mother persisted. 'He'll get called up when he's nineteen. And I bet,' she added bitterly, 'it won't be long before they lower the age for call up.'

'But he'll work on the farm. Dad can apply for a deferment for him. He won't have to go,' Fleur had argued.

'But he *will* go.' Betsy's voice had risen hysterically as she'd said accusingly, 'Because he'll copy you. He idolizes you. You can't do anything wrong in his eyes.' There was more than a tinge of jealousy in Betsy's tone. It was she who idolized her son, and she made no effort to hide her possessiveness. Miraculously, the boy himself was unspoilt by her favouritism and Fleur enjoyed an easy, bantering relationship with her brother.

'It's the mother–son and father–daughter thing,' he'd once said laughingly, showing a surprising insight for one so young. 'You're Dad's favourite.'

But Fleur wouldn't allow that. 'No, he doesn't have favourites. You know that. But maybe he's a bit more protective of me because I'm a girl.'

Kenny had grinned. 'Nobody's ever going to be good enough for his little girl, eh?'

Fleur had laughed. 'Something like that.'

It hadn't mattered then – there'd been no young man she'd been serious about. But now...? Well, now it was different.

'As a matter of fact,' she said carefully, 'the young man I went home with wasn't a complete stranger.'

Jake's face cleared. 'Oh, it was someone you know?'

'Not exactly,' she said carefully. 'Someone *you* know, or at least, used to know.'

The frown was back, but this time it was a puzzled look rather than a worried one that creased Jake's craggy features. And, strangely, there was a touch of wariness in his eyes.

'Do you remember someone called Mrs Rodwell and her son Robbie?'

Before Jake could answer a cry escaped Betsy and, her eyes wide, she pressed her hand to her mouth. And then to Fleur's utter amazement, Betsy began to scream. 'No, no, not her. Oh, not her. I thought she'd gone for good. I thought–' She clutched wildly at her daughter, her fingers digging painfully into Fleur's arm. 'You're to have nothing to do with him. Do you hear? He's a bad lot.'

Jake moved forward at once and put his arms about his wife. 'Now, now, Betsy love, don't take on so. Surely, after all this time–?'

Betsy twisted to face him. 'Leopards don't change their spots, Jake. She'll never change and her son'll be like her. Self-centred, devious, spiteful.' She rounded again on Fleur. 'What did she say? Does she know who you are?' Betsy was still like a wild thing, screaming questions at her daughter. Fleur stared at her. She'd seen her mother in some tempers, but never – in all her life – had she seen her quite like this. Completely out of control.

'Mum–' She reached out but Betsy slapped her hands away as if her daughter's touch was suddenly abhorrent.

Fleur let her arms fall to her side. 'Actually,' she said flatly, realizing that the tentative romance that had already begun between her and Robbie was doomed. 'She was as shocked as you are when she heard my surname, but she ... she didn't react quite as ... as...' Fleur faltered and her voice dropped to a whisper. 'Well, not like this.'

'She took you in, you say?'

Fleur nodded.

Betsy's voice hardened. 'So – what was in it for her?'

'Mum!' Fleur was appalled. She'd liked Robbie's mother. She couldn't believe the things her own mother was saying about her. Mrs Rodwell had been so kind, so welcoming. And the old man; she hadn't had much of a conversation with him, but he'd seemed a dear old boy.

Fleur sighed and said flatly, 'I don't know what you're getting at, Mum. But there was nothing "in it" for her, as you put it. She was just nice to me. Cooking breakfast for me. Apologizing because she had no eggs when there I was – a complete stranger – taking their rations.'

'But you're not a stranger.'

'I was then. She was doing all that before she knew my name. And Robbie says she works for the WVS. That she's always taking home waifs and strays. And she looks after the old man–'

'Ah! I knew it! She's got another poor old boy in her clutches.' Betsy was scathing now. 'Well off, is he?'

'An old man?' Even Jake was curious now, but Fleur was startled by the sudden bleak look in his

36

eyes. 'Who was he? Her husband?'

'I ... I don't think so. Robbie called him "Pops". And ... and ... yes, she called him "Dad".' Fleur looked from one to the other, puzzled and more than a little alarmed by their reaction. 'He must be her father.'

'Her *father!*' Now Jake was shocked. 'My God!' he murmured, and he was obviously stunned. 'Her father.'

'Huh!' Betsy pulled her mouth down at the corners. 'It'll more likely be a fancy man who's old enough to *be* her father.'

But Fleur was watching the strange, thoughtful look in Jake's eyes.

Betsy's voice was still high-pitched, demanding, 'I want to know what she *said.*'

'She asked how Dad was.'

'I bet she did. Oh, I bet she did!'

Fleur blinked under the vehemence in her mother's voice. She glanced at her father, but he was far away, lost in his own thoughts. She looked back at her mother, hoping to placate her. She couldn't know that it was entirely the wrong thing to say as she added, 'And she asked about you, too.'

'Wanted to know if I was still around, I suppose. Hoping I wasn't. Hoping I was dead and in my grave.'

'Mum!'

'Betsy!'

Jake and Fleur spoke together, shocked by Betsy's hysterical outburst. Jake went on, 'Now that's enough. You've no call to–'

'No call? No call, you say? Look at the lives she

37

ruined with her ... with her carryings on.' The venom was spitting out of Betsy's mouth. 'But you still love her, don't you? All these years you've never stopped loving her, and if she so much as crooked her little finger you'd go running.'

Fleur gasped and felt the colour drain from her own face as she listened to her mother's terrible accusations.

Jake's face was dark with anger, any sympathy and understanding gone from his expression. His wife was pushing him just a little too far now. 'That's not fair, Betsy, and you know it. I've always loved you and our children. I've done my best to be a good husband and father, haven't I?' He turned his head slightly and now his question included his daughter. 'Haven't I?'

Fleur moved swiftly to his side and linked her arm through his, hugging it to her. 'Oh, Dad, of course you have.' She turned towards her mother. 'Mum–'

'You stay out of this.' Betsy's voice was still high-pitched. 'It's nothing to do with you.'

'Well, as a matter of fact, I think it has. You see – I'm sorry – but I invited Robbie to come out here to tea this afternoon. And ... and I said he could bring his mother if ... if he wanted.'

For a moment Betsy stared at her. Then she let out a chilling scream and began to pull at her own hair like someone demented. Jake released himself from Fleur's grasp to take hold of his wife, but she struggled against him, beating his chest with her fists, crying and screaming, even kicking out at him. Jake winced as the toe of her sturdy shoe caught him on the shin.

'Dad?' Fleur raised her voice above the noise her mother was making. 'Shall I fetch the doctor? Shall I call Dr Collins?'

There was a sudden silence in the kitchen as the screaming stopped abruptly. But then Betsy began to laugh – a hysterical sound that was more chilling than her crying.

'Oh yes, oh yes. Call Dr Collins – and his wife. Let them all come. Let them all meet. I'm sure Dr Collins would like to meet his–'

To Fleur's horror, Jake suddenly clamped his hand across Betsy's runaway mouth. 'That's enough,' he bellowed in a tone that brooked no argument.

Four

Middleditch Farm lay five miles from the small town of South Monkford amidst gently rolling countryside. Robbie – and his mother, if she came – would have to take the Nottingham to Lincoln train, get off at the Junction and catch the little train that the locals called 'the Paddy' out to South Monkford. Fleur hadn't dared to ask her father to meet the train. Not now. So, from the town railway station they would have to hitch a lift out to the farm. That afternoon Fleur walked down the lane some distance from the farmyard gate to waylay Robbie and – more importantly – his mother. Fleur frowned as she went over in her mind every little detail of her own mother's frenzied outburst. Her father was tight-lipped about it all. He would explain nothing.

Jake had released his hold on his wife, glared at her for a moment, then turned on his heel and gone outside into the yard, slamming the back door behind him. Betsy had stared after him, pressing trembling fingers to her mouth.

Fleur had stepped towards her, holding out her arms. 'Mum–?' But Betsy had let out a sob, turned her back on her daughter and run up-stairs to her bedroom, slamming the door just as Jake had done.

Fleur had winced and stood alone in the kitchen, biting her lip. After a moment, she'd followed her father outside and found him leaning on the gate, staring with unseeing eyes at the spread of land before him that was now all his. She'd stood beside him, resting her arms on the top of the gate.

'Dad–?'

'Leave it, Fleur.' He'd sighed heavily, his anger dying as swiftly as it had come. 'It all happened a long time ago and it's best left buried. It's over and done with.'

'It doesn't sound like it as far as Mum's con-cerned,' she'd retorted. Immediately she regretted her words when she saw the bleak expression that flitted across her father's face.

'Oh, Dad,' she'd said, putting her hand on his arm and trying her most cajoling tone. 'Won't you tell me what it's all about?'

His hand had covered hers as he'd replied softly, 'I … I can't, love. They're not my secrets to tell.' And he'd refused to say any more.

For mid-April, it was surprisingly hot and still in

the lane, sheltered from the light breeze by hedges on either side. Fleur spread her greatcoat on the grass and sat down beneath the shade of two huge trees, the branches rustling gently above her. She leant back against one of the trunks, her gaze still on the corner of the lane. She wanted to see him again – even wanted to see his mother again. She'd liked her. But part of her wanted them to stay away. For, if they did come, how was she going to explain that they weren't welcome at Middleditch Farm? She certainly couldn't risk taking them home. She didn't want her mother throwing another fit. Nor did she want to see that terrible haunted look on her dad's face.

Fleur loved her dad – loved both her parents, of course, but she was fiercely protective of her father. She didn't really understand why – couldn't have put it into words – but for as long as she could remember she'd sometimes seen a strange, sad, faraway look in his eyes and, even as a little girl, she'd felt the instinctive desire to shield him from hurt. Only the touch of her tiny hand in his had brought him back to his happy present, as he'd hugged her to him or ruffled her hair affectionately. As she'd grown older she'd thought his moments of melancholy were because of Betsy's preoccupation with Kenny, believing her father felt neglected and excluded. It had drawn her even closer to him.

But now, she wondered, was that sadness, buried deep, to do with Robbie's mother? If it was, the re-minder of it had made her own mother hysteri-cal...

There was something tickling her nose.

Drowsily, she brushed it away, and then she heard his soft chuckle and opened her eyes.

'Sleeping Beauty,' he teased. He was lying beside her, leaning on one elbow and tickling her with a piece of grass.

She gave a startled cry and sat up. 'I must have fallen asleep.' She blinked and rubbed her eyes as she looked around her. 'Where's your mother?'

'She hasn't come.' For a moment, his eyes clouded. 'Said it wouldn't be right.' He shrugged. 'I don't understand why though.'

'I do,' Fleur said promptly. 'At least, part of it. I think I know why she hasn't come.'

She lay down, leaning on her elbow so that they were facing each other. 'There's something gone on in the past between them all. I don't know what it is – they won't tell me – but it must be something pretty awful 'cos my mum threw a ducky fit.'

'A what?' He was laughing in spite of himself.

Now Fleur grinned too. 'Sorry. It's something one of the girls I met while training was always saying. It must be catching.'

'I take it your mother wasn't best pleased?'

'That's an understatement if ever there was one. I've never – in my whole life – seen her act like that. Oh, she gets a bit het up about things. Fusses and flaps about anything and everything – usually about our Kenny – but this morning she was screaming and shouting and hitting out at my dad when he tried to calm her down.'

'Good Lord!' Robbie frowned thoughtfully for a moment and then said slowly, 'My mother was sort of – well – odd. Not hysterical or anything,

42

but you saw how shocked she was when she heard your surname.'

Fleur nodded. 'Did she explain why?'

Robbie shook his head. 'No. Shut up like a clam. She went very quiet and seemed lost in a world of her own. I couldn't reach her, if you know what I mean.'

'Oh, I know exactly what you mean. I bet it's the same sort of look my dad sometimes has. As if he's lost in the past.'

'That's it. That's it exactly.' They stared at each other for a moment before Robbie said slowly, 'You … you don't think there was – well – something between them, do you? Between your dad and my mother? Years ago?'

Fleur nodded. 'There must have been because … because in amongst all my mum's shouting and hysterical crying she said, "All these years, you've never stopped loving her."'

'And you think she meant my mother?'

Again, Fleur nodded, but now she said no more. She couldn't for the heavy feeling growing within her chest, a feeling of ominous foreboding.

Robbie blew out his cheeks as he let out a long sigh. 'Crikey! Now I see why Ma wouldn't come with me today and why you're waiting for me in the lane.' His blue eyes were dark with disappointment. 'I take it I'm not welcome at your home?'

She shook her head, not trusting herself to speak for the lump in her throat.

He sighed again and sat up, resting his arms on his knees and linking his fingers. His back was towards her as he said flatly, 'So, you don't want to see me again?'

Fleur sat up too and touched his arm. Slowly, he turned to face her. They gazed at each other for a long moment before she said, 'I *do* want to see you again. I mean – that is – if you want to see me.'

'Of course I do.'

She smiled and felt a warm glow at the swiftness of his reply. 'But,' she went on, 'we've just got to realize what we might be getting ourselves into. We won't be able to visit each other's homes.'

'You can come to mine. Ma won't mind.'

'Are you really sure about that?'

'Well...' She could see the sudden doubt on his face.

'She was very kind to me last night,' Fleur went on, 'and even after she knew who I was, but that doesn't mean she'll want to see me again. Have me visiting, reminding her...' There was a long silence before Fleur said, 'So do you see why I say, "as long as we realize what we're getting ourselves into"?'

'Yeah,' Robbie's mouth tightened. 'Right into the middle of a Shakespeare play by the sound of it.'

Fleur laughed, stood up and held out her hand to pull him up. 'Just so long as you know I've no intention of committing suicide over you like Juliet.'

He stood close to her, still holding her hand and looking down into her dark brown eyes. 'And that's another thing.'

'What is?' she whispered, suddenly frightened by the serious look in his eyes.

'Death. Not by suicide, of course. But I face it

every time we take off on a bombing run. And you're not in exactly the safest job there is, are you? Airfields are constant targets for the enemy.'

'I know,' she said quietly. 'But we're only in the same boat as thousands of others. We ... we've all got to take our happiness when we can, haven't we?'

Robbie nodded. 'Damn right we have. And damn the past and all its secrets. We're living in the present.' Though he didn't speak the words aloud, as he took her into his arms and bent his head to kiss her Robbie was praying silently: Dear Lord, grant me a future with this lovely girl. Don't let me end my days in a burning plane, or her buried beneath a pile of rubble on a bombed-out airfield. Let us grow old together, with our grandchildren at our knees...

Five

'There's something else I want to ask you.'

'Fire away,' Robbie said, resting his elbows on the small table in the cafe where they were sitting. They were determined to spend the afternoon together, even if they were not welcome at Middleditch Farm, and had walked back to South Monkford, hitching a ride on a farm cart for part of the way.

'Who's the old gentleman who lives with you?'

'Pops?'

Fleur nodded.

'My grandfather.' There was a pause before Robbie asked. 'Why?'

Fleur stirred her tea, even though, with wartime rationing, she had stopped taking sugar in it. She avoided meeting his gaze. 'Your mother's father?'

Robbie nodded.

'Has he always lived with you?'

Robbie wrinkled his forehead. 'No. I must have been about eight or nine when he arrived out of the blue. I think – no, I'm sure – before that there was just me and Ma. My father died before I was born. I told you that, didn't I?'

'Mm.'

Slowly, as if he was reliving a memory he'd not thought about in years, Robbie went on, 'There was a knock at the door one day and I ran to answer it. You know how when you're a kid, you love to be the one to answer the door?'

Fleur nodded but did not speak. She didn't want to break his train of thought.

'This chap was standing there. I thought it was an old tramp asking for food. He was wearing scruffy clothes, had a full straggly beard and long greasy-looking hair.' He grinned. 'Mind you, it wasn't the first time I'd seen a gentleman of the road knocking at our door or sitting in our kitchen being fed.' He laughed. 'They reckon tramps leave signs for one another pointing the way to a house where they'll likely get a meal.' The smile faded and the thoughtful frown returned. 'But when Ma saw this particular chap, I thought she was going to faint. I do remember that. Then she hustled me away – sent me to my bedroom. Next morning the old boy was still there. Clean

46

clothes, shaved, hair neatly trimmed. Ma's a dab hand with her scissors around hair as well as material. He was sitting in the chair by the fire just as if he'd taken up residence.' Robbie laughed again. 'And he had. He patted my head and said, "I'm your grandad, son."'

'And he's lived with you ever since?'

'Yup.' She felt his searching gaze on her face. 'Why all the interest?'

He'd seen through her. She laughed self-consciously. 'I can't hide anything from you, can I?'

'Nope.' His wide smile was back.

'It was just – well – when I mentioned him at home, my dad seemed flabbergasted.'

'Oh? I wonder why.'

'Mm. So do I.'

They sat in thoughtful silence drinking their tea, until Robbie, leaning forward, whispered, 'Don't look now, but there's a woman over there who can't seem to take her eyes off me.'

Fleur giggled. 'Must be the uniform. There are some women who'll do anything for a man in uniform.' She held up her hand, palm outwards. 'And before you say it, I'm not one of them.'

Laughter crinkled his face and his bright blue eyes danced with merriment. 'Shame,' he murmured and his glance caressed her. She felt as if she were wrapped in his arms even though the table separated them. A pink tinge coloured her cheeks but she returned his gaze boldly. Fleur was no shrinking violet who simpered and tittered under a man's admiring eyes. She'd been a WAAF long enough to fend off ardent advances, but she had no wish to fend off Robbie Rodwell.

If only...

'Look out,' Robbie muttered suddenly, 'she's coming over.'

As the woman approached, Fleur looked up and then she smiled. 'Why, it's Aunt Louisa.' She jumped up and kissed the woman's cheek before pulling out a chair and inviting her to join them.

As she introduced her to Robbie, the young man stood up and held out his hand. Louisa gazed up at him as if mesmerized, allowing him to take her limp hand in his broad grasp. 'I'm pleased to meet you.'

'She's not really my aunt but I've always called her that. She's Mrs Dr Collins.' Fleur laughed. 'That's what folk call her, isn't it, Aunt Louisa?'

'Yes,' Louisa mumbled weakly, still unable to drag her gaze away from Robbie's face.

'And this is Robbie Rodwell. We only met last ni...' Her voice faded away as she watched Louisa's face turn pale. The older woman seemed to sway and sink down into the chair Fleur had placed for her. But, still, she was staring up at Robbie.

'Aunt Louisa – what is it? Whatever's the matter?'

'Rodwell,' Louisa murmured. 'You're – you're Meg's boy, aren't you?'

Robbie, too, sat down. 'Yes, I am, and I'm very sorry if meeting me is distressing you in some way. It seems–' he glanced up at Fleur, seeking her permission to say more. Fleur gave a tiny nod and he turned back to face Louisa. 'It seems there are a lot of things that Fleur and I don't know about.'

Louisa was regaining her colour now and some of her composure, though her hands still

48

trembled. 'Oh yes,' she said, a bitter edge to her tone. 'There are a lot of things you don't know. But I'm not the one to tell you.' She struggled to her feet and, automatically, Robbie and Fleur rose too. Robbie put his hand out to steady her, but she snatched her arm away as if she couldn't bear him to touch her. She stared at him for a moment and then said, 'You ask your mother, if you want to know. Yes, you ask her. Ask her...' She made a gulping noise that sounded suspiciously like a sob. 'Ask her about your ... your *father*.' Then she swung round towards Fleur. 'But don't you go asking your dad anything – and certainly not your mother. Don't you go hurting my little Betsy. Not again.'

With that, Louisa turned and hurried from the cafe, her shoulders hunched and holding a handkerchief to her face. The young couple stared after her, concerned by the woman's obvious distress yet still mystified.

'Seems everyone knows what this is all about – except us,' Robbie said.

'Yes,' Fleur agreed slowly. 'It does, doesn't it?'

Robbie caught hold of her hand. She turned to face him and he put his hands on her shoulders. Looking down into her face, his expression was serious. 'You ... you won't let this come between us, will you? Whatever it is?'

Fleur was anxious too, but she said firmly, 'No, I won't. *We* won't.'

And there, in the cafe, oblivious to onlookers, he bent and kissed her. Those around them who noticed merely smiled and turned away a little sadly. So many partings, they were thinking. So many young couples snatching brief moments together before the war tore them apart again. Not so long ago, such a public display of affection would have been frowned upon, but now no one said a word.

They walked back to the railway station, their arms around each other. It felt quite natural, even though they had only known each other such a short time. They were living in strange times – times when happiness had to be grabbed whenever and wherever it happened.

'There's only one thing I can think of.'

'I know.'

'It must be that your father and my mother were in love.' Robbie was the one to voice aloud what they were both thinking. 'Or at least that your dad was in love with my mother and your mum was … well...' He didn't like to say the word, but Fleur finished the sentence for him. 'Jealous.' She was quiet for a moment before whispering, 'Do you think they had an affair?'

Robbie wrinkled his forehead and blew out his cheeks. 'Who knows? Let's face it, they lived through the last lot, didn't they? Maybe they met in the last war and … and felt just like we do now.' He turned and brushed his lips against her hair. 'Oh, Fleur, Fleur. I'm so glad I met you.'

'But my parents were married then. I was born just after the war ended.'

'So was I. Well – in the following June to be precise.'

Now they stopped and turned to face each other.

'You don't suppose–' Robbie began, as an appalling thought crept its way into his mind. So in tune with each other were they that Fleur ended the sentence yet again.

'That we're half-brother and sister?'

They stared at each other, stricken. They had promised each other that nothing would keep them apart. Nothing that had happened in the past was going to come between them. But now, with growing horror, they realized that there was something that could do just that.

'But my mother would've said if it had been that.' She paused and then asked doubtfully, 'Wouldn't she?'

'I don't think so. You said she was hysterical – like you've never seen her before?'

'Yes.' Fleur's voice was low.

'And she forbade you to see me again?'

'Yes.'

'And that woman in the cafe. She knows something. She reacted just the same as my mother and your mother did.'

'But surely my dad would have said–'

Robbie shook his head. 'I bet your dad idolizes you, doesn't he?'

Fleur nodded.

'Then do you really think he'd want you to find out something like that about him?'

Mutely, Fleur shook her head.

'And there's something else too,' Robbie said solemnly. 'Something I should have realized before.'

'What?'

'Your dad's name? It's Jake, isn't it?'

Fleur nodded.

'That's my middle name. I'm Robert *Jake* Rodwell.'

'Oh no!' Fleur whispered.

He put his arms around her and held her close, trying to lessen the pain his words would bring. 'I really think we'd better find out what all these secrets are, don't you?'

Against his chest, he heard her muffled 'Yes.' Then she raised her head. 'But how are we going to find out?'

Robbie's face was grim. 'We'll have to ask them. I shall tell my mother that we've fallen in love.' For a moment he stroked her hair tenderly and kissed the end of her nose. 'And that we need to know. We have a *right* to know.'

'Would it be best if I asked my dad?'

He pondered for a moment. 'No, I'll ask my mother first. We've always been close. I think she'll tell me the truth. Your dad might...' He hesitated, not wanting to say what was in his mind, but uncannily she knew.

'You mean, he might not tell me the truth for fear of hurting my mum?'

Robbie nodded.

'Yes, you're right.'

'So I'll ask my mother. Don't worry, darling. I'm sure there's a simple explanation.'

But when they parted they were still both anxious and the kiss they shared was tentative, as if they were each holding back. Just in case...

Six

Louisa Collins sat in the darkness of her sitting room in the big, double-fronted house that was both their home and her husband's medical practice. The room to the right of the central front door was their private sitting room, whilst across the hall was Philip's surgery and dispensing room. Patients waited in the spacious hallway and Louisa, acting as her husband's receptionist, welcomed them with words of comfort and reassurance and ushered them into his room when their turn came.

The blackout curtains were drawn and the only light in the room came from the fire in the grate of the ornate fireplace, the flickering flames casting eerie shadows around the room, glinting on the heavy, old-fashioned but lovingly polished furniture. The light settled for a brief moment on the oil paintings on the wall and the delicate china in the glass cabinet and then flitted away again.

She sat perfectly still, yet her mind was busy with darting thoughts and fleeting memories and dark suspicions that refused to be buried any longer. She hadn't thought about all that for years. Only now and again when she saw Jake and Betsy was she reminded, but even then, as the years had passed, she had managed to stop her thoughts dwelling on those times they had all shared but never spoke of now.

She had loved Philip, body and soul, ever since she had first met him. There had never been anyone else for her but him. Her only regret was that she had never been able to give him children. The sob rose in her throat and she pressed her fingers to her lips to stop the sound escaping, even though there was no one else in the house to hear. She had shed many tears over it through the years, mostly alone, but sometimes against her husband's shoulder whilst he held her and patted her and told her it didn't matter. They were happy, weren't they? Just the two of them? They had each other and more than likely it was all his fault anyway. Being gassed in the Great War had left its mark on him and he was sure that could be the reason. But Louisa knew that he was trying to be kind, trying to spare her the dreadful burden of being barren – of not being able to give him a child.

And now, today, she'd seen Meg's son. And – of all people – he'd been with Fleur. She'd seen the way they'd looked at each other and she shuddered. If ever she'd seen two people on the brink of falling in love, it had been those two. Then, stupidly, oh so foolishly, she had lost control of her emotions. She'd said far too much to them, far more than she should have done. A fresh panic swept through her. They would be sure to ask questions after the way she'd acted. He would ask Meg and – despite her plea – she was sure that Fleur would ask her parents too.

Now she groaned aloud to the empty room and dropped her head into her hands.

'Oh, what have I done?' she whispered. 'What

have I done?'

At Middleditch Farm, Betsy, too, was sitting in the dusk beside her bedroom window. There was no light in the room behind her so the blackout blinds were not drawn. She looked down into the yard, watching Jake finishing the evening milking and driving the cows out of the byre, through the gate and down the lane back to the field.

She should have been helping him. With Fleur gone, he was always short-handed nowadays, even though Kenny lent a hand whenever he could. And that was another worry. Where was Kenny? He should have been home from school hours ago. They had persuaded their son to stay on at school into the sixth form, with the hope that he might go on to university afterwards. Anything to try to keep him out of the war for as long as possible.

Betsy craned her neck, trying to see further up and down the lane through the gathering gloom. She opened the window and leant out, straining to hear the sound of his whistling. Kenny was always whistling as he rattled homewards on his bicycle. She'd hear him long before she saw him... But the evening air was still, the only sounds the occasional bark of their dog as he helped herd the cows along the lane.

And Fleur – where was she? She'd not come back since going out to meet that boy. Meg's boy. Betsy had watched her go from this very window – had seen her walk down the lane. Watched her turn the corner until she was out of sight.

The very lane that Meg had walked down all

those years ago as she left with her baby. The day that Jake had said 'goodbye' to her for ever. The day he had chosen to stay with Betsy and their daughter, and they had stood together in the yard and watched Meg walk away.

Betsy sank back into the chair, her arms resting on the sill, and dropped her head onto her arms. It was as if the intervening years had never happened. As if all the love and care Jake had lavished on his children and, yes, on her too, she had to admit, had never happened.

It seemed like only yesterday that she'd stood beside him as he'd waved goodbye to Meg.

'I'll drop you at the main gate for you to book in at the guardroom,' the driver of the RAF lorry that had met them at Lincoln railway station told them, as he drove through Wickerton village and turned into the gateway of the RAF station. Robbie and Fleur had met up on the Nottingham to Lincoln train as they had planned and travelled the last few miles together.

'Here we are, then,' the driver said as he slowed the vehicle to a halt just in front of the barrier. Whilst they waited for the sentry to approach them, he added, 'You'll need to report in at the main guardroom here first, but all the living quarters are set well away from the actual airfield itself. The Waafery's that way, miss.' He pointed along the road to the left. Fleur giggled inwardly at the nickname given to the WAAF buildings.

'That's where you need to go and they'll tell you where to go from there, but you, sunshine' – he nodded at Robbie – 'will have a bit of a walk.'

His grin widened as he added, 'I reckon they've built the fellers' quarters as far away from the lasses as they can.'

Robbie laughed. 'I shouldn't wonder!'

'Over there, see.' The driver jerked his thumb to the right, towards several buildings of all shapes and sizes, scattered across a vast area some distance away. 'That's the men's quarters. There's the CO's quarters, officers' mess, sergeants' mess, airmen's mess, NAAFI, gym, chapel and the sick quarters. Let's hope you don't see much of that place, though.' He winked at Robbie. 'I wouldn't mind meself. There's a couple of nice nurses there, so I've heard.'

Robbie jumped down and held out his hand to help Fleur. 'Home for the next few months at least.'

As the lorry drove off further into the camp with a series of splutters and bangs, they looked about them.

Fleur shaded her eyes against the setting sun beyond the distant airfield, its huge, camouflaged hangars black silhouettes against the golden glow. A little nearer several aircraft stood in a silent row.

'What are those?' Fleur asked. Though she'd studied pictures of various aircraft, she'd never been so close to one.

'Hampdens,' Robbie murmured. 'I wonder if one of them's ours.'

Fleur gazed at the planes and shuddered. Soon Robbie might be flying night after night in one of them. And she would be left watching and listening and waiting.

'Come on,' he said, picking up his belongings

and Fleur's kitbag too. 'We'd better do as we've been told and then I suppose we'll have to go our separate ways.' The regret in his tone mirrored her feelings.

'But we'll see each other, won't we? About camp, I mean?'

He grinned at her through the gathering dusk. 'Just let 'em try to stop us.' But his hearty tone was forced now. The worry was still in both their minds. Should they even be meeting at all?

When they'd reported in, they stood together for another few minutes, in the middle of the road, both reluctant to make the final move to part.

'There doesn't seem to be anyone about,' Fleur said. 'I thought the place'd be teeming with activity.'

'You'd think so, wouldn't you? Maybe it's supper time or something.'

'That'd explain it.'

'Or maybe they're flying...'

Again, a silence, but neither of them moved.

Robbie nodded towards the WAAF buildings. A few were obviously still under construction. 'I'd heard this was a newish station. Looks like it's not finished yet.'

Fleur looked about her and then said reluctantly, 'We ... we'd better go, hadn't we?'

Robbie grinned. 'Trying to get rid of me already, are you?'

'Course not.' Fleur pretended indignation that he could even think such a thing. 'I just don't want you in trouble on your first day. I ... I'm not quite sure how they'll view the men and women mixing, especially different ranks. You know...?'

Robbie laughed aloud. 'Shouldn't think they'll be able to stop it even if they try.' His blue eyes twinkled at her through the gathering dusk. 'Not with us they won't. Will they?'

'Not likely,' Fleur grinned, then she sighed. 'I'd better report in at the Waafery.'

'And I'd better go and find the rest of the chaps, I suppose,' Robbie said and handed over her kitbag. 'So – this is it then?'

Fleur nodded and tried to smile. 'Looks like it. I ... I'll see you around, then.'

'You most certainly will even if I have to break into the Waafery at night.'

'Don't you dare...' she began and then realized he was teasing. Instinctively, she knew he wouldn't do anything that would get her into trouble, even if he didn't mind for himself.

As she moved towards the WAAF buildings, Fleur glanced over her shoulder and waved as Robbie's long strides took him along the road in the opposite direction further and further away from her. At the same moment, he turned and raised his arm in the air and then strode away, quickening his pace.

With a small sigh, Fleur shouldered her heavy kitbag and walked towards the Waafery. As she did so, a WAAF came out of the nearest building, slamming the door behind her. As she drew nearer, Fleur could see that she was short and round, her uniform buttons straining to stay fastened across her ample bosom. She was a good few years older than Fleur and her plump cheeks were florid, her small eyes almost lost in

59

the fatness of her face.

The woman – a Flight Sergeant – would have walked straight past without even glancing at her had not Fleur said, 'Excuse me. I've just arrived. Could you tell me where I have to go?'

The WAAF stopped, looked Fleur up and down, and then snapped, 'Name?'

Fleur reeled off her number, rank and name.

'You're late. Supper's nearly finished, but you'd best go to the dining room.' She nodded towards the building she had just left. 'You might get something.' She didn't sound very hopeful and seemed to care even less. 'Find Morrison. You're billeted with her. In the village. And report to Flight Sergeant Watson in Control in the morning. They work a system of shifts in the watch office: a four-hour and then an eight-hour, times varying of course, so between all the operators, the twenty-four hours are covered, with always at least two on duty. More sometimes, when they're flying. The rota's posted on the board in the office. Because you work a twelve-hour day and often through the night, the time off is very generous.' It sounded as if she heartily disapproved of the WAAFs being given any time off. No doubt she was a great believer in the 'idle hands' saying.

'Thank you,' Fleur said carefully.

The older woman eyed her critically. 'Your hair's too long. It's touching your collar. Either mind it's tied up properly under your cap or get it cut.' Then she turned and marched away.

'Well,' Fleur murmured as she watched her go. 'I hope the other girls are a little friendlier than you!'

60

Seven

As Fleur entered the dining room, the noise of chatter and laughter hit her. She stood, blinking in the bright light, and looked around her, not sure what to do.

Catching sight of her, a plump, merry-faced girl with unruly fair curls rose from her seat at one of the long tables and came bouncing towards her. 'Hello there. Come and sit with us and I'll get you something to eat. Leave your gear there. We'll sort it out in a mo.'

She caught hold of Fleur's arm and pulled her towards the place where she'd been sitting. 'Budge up, you lot. Room for a little 'un. Sorry about the squash. We're having to make do with trestle tables at the mo, though they keep telling us that proper dining tables and chairs are on order.' Then she rushed away towards the counter where the food was being served.

As they shuffled along the bench seat to make room for her, the other girls smiled at her. 'Just arrived, have you?'

Fleur nodded. 'Yes. Thanks,' she added, as she squeezed into the space they'd made for her. The girl who'd greeted her arrived back carrying a plate of cheese on toast and a mug of tea. 'There. Get that down you. Bet you're hungry. Come far, have you?' She hardly paused for breath as she sat down again. 'I'm Ruth Morrison, by the way, and you'll be with me. We're billeted in the village. Most of the girls are.' She nudged Fleur and winked. 'Don't reckon they trust us to stay on the camp with the fellers.'

'It's nothing of the sort,' a fair-haired girl sitting opposite retorted. 'Don't listen to her. I'm Peggy Marshall.' She held out her hand across the table and Fleur took it.

'Fleur Bosley. Hello.'

'And don't believe a word our Ruth tells you. Truth is, they haven't got the sleeping quarters finished yet, so most of us are billeted out...'

'Not all of us.' A dark-haired girl further down the table remarked. There was a distinct note of resentment in her tone, though, as Fleur glanced at her, the girl winked. 'Some of us,' she went on dryly, 'have to put up with sleeping in a draughty hut on hard biscuit beds and eat forces' fare whilst the rest of you languish in feather beds and are plied with delicious home cooking by the locals.'

There were cries of derision and someone threw a dry biscuit at her, but the girl just smiled, her dark eyes sparkling with mischief.

'That's Kay Fullerton, by the way. As you can see, she's a corporal,' Ruth said. 'The rest of us are just lowly ACWs.'

Fleur nodded. 'Me too.'

Ruth nodded towards Kay as she added, 'She doesn't mean it – about the sleeping arrangements, I mean.'

'Oh yes I do. Why should all the newcomers get the best billets, I'd like to know?'

Fleur looked up and met the girl's belligerent expression. 'Well, I don't mind sleeping here if

62

you want to swap,' she offered.

Kay stared at her for a moment until someone else put in, 'Kay's all talk. She'll not leave camp – she's already got her eye on one of the new pilots that's just arrived.'

The remark was greeted by loud guffaws and even Kay smiled sheepishly. 'No, you're OK, but – thanks for the offer.'

As there was a general movement to get up from the table, Kay came up to Fleur and held out her hand. 'You're the first one to do that.'

Closer now, Fleur could see that the girl had the most unusual dark blue eyes – so dark they were almost violet. Her skin was smooth and flawless, and her black hair was so shiny it seemed to glint in the light as she moved. She was really very pretty.

'She gives all the new ones a hard time over it,' Ruth explained, 'just to see how they react.'

Kay laughed. 'Most of them go all red and embarrassed, but none of them have ever offered to swap. You're all right, Fleur Bosley. In my book anyway.'

Now it was Fleur's turn to look a little embarrassed at the unexpected compliment.

'Not one to hold back is our Kay. You'll get it straight John Bull from her,' Ruth said. 'If she likes you, she'll tell you so. And if she doesn't – well, she'll tell you that an' all.'

'What job will you be doing? Do you know?' Kay asked.

'R/T operator.'

Kay's eyes lit up. 'Oh, then you'll be with me in Control. That's good. Welcome aboard, Fleur.'

Then she spun on her heel, adding, 'Must go. Things to do, people to see. See you tomorrow.' And before Fleur could say a word, she had marched down the long room and out of the door.

Ruth spluttered with laughter. 'She's a caution, that one, as my mother would say.'

Fleur smiled. She was feeling very much at home already. She liked Ruth and had taken to the girl she now knew would be working with her. She wondered if she'd be working with Ruth too. 'What do you do, Ruth?'

'I'm in intelligence. I help at briefings and then debrief the crews when they come back from a raid.'

'That must be tough,' Fleur murmured sympathetically.

Ruth's hazel eyes clouded for a moment. 'It is a bit. An RAF intelligence officer usually asks the questions and I write down their answers. But if it's been a rough one and the crews are dog tired, sometimes their stories take a lot of unravelling. Still, it's an interesting and – I think – worthwhile job. Though you're right, it's harrowing at times.'

Fearing she had touched on something sensitive, Fleur changed the subject swiftly. 'So – how do I find this billet we're sharing?'

Ruth's expression lightened at once. 'I'll take you. I'm not on duty for a couple of hours or so when the first planes start coming back.'

'There's a raid on tonight then?'

'Mmm. Not a very big one, just a gardening run...' She grinned. 'Mine-laying, you know, but we still have to go through the routine, of course. Come on. Let's get your gear. We're only a few yards down the road on the outskirts of the village. With a widow. She's a nice old dear. Fusses a bit, but then I think she's lonely. Her husband died a few years ago and all her chicks have left home. Oh, you'll get the full family history within the space of ten minutes, believe me.'

As they walked out of the main gate and along the road, following the pencil-thin beam from Ruth's torch, she chattered. 'I'm from Lincoln. I live with me mam and dad and two sisters. They're younger than me and keeping their fingers crossed that the war's going to last long enough for them to join up.' She pulled a face. 'Selfish little devils – fancy anyone wishing such a thing!' But Fleur heard Ruth's soft chuckle through the darkness. The girl linked her arm through Fleur's as she confided, 'Mind you, it could be my fault. I'm always telling them what a great time we have and how we're surrounded by all these handsome chaps.' Then her voice faltered as she added sadly, 'I can't bring myself to tell them the truth, see. Of course, we do have fun, but ... but it's no fun, is it, when you wave all the bombers off at night and know what they're going to face? And then, when they come back, counting them all. One by one. Only they're never all there, are they? They never *all* come back, do they?'

Fleur shook her head. 'Not very often.'

Ruth squeezed her arm and forced jollity back into her tone. 'Hark at me, getting all serious. As if I need to tell you. You've worked on another operational bomber station, haven't you?'

Fleur nodded. 'Yes, down south, but I applied to remuster as an R/T operator and hoped I'd get a posting a bit nearer home and here I am.'

'Me too. I was up north for a while straight after training and I've been very lucky to get a posting so near home. What about you? Did you manage it?'

'What?'

'To get a posting nearer home?'

'Oh yes. I live at South Monkford. Do you know it?'

'Near Newark, isn't it? Well, you should be able to get home on leave easily enough. Even on a forty-eight-hour pass. You might have to hitch, but we're really lucky. Some of the girls are hundreds of miles from home. Peggy's from Newcastle. And Kay's from London. They can really only get home about once every three months.'

At the mention of Kay, Fleur remembered what had been said at the table. 'Has ... has Kay got a boyfriend here then?'

'Yes, she has,' Ruth said with a snort that sounded very much like disapproval. 'Silly mare!'

'Why do you say that? Haven't you got one?'

'Me? Oh no. Fancy free, me. And I mean to stay that way.' Again there was a sniff. 'It doesn't do.'

Alarmed, Fleur said, 'What do you mean? Isn't it allowed?'

'Well, you have to be careful, but they can't stop it, even if they'd like to. No, what I mean is, you're stacking up a load of heartache for yourself if you let yourself get close to anyone.'

Fleur thought she detected a note of real pain in the girl's tone and she was about to ask gently if she had lost someone close to her, but before she could form the words, Ruth said brightly, 'Here we are. Rose Cottage. "Home, Sweet Home".'

She pushed open the wooden gate and they crunched up the narrow cinder path.

'Watch yourself. The garden's so overgrown the long grass falls onto the path. When it's wet, your ankles are soaking by the time you reach the door.'

In the wavering torchlight, Fleur caught glimpses of the neglected front garden. The grass looked so long it would need a scythe to cut it now, she mused. As if answering her unspoken question, Ruth said softly, 'Poor old dear loves her garden. Her old man used to keep it immaculate, she says, but since he's gone it's got topside of her. She's got a huge back garden with an orchard at the end of it. Used to grow veg and all sorts. But she's got arthritis, see, and can't cope with it. But she won't move. Says she came to this cottage as a young bride and she'll die here.'

Briefly, Ruth flashed the torch over the low, oblong shape of the cottage. 'Typical "roses-round-the-door cottage" we all dream of, eh? But she really got it.'

'Mm,' Fleur murmured. 'No wonder she doesn't want to leave it.' Even before she had met Mrs Jackson, she knew she was going to be a sweet old lady who'd lived a lifetime of love in her little cottage. Fleur had a sudden mental picture of a young bride being carried over the threshold to start a long and happy life with her groom in the idyllic little house. However, the image in her mind's eye was not of the unknown Mrs Jackson but of herself and Robbie.

'I'm surprised the authorities haven't been on to her about her garden,' Fleur said, dragging herself back to the present. '"Dig for Victory" and all that.'

'I think they did try. Got some local boy scouts to come and dig the back garden, but they made a right pig's ear of it.' She giggled in the darkness. 'There was even talk of them building her an Anderson shelter, but after a couple of spadefuls, they gave up, so she says.'

'Not got a shelter and living so close to an airfield!' Fleur was shocked. 'Well, we'll have to see about that.'

'Come on, then,' Ruth urged. 'We'll go round the back. Tell you the truth, the front door's stuck and she can't open it.'

They followed the narrow path round to the back, brushing through long wet grass so that by the time they arrived in the unevenly paved back yard their ankles were quite damp, just as Ruth had predicted. She shone the torch and nodded towards a brick building a few steps across the yard from the back door. 'That's the lav.' She leant closer and whispered, 'It's a bit basic. No indoor facilities, but the old dear cooks like a dream.' Ruth patted her stomach. 'Makes up for a bit of discomfort in other areas. 'Sides, she provides us with a potty under the bed so we don't have to come tripping out into the back yard in the dark.' Ruth giggled again as she added, 'She calls it a "jerry". I always imagine I'm piddling on Adolf's head if I use it in the night.'

Fleur laughed softly. 'Home from home, Ruth. It's what I'm used to. We've no inside lav either.'

Ruth's eyes widened. 'But I thought you said you lived in South Monkford? It's a town, isn't it?'

'A small one. But I live on a farm about five miles from the town itself. Right out in the wilds.'

'You're a country girl, then?'

'Born and bred.' Fleur moved carefully across the cobbled yard towards the rickety little gate leading into the back garden. As her eyes became accustomed to the darkness, she could see the shapes of trees silhouetted against the night sky. Ruth came to stand beside her and shone the torch and now Fleur could see that the whole area was as overgrown and choked with weeds as the front one.

'There's raspberry and gooseberry bushes and all sorts down the bottom there. The old dear said they even had a strawberry patch once. And you can see the fruit trees. There's a lovely old apple tree with a little bench seat under it. It's where her and her Arthur used to sit on a summer's evening, she said.'

'You know,' Fleur suggested, 'we could help her, in our spare time.'

'Hey, hang on a minute. I'm a city girl. Born and bred in Lincoln. That's why I chose the WAAFs instead of the Land Army. You're welcome to go grubbing about in Mother Earth but don't ask me to join you.' The words could have been tart and dismissive, but they were spoken with such a warm humour that Fleur laughed.

'We'll see,' she teased, as Ruth grabbed her arm and pulled her towards the back door. As she pushed it open, it scraped and shuddered on the uneven floor.

'Coo-ee, Mrs Jackson. You in?' She turned and whispered. 'She hardly ever goes out, 'cept to church on a Sunday and sometimes as far as the village shop, but her legs are getting that bad, poor old thing. She walks with a stick as it is, though she can move about the house without it. Come on in. Mind the blackout curtain. It's a bit long and trails on the floor. It gets caught under the door if you don't watch out.'

They moved through the back scullery, which housed a deep white sink and wooden draining board with shelves of pots and pans above. There was also a cooker to augment the range that Fleur knew would be in the kitchen. Ruth flung open the door into the kitchen-cum-living-room where an elderly lady was struggling to lever herself up out of her armchair in the far corner of the room beside the black-leaded range that Fleur had expected to see. A fire burned in the grate and a kettle stood on the hob. It really was just like home, Fleur thought.

'Don't get up, Mrs Jackson,' Ruth was saying. 'I've brought another lodger for you. This is Fleur Bosley. She's just come to work in the watch office.'

The old lady sank back thankfully into her chair, but she beamed up at Fleur with such a wide smile that her rounded cheeks lifted her spectacles. She was a plump little woman, with her white hair pulled back and wound into a roll at the nape of her neck. She wore low-heeled lace-up shoes and lisle stockings, and her striped blouse and navy skirt were almost hidden by a paisley overall. Fleur smiled. It was identical to the one her mother wore. This woman could be Betsy in thirty years' time, she thought, though she couldn't imagine her mother welcoming complete strangers into her home the way this woman was doing. Her mother wouldn't even make someone she knew welcome, Fleur thought wryly, thinking of the uncomfortable last few hours she had spent at home. It was a sad fact – and it hurt even to think it – but she'd been glad to get away.

Fleur quickly scanned the room, taking in the other armchair on the opposite side of the range and the table with its white lace runner and two chairs set against the wall. On a small table beside the old lady sat a wireless with a polished oak cabinet, silk front and black Bakelite controls. It seemed out of place in the old-fashioned cottage, yet Fleur knew that the wireless had become almost a necessity in the homes of those anxious for news of the war.

Fleur crossed the room to stand on the pegged hearthrug. 'Hello, Mrs Jackson. I'm pleased to meet you.'

'You're very welcome, lass,' the old lady said, her faded blue eyes smiling up at Fleur. 'Mek yourself at home. Ruth'll show you your room upstairs. I can't get up there now.'

'Mind your head,' Ruth warned, as she led Fleur up the narrow staircase to the two attic bedrooms under the eaves. 'There's only us here. We have a room each. I'm in the bigger room with the double bed and you'll be in here...' she said, opening the door into a small room that only had space for a single iron bedstead, a wardrobe and narrow dressing table. But the bed was covered with a cheery patchwork quilt and there was a pegged rug beside the bed to step

71

onto instead of the cold floor.

'Do you mind?' Ruth glanced back over her shoulder.

Fleur smiled reassuringly. 'Course not. Don't be daft. It's fine. It's not much smaller than the one I have at home. Honest.'

'The old dear sleeps downstairs in her front parlour now. Bless 'er. I'll show you when we go down.'

As Ruth helped her unpack her belongings, hanging her clothes in the narrow wardrobe with a creaking door, she pulled a face and said, 'At least staying here we don't get those dreadful kit inspections every morning. Mind you, I'll warn you now. Ma'am has eyes like a hawk so it pays to keep your uniform spick and span. And she has been known to make an unannounced inspection of our billet now and again.'

'Is she very strict?'

Ruth turned surprised eyes towards her. 'Who? Mrs Jackson? Heavens, no!'

'I didn't mean her.' Fleur laughed. 'I meant the WAAF CO. I mean, are we allowed to meet the RAF lads?'

Ruth stared at her for a moment. 'Well, of course we meet them at work. And there's the dances on camp, usually in the men's NAAFI or sometimes in the sergeants' mess. Then there's the Liberty Bus on a Saturday night.'

'What on earth is the "Liberty Bus"?'

Ruth grinned. 'A bus laid on to take us into Lincoln. To dances or the pictures.'

She was silent a moment, watching Fleur sort out her underwear and put it away in one of the drawers in the dressing table. Then Ruth said quietly, 'Why all the questions? Do you know someone on camp? Someone – special?'

Fleur felt the blush creep up her face and knew she couldn't hide the truth. 'Well, sort of. I've only just met him. We bumped into each other – literally – on Nottingham station. He's just been posted here an' all. That's how we met.'

'Oh, Fleur!' Ruth flopped down onto the bed. The springs protested loudly, but neither of the girls noticed. 'Don't get involved with someone – with anyone. Not if he's a flier. He is, I take it?'

Fleur nodded. 'He's a wireless operator on bombers.'

Ruth groaned and then sighed heavily, regarding her new-found friend with a hangdog expression. 'I don't suppose anything I say's going to make any difference, is it?'

Fleur grinned. 'Not a scrap.'

Ruth heaved herself up. 'Well, my shoulder's ready when you need it.'

'Don't you mean "if"?'

Ruth stared at her for a long moment before she said seriously, 'No, love. I'm sorry, but I do mean "when".'

Eight

As Fleur approached the control tower early the following morning, her heart was beating faster. Although she had been thoroughly trained and had been briefed on how to cope with every emergency possible, she was still a little apprehensive. This was her first posting as a fully fledged R/T operator and she knew that 'the real thing' would be very different. Mistakes in training hadn't mattered. Now they did.

She stepped into the ground floor of the watch tower. The concrete steps leading to the upper floor were on her right, but first she was curious to see what else the building housed. The first room on the left was the met office, with maps spread out on the waist-high table against the wall. A WAAF sat at a telephone switchboard; another stood in front of a teleprinter, which was noisily chattering out a message. A nearby desk was cluttered with telephones, a black typewriter and papers. Next door to the met office was the duty pilots' rest room. It was empty and silent, newspapers flung down untidily amongst the battered easy chairs. Dirty mugs, an overflowing ashtray and dog-eared books littered the table almost hiding the telephone. It seemed, even here, there was no escaping the call to duty. Near the door was the compulsory sand bucket – the ever-present reminder of the war and all its dangers.

Fleur climbed the stairs to the upper floor. The smell from the freshly painted cream and green walls reminded her that this was a new station, still in the process of being built. She peeped into the signals' room with its wirelesses, typewriters and teleprinters. For a moment she stood listening to the morse code blips that filled the room, mentally translating a few words in her head. Directly opposite the signals' room was the rest room, but Fleur ignored this for the moment and, taking a deep breath, moved to the end of the narrow passageway and opened the door into the watch office.

This was the largest room in the building. Directly in front of her was the long desk where the R/T operators sat. In one corner the duty officer sat at his desk, overseeing all that was happening. Flight Sergeant Bob Watson was in his mid forties, Fleur guessed. He was tall and thin and had dark, Brylcreemed hair and the usual moustache that was fast becoming the trademark of the RAF. Fleur was to notice that he stroked it continuously when the tension mounted in the watch office and that he would pace up and down behind the operators as the aircraft took off one by one and again when they landed.

As she entered the room, Bob Watson greeted her informally with a friendly smile. 'You must have made an impression already. Fullerton has already asked if you can work with her.'

Fleur smiled and felt a faint blush creep into her cheeks. 'I'd like that, Flight, if it can be arranged. I think we'd work well together.'

He eyed her keenly. 'You think so? Some of the

younger girls find her – well – a bit abrasive. She doesn't suffer fools at all – let alone gladly, as they say. Mind you,' he said arching his eyebrows, 'neither do I, but I suppose they expect it from me.'

Fleur remained silent. He stroked his moustache thoughtfully. 'Well then, I'll adjust the rotas so you work with Fullerton. And in that case, you'll be on from tonight, but only if they're flying. Come on duty a bit early and we'll show you the ropes – how we do things in this watch office.'

'Thank you, Flight.'

So, she thought, as she went down the steps, I've the rest of the day off. I wonder what Robbie's doing.

Ruth brought her the news in the NAAFI at midday. 'I don't think you'll see much of him for the next few days. The new crews are getting to know one another. They might even get a few practice flights in to make sure they gel before they're sent on a mission. Mind you, they could be flying tonight if Tommy thinks they're ready. He's done quite a bit of flying on Hampdens already evidently and...' But Fleur was no longer listening. She was far too wrapped up in her own disappointment that she wouldn't be able to see Robbie and – worse still – there would be no chance for him to get home on leave for quite a while. No chance for him to ask his mother some very delicate – yet to them very important – questions.

With time on her hands, Fleur went back to the cottage and changed into civvies – a pair of old trousers and a thick sweater.

76

'Are you hungry, dear?' Mrs Jackson asked as Fleur came downstairs.

'No, thanks. I ate in the NAAFI, but I wouldn't mind a cup of tea, if you can spare one.'

'Of course. I get extra rations with you two here.'

'I'll make it. You sit down.'

The old lady sank thankfully into her chair and took up her knitting. 'Socks for the troops.' She smiled. 'A nice WVS lady brings me the wool and collects them. It gives me something to do and I feel I'm helping.'

'You're helping a lot already, putting up with us two.'

Mrs Jackson's face creased into smiles and her spectacles wobbled. 'Oh, that's no hardship, dear. I enjoy the company.'

Fleur set a cup of tea on the small table beside the old lady. She was about to sit in the chair on the opposite side of the hearth when she paused and asked quietly, 'Is it all right for me to sit here?'

There was the slightest hesitation before Mrs Jackson said, 'Of course, dear. My Arthur would have been tickled pink to think that a lovely young WAAF was sitting in his chair.'

Fleur sat down, balancing her cup carefully. 'When...' she began tentatively, thinking that this was as good a time as any to broach the subject of the garden, 'When did your Arthur...?'

The old lady's face dropped into lines of sadness. 'Three years ago next month. Very sudden. Heart attack. Out there in the garden.' She smiled fondly. 'But it was just the way he'd've wanted to go. With a spade in his hand, doing what he loved best.'

'And the ... er ... um ... garden?'

Mrs Jackson sighed deeply. 'It makes me so sad to see it like that. Poor Arthur. All his hard work overgrown and so quickly too. Who'd have thought it could've gone wild in only three years?'

'Would you mind if I worked on it when I'm off duty? I mean, if you'd rather I didn't,' she began, fearing she might have upset the old lady, but Mrs Jackson's face was alight with joy.

'Oh, my dear, that would be wonderful. Really wonderful.' Her face clouded. 'But do you really want to? I mean surely a young lass like you wants to be out enjoying herself. And besides, I mean, do you know much about gardening?'

Fleur laughed. 'Born and bred on a farm, Mrs Jackson. What I don't know already my dad will tell me.'

The old lady laughed along with her. 'Well, you won't have to go very far for a bit of advice, love. Old Harry next door will be only too pleased to help. In fact' – she smiled – 'you'll have a job to stop him.'

'Right then,' Fleur said jumping up, glad to have something physical to do. With her first duty looming and maybe with Robbie flying with his new crew for the first time, she needed something else to concentrate on. 'No time like the present.'

Mrs Jackson's garden shed in the back yard was cluttered; there was hardly room to step inside it.

'Another job for a rainy day,' Fleur murmured as she unearthed some rusty gardening tools. There was a sickle but no scythe, and cutting the

78

grass at the front of the cottage and the overgrown kitchen garden would be a long and back-breaking task on her hands and knees.

'Mrs Jackson?' she said, going back into the house. 'Do you know anyone who's got a scythe?'

The old lady washing up at the deep sink in the small scullery turned in surprise. 'Whatever do you want a scythe for?'

'To cut all the overgrown grass back and front. If I get it dug over there's still time to plant some vegetables.'

Mrs Jackson's eyes were filling with tears. 'D'you know, when Arthur was alive I never 'ad to buy vegetables all year round.'

'You'll have to tell me what he used to grow,' Fleur said gently. 'I'm sure he'd be pleased to think we'd got it like it used to be.'

'Oh, he would, he would.' Mrs Jackson wiped the corner of her eye with the back of her hand and sniffed, but she was smiling through her tears. 'A scythe, you say? Harry next door might 'ave one or 'ee'd know someone who has.'

'Right then.' Fleur began to turn away but then paused to ask, 'What's his surname, Mrs Jackson? I can hardly call him "Harry".'

The old lady chortled. 'Oh, Harry wouldn't mind. He's a one for the pretty lasses.' Her face fell into sad wrinkles. 'He's on his own like me now. His wife, Doris, died two years ago. His name's Harry Chambers.'

Fleur went through the front gate and along the lane to the next-door cottage. She walked round to the back and as she turned the corner of the house, she gasped in surprised delight. The layout was the same as Mrs Jackson's cottage and garden, but there the similarity ended: beyond Harry Chambers' back yard lay a lovingly tended kitchen garden. But after her initial pleasure, Fleur frowned. If he could do his own garden, why didn't he help the old lady next door? The way Mrs Jackson had spoken of her neighbour, they were friendly, so why...?

As she lifted her hand to knock tentatively on the back door, Fleur bit her lip, wondering, after what Mrs Jackson had said, just what she was going to have to deal with. But she needn't have worried. When Harry Chambers opened the door, she saw that he was as old and bent as her landlady, yet there was a mischievous twinkle in his rheumy eyes and a wide, toothless smile.

'By heck – have I died and gone to heaven? A pretty young lass knocking at my door. Come away in, lass.' He turned away and shuffled back into the kitchen. Smiling inwardly, Fleur followed. Now, the question in her mind was not why he didn't help his neighbour, but how on earth did he manage to keep his garden so immaculate? As she stepped into the kitchen, she saw the answer. The inside of his home was like a rubbish tip. The range was dirty, the floor filthy and every surface was littered with newspapers and unwashed pots. The old man swept aside a pile of clothes on a chair. 'Sit down, sit down,' he insisted, beckoning her forward.

Thankful that she was wearing her old trousers, Fleur sat in the rickety chair. The old man let himself down into the dusty armchair near the range and beamed at her. 'A' you one of them lasses at Mary's?'

'Yes. I only arrived yesterday. I'm just getting settled in, but I'd like to make a start on getting the garden in order for her.'

'Aw lass...' To Fleur's horror, tears filled his eyes. But at his next words she realized they were tears of joy too, just like Mrs Jackson's had been. 'That'd be wonderful for 'er. I'd've liked to have kept it right but I've more than I can manage with me own bit.' He wiped the back of his hand across his face. 'Her ol' man, Arthur – we was mates.' He laughed wheezily. ''Cept when it came to the village show and we was both entered for the biggest marrow competition. Then it was "gloves off" time. Eee, lass, but I miss him. You don't know how much I miss our little chats over the fence.'

Fleur smiled but didn't know what to say so she let the old man ramble, reliving happier times. But he was laughing along with his tears. At last, he came back to the present.

'So what can I do for you, lass?'

'Mr Chambers, have you got a scythe I can borrow?'

He gaped at her. 'A scythe, lass? Aw now, I don't know if I should let a young lass like you loose with a scythe. Them's dangerous things if you don't know what you're doing...' He leant towards her, screwing up his eyes in an effort to see her better. Then he chuckled. 'I can see by the look on your face – you *do* know, don't you?'

Fleur nodded, her eyes brimming with mischief. 'If my dad could hear you, Mr Chambers, he'd say, "No daughter of mine's going to grow up without knowing how to use a scythe." I was born and brought up on the farm.'

The old man blinked. 'Then what are you doing here? In the WAAFs? I'd've thought they'd've needed you at home.'

Fleur sighed as she felt a sudden stab of guilt. 'They do,' she admitted, 'but I wanted to get away. To see something of the world outside me dad's stackyard. I still want to do my bit, but...'

The old man watched her for a moment as she bit her lip. 'I can understand that,' he said gently. 'I volunteered for the last lot even though I could have stayed safely at home 'cos I was getting on a bit for service life. My Doris begged me not to go, but I would have me own way.'

'So did my dad. I think he understands why I wanted to join up, but me mum...'

'Aye well, she's your mother, lass,' was all he said as if it explained everything. There was a moment's silence between them and then he began to chuckle. 'And now here you are, wanting to dig up Mary's garden. Seems you can't get away from it, eh, lass?'

Fleur spluttered with laughter. 'Just serves me right, doesn't it?' And they rocked with merriment.

'Ee lass, you've done me a power of good. I don't know when I last laughed so much. It's the best medicine, they say. I'll be throwing all me pills away if you're staying long.'

'I'm staying.' Fleur nodded as her thoughts turned to Robbie. 'Oh, I'm staying, Mr Chambers.'

'Right then, lass,' he said as he levered himself up from the battered chair. 'Then you'd best start calling me "Harry". I don't know who on earth you're talking about with all this "Mr Chambers" business. Now, let's go and see if I can find this 'ere scythe for you.'

When he opened the door of his shed, Fleur could not prevent a gasp of surprise escaping her lips. All the gardening tools were neatly stacked against the walls or lined up in order along the shelves or hanging from hooks. Each item had been cleaned and oiled before being put away. She almost laughed aloud to see the contrast between the old man's garden shed and the state of his house. But, she reflected, the smile dying on her lips, this was his domain; the house had been his wife's and he'd lost her.

''Ere we are,' Harry said, carefully unhooking the huge scythe from its nail. 'It's a big 'un, lass. Sure you can manage one this size?'

Not wanting to sound boastful, Fleur said, 'I think it's the same size as me dad's.' She took it from his hands, feeling the weight. 'Yes, I'm sure it is. Anyway, I'll soon know.'

'Just you be careful, lass.' Harry was still anxious.

'I will,' she smiled. 'And thank you.'

'Don't mention it. There'll be no one more pleased than me to see old Arthur's garden looking a picture again. I just wish...' His voice faded away and a sad, faraway look came into his old eyes as he glanced back towards his own house.

'What do you wish, Harry?' Fleur prompted softly, but he sniffed and forced a smile. 'Nothing, lass, nothing at all.'

But as she walked past the open back door and saw again the cluttered state of the old man's kitchen, she thought she knew what he had been going to say.

Of course, as she thought might happen, Harry leant on the fence between the two gardens to watch her taking the first few sweeping strokes. Soon she was into a steady rhythm. When she paused for a breather, she looked up to see him nodding at her.

'Aye lass, you're right. You can do it. Never seen a lass frame so well, I haven't. In fact' – his expression was comical – 'I can't say I've ever seen a lass scything afore.' He levered himself off the fence. 'Well, can't stand here all day chatting. I'd best be getting on with a few jobs mesen.'

'Harry, before you go, could you pass the sharpening stone over? I'm going to need it.'

'Right you are, lass. Ah, and here comes Mary with a cuppa.' Fleur turned to see Mary Jackson tottering along the mud path down the centre of the garden. Laying down the scythe, Fleur hurried towards her. 'Oh, you shouldn't have bothered,' she scolded the old lady gently, but reached with eager hands to take the mug. 'Mind you, it's thirsty work. I'm ready for it.'

'Any left in the pot, Mary?' Harry called out and the old lady chuckled.

'Course there is, Harry. Think I'd forget you?' And she turned to walk stiffly back towards the cottage.

'Don't you be struggling out again, lass,' Harry called. 'I'll come round.'

Fleur stifled her giggles to hear the old lady called 'lass', but maybe they'd lived side by side

84

for years and that's how he still thought of her.

Before long the two elderly people were sitting on a couple of old stools in the back yard chatting amiably – Harry's jobs forgotten – whilst Fleur worked herself into a sweat cutting the long grass. She was still at it when Ruth appeared round the corner of the cottage.

'Well, it's all right for some. 'Ello, Harry – Mrs Jackson.' She shaded her eyes and looked down the garden. 'What on earth is she doing?'

'Cutting the grass. Mekin' a good job of it an' all,' Harry said with a note of pride, almost as if he had trained Fleur himself.

'Then what's she goin' to do?' Ruth turned wide eyes on Harry. 'She's never going to dig that lot?'

Harry began to chuckle and Ruth cast her glance skywards. 'Don't tell me! She is.'

At that moment, Fleur, red faced and breathing hard, paused and looked up. Seeing Ruth, she waved.

'I've got a message for you,' Ruth shouted. 'From Flight Sergeant Watson and...' Her eyes were full of mischief. 'From lover boy.'

Fleur dropped the scythe and pushed her way through the long grass, her eyes anxious. 'What is it? There's nothing wrong is there?'

Ruth shook her head. 'Far from it. Flying's cancelled tonight. Low cloud over the target.' She pulled a face. 'Wherever that was. So he's got the night off.' She grinned. 'And so have we, 'cos we're not needed if they're not flying. A gang of us – including your Robbie – are going to the Mucky Duck in the village.'

Fleur's eyebrows rose. 'The Mucky Duck?

85

What on earth is that?'

She heard Harry's deep, rumbling chuckle and saw Mrs Jackson's smile. 'It's the locals' name for our pub – the White Swan. It's been called the Mucky Duck for as long as I can remember.'

'Right,' Fleur said. 'I'll just clean the scythe and–'

'No, no, lass,' Harry said, pulling himself up off the stool. 'I'll see to that. You get off and enjoy yourself.' He seemed about to say more, but then cleared his throat and, instead of whatever he had been about to say, added, 'You've earned it.'

'Thanks, Harry. Can I borrow the scythe next time I get some time off?'

'Course you can, lass. Any time. Just come round and help yoursen out o' me shed.'

'And I'd better get you girls a bite to eat if you're going out.' Mary was struggling to pull herself up. Ruth and Fleur held out their hands to haul the old lady to her feet. 'Thank you, my dears. Now off you go and make yourselves pretty.'

'That won't take too long to do,' Harry laughed. 'Pretty as a picture already, they are.'

'By the way,' Ruth said. 'Sorry, but we have to wear uniform. Ma'am's orders.'

Fleur shrugged. 'I don't mind. I'm proud to wear my uniform.'

'You might change your mind when you see all the local girls in their pretty dresses being chatted up by all the fellers.'

'There's only one I want to be chatted up by and he'd better not be looking at other girls while I'm around – uniform or no uniform.'

The two girls laughed and hurried into the

house to wash at the sink in the back scullery and change their clothes.

The two old people watched them go. Quietly, Harry said what he had stopped himself from saying earlier. 'Aye, let 'em enjoy themselves, eh, Mary? While they can.'

Nine

The moment Fleur and Ruth stepped into the public bar of the pub, she spotted Robbie with three other airmen. Kay and Peggy were already sitting with them. Robbie must have been watching the door for he rose at once and threaded his way around tables to reach her. He didn't kiss her, but took her hands in his and squeezed them warmly. 'Come and meet the rest of the crew. They're great lads.'

He pulled her behind him, weaving his way through the crowded bar room, and made the introductions. He reeled off the names. 'This is our skipper, Tommy Laughton. And these two reprobates are Alan Hardesty and Johnny Jones.' Then Robbie waved his arm to encompass other airmen sitting in small groups around the bar room. 'We'll no doubt get to know a lot of the other chaps on our Flight in time. They all seem a great bunch.'

Tommy unfolded his lanky frame and shook her hand warmly. He was thin faced with sharp eyes that missed nothing and he sported a moustache that stuck out on either side of his upper lip like a stiff, bristly shaving brush.

It was a merry evening. The beer flowed as did the conversation and laughter. They talked about anything and everything. Everything, that is, except the war. But Fleur was acutely aware that perhaps the jollity was a little forced, the laughter just a little too hearty.

'Fleur, you must meet Bill Moore, the landlord.' Tommy Laughton, the pilot of the newly formed crew, got up and held out his hand to her. 'Come on. You can help me get the next round in and I'll introduce you.'

Fleur glanced at Robbie, who stood up to let her move past him.

'Bill,' Tommy called to the middle-aged man behind the bar. The landlord was dressed casually in a collarless striped shirt, the sleeves rolled up above his elbows, and a black waistcoat. His strong arms pulled pint after pint effortlessly. What hair he had left was dark, yet the pate of his head was bald, and he sported a black moustache that drooped over the corners of his mouth.

'This is Fleur Bosley. She's come to work in Control. She's the lovely voice we'll hear when we're coming home. And a very welcome voice it'll be too, I can tell you.'

'Of course, it could be mine,' Kay chipped in. 'You'd better be able to tell the difference or there'll be trouble.'

As Tommy grinned over his shoulder at Kay and winked, Fleur realized that the newly arrived pilot that Kay had 'got her eye on', as Ruth had said, must be Flying Officer Tommy Laughton.

'Pleased to meet you, love.' Bill Moore enveloped her hand in his huge paw. She felt the calluses on his work-hardened hands – strong, capable, reliable hands. The sort of hands you could trust...

'Pleased to meet you, Mr Moore.'

'Eh now, lass. None of that there "mister" stuff. Bill's the name.'

Standing behind the bar amongst the pumps, the bottles and the glasses sparkling against the polished wooden surface of the bar, Bill Moore was master of all he surveyed. Fleur smiled. The man was just like Harry had been when they had first been introduced. No standing on ceremony. What a friendly bunch these locals were. Actually, she was surprised. She would have thought that the locals would resent having the airfield quite so close to their village. Despite the custom that came the pub's way and maybe to the local shop too, she was sure the disadvantages of noisy aircraft day and night and the danger of attacks, not to mention having a lot of strangers milling about the place, would far outweigh any advantages.

But it seemed she was wrong. The locals – young and old alike – were mingling freely and in a friendly manner with the RAF boys. Especially, Fleur noticed with a wry smile, the local lasses, who were being very friendly with the handsome RAF lads in their smart, blue uniforms. And the only looks of resentment were on the faces of one or two local youths not in uniform and obviously feeling that their noses had been pushed very much out of joint.

As Fleur began to ferry the drinks back to their

table, Johnny jumped up and said, 'I'll give you a hand, Fleur.' He went to stand beside Tommy, but at once a young blonde girl in a short-skirted dress sidled up to him and tapped him on the arm.

'Hello, Johnny.'

'Hello, Kitty. Would you like a drink?'

'Ta. Don't mind if I do.'

Johnny bought her a drink and they stood at the bar chatting.

'I reckon we could have trouble from one or two of the local lads,' Fleur whispered to Robbie as she took her seat beside him again. 'See that lad in the white shirt and sleeveless green pullover? Over there – near the fire.'

Robbie glanced casually around him. 'I see him. What about him?'

'Well, just keep your eye on him for a few moments. He's watching Johnny talking to that lass, and if looks could kill, Johnny would be feeling decidedly ill.'

Robbie didn't seem perturbed. 'I expect the girl old Johnny's chatting up is the lad's girlfriend.'

'Did you ought to warn Johnny, 'cos I don't think he's noticed?'

Robbie chuckled. 'No. He's otherwise occupied, isn't he? And Johnny can take care of himself. Besides, there's plenty of us here if–'

As if on cue, the youth in the corner got up and brushed back the flop of hair from his face. Then he stumbled his way between the tables, knocking against a chair and then someone's arm.

'Watch it, young 'un. You're spilling me beer.'

But the young lad took no notice. His eyes, bleary with drink, were fixed on the girl who was now sitting with Johnny and cuddling up to him quite openly.

'I really think you should do something, Robbie,' Fleur muttered.

Robbie put down his beer and unfolded his tall frame. He held out his hand. 'You're right. I should get you out of here before any trouble starts.'

'I didn't mean that. I meant–' Fleur began, but at that moment the landlord's thunderous tones cut through the chatter and laughter. 'Now then, young Alfie. I want no trouble in my pub.'

Alfie stopped in his tracks and stood swaying unsteadily in the middle of the bar-room floor.

'Go home, lad, an' sleep it off. Kitty's doing no harm. She's only being friendly, like.'

'A bit too – friendly,' the lad slurred his words. 'Kitty! You're my girl. You come here this minute.'

Now all eyes were turned towards Alfie or on Kitty sitting with her blonde head against Johnny's shoulder. She raised it briefly and waved her hand towards Alfie as if brushing him away. 'Oh, go home, little boy.'

Incensed by her dismissive taunt, Alfie launched himself towards the pair, knocking over drinks and tables.

'Steady, lad.'

''Ere – watch what you're doing.'

With one accord, the rest of the crew – including Robbie – rose to their feet and moved together. Tommy and Alan caught hold of the youth's arms and Robbie grasped his kicking legs.

'Calm down, mate, calm down,' Johnny said. 'No offence meant. If she's your girl, then–'

'I'm not his girl,' Kitty piped up. 'Only he'd like to think so. Tek no notice of him. He's nowt but a kid. Ought to be in uniform, he did. He's old enough.'

There was a brief silence whilst the locals glanced at each other uncomfortably.

'Now, now, Kitty,' Bill said gently. 'No need for that sort of talk. The lad works on a farm. He's doing a good job.'

Kitty said no more, but her lip curled disdainfully.

'So why aren't *you* in uniform?' Alfie spat back at her, struggling to free himself, but the young airmen were holding him fast. 'Like that lass there.' He nodded towards Fleur, who felt embarrassment creep up her face. 'Or are you "doing your bit" another way?'

His crude meaning was obvious to everyone listening and a gasp rippled around the room. But Alfie turned his attention to the young men holding on to him. He glared into the face of each one of them and then, slowly and deliberately, he said, 'And I hope your bloody plane crashes.'

Now there was a shocked silence through the whole bar. For a moment, no one moved. Then Fleur leapt to her feet, her eyes blazing. 'That's a wicked thing to say!'

'Steady on, lass. He doesn't mean it–'

'Oh yes, I do,' the youth muttered.

'He's had one too many – he dun't know what 'ee's sayin',' Bill said and moved from behind the bar to step between the airmen and take firm hold of Alfie himself. The burly man held the lad quite easily. 'Time you was going home, Alfie

Fish. You've said quite enough for one night. More than enough. Now, I don't want to 'ave to bar you from my pub, but if you can't behave ya'sen, I will. Mek no mistake about that. These lads' – he nodded towards Robbie and the rest – 'and those lasses there an' all' – now he included Fleur and the other girls too – 'are all here for a very good reason. They're fighting this war for us. They're in the front line, as it were. Now, to my mind, we're all doing our bit. You're working on the land, providing us all wi' food. I'm doing my bit, giving these young 'uns a bit of fun on their time off. So, we're all doing our bit one way or another. Everybody here.' Now he swept his arm wide to include everyone sitting in the bar room. 'So let's have no more fighting amongst oursens. We've got enough on, fighting old Adolf. And as for Kitty – well – you're hardly going to keep her with this sort of behaviour, now a' ya?'

Suddenly, the fight seemed to go out of the young man and he slumped against Bill. The older man took his full weight and the airmen released their hold. With a shake of their heads the locals resumed their conversations and took a swallow of their beer, whilst Bill helped Alfie from the bar room out into the night.

As Bill returned, he nodded towards Robbie and the others. 'Sorry about that, lads. Just give him a minute or two to get hissen down the road home afore you leave.' He winked at them meaningfully. 'I 'aven't got so much authority on the public highway and PC Mitchell's nowhere to be seen when you want him.' He laughed heartily. 'Mind you, it's a good job sometimes if I'm a bit

93

late closing.'

After about fifteen minutes, Tommy said, 'We'll have to get going, chaps, else we'll be late back at camp. 'Specially if we've to escort these lovely young ladies back to their billets.'

'No need,' Ruth said brusquely. 'We'll be fine.'

'And I, of course,' Kay remarked dryly, 'am going the same way as you lot anyway. Back to my biscuit bed in a draughty hut.' She cast a mock resentful glance towards Ruth and Fleur, who merely grinned in return, refusing to rise to her bait this time.

'Right then. Time to go,' Robbie said, standing up and holding out his hand to Fleur. As they moved towards the door, calling 'goodnight' to Bill, and out into the darkness, none of them noticed the three youths who had been sitting with Alfie in the corner rise to their feet and follow them out.

The youths came at them out of the blackness, launching themselves at their perceived enemies with the same ferocity as any trained solder with a bayonet in his hand.

'Look out!' Fleur's cry came too late and, as she found herself pushed to her hands and knees on the rough road, Robbie and the rest were under attack.

It was an unequal fight, even though it was four against four. Alfie too had appeared out of the shadows. The airmen, though fit from drill and gymnastics on camp, were no match for the brawny strength of the young farm workers. Fists flew and solid punches found their mark. Grunts and shouts filled the night air, whilst the four girls peered through the gloom, watching helplessly.

'Ouch! You little sod!'

It was Robbie's voice that galvanized Fleur. 'Stop it! Stop it this minute!' she cried and then launched herself at the youth attacking Robbie. She clung to his back and wound her arm around his throat. Suddenly, all the play-fights she had ever had with her younger brother came back to her. She hooked her leg round Robbie's attacker and pulled him backwards so that he lost his balance and fell to the floor.

'Ruth!' she yelled. 'Come and sit on this one.'

'Attagirl!' Ruth whooped and threw herself bodily across the prone figure, satisfied to hear his weak groan of futile protest as her weight knocked the last ounce of breath from his body.

Squinting through the darkness, Fleur saw that Tommy was taking a real battering.

'Come on.' Now she heard Kay's voice at her side and together they launched themselves against Tommy's assailant. A moment later, he too was lying on the ground with Kay sitting astride him.

With both Robbie and Tommy now free, Alan and Johnny's attackers were soon dispatched. They fled into the darkness and only then did Ruth and Kay release their captives.

Panting heavily, the airmen and WAAFs stood in the lane listening to the pounding feet growing fainter in the distance.

'Now we'll be for it,' Tommy muttered. 'Fighting with the locals. We'll be on a charge and no mistake.'

Ten

'Well, I'm going to say I fell over in the dark. That'll explain my laddered stockings,' Ruth declared next morning. 'What about you?'

Fleur bit her lip. She'd never liked telling lies. She'd always owned up to any misdemeanour either to her parents or to her teachers. But now, others were involved and she didn't want to get anyone else into trouble. 'I wonder how the lads are faring.'

'It's a clear forecast for tonight – so Peggy was saying,' Ruth told her as they left the dining room together after breakfast. 'They'll be flying for sure. I doubt a word will be said as long as no one from the village makes trouble. And I don't think they will. You heard what Bill Moore's attitude is. And I reckon most of the villagers feel the same.' She laughed wryly. 'More likely those lads will get a leathering from their dads for being such idiots.' She nodded wisely. 'The station brings a lot of trade to this area to say nothing of the little treats that find their way from our NAAFI onto the tables of the villagers.' She tapped the side of her nose. Fleur laughed, hoping fervently that Ruth was right.

As she climbed the steps to the watch office that evening, Fleur found her heart was hammering inside her chest and she felt sick. Already, the vehicles were ferrying crews out to their aircraft as she took her place beside Kay. Although she'd spent four hours earlier in the day familiarizing herself with how things were done in this particular flying control, this was her first time on duty during a mission. Kay was a good teacher, brusque and to the point as was her manner, but in no way irritable or impatient. Fleur, meticulous as she had always been since the day she'd signed up, welcomed the other girl's professional attitude. Bob Watson was on duty that night. He smiled and nodded at Fleur as she took her seat, rearranged her writing pad and pens in readiness for the notes and lists she would be required to jot down through the busy night. She adjusted her headphones and the microphone around her neck for comfort as, behind her, other members of the team readied themselves too.

On the walls around the room were maps and clocks, and blackboards giving local weather conditions and target information. The most interesting one to Fleur was the operations blackboard with 'WICKERTON WOOD' painted in white at the top. Beneath it, the station's call sign 'Woody' and the numbers of the two squadrons operating from Wickerton Wood with their respective call signs, Lindum and Pelham. In the centre of the board was the word 'RAID' with a space for the name of the target to be chalked in each time. Below that was a white painted grid where Peggy was already filling in all the details of each aircraft and the pilot's name for tonight's raid. As each one took off she would fill in the time. And then, lastly, there was the blank column that everyone watched most anxiously: 'RETURN'.

Fleur glanced over her shoulder to see Peggy writing in Tommy Laughton's name. Now there could be no mistake. Robbie was definitely on tonight's raid.

She glanced out of the window, criss-crossed with tape, in front of the long desk where the R/T operators sat with all their instruments and telephones overlooking the airfield's runways. Her heart skipped a beat. In the distance she could see the airmen climbing into their planes. She strained her eyes but could not pick out Robbie. Good luck, darling, she said silently. Safe home.

One by one, dozens of engines burst into life, their throbbing filling the night air and almost shaking the ground as they taxied from the various dispersal points, forming up to take off at orderly, timed intervals. At the end of the runway each aircraft waited for the controller's red light to switch to green before, revving its engines, it began its cumbersome, breath-holding take-off. One by one the Hampdens, heavy with fuel and bombs, lumbered down the runway.

On take-off and until the aircraft reached the target there was radio silence, unless in a dire emergency. Landing back at base, when security no longer mattered quite so much, was when the girls in the watch office would have radio communication with the aircraft. But they were all on duty for take-off, listening in, ready to help if needed.

'Right, ladies and gentlemen,' Bob Watson said. 'Let's see these lads into the air.'

There was a clatter of footsteps outside and the door burst open. A breathless Ruth came to attention in front of Bob's desk. 'Permission to go up to the roof, Flight?'

With a small smile, Bob nodded and Ruth rushed out of the room.

Fleur blinked and turned questioning eyes towards Bob Watson, who said shortly and with a trace of sarcasm, 'Your friend seems to think it vital that she waves off every mission from the roof of the watch tower. Some silly superstition of hers. She comes in even when she's not on duty herself and, if she's on leave, she makes someone promise to do it for her.'

Fleur said nothing. She understood about superstition and 'good luck' charms that the airmen carried. Why, at this moment, one of her initialled handkerchiefs nestled in the breast pocket of Robbie's uniform. No, she didn't blame Ruth one bit for her 'silly' superstition.

It was a long night. Once the flurry of activity of watching all the aircraft get safely airborne was over, there was nothing for the team in Control to do but wait.

'You girls can take it easy for a while. It'll be several hours before they're back,' Bob said. 'Get a cup of tea in turns ... er ... write letters, knit or do some ... er ... mending...' Fleur noticed that Bob was looking hopefully at Kay, who was studiously avoiding his eyes.

Fleur chuckled. 'I think Flight has a job he'd like you to do, Corp,' she said, pretending inno-cence.

'Then he can think again,' Kay said tartly, but Fleur caught the twinkle in the girl's eyes and she sent Fleur a surreptitious wink. She was toying with Bob, who looked crestfallen. Suddenly Kay swivelled round on her chair. 'What is it this time? Socks? Shirt buttons?'

'Actually – it's a button on my jacket...'

'Oh, now that is serious,' Kay mocked. 'Just think if you were called to the CO's office with a button missing on your jacket. Tut-tut.' She winked at Fleur. 'You any good with a needle, Fleur?'

Fleur caught the mischief in Kay's eyes and shook her head. 'Terrible! My mother despaired of me.' She could hardly stop the giggles that were welling up inside her from spilling out. The truth was that Betsy had brought her up to sew, mend and make do. She was quite expert with her needle and thread and no slouch with a sewing machine either.

Now the two girls dissolved into laughter whilst Bob stood looking at them helplessly. Peggy joined in the conversation. 'You're rotten, you two.' She turned to Bob. 'I'd offer, but I really am useless at needlework. I bet that one' – she jabbed her finger at Fleur – 'is pulling your leg. She's been brought up on a farm and I bet she could knit you a jumper straight off a sheep's back.'

Fleur wiped the tears of laughter from her eyes, thankful that for a few moments she had been able to put aside her anxiety over Robbie. 'Not quite, Peggy, but I am teasing. Yes, I can sew. My mother would have a ducky fit if she heard me denying all her teaching. Hand it over and I'll see what I can do.'

As she fished in her bag for her 'housewife' with, amongst other items, its sewing needle, blue thread and tiny pair of scissors, Bob brought his uniform jacket to her, holding out the shining button in the palm of his hand. 'Lucky I didn't lose this.'

'Well, on your own head be it, Fleur,' Kay remarked. 'Don't say I didn't warn you. Word will go round this place like wildfire that you've set up as the camp seamstress. You'll have all these ham-fisted fellers beating a path to your door.'

'I should be so lucky!' Fleur quipped as she threaded her needle.

'There's just one thing,' Bob said seriously. 'Don't let the CO catch you. He's a stickler for the rulebook.'

'Then you'd better keep an eye out.' She grinned up at him. 'At least while I'm doing *your* jacket.'

'I'll get us some tea,' Peggy offered, whilst Kay turned back to study her notes and the jottings she had made during take-off.

The hours of waiting seemed interminable, especially on the eight-hour night watch, but Fleur was glad to be here. It helped her to feel closer to Robbie, even though she had a hollow, sick feeling in the pit of her stomach that she knew would not go away until he had landed safely. But tomorrow she could look forward to a day off after the long night duty. She hoped Robbie would have some time to spend with her.

As the time drew near for the aircraft to return, the relaxed atmosphere in the watch office disappeared and became businesslike once more.

Just as the voice from the first homecoming aircraft came crackling over the airwaves, a red air-raid warning came in and at once the runway lights went out. Hurriedly, but with surprising calm, Kay gave warning to the homecoming crew about what was happening.

Though her hands were shaking, Fleur managed to speak calmly into her own microphone, warning each aircraft as it called in of the danger. They were all given the command to orbit at a certain height, though several were already low on fuel and wouldn't be able to circle for long. Fleur bit her lip, her ears tuned for the call sign of Robbie's plane, D-Doggo.

Then they heard the incendiary bombs falling. Thud! A silence and then another thud. Closer now. Another, even closer, and then came a thunderous boom very close to the control tower. The whole room seemed to shake and the glass rattled, but Kay continued to speak calmly into her microphone. 'Hello, G-George, this is Woody receiving you, strength niner, over...' Then she wrote rapidly on her notepad, her hand moving smoothly over the page, without any telltale shake.

Fleur took a deep breath. 'Hello, P-Poppy, this is Woody...' She was gratified to find that her voice was level and calm too, but her heart was pounding so loudly in her chest, she was sure they could hear it over the airwaves.

They waited for the next bomb to fall, convinced it would be a direct hit on the watch office. Well, there's one thing, Fleur thought irrationally. If I'm to die so soon, my mother will have been proved right!

But no more bombs fell and in a few moments the all-clear was declared.

'Just a lone raider dropping a stick of bombs, I expect,' Bob said, smoothing back his hair, which had become distinctly ruffled during the last few minutes. The landing lights came on and, as soon as the runway was declared damage free, instructions to land began at once.

Later Fleur was to learn from Ruth that one or two aircraft had landed on almost empty tanks.

One of the last aircraft to land was D-Doggo. Finally, Fleur could breathe again. Robbie was safely back.

If every night was going to be as bad as this one had been, Fleur wondered how she would cope. But cope she would; she had to for Robbie's sake. It wouldn't help him if she let him see how dreadfully anxious she was. And yet she needed to let him know how very much she cared for him, how very much – already – she loved him.

She smiled. But he knew that, just as she knew how much he loved her.

There were no doubts between the two of them about their feelings for each other. If only he had been able to talk to his mother...

Eleven

'Hi, Sis. Thought I'd bike over and see how you're getting on.'

'Kenny! What are you doing here this time of the morning? Whatever time did you set off?'

He was waiting for her as she came off duty after the long night. She wouldn't see Robbie until later – they both needed to sleep. Kenny had arrived at the guardroom at the main gate and a message had been sent to Fleur.

'There's nothing wrong at home, is there?' Fleur was still anxious.

Kenny grinned. 'No more than usual. Mum's still going on about you joining up and me following you. I shan't wait till I'm called up, though. I shall volunteer as soon as I can.'

'Oh, it'll all be over by the time you're old enough,' Fleur said, hoping she sounded more convincing than she felt.

'Hope not,' Kenny said cheerfully with the thoughtlessness of youth. 'I want to see a bit of the action myself.'

Fleur sighed heavily but couldn't prevent a smile. 'And you know who'll get the blame if you do "see a bit of the action"?'

'You will.' He grinned, draping one arm around her shoulder and wheeling his bicycle with the other hand as they began to walk down the lane towards Rose Cottage. Although five years younger than Fleur, he was already a head taller.

'Exactly!' she said with wry humour, but then her tone sobered. 'But seriously, Kenny, I couldn't bear it if something happened to you. No more than Mum and Dad could. You do know that, don't you?'

He gave her shoulder a squeeze. 'Course I do,' he said softly, but then teased, 'now don't start getting all soppy on me. But I'll tell you now, if the war is still going on, I shall join up. I'm not having anyone calling me a coward.'

'Oh, Kenny, they wouldn't. Farming's acknowledged as a reserved occupation.'

'I know, and *I* don't blame those who stay, but you've seen for yourself the looks that young, unmarried fellers get.'

Fleur was silent, thinking of Kitty's scathing remark about Alfie. She'd seen for herself now how hurtful such comments could be.

'And it's not your fault either. I'd've gone anyway, whether you had or not, and I shall tell Mum so when the time comes.'

Fleur slipped her arm around his waist and laid her head against his shoulder as they walked side by side.

'It makes no difference whether Mum blames me or not, love. I shall blame myself.' There was a pause and then she said, 'I just wondered why you're here so early, that's all.' She sighed. 'It's a sign of the times. I immediately thought something was wrong.'

'I just thought I'd like to spend the day with you. I've no school today and Dad said he'd manage the morning milking on his own, so I set off at the crack of dawn.'

'How long does it take you?'

Kenny wrinkled his forehead. 'Couple of hours, I suppose. Bit more, p'raps. I use all the back roads and lanes, cutting across country. It's quicker.'

'Well, it's great to see you,' she said, giving his waist a quick squeeze.

As they rounded the last corner towards the two cottages, Fleur glanced up and saw Robbie waiting by the gate, arms akimbo, watching them approach. His fair hair was ruffled by the breeze, his jacket and shirt collar undone, his tie hanging loose. She pulled in a sharp breath and Kenny looked down at her.

'What is it, Sis?' Then, as he saw the brightness in her eyes, he followed the line of her gaze. 'Oho,' he said softly, 'so this is the feller all the trouble's about, is it?'

'Yes,' Fleur breathed. 'That's him. That's Robbie.'

'Then you'd better introduce me and I can report back to Mum.'

'It won't make any difference,' Fleur murmured sadly. 'There's something that happened in the past, but we don't know what and no one will tell us. Look, Kenny, be a dear. Don't say anything in front of Robbie, will you?'

'Course not if you say so.'

They were too close now to be able to say more without him hearing, so, releasing herself from Kenny's arm, Fleur ran towards Robbie.

'What's this?' he said, smiling down at her. 'A rival already, have I?'

'Absolutely! This is the man I've loved all his life. Robbie – this is Kenny, my ... my brother.' For a brief moment her voice faltered and they exchanged a stricken glance.

What if ... oh, what if...?

But then Robbie had mastered his expression and was turning towards Kenny, his hand out-stretched. 'I'm very pleased to meet you,' he said warmly, but Fleur was still battling to control her runaway emotions. What if she were at that moment introducing half-brothers to each other?

A shudder ran through her and it was Robbie's arm that now tightened around her, silently encouraging her to stay strong.

Kenny held out his hand. Although he favoured their mother's colouring – fair hair and blue eyes – there were times, like now, when his face creased in smiles just like their father's did when he laughed. 'Pleased to meet you.' The younger man looked Robbie up and down. 'Smart uniform, though I was thinking of the army mesen – when the time comes.'

'You'll probably see more of the world than I will stuck up there in a plane. But I fancied the flying.'

Kenny nodded. 'Yeah. Now you come to mention it,' he said thoughtfully, 'it must be thrilling, though I think I'd prefer fighter planes. Bit more exciting, that one-to-one stuff.' And they laughed together, comrades already.

Fleur stepped between them and linked her arms through theirs. 'Right, now I'll take you to meet Mrs Jackson and Harry – if he's about. And Ruth should be home soon.'

'Well, I'd come to tell you that I'll give you a hand this afternoon with this overgrown garden you were telling me about,' Robbie said. 'I felt like some fresh air and a bit of real work when I've had a few hours' kip.'

'Me too,' Fleur agreed. She was delighted to see Kenny, but after the long night of anxiety she felt she could fall asleep standing up.

'But I needed to come and make sure you were all right after the air raid.'

'Air raid? What air raid?' Kenny asked at once before Fleur could even reply.

'Oh, it was nothing, just a lone raider dropping a stick of incendiaries,' Fleur said airily, as if it was a daily occurrence and nothing to get excited about. She squeezed Robbie's arm, warning him not to make too much of it.

Catching on at once, Robbie adopted a light, bantering tone. 'Well, it was just an excuse to see you really.'

Kenny glanced at Robbie above Fleur's head and, despite Robbie's affected nonchalance about the raid, Kenny could still see the worry in his eyes. The young man knew that they were both trying to make light of the incident in front of him.

Softly, he said, 'You can tell me the truth, you know. I won't go running home to tell Mum. I know an airfield's a dangerous place.' He looked down at Fleur. 'You've been on duty all night, haven't you? And you,' he said, glancing up again at Robbie, 'have been flying?'

Robbie laughed softly. 'Seems there's no keeping any secrets from this brother of yours, darling.'

Fleur smiled ruefully. 'No,' she said wryly. 'I

don't think there is. Not about anything.'

'So, you both need to get some sleep,' Kenny began, but Fleur cut in saying, 'Well, yes, but don't go. I've the rest of the day off. In fact, I'm not on duty until the afternoon shift tomorrow.'

'And our aircraft's out of action until tomorrow. We encountered flak coming back across the coast and there are a few holes here and there.' Again, he was trying to make light of it. 'We'll just need a couple of hours and then we can spend the afternoon with you, Kenny.'

'Right-o,' Kenny said cheerfully. 'In the meantime, I can maybe make myself useful. What's all this about a garden?'

Fleur laughed. 'Careful – I might set you on.' Swiftly, Fleur explained about the state of the old lady's garden. 'It must have been a wonderful kitchen garden when her old man was alive, but now...' She shrugged. 'Well, you'll see the state of it for yourself. I scythed about half of it yesterday and then it'll want digging over. There's a lot of work, but it'll be worth it if I can get it right. And it's still only April. There'll be time to plant a few veggies.'

They went in by the front gate and around the corner of the house and then moved to the little gate leading into the back garden. The two men stood looking at the neglected ground.

'Grow a lot of stuff, that would,' Kenny mused. 'And the government's shouting for us all to use every spare bit of ground. I'm surprised they haven't sent a couple of sturdy Land Army girls to do it for her. Dad's got two coming, since you left.'

Fleur laughed. 'Now there's a compliment! Takes two to replace me, does it?'

Kenny grinned. 'That's about the size of it, Sis.'

'It's a lot to tackle on your own,' Robbie said. 'Is Ruth helping?'

'She's a city girl. Wouldn't know a 'tatie from a turnip. Mind you' – Fleur's eyes sparkled with mischief – 'I've got another little job lined up for her – though she doesn't know it yet.'

'Well, I don't mind lending a hand when I'm off duty. Be good to get my hands dirty for once,' Robbie promised.

'Maybe I could bring you some tools–' Kenny began, but Fleur shook her head. 'No need. What Mrs Jackson hasn't got in her shed, Harry'll lend me. Come on in and meet my landlady.'

Fleur led the way into the kitchen and watched the old lady's eyes light up at the sight of the two handsome young men. The introductions over, Fleur made tea whilst Robbie sat down opposite Mrs Jackson with Kenny next to her. From the back scullery, Fleur heard them all laughing. It was the first time she had heard the old dear laugh aloud and when she carried the tea tray into the room and set it on the table, she saw that Mary's face was pink with pleasure.

'Coo-ee, it's only me,' a voice shouted as the back door was thrown open and Ruth appeared like a whirlwind. 'Why didn't you wait for me–?' she began as she stepped into the kitchen, but she stopped short as she saw the two young men. She'd met Robbie during the evening at the local pub, but her eyes widened as she spotted Kenny. Her mouth twitched with amusement as she said

110

with mock severity, 'Well, I can see why now. Wanted to keep this handsome pair to yourself, did you? I call that greedy, don't you, Mrs Jackson?' She stuck out her hand towards Kenny. 'Hello. I'm Ruth. Fleur's very *best* friend.'

Kenny scrambled up, the colour rising in his face. 'H-hello. I'm Kenny. Fleur's brother.'

Fleur watched with mixed feelings as her little brother – not so little now, she noticed with a pang, for he towered over Ruth – took the girl's hand in his, his gaze fastened on her pretty face. Ruth smiled, the dimples in her round cheeks deepening. She took off her cap and shook her wayward curls. 'Nice to meet you, Kenny.'

She let go of his hand and turned towards the table. 'Any tea in the pot? I'm parched.'

Kenny sank back down into the chair, but his gaze never left Ruth as she busied herself freshening the pot and pouring herself a cup. She sat in a chair near the table, crossed her shapely legs and smiled round at everyone.

They sat chatting for several minutes until a knock came at the back door, which then opened. 'You there, lass?' came Harry's voice. 'I saw you come in. I've brought you the scythe round.' He reared the implement against the wall and stepped into the house. 'Oh, sorry. Didn't realize you had company.'

The old rascal, Fleur thought. If he saw me come home then he must have seen the lads with me. He's just come round to see what's going on. Then, remembering how lonely the old boy must be, she introduced him to Robbie and her brother.

Harry nodded at them in turn. 'How do?'

111

'How d'you do?' Robbie said, getting up. 'You must be Mr Chambers. Fleur has told me about you.'

'Call me 'Arry, young feller. Everybody does.'

'Well then, pleased to meet you, Harry.'

'Well,' Fleur gave an exaggerated sigh. 'I'd best get me head down for a couple of hours and then into me gardening clothes. You're a hard task-master, Harry, an' no mistake.'

'No, no, lass, if you've got company, I'll take the scythe back again.'

'It's OK,' Kenny said at once. 'I'll have a go while Fleur has a sleep. I'll do all the grass under the fruit trees and bushes at the bottom of the garden. Have you got a sickle I could use as well, Mr Chambers?'

'I have, lad, and I'll fetch it round for ya, but only if you call me "Harry".'

'And I'll be back this afternoon,' Robbie promised. 'And we'll all do a spot of digging.'

Kenny, red to the roots of his hair, said, 'You know I could bike over now and again and lend a hand, if you like, Sis.' But she noticed that his eyes went to Ruth as he made the offer.

Struggling to keep a straight face, Fleur said, 'That'd be great.'

'Well, young feller,' Harry put in, 'if you're as handy with me scythe as your sister, you should get that grass cut by the end of the morning.'

'You're on, Harry.' Kenny grinned.

That afternoon, Robbie returned. As he took off his jacket and hung it on a nail in the shed, he glanced down the garden to where Kenny was mowing the last patch of long grass, with Ruth sitting on the bench under the old apple tree, watching him.

'You know,' he said softly to Fleur, 'I think your little brother is smitten with Ruth.'

'Mmm, I noticed. But he's not so little now, is he?' she added wistfully and felt a shudder of apprehension at the thought that in the short space of a year her beloved Kenny would be old enough to enlist. 'Come on,' she said, determined not to let thoughts of the war spoil this sunny afternoon. 'Let's go and help.'

'What do you want me to do?'

Fleur grinned at him. 'How are you at digging?'

Twelve

It was a happy afternoon. Robbie and Kenny tackled the digging – a tough job, for the ground was hard and the grass and weeds had taken a firm hold – whilst Fleur finished the last bit of scything.

Harry sat in the house, chatting to Mary Jackson in between making little forays into the garden to see how the work was progressing, whilst Ruth kept everyone supplied with tea.

'The old dears have fallen asleep,' Ruth said about the middle of the afternoon. 'Harry's snoring with his mouth wide open. But they look so sweet,' she added fondly. 'You'd think they were an old married couple instead of just neighbours.'

113

Kenny, his face red from exertion, took a breather leaning on his fork. 'Thanks,' he said, the colour on his face deepening as he took the mug of tea from Ruth.

Hands on her hips, Ruth surveyed their work. 'Well, I feel like a spare part. But I wouldn't know where to start.'

Fleur rested on the scythe for a moment. 'You could rake this grass up if you like, but mind you don't get near me.'

'Huh! Not likely when you're wielding that thing.'

'Well, you're doing a great job keeping us supplied with tea for today. It's thirsty work.'

'I'll stick to that then. Mind you, I suppose I could do a bit of raking. Seems easy enough.' She was about to move away to rummage in the conglomeration of Mrs Jackson's shed to find a rake when she turned back and eyed Fleur suspiciously. 'What did you mean "for today"? Sounds as if you've got something else lined up for me. I told you, I'm a city girl.'

'I know – but how are you at housework?'

Ruth's eyes lit up. 'Oh, I'm a dab hand at that. I like everything spick and span.'

'I know,' Fleur said ruefully. 'I've seen your bedroom.' She was having a hard time keeping her own room as neat and tidy as her fellow WAAF's.

'We live in a council house back home,' Ruth went on. 'And me mum keeps it like a little palace.' She frowned. 'But Mrs Jackson's cottage is spotless. I don't see–'

'I wasn't thinking of here.' She paused, leant towards Ruth and lowered her voice. 'Have you

114

seen Harry's place?'

Ruth stared at her and shook her head. 'Harry's place?' she repeated. 'No, I've never been inside.'

Fleur laughed. 'Well, take my word for it. It's a tip.'

'But – but he keeps his garden immaculate.'

Fleur nodded. 'I know, but I reckon that was his domain and the house was his wife's, and since she's gone...'

'Oh, I get you. Not much of a housewife, is he?'

'That's an understatement, love,' Fleur said wryly.

'But – but how can I offer to help? I mean, I don't want to hurt the old boy's feelings. He's a pet.'

'Go back into the house and say you feel a bit – well – a bit useless out here.'

'Oh, thanks!'

'You know what I mean. You've got to lay it on with a trowel.'

'I told you – I'm no good with trowels.'

They laughed, sparring with each other, until Ruth nodded and said, 'I'll go in and ask Mrs Jackson if there's anything she wants doing. I know she'll say "no" 'cos I've asked her before and there's only so many times I can clean my bedroom from top to bottom. And then I'll turn to Harry and ask him if he wants any ironing doing or the washing up. That'd be all right, d'you think?'

'Perfect,' Fleur grinned.

'Right.' Ruth took a deep breath. 'Here we go, then.'

The grass forgotten, Ruth headed for the

115

cottage and a few moments later she emerged, her arm linked through Harry's. Behind his back she gave Fleur the 'thumbs up' sign and called, 'Mrs Jackson's taking over tea-making duties. Let her know when you want another.'

At the sound of her voice, Kenny looked up. 'Where's Ruth going?'

'Just next door. Give Harry a bit of a hand. She's not one for the outdoor life, it seems.'

'Oh.' His disappointment was clear to see. 'Will she be back before I have to go?'

'I expect so, but if not, you can nip next door and say "cheerio".'

The grin was back on his face as he attacked the solid ground with his fork. Unseen by Kenny, Robbie winked at Fleur just as Mrs Jackson appeared in the back doorway with a plate of scones in her hand to go with the tea Ruth had brought out.

As they stood leaning against the outer wall of the cottage, drinking tea and eating scones, Robbie declared, 'D'you know, I'm a townie like Ruth, but I have to say I'm enjoying a bit of physical work.'

'You'll suffer for it tomorrow.' Fleur grinned. 'You'll ache in muscles you didn't know you'd got.'

Robbie pulled a face. 'Quite likely, but it'll be worth it. It's good to get away from camp and to concentrate on something other than what we've got to do at night. And that reminds me.' He glanced at his watch. 'I'll have to go in about half an hour. There's a final briefing in an hour's time and even though I'm pretty sure our crew's not flying tonight, I'd better be on hand just in case.'

'Yes, and I'll have to report in too. Someone might have gone off sick and I'll be needed to take their place. Ruth too.'

As she collected the cups and plates, Kenny said, 'Look, you two go off – for a walk or summat. Have a bit of time to yourselves. I'll carry on with the digging here. I can stay till you have to go, Sis.' He glanced at the cottage next door.

'Right you are, Kenny. Thanks.' Deliberately casual, she said, 'And don't let me forget to give Ruth a shout. We'll both need time to get back into our uniforms.'

Kenny grinned. 'No, I won't forget.'

'I bet he won't.' Robbie laughed softly as they walked, hand in hand, out of the squeaking gate and a little way down the lane to where the houses stopped and the countryside began. They headed for a little copse at the edge of a field that would afford them a bit of privacy. Climbing over the gate, they headed for the shelter of the trees.

Robbie took her in his arms, but Fleur was stiff, afraid to respond. 'Oh, Robbie,' she whispered, tears filling her eyes. 'Did we ought to?'

He sighed heavily and rested his cheek against her hair. His arms were still about her but comforting rather than desirous. 'Darling, I'll try to speak to Ma as soon as I can. I promise. Maybe I could wangle a day's leave on compassionate grounds. I got a letter from her this morning and she says Pops has a very bad cold and it's gone on his chest. She's quite worried about him, I think.'

Fleur pulled a face. 'I doubt you'll manage it unless the weather gets bad and you can't fly.'

So much taller than Fleur, Robbie kissed the top of her head. 'Then we'll just have to pray for snow.'

Fleur laughed, despite the worry clouding their time together. 'What? In April?'

'It's been known. Pops reckons he remembers it snowing in the middle of May in nineteen hundred.'

'Really?'

'So he says.'

They stayed for the half-hour, just happy to be together, and yet they dared not kiss – it felt wrong until they knew for sure.

'Oh I wish we knew. I wish we knew the truth,' Fleur moaned as they walked back to Mrs Jackson's cottage. Robbie squeezed her hand. 'I'll find out as soon as I can. I promise.'

The snow that they'd wished for didn't arrive and there were operations on each of the following three nights. The watching and waiting didn't get any easier and Fleur breathed a sigh of relief each time D-Doggo landed safely. On the fourth night, however, there was a weather report of bad visibility over the target area that cancelled the mission. All aircrews were stood down and Robbie went at once to see Tommy Laughton.

'Skip, is it absolutely definite that we won't be flying? Because, if it is, I could do to nip home for twenty-four hours.'

'It's definite, old boy, so it should be OK. Mind you fill in a two-nine-five.' Tommy reminded him to submit the usual application form. 'But can you be sure to be back by thirteen hundred

118

tomorrow? If there's flying tomorrow night, briefing's likely to be at fourteen hundred.'

Robbie nodded. 'I'll hitch if the trains don't fit up. Folks are very decent about picking up servicemen.'

Tommy stroked his bristly moustache thoughtfully. 'Tell you what, nip along to MT. They might have a lorry going your way.'

'Thanks, Skip. I will.'

When he went in search of Fleur, it was to find that she too had been given permission to go home for a brief visit because there was no flying that night. He squeezed her arm. 'I've got a lift all the way to Nottingham. I'll ask the driver if he can take you too.'

They parted in Newark.

'Could you drop me outside Castle Station, please?' Fleur asked. 'I rang home and my father had to come into Newark anyway today so he said he can pick me up there.'

'What if he sees me?' Robbie asked worriedly.

The WAAF driver smiled knowingly, but made no comment as Fleur said cheerfully, 'I don't care if he does. You've got to meet each other some time.'

The lorry came to a halt and Fleur leant over and kissed Robbie's cheek before climbing down. As the vehicle pulled away, she turned towards the station to see Jake standing beside his battered Ford. She caught her breath. He must have seen Robbie. When she got closer she was shocked by the look on her father's face. Even though he was tanned by the outdoor life he led, the colour had drained from his face and his eyes

119

were haunted. He looked as if he had just been dealt a devastating blow. The thought terrified Fleur. Had her father believed he was looking at his own son for the first time?

Her voice shook as she said, 'Dad? What is it? What's the matter?'

He was breathing heavily. 'Is that him? Is that Meg's boy?'

'Yes,' Fleur said hesitantly. 'He ... he couldn't stop now. He's on his way home. His grandfather's ill. He–'

'Are you *sure* it is his grandfather?' There was still disbelief in Jake's tone.

'Yes. I asked him. It's his mother's father.'

Jake shook his head as if he couldn't believe what she was saying. 'You do surprise me,' he murmured, but he was speaking more to himself than to her.

Fleur took a deep breath and put her arm through her father's. 'Dad – Robbie and I – well, we've fallen in love, and unless you tell me that there's a good reason why we can't see each other–'

'Isn't upsetting your mother good reason enough?' he demanded harshly.

Fleur kept her voice calm. 'No – not on its own. I'm sorry, but it isn't.'

'Don't you think she's got enough to worry about with you gone and Kenny just waiting for the day when he's old enough to join up without you taking up with someone – with someone – unsuitable?'

'But *why* is he unsuitable, as you put it? If only you'd tell me then perhaps I could understand.'

120

Jake's mouth was a hard, unyielding line. 'I've told you once and I won't tell you again.' It was as if she were small again and he was chastising her for some childish escapade. 'It's not my secret to tell.'

'Are you sure?' Fleur cried passionately, no longer able to stay calm. 'Are you quite sure it has nothing to do with you?'

The bleak look on her father's face tore at her heart and when he pulled himself free of her grasp, picked up her bag and marched towards the car, she knew it would be fruitless to ask any more questions.

'I just hope Robbie's having better luck with his mother,' she muttered angrily as she followed Jake.

They drove all the way from Newark to South Monkford in an uncomfortable silence. As he drew the vehicle to a halt in the yard, Jake said, 'Not a word to your mother about all this. You hear me?'

If she didn't want to spoil her leave completely, Fleur gave the only answer she could. 'Yes, Dad.'

Thirteen

'Oh, it's you.'

'Well, that's a nice greeting, Mum, I must say.'

'What do you expect?' There was no smile from Betsy, not even a hug. 'It was bad enough you leaving us in the lurch, but now Kenny's taken it

121

into his head to come cycling over to see you every spare minute instead of helping your father.'

'Mum, he's been over *once*...'

But Betsy was in no mood to listen. 'He *says* it's to help some poor old dear with her gardening.' She gave a disapproving click of her tongue. 'But there's more to it than that.' She wagged her finger in Fleur's face. 'He's done nothing but talk about a girl called Ruth. Who is she, I'd like to know?'

Fleur took off her uniform jacket and hung it up on the back of the door. The teapot – as ever – was standing on the hob in the range. She picked it up, moved to the table and poured herself a cup of tea.

'Well,' Betsy demanded impatiently.

Fleur sighed as she sat down at the table. 'She's the other girl in the billet with me and the old lady is our landlady. She's a sweet old dear, but she's crippled with arthritis. Her husband used to keep the garden lovely, but since he died three years ago, it's been neglected. I just thought I'd help tidy it up in my spare time, get some veggies growing. You know, like the government's always telling us to do.'

'It's here you should be helping.' Betsy prodded her forefinger towards the floor. 'Not digging some stranger's garden *and* enticing your brother away from his duty too.'

'I didn't *entice* him, as you put it,' Fleur said wearily. 'I didn't even ask for his help. He came over to visit me and saw what I was doing.'

'Huh! And I expect you're trying to set him up with this Ruth girl? He's far too young to be thinking about girls. He's still at school, for heaven's sake.'

'Only because you've made him stay on. Still want him to go to university, do you?'

'No,' Betsy said promptly. 'Agricultural college.'

Fleur raised her eyebrows. 'That's a new idea. I've not heard that before. When did you think that one up?' Her eyes narrowed thoughtfully as she stared at her mother. 'Oh, I get it. You think it will keep him out of the war, don't you?'

Betsy wriggled her shoulders. 'Can't blame a mother for trying.'

Fleur was about to say, No, though you're trying much harder to stop Kenny going than you ever did with me. But she bit back the retort. It was the mother/son thing. She knew that. She sipped her tea in the tense silence.

Almost as if she had read her daughter's thoughts, Betsy blurted out, 'I'd've thought you'd have done what your dad wanted, even if you'd take no notice of me. But no, you had to go, didn't you?' Tears filled Betsy's eyes. 'And now there'll be no stopping Kenny.' Her voice rose hysterically. 'He'll go and it'll be all your fault. If you'd stayed here at home, he would've done an' all. But now...'

Fleur set down her cup with deliberate care. 'I know you won't believe me, Mum, but I've asked him not to go. But I don't think anything any of us can say will make any difference. And – and he said he'd go anyway – that it has nothing to do with me...' She saw her mother's sceptical glance but ploughed on. 'He doesn't want to be thought a coward. He says he gets some funny looks even now because he's not in uniform – because he's so tall for his age.'

Now Betsy leant over the table towards Fleur, almost menacingly. 'I'd rather him be thought a coward,' she said slowly, emphasizing every word, 'put in prison for it even – if it keeps him alive.'

'Oh, Mum!' Now Fleur's eyes filled with tears as she felt an overwhelming pity for her mother. 'That's not our Kenny. Can't you be proud of your son that – that he wants to do his duty for his country?'

Betsy banged the table with her fist. 'His duty's here. Helping his father on the land. Why else would the government make farming a reserved occupation? He'll be helping his country just as much. More, if truth be known, than becoming cannon fodder.' Fleur gasped as her mother ranted on. 'I've been through all this before, you know. Your father was in the last lot. Oh, he married me before he went – so that I would get his pension.' Her face twisted. 'His pension! What good is a pension compared to a lifetime of loneliness?'

'But Dad came back.'

'Aye, he did. I was lucky...' For a moment her eyes glazed over and she was lost in the past. 'I was lucky he came back – that he came back to *me* – that he stayed with *me*.'

Fleur felt as if ice-cold water was running down her spine. 'Mum – what d'you mean – came back to *you?*'

Betsy blinked, back in the present. 'Eh? Oh – oh nothing. Nothing.' She bit her lip and turned away, murmuring, 'Yes, you're right. I was lucky.' And then adding ominously, 'That time.'

The atmosphere lightened noticeably when Kenny breezed in from school, slung his satchel in the corner, hugged Fleur and then lifted his mother in a bear hug and swung her round. Betsy laughed and slapped him playfully. 'Oh, you bad boy! Put me down, put me down. I've your tea to get...'

She bustled about the kitchen and scullery with renewed vigour, a smile on her face now that her beloved son was home. She placed an overloaded plate of hot food before him, fussed around him, stroking his hair and patting his shoulder.

How does he put up with it? Fleur thought, gritting her teeth, realizing that she was glad she was not her mother's favourite if that was what she would have to put up with. She glanced across the table at her father, but Jake was eating his meal, outwardly placid, his face expressionless. But she wondered what exactly he was feeling inside.

'How's Ruth?' Kenny mumbled, his mouth full of meat and potato pie.

Before Fleur could answer, Betsy, sitting down next to Kenny, said, 'Don't talk with your mouth full and never mind about her. Did you see the careers master today? Did you ask him about agricultural college like I told you?'

Kenny stopped chewing and laid his knife and fork down on his plate, though his meal was only half eaten. He swallowed.

'Mum,' he began, his face unusually serious. He put his arm along the back of her chair and touched her shoulder. 'I don't want to go to college or university or anywhere. Not yet. When I

125

leave school, I'm going to join the RAF. I want to be a pilot. A fighter pilot.'

For a moment there was complete stillness in the room until the air was rent with Betsy leaping to her feet, pointing at Fleur and screaming. 'See? See? I told you. It's all your fault. If it hadn't been for you, he'd never even have thought of the RAF. If – if he's killed, it'll be your fault. All your fault.' She swung round towards Jake. 'And you're no better. You should have forbidden her to go. But you're too soft, too – too...' Betsy couldn't find the words to describe what she felt about Jake. She sank back into her chair, covered her face with her hands and broke into noisy sobbing.

'Oh, Mum, don't.' Kenny hugged her awkwardly, but it was to no avail.

Above the noise, Jake said, 'Betsy, now that's enough. You know I won't interfere with what either of them wants to do. I went myself last time, didn't I? I can hardly start playing the heavy-handed father this time round. Besides, if you want the truth, I'm proud of them. Proud of them both that they want to do their bit.'

Fleur and Kenny gaped at him, a mixture of emotions on both their faces. Gratitude for his understanding and because he'd spoken up in their defence, but at the same time shock because it was the first time they'd ever heard him criticize their mother. At least, in front of them. What perhaps passed between their parents in private they weren't to know.

Betsy's sobs subsided and she let her hands fall away from her face. In a flat voice she said, 'Then you don't care if they get hurt or even killed?'

126

'Of course I care.' Jake's voice was rising in anger now. 'How can you accuse me of not caring? But the whole country is in the same boat. Every mother's son is in danger.' He looked at Fleur and added, 'And a lot of fathers' daughters too.'

'I don't care about anyone else,' Betsy said and now her quiet tone was more frightening than her screaming. 'I only care about my own.' And she leant towards Kenny to emphasize just where her concerns lay.

'Then that's very selfish of you, Betsy.' Jake pushed back his chair and rose. As he was about to turn away, his wife said, 'I bet *she's* only bothered about her own precious son.'

Jake was very still and Fleur held her breath. Slowly he turned back to look down at Betsy. There was sadness on his face, a sorrow that was far deeper than disappointment in his wife's attitude. He was struggling to hold his tongue, to end the argument, but he lost the battle as he said quietly, 'He's a fine boy.'

Betsy stared up at her husband, her eyes wide with shock, whilst Fleur and Kenny could only watch in silence, mystified by what was being said. 'You've seen him?' she whispered. 'You – you've met him?'

'No, but I saw him – at a distance.' Without thinking, his glance went automatically to Fleur. It was enough for Betsy.

'He was with her? At the station? You saw him there? Today?'

Jake sighed. After all his warnings to Fleur, it was him who'd let the secret out. 'Yes, he was.'

127

His eyes were hard as he held his wife's gaze. 'He's a fine-looking boy, Betsy.'

'I bet he is. Oh I bet he is.' Tears ran down her face once more. 'I expect he's just like his *father!*'

There was a breathless pause before Jake said, with surprising calm now, 'Yes, Betsy, he is. He's the spitting image of his father.'

Fourteen

'I seem to say nothing but "I'm sorry, darling", don't I?' Robbie said ruefully.

They had arranged to meet in Newark and travel back to Wickerton Wood together.

'So – I take it you didn't get to ask your mother?'

Robbie shook his head. 'I felt very guilty asking for compassionate leave when the old boy had got no more than a cold, but in actual fact, when I got home, he was in hospital. Pneumonia, they say.'

Fleur gasped. 'Oh no! Will he be all right?'

'I hope so. Ma will be devastated if anything happens to him. Specially now with me... You know?'

There was no need for him to say more: Fleur knew exactly what he meant. If anything happened to Robbie, then the old man was the only person his mother would have to cling to.

Interrupting her thoughts, Robbie said, 'I just couldn't worry her at the moment.'

'Of course you couldn't.' Fleur was quick to reassure him. 'But there is a glimmer of hope.'

'Really?' His eyes lit up.

Over their tea, Fleur recounted the strange, mystifying argument between her parents. 'And when Mum said she expected that you're just like your father, Dad said, "Yes, he is. He's the spitting image of his father." She reached across the table and clasped his hands, leaning towards him to say earnestly, 'But you're nothing like my dad. You're fair and he's dark. He's starting to go a bit grey now, but he has brown hair. You've got blue eyes – really bright blue eyes – and his are brown. You're tall. He isn't particularly. So, where's the resemblance? I can't see it. Admittedly, your face creases up when you smile, a bit like his does, but then so do a lot of people's.' She paused and laughed. 'Old Harry's does, for a start.'

Robbie's face creased as he chuckled. 'Yeah, but he's got a lot more laughter lines on his face than I've got at the moment.'

'At the moment'. How poignant that simple phrase was. In these dangerous days how many handsome young men would never grow old enough to have a wrinkled face like Harry's?

Fleur deliberately tried to lighten their thoughts. 'Laughter lines, you call them?' she quipped. 'Nothing's that funny!'

Returning to the comparison between Robbie and her father, she went on, 'You've got a much squarer jaw than my dad and...' Suddenly, her voice faded away as she stared across the table at Robbie.

'What? What is it? Grown another nose, have I?'

Fleur shook her head, but she was still staring at him. 'You know, you do remind me of someone. Not my dad,' she added hastily, 'but someone... But for the life of me, I can't think who.'

Robbie grinned. 'Some handsome film star, I've no doubt.'

Fleur laughed out loud so that one or two folk at nearby tables smiled fondly. It was good to see two young people in uniform enjoying themselves.

'Of course,' Fleur teased. 'That must be it.'

They rose from the table, put a tip beneath the plate for the waitress and left the cafe, their arms about each other, suddenly a little freer to let their feelings show. And yet, they wouldn't be certain, not absolutely certain, until Robbie had spoken to his mother. Not until then would they allow themselves to be real girlfriend and boyfriend. Until then, they must act like the brother and sister that – God forbid – they might really be.

'You really are a grand pair of lasses to be helping us old folk like you are,' Mrs Jackson said as she shuffled across the room to set the table in time for an early tea. Both Ruth and Fleur were due to report back to camp for the evening shift. The lads – including Robbie – were flying tonight.

'It keeps us out of mischief,' Ruth laughed. 'I mean, if we weren't doing that we'd only be down the pub–'

'Or dancing–'

'Or shopping–'

They glanced at each other in mock horror.

'What *are* we thinking of?' Ruth said and Fleur giggled.

Ruth put her arm round the old lady's ample waist. 'Don't you fret, Mrs Jackson. I'm one of these strange people who actually enjoy housework. And – if I'm not mistaken – Fleur is going to get a lot of satisfaction when she sees leeks and potatoes and whatever else she's going to grow in that garden of yours.'

Fleur nodded. 'I've got it all planned out. I was asking my dad for advice when I was home at the weekend and he's given me a list of what to plant and when to plant it. I've written it all down in an old diary. I'm going to plant carrots, potatoes and cauliflowers, maybe leeks and onions too. And that rhubarb patch we unearthed when we cut the grass needs looking at. And I'll start a compost heap in the far corner. And in the other corner, I'm going to build you an Anderson shelter, Mrs Jackson.'

'Oh, don't worry about that, love. I don't think I could get there quick enough anyway. Someone did come a while back, but I told 'em I'd go round to Harry's if we got a bad raid.'

The two girls stared at the old lady. 'But ... but Harry hasn't got a shelter either,' Ruth said.

Now Mrs Jackson looked suddenly sheepish. 'No, I know. He wouldn't accept any help from anyone and he promised the authorities he'd build one himself.'

'But he never did.'

Mrs Jackson shook her head. 'I don't think he ever intended to, the awkward ol' devil!' She smiled fondly.

'Well, you really ought to have one,' Fleur said firmly, 'especially living so close to the airfield, so we'll build one for the two of you. We'll put it in the corner of your garden nearest his and cut a hole in the fence for him to get through and you can share it. All right?'

Mary Jackson smiled. 'If you say so, dear.'

'Right – that's settled then,' Fleur said firmly. 'I'll make enquiries as to how to get hold of what we need to make one.'

'The local ARP people might know,' Ruth suggested.

'That's a good idea. Only thing now is – I could do to find a farmer nearby with a lot of pigs, and maybe cows and chickens as well.'

'Pigs!' Ruth exclaimed. 'You're not thinking of keeping pigs at the bottom of the garden, are you?'

'Mr Clegg at Top End Farm keeps pigs,' Mrs Jackson put in. She was smiling as if she'd already guessed what Fleur was talking about. 'All the villagers keep their scraps for pigswill for him. He collects two or three times a week.'

Fleur's face lit up. 'Great!'

'But what do you want them for?' Ruth persisted. 'You're not seriously thinking of having some here, are you?'

'I don't actually want the *pigs*, I just want what they produce. For the garden.'

'What they–?' Ruth's face was a picture as realization dawned. 'Oh my! Well, now I've heard it all!'

The bombing mission that night was a difficult one and the planes encountered heavy flak both over the target and along the route home, especially near the enemy coast. Fleur was careful to hide her anxiety as the bombers limped home, some with aircraft so badly damaged that it was a miracle they got back at all.

Anxiously, she waited for the call sign of D-Doggo. At last, she heard, 'Hello, Woody, this is Lindum D-Doggo. One engine u/s and wounded on board...'

At once, Bob Watson was standing behind the operators. 'Kay, call up number four and tell him to overshoot. Fleur, tell D-Doggo he has straight in approach. Corporal–' Bob called to the airman who manned the internal telephone. 'Call up the ambulance and fire tender.'

Fleur took a deep breath. 'Hello, D-Doggo, you are number five to land, straight in approach, runway two-zero ... switch to channel B.'

Calmly, her instructions were repeated and then they heard the drone of the aircraft as it approached the runway.

'His other engine doesn't sound too healthy,' Bob said. Everyone was holding their breath, trying to see out into the darkness. The aircraft touched down, the noise fading as it ran towards the end of the runway.

The radio crackled again. 'Hello, Woody, this is number five. Turned left off runway, but second engine now u/s. Over.'

From the clipped message, Fleur knew that the aircraft had been able to turn off the runway, but now it seemed that the second engine had given up on them and the plane could taxi no further under its own power.

'Help is on its way, number five,' she said into

her microphone. 'Well done. Out.'

Now Fleur could breathe easily again and at once began to call up the aircraft waiting to land. It had been a close call for Tommy Laughton and his crew. The rear gunner was injured, but at least they were all home. Five planes failed to come back. Debriefing revealed that one had been seen to crash in enemy territory.

'I did see parachutes, though,' one of the pilots told Ruth.

Three aircraft had ditched in the sea, though the fate of the crews was unknown and one plane couldn't be accounted for at all.

D-Doggo was badly damaged and would be out of commission yet again for two or three days whilst the mechanics worked on it frantically. Several more planes in the same squadron needed extensive repairs before they would be airworthy.

'I've got a seventy-two, so I'm going home. And this time, I really will speak to Ma,' Robbie promised Fleur. 'What about you? Can you get any leave?'

She shook her head. 'No. Sounds like there's a big op on for tomorrow night. We're on duty.'

A fleeting look of regret crossed Robbie's face. 'And I'll miss it,' he murmured. Fleur looked at him incredulously, shaking her head slowly. She said nothing, but she was wondering just what it was about these young men that made them want to be in the thick of danger. Was it the excitement? And was that excitement all the more thrilling because it was dangerous? She didn't know. All she knew was that Kenny craved that same kick.

Robbie put his arm about her waist. 'I'm sorry

you can't get leave too. We could have met up. Spent some time together.'

'I know,' she said softly, anguished at the thought of not being able to spend every precious minute with him. 'But maybe it'll be worth it if you do get a chance to talk to your mother.'

'I'll make sure I do this time. I promise.'

Fifteen

Fleur attacked the gardening work with a vigour born of anxiety and frustration. Anything, to keep her mind from wandering to Robbie and what was being said between him and his mother.

She double dug an area down one side of the garden ready for planting potatoes, then levelled an area nearby to plant carrots and cauliflowers. After that she carefully weeded the rhubarb patch. Then she marked out the oblong shape for the Anderson shelter and began to dig out the hole. The ground was hard and the effort back-breaking.

Taking a break about mid morning, she went into the house to find Mrs Jackson standing at the kitchen table rolling out pastry. Beside her was a container of shrivelled-looking rings.

'What on earth are those?' Fleur asked.

Mrs Jackson chuckled. 'Dried apple rings.'

'Dried? I've never heard of doing that.'

'Oh, they come out quite well if you soak them and then use them in a pie.'

'My mum always bottles all her fruit. She's got a cooker as well as the old range and she uses a huge metal container. A big box-like thing...' Fleur demonstrated its size with her hands. 'It holds about eight bottles at once. And she packs all the fruit into them with syrup and then boils them for – oh, I don't know how long.'

Mrs Jackson was nodding. 'Yes, I used to do something similar in the oven with Kilner jars, but since Arthur went I haven't had the heart. Truth is, I found it too hard to get the fruit picked.'

Fleur put her arm around the old lady's shoulders. 'Well, this year we'll harvest it all and we'll see what we can do then, eh?'

Mary Jackson smiled. 'That'd be lovely, dear. My Arthur would be so thrilled to think all his hard work hadn't been wasted. He planted those fruit trees, y'know, when we was first married. There's two apple trees and a Victoria plum as well as raspberry canes and gooseberry bushes. Just before our Eddie was born, it was. And he built that bench under the apple tree so's I could sit down there with the pram.'

'Eddie? Who's Eddie.'

The old lady's face fell into lines of sorrow. 'Our boy. Our son. Our *only* son.'

'And – er – where is Eddie now?' Fleur held her breath. For some reason she feared the answer.

'He was killed in the last war. On the Somme.'

'Oh, Mrs Jackson, I am sorry.' She paused, before asking tentatively, 'Have – have you any other children?'

'Two daughters. Phyllis and Joyce.'

Fleur waited for Mrs Jackson to volunteer the

136

information herself. 'Phyllis is married and lives down south. She ... she doesn't get home much, but she writes every week.'

Fleur nodded. She had seen the letters arriving regularly and had posted replies for the old lady, although she hadn't known they were addressed to Mary's daughter.

'And ... and Joyce?'

Mrs Jackson was silent for a moment, concentrating on rolling out the pastry for the apple pie. Her voice was husky with sadness when she did answer. 'Joyce was only seventeen when she started courting a lad from the village. She ... she got herself into trouble.'

Fleur said nothing, knowing that in such a small community the gossips would've had a field day.

'They got married but ... but she died having the bairn. She was only just eighteen.'

Fleur's eyes filled with tears. 'Oh, Mrs Jackson, how sad. I'm so sorry. And ... and what happened to her baby?'

'A little boy, it was, but his daddy – the whole family, in fact – moved away. They've kept in touch and I've seen him a few times while he's been growing up. I've always sent him a little something at Christmas and on his birthday.'

How sad that must be for the old lady, Fleur thought. The boy's birthday would also be the anniversary of his mother's death.

'He ... he's seventeen now.' Mrs Jackson's expression was suddenly anxious. 'I expect he'll be called up when he's old enough. If ... if it's not over by then.'

137

'Same age as Kenny.'

'That's right. Your Kenny reminds me of Simon in some ways. Same cheeky grin.' Now she smiled fondly.

'Do you mind Kenny coming here? I mean, I wouldn't want it to upset you if he reminds you—'

'Mind? Heavens, no, dear. I like him to come. He's a lovely lad.'

'Has Phyllis any children?'

Mary laughed fondly. 'Oh yes. Four. Two boys and two girls. Clever, wasn't she?'

Fleur laughed too, glad to move on to a happier note. But still, even with her other grandchildren, it seemed Mary had worries.

'One of the girls is in the WAAFs like you and the other is in the Land Army. The eldest boy is a fighter pilot. We were very worried last year when the Battle of Britain was going on. He was in the thick of it. But he's all right, thank the Good Lord. And the youngest boy, well, he's only thirteen. I hope it'll all be over by the time he reaches call-up age.'

'Oh, my goodness, let's hope so,' Fleur said fervently.

There was a silence between them as Mrs Jackson shaped her pastry to fit the pie dish.

'Has Harry any family?'

'Not now. They only had one child – a boy – and he was killed an' all in the last lot. Ypres, I think it was.'

Fleur couldn't think of anything to say. How sad it was for these lonely old people and now they were being plunged into another terrible war. Hearing about Mrs Jackson's loss and old Harry's made Fleur understand her mother's fears a little more. What she couldn't understand was Betsy's vehement hatred of Meg and her son. Surely, in such troubled times past animosities and feuds should be laid aside, forgotten and forgiven. Whatever could have happened to make her mother so bitter and resentful against Robbie's?

Outside again, Fleur eyed the area she had marked out for the Anderson shelter with a frown. She'd made a start but was getting tired now, and she had to remember that she still had a full eight-hour night shift to do.

'I'll do a bit in the front garden,' she decided. 'The ground might be a bit softer there.'

She hadn't been digging for many minutes when she heard the familiar, 'Hi, Sis.'

Fleur looked up at the sound of squeaking brakes as Kenny slithered to a halt at the gate. He jumped off his bike, reared it against the fence and straddled the gate without bothering to open it. Fleur grinned and leant on her fork. 'Hello. What brings you here?'

'To see my sister, of course.' Kenny grinned and the twinkle in his eyes told the rest.

'Really?' Fleur teased with a wry note of disbelief in her tone. Then she capitulated and laughed. 'It's good to see you – whatever the reason. But shouldn't you be at school?'

'Nope. Our school's sharing with another that got bombed out. So we go in the morning and they have the afternoons. And before you say anything – yes, I have taken this morning off to get here, but don't tell Mum, will you?'

'You bad lad!' Fleur laughed again, but Kenny knew she wouldn't give him away.

'What are you going to do here?' He changed the subject, pointing to the newly turned earth at her feet.

'I thought runner beans. I'll get them planted and then build a frame from canes for the plants to climb. I've seen a bundle in Harry's shed.' She lowered her voice. 'And Mrs Jackson said that her Arthur always used to grow her a row of sweet peas. They're her favourite flowers. I'd love to grow some for her, but I don't think I dare.'

Kenny frowned thoughtfully. 'Wait a minute. What about...?' He moved to the corner of the cottage furthest away from Harry's cottage and pointed at the end wall. 'Down this narrow border here. It's not much use for anything else, and behind that big bush she's got there near the fence, it won't be easily seen from the road. I reckon you could get away with it there. And if the authorities say anything...' he shrugged. 'Then you'll just have to rip 'em up again.'

Fleur beamed at him. 'You clever old thing. That'd be perfect. It'd just take a narrow frame, wouldn't it?'

'And it'll get a bit of sun,' Kenny added. 'Not much, but enough. Mind you, you're a bit late now for getting sweet peas sown, aren't you?'

'Dad's got some seedlings, hasn't he?'

Kenny's face cleared. 'So he has. I'd forgotten. I'll bring you a trayful next time I come.'

'Meantime, I'll get that narrow border dug over and a cane frame built, but not a word to her.'

'Won't she see it?'

Fleur shook her head. 'Doubtful. She only comes out once a week to go to church and then she walks round the other end of the cottage and down this front path.' She stood a moment and glanced towards the other end of the building. 'No, she'll not see it. Not unless she goes that end deliberately – and I don't think she will.'

'Mum's the word then, until you present her with a bouquet of sweet peas.'

Fleur hugged herself. 'I can't wait to see her face.' Then her expression sobered. 'Talking of "mum" – is everybody all right at home?'

Kenny laughed. 'Right as they'll ever be. She's still adamant that if I apply for college, I won't be called up, and nothing we say will persuade her any different.' He pulled a face. 'I reckon when the time comes, she'll march into the nearest recruiting office and tell them I'm not going and that's it.'

Fleur wasn't laughing. 'You know,' she said seriously, 'she might very well do just that.'

'Eh?' Kenny looked scandalized. 'I was only joking. Oh, Sis, she wouldn't really, would she?'

'She'll do anything to stop you going. Anything she can. She'll use the "reserved occupation" argument and anything else she can think of. She certainly might apply to the local War Agricultural Executive Committee for your exemption.'

'But it wouldn't work, would it? I mean – they wouldn't take any notice of a chap's mother, would they?'

'If she makes a proper application as your employer, then, yes, I think they might.'

'Does she know that?' he asked worriedly.

141

Fleur shrugged. 'If she doesn't yet, she'll soon make enquiries and find out. You can be sure of that.'

'Fleur, I want to go. Just like you.'

'Oh, don't say that, Kenny.' Fleur groaned. 'You make me feel so guilty.'

Kenny shook his head. 'That's not what I mean. I'd go anyway – I've told you that already – even if you hadn't volunteered.'

Fleur looked at him, wanting to believe him but not sure she could. She had set an example to her younger brother and he didn't want to be out-done by her. If anything happened to him...

'Right then, where do you want me to start?' Kenny interrupted her maudlin thoughts with his ready grin and willing pair of hands. 'By the way,' he added, trying to sound nonchalant, 'Ruth here, is she?'

'She'll be home later. She should be back before you go. But, yes, I would be glad of your help.'

Kenny grinned. 'More digging? I thought you'd've got it finished by now.'

'It is – more or less – but I want to build an Anderson shelter that both Mrs Jackson and Harry can share. Down the bottom of the garden. I've made a start, but the ground's so hard.'

'Right-o. I'll help you dig out the foundations.'

'Actually, there's something else I'd rather you helped me with today, if you would.'

'Oh yes. What's that then?'

'I've made arrangements to go up to Top End Farm and see about some manure. If I can get some for this afternoon, I was hoping to get it dug in tomorrow. I'll be off all day after tonight's

142

shift. In fact I'm not on again until the day after tomorrow in the afternoon, so I'll get a good long go at it. But now you're here.' She smiled archly at him. 'You could help me dig it in this afternoon. I was going to ask Robbie, but his plane's grounded for repairs and he's gone home to see his mother, so I thought I might twist Ruth's arm to lend a hand.'

Kenny guffawed loudly. 'I don't think you'll get either of that pair of townies to deal with a pile of–'

'Careful, Kenny,' Fleur laughed. 'Mrs Jackson's a lady. It's "manure" to her.'

Her brother's grin widened. 'I'll try to remember, Sis. She's a sweet old dear. I wouldn't want to upset her. She reminds me of Gran.'

They were both silent for a moment, remembering with affection their father's mother who had lived with them for the last two years of her life.

'She is a bit, I suppose. Gran had arthritis just like her.'

'And she's round and waddly – just like Gran.' After another brief pause, Kenny said, 'Right then, what about this – manure? How are we to get it here?'

'I saw the farmer. Mr Clegg. He said if I went up today, I could have one of his horses and his cart. I've to do the loading up that end and the unloading this end and take the horse and cart back before I go on duty.'

'Sounds as if it's a good job I've come then.'

'Bro, you don't know how glad I am to see you.'

'You only want me for my brawn,' Kenny

143

teased, flexing his muscles.

'Absolutely!' she retorted, but brother and sister smiled at each other with deep affection.

They walked the half-mile through the village until, a short distance after the houses ended, Fleur pointed to a rough track leading down a slight incline towards a farmhouse and outbuildings nestling in a natural shallow vale. Kenny glanced around him. 'Is this what they call the Lincolnshire Wolds?'

'I'm not sure. I think they're a bit further east. More in the centre of the county. And then there's the Lincoln Edge. Not so flat as people think, is it? I think it's flatter to the east – towards the sea and in the south of the county.'

'Oh yeah. What they call the fens down there, isn't it? Mind you, you can see why it's ideal for all the airfields they're building, can't you? I heard someone call it "bomber county" the other day.'

'Really?' Fleur was thoughtful for a moment. 'Well, yes, I can see why they might call it that. Right,' she said more briskly as they reached the farm. 'Now, where is Mr Clegg?'

'Well, there's his horse and cart standing over there near that pile of...' He grinned. 'Manure. And if I'm not mistaken, someone's already started loading.'

As he spoke, a forkful of manure flew up in the air and landed with a thud on the growing pile in the back of the cart. As they approached, Fleur stroked the horse's nose and patted his neck. 'Now, big feller,' she murmured.

Hearing her voice, the man at the back of the

cart straightened up. 'Na' then, lass. Thought I'd mek a start for ya.'

The farmer was a big man, tall and broad with iron muscles standing out on his arms. He wore heavy workaday boots, dark green corduroy trousers that had seen better days, a striped, collarless shirt and a checked cap. Mr Clegg nodded towards Kenny. 'Brought reinforcements, I see. Yar young man, is it?'

'My brother.'

'Pleased to meet you, young feller.'

Kenny stuck out his hand, 'Kenny Bosley, sir. Pleased to meet you, an' all.'

The farmer blinked down at the young man's outstretched hand. 'Oh, I don't think I'd better shek yar hand, lad. Not with my mucky 'un.'

Kenny laughed. 'We're used to it, Mr Clegg. Born and bred on a farm. Never afraid of good, clean dirt, our dad always says.' He nodded comically towards the manure heap. 'And especially not this that's going to do Mrs Jackson's garden a power of good.'

The big man laughed loudly. 'Ah well, in that case, lad, put it there.' And the two shook hands.

'It's very good of you to let us have it,' Fleur said.

'Pleased to get rid of some of it. I keep pigs, cows an' chickens so there's plenty to go at. Mind you, you'd be surprised at the number of folks asking for it nowadays. Now then, if I can hand over to you, I must get on wi' me other work. Just mind you have old Prince here back for 'is tea, else 'ee's likely to get a bit cussed and take off on his own. Trouble is,' he added, laughing, 'he

145

knows 'is way home so 'ee won't think twice about it.' He paused and eyed Kenny again, his gaze running up and down him as if assessing him. Bluntly, though not unkindly, Mr Clegg said, 'Home on a spot of leave, a' ya, lad?'

The flush rose in Kenny's face at once. 'Well, no, actually...'

'Ah, reserved occupation, is it? On yar dad's farm?' Now there was the tiniest note of disapproval in his tone.

Fleur caught and held the big man's gaze. Quietly, she said, 'Kenny's only seventeen, Mr Clegg.'

'I'll be joining up next year,' Kenny put in. 'Soon as I can.'

Mr Clegg smiled. 'That's the spirit, lad. Pleased to hear it.' His face sobered. 'Same as me own boy. He joined up, though his mam wanted him to stay wi' me on the farm. But I was in the last lot. Two years in the trenches, I was, and never a scratch.' He paused before saying in a low voice, 'I was lucky, though. I know that.'

Fleur nodded. 'Our dad was too. He was wounded and has a stiff leg, but at least he came back.' She bit her lip before she added quietly, 'A lot from the town never did.'

'Aye,' the big farmer sighed heavily. 'Bad business, it was. And now they've no more sense than to get us involved in another one.' He sighed. 'Aye well, I wish you luck, young feller. When you go. Good luck to you.'

Kenny nodded. 'And I hope your son's – all right.'

'Aye, so do I, lad. So do I. He's all we've got. If

146

owt happens to him, the missis will never forgive me.' His voice was low as he added, 'Won't forgive mesen, if it comes to that.' Then briskly he shook himself and smiled. 'Aye well, let's not dwell on all that. Not when there's work to be done. Look, I tell you what, you carry on here now loading up and if I've got me own work done, I'll see if I can come with you. Give you a bit of a hand, like.'

'Oh, Mr Clegg. Are you sure? You must have such a lot to do, 'specially if you're on your own now.'

'Aye, there is. But I'm never too busy to help a neighbour. Old Arthur Jackson used to work for me, see? Good man, he was. Worked on this farm most of his life – well, the latter part of it anyway. I'd like to help his widow.'

Fleur and Kenny grinned at him. 'Then we'll gladly accept your offer,' Fleur said.

'Right you are, then. Come and find me when you're ready to go. In fact, come to the back door of the house. I'm sure the missis will find you a drink and a bit of summat to eat.'

'There you are, you see,' Kenny said, as the farmer moved out of earshot. 'What did I tell you? Even a nice man like Mr Clegg questions why a big lad like me isn't in uniform.'

'Yes, but you soon will be, won't you?'

'Yeah,' Kenny said, firmly. 'And the sooner the better.'

At that moment, a cloud crossed the sun and a sharp breeze brought a chill to the bright day. Fleur shuddered, then snatched up the fork and attacked the pile of manure as if her life – and

Kenny's too – depended upon it.

'By heck, you've done a grand job with this back garden,' Mr Clegg said three hours later as he stood surveying all their hard work.

'My sister's done most of it,' Kenny said and then, as Fleur walked away from them to fetch mugs of tea, he added slyly, 'when she's not on duty at the airfield.'

The farmer's eyebrows rose. 'Yon lass? She's in the forces?'

Kenny nodded. 'She's a WAAF. She's an R/T operator. Talks to all the aircraft when they land. That sort of thing.'

Mr Clegg pulled a face. 'Tough job. Specially if you get to know the airmen, like.'

'There's one she's particularly close to,' Kenny confided.

'Not the best place to be then,' the big man murmured, but as Fleur came back their conversation ceased.

'How are we going to get it all round to the back?' she asked, handing out the mugs of tea.

'Tell you what,' the farmer suggested. 'I'll take it round into the field at the bottom of her garden and tip it there. It'll be easier to chuck it over the fence.'

Fleur eyed the grass field where cows grazed contentedly. 'Will the farmer who owns that field mind, d'you think?'

The big man laughed. 'Shouldn't think so. Them's my cows and it's my field.'

148

When Ruth arrived home, she stood staring in astonishment at the farmer on top of a pile of manure in the neighbouring field, rhythmically flinging forkfuls over the fence into the garden. Then at Fleur and Kenny, who were moving it and spreading it over the surface of the garden and digging it into the earth. All three of them were red faced and sweating, but they worked on as a team.

Kenny looked up and grinned at her. 'Hi, Ruth. Come to lend a hand?'

Fleur looked up and grinned mischievously. 'There's another fork over there.'

'Not on your nelly!' Ruth was horrified. She wrinkled her nose. 'Pooh, what a pong.'

Fleur closed her eyes and breathed in deeply. 'Nothing like it. Best perfume in the world.'

'Dead right there's nothing like it, but I don't know about the last bit. *Eau de cochon?* No thanks! Count this townie out. Tell you what, though, I'll make you all a nice cuppa. Will that do?'

There was a heartfelt unanimous chorus of 'Yes, please', and Ruth held up her hand, fingers spread out. 'Give me five minutes to get out of my uniform.'

'Sounds heaven,' Fleur called.

The promised minutes later, they stood in the tiny back yard, drinking tea, eating scones and admiring their handiwork.

'What a' ya thinking of planting, lass?' Mr Clegg looked to Fleur as the leader of the venture.

'Potatoes, carrots, leeks, cabbages. Runner beans in the front garden. Oh don't let's forget to take some of the manure round the front.'

'It'll cost you a fortune to grow all that lot,'

149

Ruth exclaimed.

'Dad's promised me some seeds.'

'Now mebbe I can help you there,' the farmer put in. 'I'll have a word with the locals and see if we can put a bit of a collection together. Not money, lass,' he added hastily. 'But a few seed 'taties, an' that.'

Fleur's eyes filled with tears. 'Oh, how kind of you. That'd be wonderful.'

'Aye well,' the man said gruffly, touched by her gratitude, 'we've all got to pull together. All got to do our bit. There is—'

And they all chorused together, '...a war on, you know.'

Sixteen

Later the following morning, after a few hours' sleep, Fleur reluctantly returned to digging out the foundations for the Anderson shelter. She'd managed to dig the oblong shape to a depth of about a foot when the curved sheets of corrugated steel arrived for the shelter.

'Ya'll need to be another three foot down, luv,' the man who made the delivery advised, nodding his head towards the hole.

'I know. It's harder than I thought. This ground hasn't been dug over for some time and certainly not four-foot deep.'

'Ah, well, I wish I could give you a hand but I've still three more shelters to deliver today. I'd best be getting on...'

'Would you like a cup of tea?' Fleur asked.

'Nah, lass, ah'm all right. Had one at the last house.' He set off back along the narrow garden path, having deposited his delivery near where Fleur was working. 'Good luck, lass. I reckon you're going to need it.'

'Thanks!' Fleur muttered wryly but she gave him a cheery wave.

She'd dug for another ten minutes and then sat on the edge of the hole for a breather when she heard the chugging sound of an engine that sounded vaguely familiar. 'Can't be,' she muttered. The noise died away and she shrugged, stood up and, with a sigh, picked up her spade once more.

She'd dug five more spadefuls when a voice said, 'You look as if you could use a little help, love.'

Fleur stopped, looked up and then dropped her spade with a squeal of delight. She flung her arms wide as she scrambled out of the hole. 'Dad! And Kenny too! Whatever are you doing here?' Her face clouded. 'Oh, there's nothing wrong, is there? Is Mum all right?'

'She's fine,' Jake laughed as he gathered his daughter, earthy hands and all, into a bear hug.

'Then why are you here?'

'A little bird told me you were planning to put up an Anderson for the old folk to use and finding the digging a bit tough.' He shrugged. 'So, here we are. We thought a little help wouldn't come amiss.'

'Come amiss!' Fleur echoed. 'You're heaven sent!'

151

'Right,' Kenny grinned. 'I'll go and get the tools out of the boot while you take Dad to meet Mrs Jackson. And I've no doubt Harry will be popping his head over the fence any minute now...'

Right on cue, as they moved towards Mrs Jackson's cottage, the old man appeared round the corner with his usual greeting, 'Now then, lass.'

Fleur and Kenny leant against each other, unable to stem their laughter, but Jake merely smiled broadly and moved towards the old man, his hand outstretched. 'You must be Harry. I've heard a lot about you. I'm Jake Bosley, Fleur and Kenny's dad.'

Harry beamed as he shook hands. 'I'm real glad to meet you. You've a fine couple o' bairns, Mr Bosley.'

'Jake – please.'

If it could, Harry's beam widened even further. 'Have you met Mary yet?'

'No. We were just on our way in to say "hello" before we get digging.'

'Ah. Come to give the lass a bit of a hand have you. It's a big job on her own and I'm afraid I'm past that sort of digging mesen else I'd've...'

'Of course,' Jake said and put his hand on the old man's shoulder.

'Well, come and meet Mary. I'll introduce you. She'll be glad to meet you an' all. Thinks a lot of yon lass, an' that lad o' yourn an' all. Tells me he can't wait to join up.'

Jake's face sobered. 'Aye.'

Harry stopped on his way towards the back door of the cottage and faced Jake in surprise. 'You don't sound too pleased about it.'

Jake sighed. For some reason he couldn't at this precise moment fathom, he felt he could confide in the old man. 'It's not me, it's his mam. She ... she wants to keep her chicks safely at home and because we live on a farm she can't understand why they even want to go.'

'Were you in the last lot?'

'Aye. I volunteered.'

'Then *you* know why they want to be involved?'

Jake nodded. 'Oh yes. I know why.'

'We lost our lad in the last war. Nearly broke my Doris's heart when the telegram came. But we were still proud of him. To this day, I'm proud of him. The only sad thing is that these young-sters have got to do it all again now. Don't seem right, does it?'

'No. It doesn't. But they'll do it. They'll do it all right.'

'Oh, I know that. Whilst we've got young 'uns like yourn there...' He nodded towards Fleur and Kenny. 'And that young feller of hers, then we'll win. No doubt about that. It's just – well – what we might lose along the way, eh?'

Now Jake couldn't speak for the sudden fear that arose in his throat, so he just gently squeezed the old man's shoulder.

Harry nodded understandingly and then opened the door and called cheerily, 'Hello, Mary, love. Got a visitor for you. Fleur's dad.'

Mrs Jackson was standing at the kitchen table, her hands floury as she rolled out pastry. She looked up and smiled a welcome as Harry opened the door and ushered Jake into the room.

'Sorry I can't shake hands but come in, do.

153

You're very welcome.' She glanced beyond him. 'Is your wife with you?'

'Er – no. She stayed to mind the farm. But Kenny's here.'

Mrs Jackson's beam plumped up her cheeks so that her glasses rose. 'He's a lovely boy. So helpful. Please, Mr Bosley, do sit down. I'll make a cup of tea.'

'No, no, don't trouble just now. We've come to help Fleur with the shelter for you both.'

Mrs Jackson gasped and pushed up her glasses to wipe a tear away, leaving a smudge of flour on her face. 'How kind you all are.'

At that moment Kenny pushed open the back door and deposited a box on Mrs Jackson's table. 'Just a few eggs and a bit of butter from our dairy. And I think there's a chicken in there.' He grinned. 'Plucked and dressed with my own fair hands.' He nodded towards Harry. 'It's for you both. And we killed a pig last week. Dad's got a licence, of course. So there's some sausages and a piece of pork. Oh, and a couple of rabbits as well, but I haven't had time to skin them. But Fleur can do them for you.'

'Oh, I don't know what to say. I really don't.' Mrs Jackson was lost for words.

'You're looking after Fleur for us, Mrs Jackson. It's the very least we can do,' Jake said softly. 'Now, where's that pick we brought, Kenny? We'd best get cracking.'

The earth yielded willingly to Jake's experienced wielding of the pointed pickaxe. When he paused for a breather, Kenny shovelled out the broken-up earth whilst Fleur ferried mugs of tea down the path. The hole sank steadily deeper. 'Don't make yourself late, Dad. You ought to get home before milking time.'

'Just a few minutes more, luv, and I think it'll be deep enough. Can you manage to put up the shelter?'

'Yes, Robbie and Ruth will give me a hand with that as soon as they can.'

'Where is Ruth? Is she due back soon?' Kenny asked, pausing for a breather and mopping his forehead.

'No, sorry, she's on duty.'

Kenny's face fell. 'Oh well, give her my love, won't you?'

Jake climbed out of the hole and brushed the earth from his trousers. 'There. I think that'll do.'

As they gathered the tools together to take back to the car, Fleur said, 'Where've you built one at home?'

'I haven't.' Jake laughed. 'I can't see us getting bombed in the middle of nowhere, can you? It's different for these folk here, though. They're likely to catch a few stray bombs being aimed at the airfield.'

'Oh, Dad, I think you should build one. You never know.'

'But we can't even hear the sirens, love. Only very faintly in the distance and then only if we happen to be outside. If we're in bed asleep, we'd never hear them anyway. Besides, your mam'd never use it. "Can't waste my time sitting in here when there's work to be done," she'd say. You know she would.'

'You might have to build one if you're going to

155

have Land Army girls.'

'I don't think I need them. Old Ron says he'll lend a hand when he can.'

Old Ron, as Jake now called him, and his family had lived in a cottage on Middleditch Farm for as long as Fleur could remember. He'd worked for her father and for the Smallwoods before that until his retirement a few years earlier. He was still fit and healthy and liked to help out at lambing and at harvest time.

'You will when I go, Dad,' Kenny said, throwing the spades into the back of the car.

Jake sighed. 'Aye well, I'll think about that when the time comes.'

'You off, then?' Harry hobbled round the corner of the cottage and stood beside Fleur as they all said their goodbyes.

'Well, I think so, unless you can come back with us, Fleur? Kenny said he didn't think you were on duty until tomorrow afternoon. Will it be all right? We could be sure to get you back tomorrow morning.'

Fleur forced a smile. Part of her didn't really want to go home, didn't want to face more antagonism and censure from her mother, yet she could see that both Jake and Kenny wanted to snatch another few hours with her. 'I'll risk it. I'll just get my things...'

As she ran upstairs she was thinking: at least it might keep my mind off Robbie; but in her heart she knew it wouldn't. Oh I wonder if he's asked her yet, she couldn't help thinking as she slipped out of her workaday clothes and back into her uniform. I wonder if he knows already...

Seventeen

'Mother dear...' Robbie began, using the more formal address he'd adopted as quite a young boy when he was trying to wheedle his way around her.

Meg smiled archly at him. 'Oho, and what is it you're wanting now?'

He took her hand and led her to sit on the sofa in front of the fire. 'I need to talk to you.'

He'd been at home for two days and was due to return to camp the next morning. He was glad to have been there for he'd been on hand to help his mother bring his grandfather home from the hospital. The old man was much better, glad to be home and tucked up warmly in his own room upstairs. And now was Robbie's last chance to talk to his mother.

'Oh dear, this sounds serious,' Meg said gaily. 'What have you been up to now? Have I got to write an apologetic letter to your commanding officer – just like I had to so many times to your headmaster?'

Robbie forced a laugh, though at this moment he didn't feel like laughing. His mother, sensitive to her beloved son's feelings, said softly, 'What is it, love? Something's troubling you, I can see that.'

'Ma – I want to ask you about my father.'

He heard her pull in breath sharply and her

157

green eyes were suddenly round, dark pools of anxiety.

My God, Meg was thinking. He's heard something. They've told him something. It must have been that day just after he'd first met her. He must have gone to the farm, met Fleur's parents ... They must have said something.

I should have tried to stop him seeing Fleur, she thought in panic. But how could I, she asked herself, her mind in a turmoil, when they're stationed on the same camp? She licked her dry lips and said unsteadily, 'What about your father?'

'There's no easy way to put this, Ma, so I'll just come right out and say it.'

'Don't you always?' she murmured, though her heart was thumping madly in her chest. Her son was one of the most honest, reliable and straight-forward people she had ever known in her life. Even more so than Jake.

Jake, oh Jake! What did you say to him? Are you still so bitter after all this time that you would wreak such a revenge on me?

Clasped in his huge, warm hands, Meg's own hand trembled. Robbie felt it. 'It's all right, Ma. I don't want to upset you, dearest, but I have to know. It's important to me. To me and Fleur.'

Meg's head shot up. 'You – and Fleur?'

'Uh-huh. We ... we want to go on seeing each other, but there's something going on that we don't understand. That we don't know about. Ever since we met, it's ... it's been very...' He sought for the right word. 'It's been very strange. In fact, it started that very first day when you were so surprised to hear Fleur's name.'

Meg tried to pull her hand away from his, but he held her fast, though gently. She gave a huge sigh and sagged against his shoulder. She closed her eyes for a moment and two tears squeezed their way out from under her eyelids and ran down her face, making a salty rivulet down her carefully applied face powder.

'Oh, Ma, don't cry. I hate to do this, but we *have* to know.' Gently, he wiped her tears away. It was so like Jake's tender gesture all those years before – the very last time she had seen him – that her tears just flowed all the harder. 'And then when you thought it best if you didn't go with me to Fleur's home. And you were right. When I got there – well, to tell the truth, I didn't even get as far as the farm. Fleur met me in the lane and said that when she'd told her parents about me, her mother had become hysterical, shouting and screaming and saying all kinds of – well – odd things. Things that Fleur couldn't understand.' He paused but his mother was silent, trying to put off the dreaded moment for as long as possible.

I'll lose him, Meg was thinking. If he finds out the truth, he'll have nothing more to do with me. Oh, and I've tried so hard over the last few years to make amends for all the wicked things I did. I've tried so hard, Jake, I truly have. She took a deep breath and said, 'All right. What is it you want to know?'

'Was ... was Percy Rodwell my real father?'

Meg raised her head slowly and looked into his eyes – her dearest, darling boy who'd been conceived in a few moments of passion with a man she now realized she'd never truly loved. A man

159

who, though infatuated with her, had been too afraid of losing his standing in the eyes of the community. A man who'd deserted her when she had needed him most. There was only one man she'd ever really loved in her whole life, only she had been too blind, too grasping, too afraid of living a life of poverty, to recognize it. And now this son of hers, who'd grown up to be such a wonderful human being, the son whom she had almost given away to that dreadful woman, was going to find out all about her. All her sins were going to be revealed and she would have to pay the price. This was to be her punishment.

She was going to lose him.

His hands tightened around hers until he was hurting her. 'Who is my father, Ma?' he demanded harshly. 'Is it Fleur's dad? Are we ... are we half-brother and sister?'

'Jake!' The relief flooded through Meg. So this was what it was all about. 'Oh no, no, it wasn't Jake.' She laughed, light-headed with relief.

He was still holding her hand tightly, but now she didn't mind. 'Is that really true? We're not related in any way? Me and Fleur, I mean?'

Meg shook her head. 'No, you're not.'

His grip on her relaxed and he let out the longest sigh she'd ever heard as if releasing all the tension inside him.

She swallowed and tried to ask casually, 'Whatever gave you that idea?' She was regaining her composure now enough to pretend offence. 'And fancy thinking such a thing of your mother.'

'Oh, Ma, I'm sorry.' He drew her into his bear hug and she stayed there, closing her eyes with thankfulness. 'It's just ... it's just some of the things Fleur's mother said when she was having her "ducky fit" as Fleur called it.'

An inner voice was telling Meg to let it lie, to ask no more, but before she could stop the words coming out, she'd said, 'What did she say?' And when he told her, she closed her eyes again. Was it true? Had Jake loved her all these years, just as she had loved him? But Robbie's voice was dragging her back to the present and now his words filled her with dread once more.

'And there was something else funny happened. We met a woman in a cafe in the town and she seemed about to pass out at the sight of me. Fleur called her "Aunt Louisa". She was the local doctor's wife.'

'My dear, what is it? You don't seem yourself? Are you ill? I could prescribe something for you if–'

'Don't fuss, Philip. I'm perfectly all right.'

Philip Collins blinked. It was so totally out of character for his wife to snap in such a way. Louisa was usually so calm, serene and in control of herself. She was the perfect wife for a doctor, for any man, if it came to that. And yet... He sighed inwardly. She was beautiful. She dressed elegantly and was a perfect receptionist for his patients. She soothed them and marshalled them with a gentle hand. She smoothed his path through life and had supported him in everything he had ever done.

So why, oh why, could he not forget the red-haired firebrand with whom he'd once fancied himself in love? He'd almost given up everything for her; his infatuation for the passionate,

161

persuasive young woman had nearly been his downfall. But he'd not had the courage, if that was the right word to apply to what would have been such an act of betrayal. Betrayal of his wife, his upbringing and his vocation. It would have meant the end of his career as a doctor, and he'd realized that he loved that more than any human being. More even than *her*.

So he had turned his back on his mistress and her son and for the last twenty-two years he'd lived a model life as the caring doctor, the dutiful husband with a perfect wife. There was only one thing that disappointed him and now it was never spoken of between them. It was the tragedy of their lives that he and Louisa had never been blessed with children. Was it a punishment, he had so often wondered, because he had not been man enough to shoulder his responsibilities, as a man of honour would have done?

He had always loved Louisa – of course he had, ever since he'd met her when she was a lowly schoolmarm, struggling to support her widowed mother. But he had to admit now that he'd never quite loved her with the unbridled passion he'd felt for—

Louisa was reaching out to him across the dinner table. 'I'm so sorry, Philip dear. I didn't mean to be snappy. It's just this war. All the privations, the anxiety I see on the faces of all your patients, especially those with husbands or sons or sweethearts in the services. I ... I...' She hesitated, about to touch on something which had always been a painful subject between them. 'I never thought I'd say it, Philip,' she whispered.

162

'But I'm almost glad we didn't have children, if that's the heartbreak it brings.'

Philip patted her hand and smiled thinly. His blue eyes were kindly yet shadowed with hidden thoughts and memories, but he said nothing. Whatever he was thinking, he kept it to himself.

She couldn't tell him the truth, the real reason for her bout of bad temper; she was worried sick in case he ever came face to face with the young man she'd seen with Fleur Bosley. Robbie Rodwell. Meg's boy. What would happen if Philip saw him? She felt sick at the thoughts that tumbled around her mind in a riot of fear. Would he see the likeness? Of course he would. It would be like turning the clock back and looking into the mirror of his youth. She wondered if he'd always known. She remembered Meg coming to the house once with the child in her arms, but what had passed between doctor and patient remained a secret behind the surgery door.

Had Philip known Meg's boy was his son? Perhaps he had and he'd kept the secret from her, his wife, all these years. So, Louisa thought bitterly, the whispered gossip all those years ago had been true. There had been something between Philip and Meg. It was obvious now and, surely, neither of them could deny it any longer. You only had to look at the boy to see the truth.

She wasn't sure which hurt her the most. The fact that her husband had been unfaithful to her, had had a son all this time, or the fact that he had never told her about any of it.

So, Meg was thinking at that very same moment,

Louisa has seen him. Mechanically, she tucked her father in bed and saw that the lamp and the glass of water were in easy reach on the bedside table, but her mind was elsewhere. She was so thankful her father was home from hospital and out of danger, but he'd need careful nursing for some time. Kissing the old man's forehead, she turned off the light and went downstairs. Robbie was in bed and sleeping soundly now that she had given him the answer he wanted. He'd be up early in the morning and on his way back to camp, back to the girl he loved. Fleur Bosley.

Meg sat down in front of the dying embers of the fire. She kicked off her shoes and sighed heavily. Why Fleur? Why *Jake's* daughter? Of all the people in the world, why did Robbie have to meet her? And fall in love with her?

Fate had played a dirty trick on Meg. Yet, she was honest enough now to admit that perhaps she deserved it. She wasn't proud of some of the things she'd done as a girl, yet she'd tried to make amends. From the moment of Robbie's birth she had changed. For the first time in her life she'd loved someone more than she cared about herself. From the moment he'd stared up at her with those bright blue eyes, she had adored him, worshipped and idolized him. She'd never loved anyone quite like that before. Not even Jake, though she now knew that he'd been the love of her life up until the time her son had screamed his way into the world and wound himself around her heart.

She stared into the glowing coals. How strange life was, she mused, that her son and Jake's

164

daughter should meet and fall in love. How ironic. And how catastrophic, for she knew without a doubt that Betsy would never agree to such a union. And yet she hadn't been able to lie to her son. It would've been so easy to tell him that, yes, they were half-brother and sister, that they couldn't – mustn't – be together. Yet she couldn't do it. She'd had to tell him the truth. There'd been enough lies and deceit in the past. It was time now for the truth to be told, whatever the consequences might be.

Much as she might have wished it all these years, Jake was not Robbie's natural father. But then, neither was her dead husband, Percy Rodwell. She shuddered afresh as she remembered Robbie's final words.

'We met a woman in a cafe in the town and she seemed about to pass out at the sight of me.'

Well, she would, wouldn't she? Meg closed her eyes and groaned aloud. Louisa would see the likeness at once.

Robbie's likeness to her own husband.

Eighteen

With trembling fingers, Louisa reached for the telephone receiver. Her heart was racing. What she was about to do was unethical, and if Philip were to find out... But she had to know. Years ago, when she'd heard the gossip about her husband's frequent visits to the little cottage near the

165

church, she had dismissed them. She'd trusted Philip completely. But seeing Meg's son – the image of Philip as a young man – she feared now that the rumours had been true.

Louisa bit her lip, pulled in a deep breath and began to dial the first number on the list in front of her.

When a woman's voice answered, Louisa said, 'I'm sorry to bother you. This is Dr Collins' wife from South Monkford. My husband...' She faltered for a brief moment over the deliberate lie she was about to utter. 'My husband has asked me to try to trace a former patient of his. She left the district without informing us and we ... we still have her medical records here. We know she moved to Nottingham...' Louisa was babbling now, a nervous note creeping into her voice. She tried to calm herself again.

The woman's voice on the other end of the telephone was stiff and uncooperative. 'The usual way is for the new doctor with whom the patient has registered to send for their records.'

'Yes, yes, I know, but...'

The woman unbent a little. 'Well, I will have a look and see if the patient has registered with us. Of course, there are several other doctors in the city.'

Louisa glanced down at the rather long list on the desk in front of her, hoping it wouldn't prove necessary to phone every one of them. 'Yes, yes, I realize that,' she said.

'What name is it you're looking for?'

'Meg Rodwell. Mrs Meg Rodwell.'

'Hold on one moment.'

There was a lengthy silence whilst Louisa grew more and more agitated. She glanced nervously towards the window. Philip was out on his morning rounds, but that didn't mean he might not arrive back home at any moment.

'I'm sorry.' The woman's voice sounded again in her ear. 'But we have no one of that name recorded with us.'

'Thank you for your time,' Louisa said. 'Goodbye.'

She tried four more numbers and was met with a similar reluctance to give out information. Two even refused to look for the name in their records. 'I couldn't possibly divulge such information. You could be anyone ringing up...'

Louisa almost slammed the receiver back into its cradle in her frustration.

On the sixth attempt a young girl's voice answered merrily, 'Good morning. Dr Gough's surgery.'

Louisa repeated her request and gave Meg's name.

'Hold on. I'll look for you.' The girl voiced no concern and Louisa felt a sudden stab of guilt that she might be getting her into trouble. But within moments the girl was back on the line. 'Yes, we have a patient of that name.'

Louisa held her breath, willing the girl to give her Meg's address without her having to ask outright for it, hoping the young receptionist wouldn't realize that Meg had been their patient for years and the story of the 'lost notes' was nothing but a ruse.

As if the gods were now smiling kindly, the girl

rattled off the name of the street and even the number of Meg's home in the city.

'Thank you, thank you very much,' Louisa said weakly. As she was about to replace the receiver, the girl said, 'So you'll send her notes through to us, will you? Have you got our address?'

'Oh – oh yes. Yes, I have it here.' It was on the list in front of her. 'Thank you for your help.'

'Don't mention it,' the girl said gaily, oblivious to the fact that she had given out confidential information to a stranger.

Louisa replaced the receiver slowly. She had not even bothered to write down Meg's address. She would remember it only too well.

When Meg opened her door, it was perhaps one of the biggest shocks of her life to see the woman standing on her doorstep.

'My God!' she breathed. 'Louisa.'

The two women stared at each other until Louisa said calmly, 'Good morning, Meg. May I come in?'

Meg looked nervously up and down the street. Robbie had gone into the city, but he could be back at any moment. The last thing she wanted was for him to run into Louisa. He might start asking more awkward questions. But neither could she make Louisa unwelcome.

'Oh yes, I'm sorry. Of course.' Meg pulled the door wider and gestured for Louisa to step inside straight into the front room of the terraced house. 'Please excuse the mess. This is my workroom – as you can see.'

Louisa looked around her. The room was

strewn with paper patterns, materials and pins. On the table in the centre of the room stood a Singer sewing machine.

'I make my living as a dressmaker,' Meg explained, gesturing nervously with a hand that still shook from the surprise. She tried to calm her whirling thoughts.

'So,' Louisa was saying smoothly. 'Your husband taught you well, did he?' She was much more in control. But then it was she who had chosen to come here. She had had time to marshal her thoughts and her emotions.

'May I offer you a cup of tea?' Meg said, ignoring the remark and playing for time. But she guessed the reason for this visit. 'Please come through to the back room. We'll be more comfortable there.' She led the way through and Louisa seated herself in front of the range whilst Meg went through into a back scullery.

As she listened to the rattle of cups and saucers, Louisa glanced about her. There was little in the room that gave any indication of Meg's former life. No photographs, no obvious relics from Percy Rodwell's house. Perhaps the only thing she had kept had been his sewing machine. No doubt, Louisa thought bitterly, it wasn't her own husband whom Meg wished to remember.

Meg came back into the room and set the tray on the table. She poured a cup of tea and offered her visitor a biscuit.

'They're rather dry, I'm afraid.' She pulled a face. 'The war, you know.'

Louisa smiled thinly and shook her head. 'No, thank you. The tea is fine.'

Meg sat down opposite, but she was still on edge, listening for any sound that heralded Robbie's return. As they sipped their tea the two women regarded each other. They each saw in the other's face the changes the years had brought.

They were each thinking that the years had been kind to the other. Louisa was dressed in smart clothes, well tailored and expensive. Whilst Meg wore a fashionable dress, she had made it herself from a length of material bought on a market stall. Louisa's complexion was smooth and well cared for. She was the epitome of a doctor's wife – serene and sweet and caring. Her hair, still black, was smoothed into a chignon and showed no sign of grey.

And Meg's too belied her age. Her luxurious red hair was swept up into waves and rolls and her figure was still slim; her legs beneath the short hem of her dress were shapely and she wore silk stockings. I wonder how she can afford those, Louisa thought uncharitably.

She was the first to speak. 'I met your son recently.'

Meg felt a sudden flush through the whole of her body and her heart was pounding so loudly she was sure Louisa must hear it. 'Oh?' Her voice was unnaturally high and she fought again to control her feelings.

'He was in a cafe in South Monkford with Fleur. Fleur Bosley.' She laid emphasis on the name.

'Oh yes.' Meg forced a smile and set her cup and saucer on the tray. She was so afraid that her trembling hands would give her away. 'Robbie brought her home. They'd bumped into each other – literally – on the station. In the blackout. She ... she couldn't get transport home that night so ... so Robbie brought her here.'

'What a coincidence!'

'Yes, wasn't it?'

There was an uncomfortable pause before Louisa, staring hard at Meg, said, 'He's a very good-looking young man.'

Meg managed to hold down the fear climbing into her throat and said, 'I think so, but then I could be biased.'

And then the question she had been dreading came.

'He's not like Percy, is he? Or you. So who does he take after?'

Louisa was looking directly into her eyes, holding Meg's gaze. It was so obvious that she had seen the likeness to her own husband in the young man's features. As he had grown, Robbie had become even more like his natural father. It had been Meg's ever-constant fear that one day someone from South Monkford would meet her son. And of all people it had to be Jake's daughter.

What a cruel and devious mistress fate was.

Meg felt suddenly calm. She knew what she must do. She had thought she could tell the truth now and, as the saying went, 'shame the devil'. But she found she couldn't do it. Once Robbie had the answer he wanted, he hadn't pushed to learn more. And now, Meg doubted he would. So, for all their sakes, she must tell the biggest lie of her life and she must make Louisa believe it. She smiled, serene now in her decision. 'He's like my father.'

Louisa looked startled. 'Your father?'

Meg nodded, growing more confident with each minute that passed and warming to her story. 'Yes. He was fair haired and blue eyed, just like Robbie. Of course,' she added, feigning innocence, as if she had just realized, 'you never knew my father, did you? He lives with us now.' She gestured to the room above them. 'But he's very frail. He doesn't get up until dinnertime. Mind you.' Meg forced a laugh. 'You'd be hard pressed to see the likeness. He's white haired and crippled with rheumatism. And he's just home from the hospital. A nasty bout of pneumonia. We're lucky he's survived it.' Silently, she prayed that her father would not choose this morning to get up earlier. There was no likeness to see between grandfather and grandson. Never could have been. Her father, Reuben, had had brown hair and eyes.

'No,' Louisa was saying, 'I never met him.' She was surprised to hear that the old man was living with his daughter. Had Meg really forgiven him – the man she had vowed never to see again? My goodness, Louisa thought, Meg really must have changed. She was tempted to ask more, but it was Meg's son who interested Louisa. If what Meg was telling her was true, then perhaps she'd been wrong. Perhaps the gossip about Philip's friendship with this woman all those years ago was unfounded. Maybe he'd been what he always said he'd been to Meg. Just a friend.

Louisa set her cup down and clasped her hands in her lap. The whiteness of her knuckles was the only sign of her inner turmoil. Her voice was

172

quite steady as she said, 'We never had children, you know. It has been a great disappointment to us both, especially to Philip.' She stared directly into Meg's eyes as she added deliberately, 'He'd have loved a son.'

Meg returned her gaze. 'I'm sorry,' she said gently. In those simple words there was a world of apology for everything that had happened in the past between them. All the misunderstandings, all the hurt. In the briefest of moments there passed between them a flash of understanding of the truth, though they both knew that neither of them would ever voice it. And Meg emphasized this again as, choosing her words carefully so that she gave nothing away but implied everything, she added, 'It has always been my greatest sorrow that poor Percy did not live. *Robbie's father would have been so proud of his son.*'

They stared at each other for what seemed an age, before Louisa dropped her gaze and said, 'Yes, I ... I'm sure he would.'

After a few moments, she stood up and took her leave. The two women kissed each other's cheek awkwardly. At the door, Louisa said solemnly, 'Goodbye, Meg.' Then she turned and walked up the street, her head held high. From the doorway, Meg watched her go, knowing it was unlikely that they'd ever meet again. Nor would she ever meet Philip again. Louisa would see to that.

Louisa's step was lighter. She would never tell Philip about her meeting with Meg. She knew, in her heart, that Robbie Rodwell was Philip's son, but Meg had given her a credible story: a story she herself would use if it were ever needed to confound the gossips. But strangely the truth was easier to deal with than the terrible doubts. Not knowing had been far worse.

Louisa smiled. Now she knew what to do. When the war ended – and surely the end must come soon – she would encourage Philip to take a well-earned retirement and move away.

The south coast perhaps, Wales or Scotland. She would let him choose. Just so long as it was miles away from South Monkford.

Nineteen

Fleur was counting the hours until Robbie got back from his leave and praying that, this time, he would be able to talk to his mother.

The first night had passed quickly enough as she'd been on duty and now, on the second night, she had come home with her father and Kenny, and the time seemed to tick by so slowly. She said nothing to her parents, did not even mention Robbie's name, but she was edgy and distracted, her thoughts miles away. Her forced gaiety, punctuated by long, uneasy silences, alerted both Jake and Betsy.

'She's still seeing him. I know she is.' Betsy was threatening to become hysterical again.

Jake tried to calm her. 'Maybe so, love. But there's nothing we can do to stop it. And you know what they say, the more parents try to stop their offspring doing something, then the more they'll want to.'

'Don't I know it. Just look at them both. Don't listen to a word we say, will they? What's the world coming to, Jake? Just think what it was like for us as kids. They don't know they're born today.'

They exchanged a glance. Their shared past was something they never spoke of – not even their children knew anything about their parents' childhood.

Jake sighed. 'It's not easy for them, love. Not with this war on.'

'We lived through a war, didn't we? We had to cope. You with the terrible life in those trenches. Me worrying every minute of every day, dreading the telegram or seeing your name in the casualty lists in the paper.'

'I know. But this one's different. It's so much closer to home with the bombing. In the last lot most of it happened abroad, but this time it's on our doorstep.' He forced a smile. 'Come on, Betsy love, let's not spoil the precious few hours we have with her. We'll both take her to the station in Newark tomorrow morning and see her off. Then you can do a bit of shopping afterwards, love. How about that, eh? Time you had a trip out and a bit of a treat. Now, let's get the supper on the table and have a nice evening – all of us together, eh?'

'Well, maybe we could,' Betsy said tartly, 'if only Kenny would come home when he's supposed to. Where is he now, I'd like to know? Dashed off out as soon as you all got home. He's missed helping you with the evening milking again. I'll clip his ear for him when he gets back.'

'It's all right, love. Fleur helped me tonight. I think she quite enjoys keeping her hand in when she's on leave.' It was the wrong thing to say and Jake could have bitten his tongue off the moment he'd said it, for it prompted his wife to say tartly, 'She'd have been better "keeping her hand in" all the time instead of swanning off to become an officer's groundsheet.'

'Betsy! I won't have you talking about our Fleur like that or any other WAAF, if it comes to that. They're a grand lot of lasses.'

Betsy pursed her lips and said no more but the loud clattering of dishes in the scullery left Jake in no doubt of her feelings.

Supper was ready on the table by the time the back door opened and Kenny burst into the house, his face wreathed in smiles. 'I've done it! I've joined up!'

Betsy gave a little scream, covered her mouth with her hand and sat down suddenly, staring at him with wide, fearful eyes, but Jake and Fleur stared at him in puzzlement.

'What are you talking about, lad? You're not eighteen till next year.'

'I know.' Kenny was still beaming.

'But ... but they won't take you till you're at least eighteen,' Fleur said.

Kenny's grin widened even further – if it were possible. 'No – but the Home Guard will. They'll take you at seventeen. I've joined the South Monkford Home Guard.'

Everyone in the room relaxed and Betsy was so overcome with relief that she almost fell off the chair. 'You bad boy – giving me a fright like that.' She pretended to smack him and then was hugging him and kissing him.

'Leave it out, Mum,' the young man said, red in the face whilst Jake and Fleur, relieved too, smiled at his embarrassment.

'So,' Betsy said gaily as they all sat down at the table and she began to serve out the rabbit pie, 'you won't need to join the forces now, will you? If you're in the Home Guard, you can stay here.'

There was a moment's silence as Kenny glanced at Jake and Fleur. 'It ... it doesn't work quite like that, Mum,' he told her quietly. 'I'm still going to volunteer for the RAF when I'm old enough.'

The plate Betsy was holding trembled slightly, and though she said no more, the light that had been in her eyes died instantly.

Determined to change the subject, Jake said, 'I think Blossom's going to calve any day now and I reckon she's carrying two.'

Robbie saw the three of them standing together at one end of the platform. Quickly, he shrank back into the carriage lest Fleur should glance in his direction. He sat well back, watching them. Strangely, it wasn't Fleur who captured his interest this morning, but her father. So this was the man who had perhaps loved his mother. He narrowed his eyes, trying to see him clearly, but the distance between them was too great. Robbie sighed. He'd dearly love to meet Fleur's dad, but...

The whistle sounded and uniformed men and women from all the services jostled each other good-naturedly as they rushed to board the train. Last farewells were said, hugs and kisses exchanged. Robbie stayed back until he saw Fleur look up and down the train, deciding which carriage to climb into. Then he moved to the open door of the carriage and leant out, calling her name and waving to attract her attention amongst all the hustle and bustle. She glanced round and, seeing him, hurried along the platform towards his carriage. Her father, carrying her bag, followed. Robbie held out his hand to her and hoisted her up into the carriage and then leant down again and held out his hand to take her bag. In that brief instant, he looked into the dark brown eyes of Fleur's father. Recognition was instant. Jake knew who he was. Robbie saw the older man catch his breath as, almost in a trance, he handed up the bag.

Fleur, standing beside Robbie, leant out too. ''Bye, Dad.' Then she waved to the woman standing like a statue on the platform, her gaze fixed upon Robbie. Fleur's wave faltered as her heart sank.

Her mother had seen him too.

The guard was moving along the platform, slamming doors and blowing his whistle. As the train began to move, there was no answering wave from her mother, nor, to Fleur's disappointment, from her father either. Though not together, they were both standing quite still, their gaze on Fleur, yet neither of them waved goodbye.

She ducked back into the carriage and sat down suddenly, her eyes filling with tears. Robbie sat beside her and took her hand.

'They didn't even wave,' she gulped.

'Darling – I'm so sorry. I should have stayed back out of sight. But ... but I so wanted to travel with you. I couldn't wait a moment longer to tell you...'

Fleur's head shot up and her eyes widened as she saw that he was beaming, it seemed, from ear to ear.

'Oh, Robbie,' she gasped. 'Is it ... is it really all right?'

He nodded and then she was in his arms, and behind them in the carriage there were whistles and catcalls and ribald laughter. But neither of them cared. They were laughing and crying and hugging each other.

As the train gathered speed and passed by the waving onlookers on the platform, through the window Jake saw it all. He sighed. Whatever Betsy wanted, he thought, nothing was going to keep those two apart. For a fleeting moment, he'd seen the joy on his daughter's face when she'd first caught sight of Robbie and hurried towards him.

It was the same joy he'd always felt when he saw Meg. And, deep in his heart, he knew that if she were to step onto the platform right this minute he would feel it again.

'What did you say to her? What did *she* say?'

As the train sped through the countryside towards Lincoln, Fleur was anxious for a verbatim report.

Robbie, all his anxiety gone now, laughed. 'This is like a debriefing. You sound just like Ruth.'

'True,' Fleur said, trying to adopt a stern tone.

'So get on with it Flight Sergeant Rodwell.'

He gave a mock salute. 'Yes, ma'am.'

Robbie recounted, word for word, what had passed between him and his mother. 'She pretended to be a bit indignant that I'd even thought such a thing of her, but I could tell she was only teasing me. It was strange,' he mused. 'When I first broached the subject she was very edgy, but when I asked her straight out who my father was – was it your father – she laughed. Yes, Fleur, she actually laughed, and like I said she pretended to be indignant.'

'But she denied it?'

'Oh yes – and it was the truth. I could see it was. But there was still – well – *something*.'

Fleur patted his hand. 'Maybe she doesn't like to be reminded of your father. Perhaps his death still affects her,' she said gently, referring to Meg's husband.

'Mmm. Maybe.' Robbie chewed his lower lip thoughtfully. 'She doesn't very often talk about him, come to think of it.' Then he smiled, determined to put it all out of his mind. They had the news they wanted – why worry about anything else? 'I'm sure you're right, sweetheart,' he murmured and, oblivious to the other passengers, he kissed her firmly on the mouth.

Twenty

Two weeks later, Fleur was busier than ever with the garden. The Anderson shelter had been constructed with the earth from the hole they'd dug placed back on top of it.

'Mek it a good thick layer, lass,' Harry had advised. 'And then you can plant summat on top.'

'Can I?' Fleur had eyed it sceptically.

'Aye, you can,' Harry had nodded. 'Lettuce or marrers. Summat that doesn't need a great depth of earth to grow in.'

So the area on top of the shelter was drawn in on Fleur's plan of the garden that she'd sketched out and kept on the shelf of the little table beneath Mrs Jackson's precious wireless.

The gifts of seed and small plants from the old lady's neighbours had been overwhelming, and now Fleur was anxious to get everything planted as soon as possible. 'These plants'll shrivel up if I don't get them in the ground,' she'd said, and had been working in the garden every minute of her spare time. Robbie still joined her whenever he could, but when a longer bit of leave came due, he said, 'Darling, I must go home and see Ma and Pops.'

'Of course you must,' Fleur said at once. 'And I should go home too, but I just can't leave here until everything's planted. I'm late with some of it now and it'd be so unfair to all the people

181

who've been so generous not to use it all. Plants and seeds are very precious just now.'

'I'm sure your mum and dad will understand.'

Fleur grimaced. 'Dad will, but I'm not so sure about Mum. Mind you,' she added as an afterthought, 'Dad did promise to come over sometime and see what I'm– Sorry' – she grinned – 'what *we're* doing.'

'I should think so too!' Robbie pretended indignation. 'Like you said I would, I'm still aching in muscles I didn't know I'd got.' His face sobered. 'But I hate not seeing you for days on end.'

They gazed at each other, their love spilling over. 'I know,' Fleur said, 'but we're luckier than most. We see each other nearly every day.'

'I know, I know. I shouldn't grumble. I'm not doing really, it's just...'

Now it was Fleur's turn to say, 'I know. I know just how you feel.' She reached up to touch him, but then, realizing her fingers were grubby, she smiled ruefully and dropped her hand.

'I can't bear to be away from you – not even for a moment. Fleur,' he said impulsively, grabbing her hands, oblivious of the earth clinging to her fingers. 'Fleur – let's get married. Now. Let's not wait any longer. Oh, darling, do say "yes".'

Fleur's eyes widened and she gasped in surprise. 'Are you – are you proposing?'

'Of course I am. Oh, I'm sorry – it's not the most romantic setting, but...'

Fleur's eyes filled with tears. 'Oh, darling, it is, it is.'

He dropped to one knee, not caring if his uniform got dirty. 'Darling Fleur, I love you with

182

all my heart. Will you marry me – please?'

'Oh yes, yes!' She flung herself at him, knocking him over so that they rolled on the ground together, laughing and crying and hugging each other.

''Ere, 'ere, what's all this, then?' Harry's voice came over the fence. 'Well, I nivver. I know the ground wants a bit of a roll when you've planted seeds, but I've never seen it done that way afore.'

Fleur and Robbie buried their faces against each other and roared with laughter.

'Come on,' Robbie said at last, still spluttering with mirth. 'We can't lie here all day.' Then he murmured against her ear, 'Much as I'd like to.' He got up and held out his hand to her to pull her to her feet, then drew her into his arms and kissed her tenderly. He turned towards the old man, still leaning on the fence.

'You shall be the first to know, Harry. This lovely girl has just consented to be my wife.'

The old man nodded and Fleur was touched to see tears shimmer in his eyes. 'That calls for a celebration, lad. You go and tell Mary to get the glasses out. I'll be round in a jiffy...'

'What's he up to now?' Fleur wondered.

'I don't know, but we'll do as he says.'

They went towards the house, hand in hand. In the back scullery, Fleur washed her hands quickly whilst Robbie brushed down his uniform. Before she could step into the kitchen to speak to Mrs Jackson, Harry was opening the back door with Ruth on his heels. She had been in his cottage ironing the old man's sheets.

'What's going on? Harry's dragged me round

183

here just when the irons are hot.' Ruth looked disgruntled. 'What's all the excitement?'

'Here we are then, lass,' Harry interrupted. 'Last bottle of my elderflower wine. Sparkling, it is. Nearest I can get to champagne.'

'It'll be better than champagne, Harry. But are you sure you want to use it? I mean...'

'Course I am.' He winked at her. 'Been looking for an excuse to open it up. I can always mek some more. I used to enjoy me wine making, but to tell you the truth, I haven't had the heart since Doris passed away. But now, well, I feel I might have another go. Now this lass has got me all straightened out in the house, I can see the wood for the trees, as they say. Come on, has Mary got the glasses ready?'

'I haven't had time to tell her yet.'

'Will somebody please tell me what's going on?' Ruth asked again, but Harry still ignored her, saying to Fleur, 'You go in and tell Mary and get the glasses ready. Come to think of it, I'd best open this outside. It might make a bit of a mess. Bring a glass, lass. Don't want to waste any...'

'What *is* going on?'

Shyly, Fleur said, 'Robbie's asked me to marry him and I've said "yes".'

Ruth stared at her. 'Oh no. You can't,' she burst out. 'Not now. Not while there's a war on. Oh Fleur!' She gripped Fleur's arm. 'Think about it. Please. What if–'

Fleur blinked. 'I don't need to think about it, Ruth,' she said stiffly, hurt that her friend didn't seem to be pleased for her. 'I love him and he loves me.'

184

'But...'

Squashed together in the tiny scullery, Harry could not help but overhear all that was being said. Gently, he touched Ruth's arm. 'Listen, love, I know what's troubling you. You're afraid that if anything should happen to that young man out there...' Harry jerked his head towards the back yard, where Robbie was still trying to remove the earth stains from his uniform. 'That she'll be terribly hurt. You're trying to protect her from that, aren't you?'

Ruth bit her lip and tears filled her eyes. 'I tried to warn her when we first met.' She glanced at Fleur. 'Didn't I?'

Fleur nodded. 'But it's too late for that now. It was even then. We'd already fallen in love. It happened so fast, I can still hardly believe it myself.'

Ruth sighed deeply as old Harry put his arm round her shoulders. 'Terrible times we live in, lass. I know that, but if you get a chance of a bit of happiness, you've got to take it. Grab it with both hands, 'cos you never know when you're going to get the chance again. Or ... or...' He hesitated to say more, but it had to be said, 'Or how long it'll last.'

'I'm sorry, Fleur,' Ruth said contritely. 'It's just ... it's just...' She took a deep breath. 'A few weeks before you came I got to know a bomber pilot. Got rather fond of him to tell you the truth and ... and...'

She didn't need to say any more – both Fleur and Harry guessed what had happened. 'Oh, Ruth!' Fleur put her arms around her. 'Why didn't you tell me?'

'I'm not the only one,' Ruth said sadly. 'It's happening to countless wives and sweethearts. I just ... I just wanted to stop you getting in too deep.' She smiled tremulously, the tears still shimmering on her eyelids. 'Seems I was too late. Oh, Fleur – of course I wish you every happiness. There's just one thing...'

'What?' For a moment, Fleur was apprehensive again.

'Can I be your bridesmaid?'

'Of *course* you can.'

Five minutes later it was a merry little party drinking Harry's sparkling elderflower wine in Mary Jackson's kitchen.

'Oo, it smells lovely, Harry,' Fleur said. 'Just like perfume. I don't know whether to drink it or dab it behind me ears.'

'So when are you getting married then?' Harry asked, his cheeks beginning to glow pink. His homemade wine was strong.

Robbie laughed and put his arm around Fleur's shoulders. 'I don't know. I suppose I'll have to ask her old man's permission.'

The words were said jokingly and everyone in the room laughed. All except Fleur. She was not smiling.

In the excitement, the joy of Robbie asking her to be his wife, she had not given a moment's thought to what her parents would say at the news.

Twenty-One

'I don't care what you say, Fleur.' Robbie was adamant. 'We're going to do this properly. I'm going to see your father.'

'Not without me, you're not,' Fleur retorted. 'There's no knowing what might happen. 'Specially if my mother's there – which she will be.'

'You really think he'd withhold his permission?'

Fleur pressed her lips together to stop them trembling. 'Yes, I do. Not because he wants to,' she added swiftly. 'But because Mum will be against it. Dead against it. And ... and he'll not want to upset her.'

'I see,' Robbie said thoughtfully.

'Did you tell your mother?'

Robbie had just returned after a brief visit to Nottingham when ops had been cancelled because of poor visibility over the target. He shook his head. 'No. I didn't think it right until I'd spoken to your father. As soon as I – as soon as we – have seen him, then I'll try to see her. I want to tell her myself. I don't want to write to her. Not with this sort of news.'

'Will she ... will she mind, d'you think?'

'Good heavens, no. She'll be tickled pink.'

'Really?' Fleur still wasn't so sure.

'Well, can we both wangle a forty-eight next weekend?'

187

Fleur nodded.

'Then we'll go together. First we'll go out to South Monkford and face your parents together and then – if there's still time – we'll go to Nottingham.'

'No – no, it'll be easier to go to Nottingham first and then come back here from South Monkford,' Fleur suggested. 'If the trains don't fit up, it might be easier hitching from there back to Lincoln.'

Robbie frowned. 'Yes, you're right. But I wanted to do it properly. To ask your dad first.'

Fleur smiled thinly. Much as she wanted to marry Robbie and as soon as possible, the days until the following weekend were filled with dread and, when the time came, she could not stop trembling and the nerves fluttering in her stomach made eating impossible. Fate, or perhaps the weather, smiled kindly upon them. There was no flying and they were both granted leave.

'There's no need to worry about Ma and Pops,' Robbie tried to reassure her for the umpteenth time as they stepped off the train and began to walk towards his home. 'I bet she offers to make you a wedding dress.'

'That's the least of my worries,' Fleur said. 'Besides, most people these days are getting married in uniform.'

'The fellers, yes. But I want to see you in the full works. Long white dress, veil and a huge bouquet of red roses from Harry's garden.'

Fleur stared at him. 'Harry hasn't got any roses in his garden. It's all vegetables.'

188

Robbie laughed. 'Haven't you been round the far side of his cottage?'

Fleur paused to think. 'Well, no, actually I haven't.'

The paths to the two neighbouring cottages were side by side. Fleur had never had need to go to the other side of the old man's cottage.

'Ah, there you are then. Harry's got a bed of red roses at that end. Well hidden from the road, it is. He says they were his wife's favourite flowers and no way was he going to dig them up, not even for Potato Pete. He's already tending them with extra loving care so they're just right for your wedding day.'

'Really!' In spite of the ever-present worry, Fleur laughed. 'And does he know when that's to be then? Because if he does – he knows more than me!'

'Roses last a fair while. He reckons they'll still be in full bloom by the time we tie the knot.'

As they arrived at the end of the street where Robbie's family lived, Fleur pulled in a deep breath. 'Well, here goes then.'

They were welcomed with open arms by Meg, and the old man by the range smiled and nodded his pleasure at the sight of them both.

'How long have you got?' Meg asked, bustling about to set the table for a welcome home meal.

Fleur giggled, anxiety making her nervous. Meg paused, glancing from one to the other. 'What? What did I say?'

Robbie, too, looked at Fleur.

'Nothing – nothing,' she said hastily. 'Honestly. It's just that my mother always asks, "When are

189

you going back?" The way you ask just sounds so much nicer. It ... it sounds as if you really want us here...' Her voice trailed away. She was explaining herself badly and sounding very disloyal to her mother too.

Meg smiled gently. 'I'm sure your mother doesn't mean it to sound the way it does. We just want to know how to make the very best of the time we've got with you.' She turned away swiftly and hurried out to the scullery, but not before Fleur had heard the catch in her voice and seen tears in her eyes. Meg Rodwell might be putting on a very brave face, but she was just as desperately anxious about her son as any other mother.

When she came back into the room, Robbie got up and put his arm about her shoulders. 'Ma, come and sit down for a moment. We've got something to tell you and Pops.'

Meg's eyes widened and the colour drained from her face. Fleur felt a tremor of fear. Had she really told Robbie the truth or had she lied to cover up her shameful past? Robbie must have noticed her reaction too, because he glanced at Fleur as he drew his mother to sit down. Still holding both Meg's hands in his, he knelt down on one knee beside her chair. 'Ma, Fleur and I are going to get married.'

Meg looked from one to another. Her mouth dropped open and she gave a little gasp of surprise, but it was relief that flooded her face. Relief and then a growing delight.

'Oh, how wonderful!' She flung her arms around Robbie's neck and kissed his cheek. Then she held out her arms to Fleur. 'It's wonderful news. Wonderful!'

In his corner by the range, the old man smiled and nodded and wiped away a tear running down his wrinkled cheek.

Gently, Robbie said, 'You looked frightened to death for a moment there, Ma. What did you think we were going to say?'

'I–' Now embarrassment crept up Meg's face. 'I just expected bad news,' she rushed on nervously. 'Nowadays – you know – I thought perhaps – there was bad news from–' She glanced at Fleur. 'From home. That ... that Jake ... I mean that someone in your family.' She pulled her scattered wits together and smiled brightly. 'But I never guessed it would be that. I mean, you've only known each other just over a month.' She looked at them both again, searching their faces. And she could see the love there, knew they were right for each other and – because of the frightening times they were living in – knew they couldn't wait. A month, a year – ten years? When had love ever taken notice of time?

'You are pleased, Ma?'

'I'm thrilled. I–' Now she allowed tears of joy to run down her face. Gently, Robbie wiped them away with his finger. Then Meg looked across at Fleur again. 'Will you let me make your wedding dress for you?'

Fleur and Robbie exchanged a look and then both burst out laughing. 'I told you, didn't I?' Robbie spluttered. 'I told you so.'

'Well, that was easy enough,' Robbie said as they climbed on the train the next morning back to South Monkford.

'Yes,' Fleur said dryly. 'Now comes the difficult bit.' As they settled themselves in the carriage, she added, 'You know, your mother never asked if we'd told my parents, did she?'

Robbie, having stowed their small overnight bags on the rack, sat down next to Fleur. 'She asked me later. When you were out the back.'

'What did she say?'

'Just asked if we'd told them yet and I said, "No, but we're going to tomorrow."'

'And?'

'She just said, "Well, I wish you luck," but it was said with a sort of wry smile.'

'Mm,' Fleur nodded. 'She knows, doesn't she? She knows how they're going to react.' She paused a moment and then bit her lip. 'Robbie – you are absolutely sure she told you the truth. Don't get me wrong,' she added hurriedly. 'I love your mother – I think she's great – but, well, I just wondered if she'd been protecting you.'

Robbie smiled, put his arm around her and kissed her hair. 'I know what you mean.'

Fleur closed her eyes, marvelling at how understanding Robbie was. He reminded her so much of her father... Her eyes flew open in horror. It was still there. Would it always be there? This terrible fear that perhaps... She dragged her thoughts back to what Robbie was saying.

'I really don't think, Fleur, that my mother would have been so delighted to hear that we're getting married if there was the remotest possibility that your father is mine too. Now, seriously, do you?'

'Well – no – but...'

He hugged her to him. 'We've got to put all that right out of our minds.' He frowned. 'There *is* something in their past, though. That's obvious – but I don't think it affects us.'

Fleur was silent. She wasn't so sure.

As they walked along the lane towards the farm, Fleur's heart was thumping in her chest and her hands were clammy. As she pushed open the yard gate, she heard Kenny's voice.

'Hey, what are you two doing here?' He loped across the yard to envelop his sister in a bear hug and to shake Robbie's hand. 'Come on in. Mum and Dad'll be pleased to see you.' He paused and then, with a wry grin, added, 'Well, Dad will be.'

He led the way across the yard, flinging open the back door and shouting. 'Mum? Mum? Look who's here.'

They stepped in through the wash house and into the kitchen just as Betsy turned round from the sink, drying her hands on a towel. For a brief moment, she began to move towards her daughter, but then her glance took in Robbie standing behind Fleur in the doorway. Betsy dropped the towel and she gave a little cry. Then she opened her mouth and screamed. 'Jake! *Jake!*'

'Mum–' Fleur began, taking a step towards her and holding out her hands. 'Please...'

'Don't touch me. Don't come near me. And get ... him,' she panted, 'out of here. Out of my house.'

Kenny was shocked, glancing helplessly between them. He'd heard Betsy ranting about Robbie, but he'd never seriously thought she would take it this far. To forbid the young man's entrance to her home.

'Mum...' he began helplessly but, at that moment, Jake opened the door that led from the kitchen into the living room, a newspaper in his hand. 'Whatever's the matter?' Then he spotted Fleur and, behind her, Robbie. 'Ah.'

'Dad – please...' Fleur began. 'We just want to...'

'Of course you do,' Jake said easily. 'Come in and sit down. Betsy, make us all a nice cup of tea, love, will you?'

'Tea? Tea? You want me to make tea?' Betsy's voice rose hysterically. 'You think a cup of tea's the answer to everything?'

'Now, Betsy.' Jake's voice suddenly held a note of firmness, a tone that all his family – including his wife – recognized at once.

Jake was an easy-going man. He liked a contented, peaceful life and rarely did he raise his voice or insist on things being done just his way. But once in a while, when he felt strongly about something, he put his foot down very firmly and all his family knew that he meant it. There was no arguing with Jake when his mouth was a firm line and his jaw hardened. Even his dark brown eyes lost some of their velvet gentleness.

He held out his hand to Robbie and shook his hand, indicating his own easy chair near the range for the young man to sit down.

'Thank you, sir,' Robbie said. There was a tension in his voice and a slight flush to his face.

Betsy stood a moment, staring at her husband, then at the young airman. Then, with a sob, she turned and fled from the room. They heard her footsteps pounding up the stairs and then the slam of the bedroom door.

'I'm sorry,' Jake said, his eyes troubled.

'Whatever's got into Mum?' Kenny was mystified.

No one answered him. Fleur just muttered, 'I'll make that tea.' And Jake sat down opposite Robbie, who leant forward, resting his elbows on his knees and linking his fingers together.

'Mr Bosley, I'm sorry to have distressed your wife. I wouldn't have come here at all, but...' He glanced at Fleur busying herself between scullery and range. 'We – I – have something to ask you. Something important and it wasn't fair to expect Fleur to do it.'

There was a moment's silence in the kitchen, and then Kenny let out a guffaw of delight. 'I know why...' he began, but earned himself a light punch on the shoulder from his sister.

'Shut up, our Kenny.' But she was smiling as she added, 'Let Robbie do it properly.'

So Kenny sat down on a chair near the table, folded his arms and looked backwards and forwards between his father and Robbie, a huge grin on his boyish face. 'Get on with it, then.'

Robbie cleared his throat and said formally, 'I'd like to ask for your daughter's hand in marriage, sir.'

Kenny tried to stifle a laugh but failed. 'Don't you want the rest of her?'

Fleur punched him again, but her gaze was on her father's face.

Jake stared at Robbie for a moment. Then slowly, his gaze came to rest upon Fleur's anxious face. 'Well, well,' he murmured at last, after what seemed an age. 'Meg's boy and my girl. Who'd ever've thought it?'

Fleur was holding her breath. She moved closer, beseeching him with her face. Their eyes met and held for a long, long moment. And then she saw the smile begin to twitch at the corner of his mouth. He rose and she flung herself against him, wrapping her arms around his neck, laughing and crying, 'Oh, Dad! Dad!'

Robbie rose to his feet as Jake held out his hand. 'It's not going to be easy, lad,' he said softly. 'I think you know that, but you have *my* blessing.' No one in the room could fail to hear his accent on the word "my".

Kenny sprang to his feet and slapped his future brother-in-law on the back. 'And mine. As if it makes any difference,' he added wryly.

'Of course it makes a difference,' Fleur cried, turning from her father to hug her brother. 'You might be the one to bring Mum around.'

There was an awkward silence until Kenny broke it by saying, 'Dad – what is up with Mum? She can't not like Robbie. She's never even met him before, has she?' He glanced at the other two. 'Has she?'

Fleur shook her head and looked to her father for an explanation. An explanation that she and Robbie needed too. But Jake shook his head. 'Don't you worry about it. I'll talk to her. Try to get her to see reason.' It should be the happiest day of their lives and Betsy was trying to rob them of their joy. He glanced sadly at the young couple as he added, 'But I can't make any promises.'

Twenty-Two

'I shan't go to the wedding, Jake, so you needn't expect me to. I don't know what you're thinking of – giving your permission. If you'd told her "no" she might've had the sense to think again.' Betsy sniffed. 'Mind you – I doubt it.'

'It was just a courtesy to ask, love,' Jake said mildly. His anger was gone now, but replaced by disappointment that Betsy refused to join in the happiness that such news should have brought. 'They don't need to. They're both over twenty-one.'

Robbie and Fleur had left and now only the three of them – Jake, Betsy and Kenny – sat around the supper table.

'Mum – why don't you like Robbie?' Kenny asked innocently. 'He seems a good bloke and he's besotted with our Fleur. And her with him. Why–?'

'It's nothing to do with you, Kenny. You're too young to understand...'

The young man flushed but he was not about to cave in. 'Mum – if I'm old enough to fight for my country, then I'm old enough to understand why–'

'You're not old enough to fight for your country.' Betsy's voice began to rise.

'Leave it, there's a good lad,' Jake said softly. There was no censure in his tone – just an infinite sadness.

197

There was a morose silence between them. Betsy's blue eyes flashed from one to the other. She was rarely angry with Kenny, but now even he was included in her malevolent gaze. At last Jake said, 'You don't mean it, Betsy love, do you? You wouldn't really stay away from your daughter's wedding. Your *only* daughter's wedding.'

Tight-lipped, Betsy muttered, 'If she marries *him*, then, yes, I shall stay away.' Her eyes narrowed as she glared at her husband. Slowly and deliberately she added, 'And if you go, I shall never speak to you again.'

Shocked, Jake stared back at her. Slowly, he rose to his feet and stood looking down at her. Sadly, but firmly, he said, 'Then this house is going to be very quiet, Betsy, for I intend not only to attend the wedding but also to give my daughter away. No one – not even you – is going to deny me that.' He began to turn away, but Betsy sprang to her feet and caught hold of his arm.

'I'm not just thinking of myself, though God knows if I never saw Meg Rodwell again as long as I live, it'd be too soon. No – I'm thinking of Fleur. He'll break her heart. He'll be devious and ruthless and selfish, just like *her*. But you can't see it, can you? Where Meg Rodwell's concerned, you're blind. Always have been.'

Jake shook his head. Quietly, and with a patience that the watching Kenny – for once – believed his mother did not deserve, Jake said, 'I'm well aware of all Meg's faults, Betsy. But I do believe that when Robbie was born, she changed.'

Betsy snorted derisively. 'How do you know? You've not seen her since...' Her eyes widened as she added accusingly, '*Have* you?'

'No, of course I haven't.' Now, even Jake's composure was wearing thin. 'Don't you trust me better than that?'

'It's her I don't trust. No man's safe around her. What about him? What about Robbie's father? His *real* father? He couldn't be trusted, could he? Poor–'

'Betsy!' Jake thundered. 'We don't talk about that.'

Guiltily, Betsy glanced at Kenny as if – for a brief moment – she'd forgotten his presence. She had the grace to drop her head. 'No,' she whispered. 'You're right, Jake. I'm sorry. I don't want to hurt–' She bit her lip. 'Innocent people.'

But then her head shot up again and she tightened her grip on Jake's arm. 'But I meant what I said. If you go to their wedding, I'll never forgive you. Never!'

He stared at her for a long moment whilst Kenny held his breath. Then Jake shook himself free of his wife's grasp, turned on his heel and strode from the house, leaving both Betsy and Kenny staring after him.

'It's the last thing I wanted,' Robbie said as they sat together in the train, holding hands. 'To upset your family.' They'd been lucky. There was one bound for Lincoln just as they reached the station.

Fleur sighed. 'I know. But there was no other way to do it.' A faint smile touched her lips. 'Unless we eloped.'

He smiled too. 'Now, there's an idea. Why on earth didn't I think of that?'

199

She touched his cheek as she said seriously, 'Because you wanted to do it properly, and besides, we couldn't hurt your mum and Pops like that.'

'No, I wouldn't do that.' He sighed heavily. 'But it looks as if I've really caused trouble amongst your folks. The annoying thing is' – his eyes clouded – 'I don't know how or why. I wish I did. Just why is your mother so ... so vitriolic against my mam? You see, Fleur, having seen her for myself now, I don't think it is actually against *me* personally. It's my mother.'

'I don't think we can worry about it any more. Dad said he'll come to the wedding and I know Kenny will.'

'And your mother?' Robbie's bright blue eyes were clouded with anxiety.

Fleur sighed. 'I don't think for a moment that she will come.'

Robbie's eyes widened. He was shocked. 'Not come to her only daughter's wedding?'

Fleur said nothing but just shrugged her shoulders.

'My God!' Robbie breathed. 'It must be something serious.'

For the rest of the journey, they were both silent, each lost in their own thoughts, yet those thoughts were much the same.

Just what on earth could have been so serious that Betsy's bitterness was so deep, her hatred of Meg so strong, that she would refuse to attend her own daughter's wedding?

'There's a notice on the board about a dance in

the sergeants' mess on Saturday night. There's rather a shortage of females on station – so all ranks are invited. You going?'

'You bet!' Fleur grinned.

Ruth rolled her eyes. 'As if I needed to ask! And I expect you'll monopolize one particular chap all night and not give any of the rest of us girls a look in.'

Fleur grinned again. 'Of course. But there'll be plenty left for you.' She paused, wondering if she dare raise a rather delicate subject. 'Anyone in particular you've got your eye on?'

'Who me? Never! Safety in numbers. That's my motto,' she said, with a forced gaiety, and her mouth tightened as she added, 'now.'

'There's one thing,' Fleur said lightly, trying to steer the conversation away from thoughts that were painful for Ruth. 'At least we'll all be in uniform. We won't have all the civilian girls in their pretty dresses to contend with.'

Ruth laughed. 'You're right and there won't be any local yokels getting jealous either.'

Fleur pulled a face as she remembered the recent fracas at the Mucky Duck. 'You know we were lucky to get away with that. We could all have been in serious trouble if anyone had reported us. Especially Tommy.'

'I don't think they would. I think all the locals – apart from young Alfie and his mates – are friendly towards all of us.'

'Maybe you're right. They've certainly been generous giving me stuff for Mrs Jackson's garden.'

'You've done a grand job, Fleur. It's coming on

a treat. Do you know, Mrs Jackson was in tears the other day?'

Fleur gasped. 'Tears? Oh no, why? Have I upset her?'

'No, no. Tears of joy, silly. She's so happy to see the garden like her Arthur used to keep it. Only thing she misses, she says, are her precious sweet peas.'

Fleur smiled. 'You haven't told her then?'

'Course not. And I've sworn old Harry to secrecy. Mind you, when he comes round now, he uses the little gate you've made through the fence near the shelter. Not round the front path like he used to.'

'But he does know about them?'

Fleur had planted a row of sweet peas close to the sunny wall on the south side of the cottage, and the plants were already growing well and climbing the cane frame.

'Yes, but he'll not say a word,' Ruth reassured her.

'Do you think she'll see them before they're ready?'

'I doubt it. She hardly ever goes out now. She can hardly get across the back yard to the lavvy some days, her arthritis is that bad. Poor old dear. Harry says she used to love going to church every week but she hasn't even managed that the last two Sundays. Shame, isn't it?'

'Mm,' Fleur said thoughtfully. 'I wonder if we could get hold of a bath chair. We could wheel her to church.'

'You'd never get a bath chair down that narrow path, would you?'

'We could take her out of the front door.'

Ruth laughed. 'Her front door is jammed shut. Just like Harry's. I bet neither of them have used their front door in years.'

'How are you getting on with Harry? I was round there the other day taking some tools back he'd lent me and he took me into his kitchen. You've got it looking like a new pin.'

'Yeah, the house is clean from top to bottom now. There's still a lot of clutter I'd like to turf out, but I can't be too hard on the old boy. Do you know, he's still got all his wife's clothes hanging in the wardrobe? And she's been dead for two years, he was telling me.'

Fleur sighed. 'I expect he can't bear to part with them. Perhaps it helps him to feel she's still close. Still around, even.'

'Maybe. But nobody would ever want to wear them again. Not now, even though there are some lovely things amongst them. They pong to high heaven of mothballs. No, I've given that up as a bad job. But there's just one thing I haven't managed to do yet.'

'What's that?' Fleur asked innocently, and then dissolved into helpless giggles at Ruth's answer.

'Get that tin bath that's hanging in his shed on the hearth in front of the fire and get Harry in it!'

The dance was a great success. It was the first that Fleur had been to on the camp, though Ruth said there had been one or two before Fleur's arrival. Half the fun for the girls was getting ready together in their bedrooms at the cottage. There was much to-ing and fro-ing across the tiny landing.

'Have you got any shoe polish?' Fleur called.

'Only a tiny bit, but you can have it. I've done mine.'

'Have you got any Brasso? My buttons look a bit dull...'

And then, from Ruth, a mournful, 'I'm down to my last pair of silk stockings. Do you think it's worth risking them getting ruined?'

'That's up to you, but don't let Brown catch you or you'll be on a charge. Silk stockings aren't exactly classed as regulation uniform, y'know. I'm saving mine for a rather special occasion...' Fleur smiled at the thought. 'So I've only got my be-ootiful lisle ones.'

'Right then. Silk, it is. Even if only to show you up.'

'Thanks, *friend!*'

'Don't mention it,' Ruth called back gaily. A pause and then, 'Do you want this lipstick? It doesn't suit me. I'm better with paler colours, but it might suit you.'

Fleur trotted across the landing. 'Let's see. Ooh, yes. That's lovely.'

'You can keep it...'

Fleur grinned. 'No, tell you what. I'll borrow it. And I'll borrow it on my wedding day. That can be my "something borrowed".'

They went down the stairs, laughing and chattering, their spirits high at the thought of being able to forget the war for a few hours and into the kitchen for Mrs Jackson's inspection.

'It was just like listening to my girls getting ready when they were going out on a date. Now, have a good time, my dears, won't you?'

Impulsively, they both kissed her on her cheek. It was like having a loving granny watching out for them.

'Oh, she is an old duck,' Ruth said as they walked through the darkness back to camp.

'She is,' Fleur agreed readily, 'but with her arthritis so bad, I just don't know how we're going to get her to the wedding.'

'Oh, she'll get there. By hook or by crook. You'll see. She was only saying the other day that she'll manage it somehow, if she has to get all the village lads together to carry her.'

Ruth couldn't know how much her remark touched Fleur. To think, she mused, that an old lady who had only known her a few weeks was prepared to make the painful effort to get to her wedding, when her own mother was flatly refusing to attend.

'Here we are,' Ruth said, interrupting Fleur's troublesome thoughts as they walked into the large hall, where the tables and chairs had been cleared away. The air was filled with cigarette smoke and the smell of beer. Chatter, laughter and music shook the rafters. Already couples crowded the floor, dancing to the band.

Robbie, standing near the bar, had been watching for them and at once threaded his way around the edge of the dance floor, Johnny following in his wake.

'May I have the pleasure...?' they chorused as Robbie held out his arms to Fleur and Johnny bowed courteously to Ruth.

'It was so nice,' Fleur commented as she and Ruth walked home through the darkness, their arms linked as they followed the tiny beam of Ruth's torch, 'to be just RAF personnel and weren't the band fantastic?'

An RAF band had been formed on camp – the girls had often heard the lads practising in a hangar, the music echoing around the silent aircraft.

'Mmm,' Ruth murmured. 'A pity though.'

'A pity? Why d'you say that?'

'There was a very good-looking lad on the drums, but of course he couldn't come and dance.'

Fleur spluttered with laughter. Ruth had been as good as her word. She'd not danced with the same man twice all the evening, yet had never been short of partners.

'What were you trying to do? Dance with every man there?'

'Something like that,' Ruth chuckled.

'Well, I was happy with just the one.'

'We noticed!'

Fleur smiled to herself in the darkness. It really had been a lovely evening. She'd been able to spend the whole time in Robbie's arms quite openly. The rumours of their engagement were already flying around the room. There'd been slaps on the back for Robbie and chaste kisses for Fleur.

Strangely, only Bob Watson had been disapproving. Fleur had tackled him about it at once. 'Do you mean I won't be able to carry on as an R/T operator after I'm married?'

He'd shaken his head. 'No, it's not that. I just don't hold with wartime marriages. 'Specially not with fliers. When he goes missing, it'll be the rest of us who have to mop up your tears.'

Fleur had been dismayed by his bluntness. And the worst of it was he had said 'when' not 'if'. That, more than anything, had shocked her. He was as bad as – worse than – Ruth. At least her friend was no longer disapproving, or if she was, then she was hiding it very successfully.

'Well, I'll tell you something, Flight, here and now. *If* it does happen,' Fleur had replied heatedly, emphasizing the word deliberately, 'then I promise you, you'll never see me cry.' And with that, she'd turned on her heel and gone in search of Robbie, who was at the bar getting drinks for them. By the time he returned to her, she'd calmed down and was able to smile and enjoy the rest of the evening.

But climbing into bed that night, Bob Watson's words came back to haunt her. Ruth seemed to have come round to the idea. She was her friend and, if the worst did happen, Fleur knew she could count on her, but there were still others who viewed a wartime wedding with scepticism and disapproval.

Including her mother. But that, of course, was for a very different reason. Whatever that reason was. Fleur only wished she knew the answer.

Twenty-Three

'I've got a darky,' Kay said calmly.

Fleur's heart skipped a beat. An aircraft in trouble. Bob sprang into action, issuing orders for the landing lights to be switched on and the crash crew to be alerted.

'Better let sick quarters know too,' he instructed Peggy, whilst Fleur threw aside her sewing and took her seat beside Kay.

Kay was speaking reassuringly to the aircraft in trouble. 'Hello, B-Beer. This is Wickerton Wood. You are cleared to land. Runway two-zero. QFE one zero two zero. Switch to channel B. Over.'

Faintly, everyone in the control room heard the intermittent noise of an engine.

'He's in real trouble,' Bob murmured, as Kay continued to talk the aircraft down. The spluttering noise came closer and closer and the crash crew, fire tender and ambulance were already moving as close as they dared to the runway. The black shape appeared suddenly, low over the perimeter hedge.

'God – he's only just missed it,' Bob muttered, straining his eyes through the darkness and pulling nervously at his moustache. 'I hope he doesn't block the runway just before all our lads are due back.'

Fleetingly, Fleur thought Bob was being callous, but then she realized the tough realism behind his remark. With the runway blocked by a crash, their own returning aircraft would be endangered. Low on fuel, they might not be able to make it to another airfield.

Everyone seemed to be holding their breath, whilst Kay kept up a serene conversation with the stricken aircraft.

Lower and lower the plane came until, with a squeal of rubber, it touched the runway, bounced once and then stayed down, trundling past the control room where every head turned to follow its progress. When the aircraft slowed and came to a halt at the far end, there was a unanimous sigh of relief as the crash crew and fire tender raced after the plane.

'I think he's OK,' Bob said, still watching. 'Well done, Fullerton. Couldn't have handled it better myself.'

'Now there's a compliment,' Kay drawled. 'Could I have that in writing, Flight?'

As the crippled aircraft was towed away, the first call came from Wickerton Wood's own squadron and the control team swung into their practised routine.

'Coming to the pub tonight?'

It had been a busy week. The weather had been good and there had been flying almost every night. With one R/T operator off sick, Fleur and Kay had been required to work extra shifts and it wasn't until the Saturday, when there was no flying, that the friends had an evening off.

Fleur stared at Kay in surprise. 'Do you think we should?'

Kay, with a little smile on her mouth, shrugged. 'Why ever not? It's a free country.'

They glanced at each other, aware that that was the very reason they were all here. Fighting to keep that freedom.

'What about the locals? I mean we ... we don't want to antagonize them any more. We might not get away with it next time.'

There had been no repercussions from the fracas outside the White Swan – much to the surprise of everyone involved.

Kay's little smile became a smirk. 'Johnny's planning something.'

Fleur's eyes widened in fear. 'Oh no! He's not planning to round up a ... a posse, is he?'

Kay laughed, her dark violet eyes twinkling with mischief. 'Johnny? The responsible navigator of a Hampden? Really, Fleur. The very idea!'

'Then – then...?'

'Ah, now that would be telling. If you want to find out, you'll just have to come along, won't you?' She swung back in her chair to face her desk, adding, with a touch of sarcasm, 'Or are you chicken?'

'Is Robbie going?'

'Of course.'

'Then so am I.'

As she heard Kay's soft chuckle, she swung round and marched out of the room. There was half an hour before she needed to be at her desk to complete her morning shift. She wanted to find Ruth.

'What do you think Johnny's planning? Trouble?'

Ruth screwed up her face thoughtfully.

'Shouldn't think so. He doesn't seem the type to me.'

'Doesn't he?' Fleur was not so sure. Johnny had had no compunction in flirting with a local girl and causing her boyfriend to be jealous.

'Well, I'll come along too. Tell you what though. At the first sign of trouble we're out of there and I don't care if they do think we're chicken. I'm not incurring the wrath of the owd beezum for anyone else.'

Fleur laughed. She knew Ruth was referring to Flight Sergeant Brown rather than the Squadron Officer Davidson, who was the most senior WAAF officer on the station. Ruth was Lincolnshire born and bred, and though her dialect was not broad there were times when it came out strongly.

'What on earth is an "owd beezum"?'

'An old hag.'

Fleur laughed louder. 'Oh, that's priceless. I must remember that.'

'Well, don't let her hear you calling her it. You'd be on a charge for sure.'

Chuckling, Fleur returned to the control room. Only a few more hours, she was thinking, and she'd be with Robbie.

Later, as Fleur brushed her uniform and polished the buttons on her jacket until they sparkled, she felt butterflies of apprehension begin to flutter in her stomach. Downstairs she found Ruth and Mary Jackson listening to the wireless. Fleur stood quietly for a moment, holding her breath. Was it more bad war news? Then she let out her breath with relief. It was only one of Mrs Jackson's favourite programmes, *In Town Tonight*.

'Oh, sorry.' Catching sight of her, Ruth jumped up. 'Ready?'

'When you are.' Though Fleur was anxious to meet Robbie, part of her would have liked to stay here safely in the cottage, listening to Mrs Jackson's wireless.

'Now, you promise to go to the shelter if the sirens start, don't you, Mrs Jackson?' Ruth said.

'I don't think I could manage the path in the dark, my dears.'

'Harry's said he'll come and fetch you. Now I want your promise. Please.' Suddenly, Ruth bent down and kissed the old lady's wrinkled cheek. 'We don't want anything happening to you, you know.'

Tears filled Mary Jackson's eyes. 'You're such dear girls. All right, I promise I'll try.'

As the two girls walked down the dark lane, arms linked and following the thin beam of Ruth's torch, she murmured, 'I suppose that's the best we can hope for. That she'll try. But I very much doubt she'll venture down that path in the dark on her own.'

'But you said Harry had promised to go round.'

'Oh, he will, he will.' Ruth laughed wryly. 'He'll go round all right. But I bet they'll just sit there listening to Mrs J's wireless and gossiping while the bombs fall around them.'

'So all that digging was a waste of time, was it?'

'Not at all. We've tried. At least it's there.' She sighed. 'Now it's up to them. But we can't make 'em go in it if they really don't want to.'

They walked on in silence until they saw the

blacked-out shape of the pub looming up in front of them.

'Now then, girls,' was Bill Moore's friendly greeting. 'The lads are already in the corner over there.'

Fleur glanced round and her heart skipped a beat as she saw Robbie, but it was Johnny who rose to his feet from his place beside Peggy and came towards them. Draping his arms around their shoulders, he said, 'Now, girls, what are you drinking? I'm in the chair.'

As Johnny ordered the drinks, Fleur looked around her trying hard not to make it obvious that she was looking for someone. Then she let out a sigh of relief. There was no sign of Alfie Fish and his cronies. Fleur carried her drink across the room to sit beside Robbie.

'Hello, darling. All right?'

She nodded. She was feeling a little easier, but not entirely relaxed. It was early. There was still time for the local lads to make an appearance. And when Johnny came back and sat down, her fears increased again. He positioned himself so that he sat opposite the door and every so often he glanced up at the entrance.

He's watching for them, Fleur thought in horror. He really is planning trouble. Her heart began to pound and her hand, held warmly in Robbie's, trembled a little.

'Darling?' he said at once, full of concern. 'What is it?'

Fleur opened her mouth to blurt out the truth about what was worrying her, when she caught

Kay's eyes. There was a gleam in those violet eyes. A gleam that seemed to say, I thought as much – I thought you were a scaredy cat.

Fleur closed her mouth and lifted her chin with a new determination. Right then. Let them come. Let them all come. She'd show 'em. She'd wade in with the rest of them and hang the consequences. It would likely be promotion out of the window, but what the hell?

She smiled brightly at Robbie and said, 'Nothing. It was just ... just a bit cold walking here, that's all.'

As it was a warm May night, her excuse was feeble. Robbie looked deep into her eyes and such was their closeness already that he seemed to be able to read her very thoughts. He leant close and whispered against her hair so that no one else should hear. 'It's all right. I promise. Don't worry.'

As he drew back, he squeezed her hand. She gave him a small smile, not in the least surprised that he'd guessed what was troubling her. The time ticked on, with much laughter and jollity in their corner. The drinks flowed. Tommy sat with his arm around Kay. She snuggled up to him and Ruth was engaged in a verbal sparring match with the ebullient Johnny, while Peggy – the quiet one of the group – listened and smiled but did not join in the banter. Thankfully, the local girl, Kitty, was nowhere to be seen and neither – to Fleur's huge relief – was Alfie.

There was only half an hour left until closing time and Fleur was beginning to relax. Surely, the local lads wouldn't come in this late. She was laughing at something Johnny had said when, behind her, she heard the door to the public bar open and saw him glance towards it. She knew by his expression that this was the moment he'd been waiting for all evening.

They were here. She knew it. Without even turning round to see, she knew it. Alfie Fish and his pals were here.

Johnny rose and moved out from behind the table and towards them. Involuntarily, Fleur gripped Robbie's hand tighter. He returned it with a comforting squeeze, but Fleur found no reassurance in the gesture.

She leant towards him. 'Can't you–?' she began, but to her surprise, he put his finger to his lips and whispered, 'Just wait and see.'

Fleur glanced at Kay but her eyes were afire and a small smile played on her lips. The chatter in the bar room had fallen silent. Everyone was watching now. Sighing inwardly with resignation for whatever was about to happen, Fleur turned round slowly to see Johnny walking towards Alfie and his mates, his hand outstretched in greeting, a broad grin on his face. Then her eyes widened and she gasped in surprise, not just at Johnny's unexpected gesture, but at the sight of Alfie.

The young man and all his friends were dressed in Home Guard uniform.

'No hard feelings, lads,' Johnny was saying. 'I'd no idea the young lady was your girlfriend, Alfie. As far as I'm concerned, she's strictly out of bounds from now on.'

He still stood with his hand outstretched, waiting for Alfie to accept his apology and shake on it.

One of Alfie's friends guffawed. 'She ain't his girl. He'd just like to think so.'

His remark cost him a sharp nudge in the ribs from another in the group. 'Shut it, Tony.'

The smile on Johnny's face never wavered nor did his hand drop. 'That's as may be, but I meant what I said. I've no wish to upset any of you local lads, especially' – he laid emphasis on the words – 'fellow comrades in uniform.'

Alfie glared. 'Are you 'aving a laugh?'

For a moment Johnny's smile faltered. 'A laugh? No. Course I'm not. What d'you mean?'

'A' you 'aving a go at us 'cos we're not in the proper services?' His mouth twisted in a sneer. 'Not one of the Brylcreem Boys?'

Slowly Johnny let his hand drop now. It seemed Alfie had no intention of shaking it. His smile faded too. 'From what I hear,' he said in a last-ditch effort to heal the breach, 'the Home Guard is doing a great job. You – and all your mates – are doing just as much as us. Let's face it.' He nodded towards all of them. 'If old Hitler does get here, you'll be the ones on the front line. You'll be the ones fighting on the beaches and in the hills, like Mr Churchill warned. And we – well – if it gets to that, we'll have failed, won't we? So, no, I wasn't having a go.' He turned away from them to go back to his seat, but over his shoulder he called, 'Bill, set 'em up for these lads, will you? Maybe a drink'll make 'em realize there's no hard feelings. At least, not on my part.'

Johnny returned to his seat, picked up his glass and drained it. Near the bar the youths stood in

216

an uncertain, embarrassed group.

'What'll it be then, lads?' Bill asked easily, though Fleur could see he was keeping a close eye on the undercurrent of tension still in the room. Then the one called Tony ordered himself a pint, and the atmosphere relaxed a little as the rest of the group followed his lead, until there was only Alfie who had not taken up the well-meaning offer. He was still glaring malevolently across the room at Johnny – indeed, at all of them, Fleur thought, quaking inwardly, though she was careful not to show apprehension on her face.

Bill had just pulled the second pint when the familiar wail of the air-raid warning siren sounded.

'Right, everyone in the cellar,' Bill roared above the din, but the Home Guard lads slammed their pints down on the bar and made for the door, Alfie in the lead, as the first bomb landed with a thud that rattled the windows and shook the doors. The rest of the locals were diving towards Bill's cellar.

'We'd best get back to camp,' Tommy said, taking the lead. 'Are you girls going down the cellar?'

Ruth glanced at Fleur. 'We ought to get back to Mrs J's. Her 'n' Harry are never going to go down the garden to the Anderson. I know they're not. Not unless we're there to drag them into it.'

'Right you are, then,' Fleur said at once. Strangely, she'd been more worried about a fight breaking out between the RAF lads and the local boys than she ever was about a few bombs falling.

'And where do you think you two are going?' Robbie said as Ruth and Fleur rose and began to head towards the door.

'Back to the cottage,' Fleur said. 'Those two old dears won't venture down to the shelter in the dark on their own.'

'Wouldn't they be safer to stay put?' Another thud, further away this time but nevertheless a warning. 'Now it's started.'

The two girls looked at each other. 'I still think we should get back to them. Be with them for once.'

'All right. I'll come with you,' Robbie said and as Fleur opened her mouth, he added, 'and no arguments.'

'Come on then,' Tommy said, 'whatever you're doing, we'd best get moving and let Bill here get down into his cellar.'

They all turned to the landlord, who was calmly clearing up, washing glasses and wiping down the smooth, polished bar top.

Another crump, a little closer again this time.

''Night, Bill,' Johnny called. 'We'll let you get down the cellar.'

'Oh, I don't bother,' the big man said calmly. 'Jerry didn't get me last time an' I doubt he will this.' He nodded towards them all. ''Night all. You tek care, now.'

They glanced at one another, shrugged and, chorusing 'Goodnight', went out into the noise of the air raid overhead.

Expecting to see the streets deserted whilst the enemy bombers wrought their havoc, they were startled to see figures running this way and that, illuminated by flames that were billowing from a building a little way down the lane opposite the pub.

Silhouetted against the bright orange flames licking the night sky was the black shape of a square tower.

'That's the church,' Ruth gasped. 'Oh, how terrible. A lot of the villagers use the crypt as a shelter.'

'Come on, lads,' Tommy said. 'We'll go and help. You girls go down to the cottage. You too, Kay. Don't try getting back to camp on your own. Not in this.'

But Kay shook her head. 'No, I'll come and help too.'

'We'll come back,' Ruth added, 'once we've got the old folk into the shelter.'

Robbie took hold of Fleur's arm. 'I don't suppose it's any good me asking you to stay in the shelter, is it?'

'Not a chance,' she retorted and grinned up at him, the light from the burning building flickering eerily on his face.

He squeezed her elbow swiftly. 'Take care, then. Give my love to the old folk. We'll all meet back here at the pub...' And then he plunged after Tommy, Johnny and the others.

Twenty-Four

'Come on, Fleur. Let's get the oldies into the shelter and then we can get back here. Else we'll miss the fun.'

Fleur swallowed a hysterical laugh. It was not

219

quite what she would call fun, she thought, as she began to run down the lane after Ruth.

Bombs were still falling with a frightening regularity, but they were further away from the village now.

'That's the airfield,' Ruth panted as they ran.

'I know,' Fleur gasped. 'I just hope everyone's all right.'

'They'll be going for the aircraft on the ground and the runways to put the whole station out of action.'

They reached the cottage and pounded down the path round the end of the house and into the back yard. Opening the back door, Ruth called, 'Mrs Jackson? Are you there?'

There was no reply.

'Come in, Fleur, and shut the door before I open the one into the kitchen. If there's a light on, the last thing we want to do is attract Jerry's bombs here.'

With the back door safely shut, Ruth opened the door leading from the scullery into the kitchen. Light flooded out and they stepped into the room to see Mrs Jackson still sitting in her chair in the corner near the range and Harry sitting in the visitor's chair. Between them the wireless blared out a music hall programme. The two old people looked up guiltily.

'I thought as much,' Ruth said, as she stood on the hearth rug, her hands on her hips, looking down at them. 'Now come on, you two. We're going to get you down to that shelter Fleur's spent so much time digging and then we've to go. But we're not going anywhere till we know you're both safe. Come on, no arguments.'

She put out her hands and grasped Mrs Jackson's. With a sigh of resignation, the old lady allowed herself to be hauled to her feet. 'We'd better do as she says, Harry, else I'll never hear the end of it.'

With a chuckle, Harry levered himself out of his chair. Fleur picked up the emergency box containing candles and matches, a bar of chocolate and a bottle of fresh water, which Ruth religiously changed every day. In the box there was also a first aid kit which everyone hoped would never be needed, but it was there – just in case. It was kept in the scullery near the back door for just such an occasion as this.

'I'd better get you a couple of blankets,' Fleur muttered. 'You go on, Ruth. I'll catch you up...'

They lurched their way down the narrow garden path. It was a short but tortuous journey in the darkness, Ruth only daring to show the tiniest light from her faithful torch.

'Where are you two going? Back to camp? Can't you stay with us?' Mrs Jackson quavered as they got her settled on one of the battered old armchairs they had put in the shelter.

'No. We're going to help out down in the village. The church has been hit. It's on fire.'

'Oh no! Not the church. Oh Harry, that's where my Arthur and your Doris are.'

'They'll be all right, lass,' he said, reaching for her hand in the darkness. 'They'll be safe.'

As Fleur and Ruth climbed out of the shelter and pulled the sacking cover across the entrance, they heard the old lady say, 'And I'm missing

Music Hall. It's one of my favourites.'

Giggling, the two girls hurried back along the pathway.

'What she'd do without that wireless of hers, I dread to think,' Ruth said.

'It's a pity we can't take it down to the shelter with her. It'd keep her happy.'

Ruth stopped suddenly and Fleur cannoned into the back of her. 'Now what?' she said a little crossly as she'd bumped her nose on the back of Ruth's head.

'Well, we can.'

'Eh? Can what?'

'Take her wireless down there. It's a battery-operated one.'

'Do you think she'd want us to?'

'It's probably the only thing that'll keep her down there.'

'Come on then. Let's make it quick...'

A few minutes later as they left the Anderson once more, it was to the sound of dance music blaring out into the night, accompanied by the distant sound of falling bombs.

The fire at the church had been put out, but at the west end of the building was a gaping, smouldering hole in the roof.

The fire-fighters, together with members of the ARP, the Home Guard and villagers, their faces and clothes blackened and smutty, took a breather as the all-clear sounded. As the noise faded away, the RAF and WAAF contingencies found each other and made their way back to the pub, where Bill had opened his doors and was serving beer again as if nothing had happened.

'It's after hours,' Johnny said, picking up a welcome pint and taking a long drink before adding, 'won't you be in trouble with the local bobby?'

Bill laughed and nodded his head towards a figure sitting in the far corner of the bar room, his face blotched with smuts, his eyes wide with weariness, his uniform rumpled and his helmet missing. 'PC Mitchell turns a blind eye on such occasions.' Bill's deep chuckle rumbled again. 'Besides, he were first in the queue.'

'You look a sight,' Kay remarked, looking Ruth and Fleur up and down.

They grinned back as they retorted, 'So do you.'

Kay grimaced. 'I expect we're going to be on a charge when we get back.'

'Depends,' Ruth murmured.

'On what?'

'What's been happening there. I reckon there's been a lot of bombs fallen on the airfield. I expect that was their target.'

'That or Lincoln,' Tommy put in and, draining his glass, added, 'We'd better get back.'

'I just want to pop down the lane and see if the old folks are all right,' Fleur said to Robbie. 'But you go with the others. We'll be all right now.'

'Aren't you staying at your billet?'

Ruth and Fleur glanced at each other. 'No,' Ruth said. 'We might be needed on camp. We'll come back.'

'All right,' he agreed as he kissed her. 'Perhaps I'd better go with the lads, if you're quite sure...'

'I am,' she said firmly.

They were all moving towards the door when it

burst open and Alfie and his cronies crowded in. For a brief moment the two groups stood staring at each other. Alfie's glance sought out Johnny and he took a step towards him and held out his hand, a wide grin breaking out over his boyish face. 'Thanks for your help tonight. Put it there, mate.'

With a laugh Johnny grasped the outstretched hand. 'Gladly.'

There were suddenly handshakes and back-slapping all round before Tommy said regretfully, 'Sorry we can't stay to have another drink with you lads, but we'd best get back to camp. We reckon it's taken a bit of a battering. We might be needed, but we'll see you all again as soon as we can.'

'Right you are,' Alfie said with a nod. 'And the drinks are on us next time.'

'You're on.' Johnny grinned.

'Oh, I do hope they're all right,' Fleur fretted as she and Ruth hurried back down the lane towards the two cottages. They were thankful to see that there was no damage to the two properties.

'They'll be back in the house, I bet,' Ruth said as they rounded the corner into the back yard and moved towards the back door. Her hand was already on the doorknob when she became still.

'Listen!'

Through the darkness the sound of dance music drifted from the Anderson.

'They're still down there. Come on, we'll help them back into the house and then go.'

But as they lifted the sacking over the entrance, above Billy Cotton's music on the wireless, they heard Harry's loud snoring.

Clutching each other and stifling their helpless giggles, they tiptoed away in the darkness.

They signed in quickly at the main gate.

'Do you know what's happened?' they asked the young airman on duty in the guardroom. His face was white, his eyes fearful. He's incredibly young, Fleur thought. He looks younger than our Kenny.

'Not really. I've been stuck here. It ... it was pretty frightening. I think the runway's been hit and one or two buildings, but I don't know what.'

'I wonder where we'd better go,' Ruth wondered aloud. 'Where can we help?'

People were running to and fro and vehicles were rushing about putting out fires that still burned here and there.

'That's an aircraft.' Ruth nodded. 'I wonder how many we've lost.'

Fleur sighed. 'One or two I expect. But at least the crews will be safe.'

It was always annoying to lose aircraft on the ground. It seemed such a futile waste when they weren't even in battle, but it did mean the airmen were unharmed to fight another day, though they hated losing their aircraft. Some pilots and crews became attached to their own particular plane like a talisman.

'Come on. Let's see if we can find Kay.'

They found her eventually in the NAAFI, sitting at a table with her hands cupped round a mug of coffee, staring into space looking stunned.

'Kay? What is it? What's happened?'

Her eyes still didn't focus properly on them. 'She's dead,' she murmured hoarsely.

Ruth and Fleur glanced at each other.

'Get us a tea, Fleur. I'm parched.' The young girl behind the counter was calmly dispensing tea and coffee as if nothing had happened. She was even singing softly to herself. It was a particular kind of courage that Fleur always admired. Carrying on, no matter what.

When she returned to the table with two cups of tea they both sat down opposite Kay.

'Now,' Ruth said firmly, but not unkindly. 'Tell us what's happened? Who's dead?'

It was strange to see the outspoken Kay looking lost. The girl blinked and suddenly seemed to see them for the first time, to recognize them.

She took a deep breath as if trying to rally herself. 'Flight Sergeant Brown – the one you call the owd beezum. She was in the sergeants' mess and ... and it took a direct hit. There's her and three of the fellers killed and one or two more injured.'

'Why on earth didn't they go to a shelter? There's one near the mess.'

'There wasn't time. The bombs started falling almost as soon as the siren started.'

'That's true. They did.' Ruth nodded.

'What can we do to help?' Fleur touched Kay's hand.

She shook her head. 'I – don't know.'

'Then we'll go to the watch office. Bob might be there. He'll know what we ought to do.'

Ruth and Fleur drank their tea quickly and stood up. 'You coming?' Ruth said to Kay, who hadn't moved.

'What? Oh – oh, yes, I suppose so.'

As they moved out into the darkness, Fleur whispered to Ruth, 'Do you think she's all right? I mean, she looks stunned. Sort of – lost. I wouldn't have expected it of her. I mean, she's always so ... so ... well, I don't quite know what to call it, but you know what I mean. On top of things. I mean, when we had that raid when I was on duty with her, she was magnificent. She was calm as you like.'

'I don't know, but we'll keep her with us. She'll be all right. Maybe it's just shock.'

The three of them ran to the control room. Bob Watson was there ranting at the enemy.

'Would you believe it?' he raved. 'It's going to take days to put this lot right.' He flung his arm out to show them the glass littering the floor and paperwork scattered everywhere.

'Right,' Fleur said, as if metaphorically rolling up her sleeves. 'Let's get stuck in, girls. Kay, you fetch a sweeping brush. Ruth, you make some tea. Flight here looks as if he could do with a cup and I'll start sorting all this paperwork out.' She glanced at Bob. 'You here on your own? Where're the others?'

He sighed and sank down into a chair as if thankful to hand everything over to Fleur. 'Sick quarters. They both got cuts from the glass.'

'They're not badly hurt, are they?'

He shook his head. 'But I expect there'll be a few that are. Have you heard? I've been here all the time.'

Fleur nodded and repeated what Kay had told them.

Bob Watson shook his head sadly. 'That's a shame. Poor old Brown. I know she was a bit of a tartar to you girls, but she was doing her duty as she saw it. She had your best interests at heart really, you know.'

Fleur was thoughtful for a moment before she nodded slowly and said, 'Yes, yes, you're right. I think she had.'

Twenty-Five

There were five fatalities that night on the airfield – three airmen, Flight Sergeant Brown and a young WAAF who had been running across the airfield to the nearest shelter but hadn't made it in time. The dead were buried side by side in the local churchyard. It was sad and touching to see the five coffins all being buried at the same time. Fleur, Ruth, Kay and seven other WAAFs formed a guard of honour around the coffins of Flight Sergeant Brown and the young WAAF. It was a grey, miserable day befitting the mood of those attending the funeral, made all the more poignant by the gaping hole in the roof at the end of the nave. A cold, damp breeze filtered into the church, chilling the mourners. It was even colder standing in the graveyard.

Afterwards, as they were about to turn away towards the pub for something to warm them, Fleur said, 'You two go on. I just want a word with someone.'

'OK. You know where we'll be,' Ruth said and linked her arm through Kay's as they walked on.

Others moved away until there was only a couple standing forlornly by the graveside of the young WAAF – and Fleur. She gave them a few moments before moving quietly towards them.

'I just wanted to say how sorry I am,' she said softly. The man turned to face her. There were tears on his face, yet he managed a smile. 'Thank you, miss. That's kind of you. Were you a friend of our Joyce's?'

'I'm afraid I didn't know her well,' Fleur said evasively. In truth, she couldn't even remember having met the girl at all. There were several WAAFs she only came into contact with on parade. She knew them by sight, but not by name. Perhaps Joyce had been one of them. Billeted off camp, Fleur really only knew the girls with whom she worked.

'She'd only just finished her basic training a month ago. This was her first posting,' his wife said, her voice tremulous. But she, too, was smiling. 'It's such a shame – a waste, but we were so proud of her for joining up–'

'We still are,' the man said quickly. 'I wouldn't want you to think we'd have it any different, even though this ... this has happened.' His voice broke and he blew his nose loudly on a large handkerchief.

His wife glanced at him and then turned back to say, 'She volunteered on her eighteenth birthday, you know?'

Fleur didn't, but she nodded anyway. 'Are you coming across to the pub? Bill – the landlord –

will have laid on refreshments...'

'That's very kind of you, miss, but we'd best be catching the bus back to Lincoln and then the train home. We've a long way. I don't expect we'll be home before nightfall.'

'Where–?' Fleur began, and then stopped. She had been about to ask where they were from. But then, she realized quickly, they would know she hadn't really known their daughter. She cleared her throat and swiftly changed what she had been about to say. 'Where will you get something to drink and eat? You ought to have a cup of tea at least.'

The man and woman exchanged a glance. 'All right, miss. You're right. We could do with something – even if it's only a cuppa.'

But half an hour later, Fleur was pleased to see them tucking into the sandwiches that Bill's wife always managed to produce when there was a particularly harrowing funeral. And today's certainly fell into that category, Fleur thought sadly. A little later she saw the couple onto the bus for Lincoln. The man – she still didn't know his surname – shook her hand warmly.

'It's been nice to meet you, miss, though I could have wished for happier circumstances. But it's a comfort to the missis and me to know that our girl had lovely friends like you. You've made today a lot easier. Thank you.'

Fleur couldn't speak for the lump in her throat. She would probably never meet these people again, but if she had helped ease their pain at all, then the little white lie that she had known their daughter was surely forgivable. As a salve to her own conscience she said impulsively, 'While I'm here, I'll look after Joyce's grave for you. Keep it tidy and that. I promise.'

The woman leant forward and kissed her cheek. 'How kind,' she murmured and dabbed away her tears.

'We'll arrange for a headstone. Perhaps you could see that it's done nicely?'

'I will,' was Fleur's parting promise to them.

Later that night, in Ruth's bedroom at the cottage, Fleur told her what had happened after the funeral and the promises she had made. 'And there's something else...' Her voice dropped to a whisper. 'When we were in the graveyard I noticed poor Mrs Jackson's husband's headstone has been broken in two. The top half's lying on the ground. I bet the bomb did it.'

'Oh, crumbs, she'll be upset. It was the first thing she thought of when we told her the church had been hit. Are you going to tell her?'

Fleur shook her head. 'No, but I'm going to see if I can get it repaired for her. Maybe she won't need to know. I'll ask my dad. He'll know what to do.'

It was several days after the bombing before Fleur got a chance to go home for a brief, overnight visit.

'Dad?'

'Ssh, listen!' Jake was sitting in his chair near the range, his head against the wireless that sat on a shelf next to the range. 'Listen!'

Fleur bit her lip, waiting impatiently, until Jake reached and turned off the wireless. 'They've got the *Bismarck*. Can you believe it? Our lads have sunk the *Bismarck!*' Jake's face was alight with triumph for a moment, then he sobered swiftly. 'It's a great victory for us, but you can't help thinking about all those poor boys drowned or shot to pieces. They reckon there must be over a thousand men lost.' He shook his head sadly. 'And I bet half those young lads don't know what they're fighting for. You know, Fleur,' he said heavily, 'lots of folks wouldn't agree with me, but I reckon the ordinary German bloke doesn't want this war any more than we do. They've just been swept along in a tide of patriotism by a fanatic who's just bent on ruling the world.'

Fleur sat down beside him and touched his arm in a gesture of understanding. 'You're right, Dad. And the loss of life on both sides, well, it's just sinful, isn't it? But what can we do? We've got to stop Hitler. We can't let him achieve his terrible ambition, now can we?'

'No, love, of course we can't.' He sighed heavily. 'But it's just so sad that all these innocent young lives are being wasted in the process. And only twenty years after the last lot. Another generation of young fellers.'

They sat in silence for a moment, until he pulled himself together and said, 'What was it you wanted, love?'

Fleur explained about the air raid and the damaged gravestone.

'Tell you what, love, I'll take you back tomorrow and see what I can do.'

'Oh, Dad, would you really? That'd be lovely – but not a word to Mrs Jackson, mind. We haven't

232

told her. I'm just hoping no one else does before we can get it mended.'

'Aye, we'll have a family outing. Mebbe your mum'll come too. And Kenny.'

But Betsy was determined to play the spoil-sport. 'I've too much to do to go gallivanting about the countryside. And you shouldn't be using petrol to go jaunting.'

'I've enough petrol to take my daughter back to camp without endangering the war effort and to do a favour for an old lady,' Jake replied, keeping his tone deliberately mild.

'You shouldn't be having to take your daughter anywhere. She should be here at home doing her duty. And now, because of her, I've likely got to put up with having strangers living here. Land Army girls, indeed. And townies! What are they going to know about life in the country, I'd like to know.'

Betsy went back into her kitchen still muttering darkly, whilst Jake winked at Fleur. 'Well, I tried. She can't say she wasn't asked to come, now can she?'

It was a merry little party that set off in Jake's boneshaker of a car the following morning. Just the three of them – even Kenny had not been able to persuade Betsy to come along.

'You shouldn't be skipping school,' she admonished. 'Not if you want to get into agricultural college...'

Kenny opened his mouth to retort that he had no intention of going to college and never would have, but, guessing his intention, Jake cut in, 'Half a day won't hurt, love. And I really need his help.'

233

They bowled along, singing at the top of their voices, above the chugging of the noisy engine, but when they arrived at the churchyard their spirits sobered as they viewed the damage and saw the five freshly dug graves, side by side.

Kenny put his arm around Fleur's shoulders and gave her a quick hug. He said nothing, but his action spoke volumes. That could have been you, Sis, he seemed to be saying.

Jake cleared his throat and became suddenly brisk and businesslike. 'Right then. Where's old Arthur's grave, Fleur?'

She led them around the end of the church that had been damaged. They paused for a moment looking up at the gaping hole in the roof. 'That's going to take a bit longer than a day's work,' Jake declared. They moved on to stand before Arthur Jackson's headstone.

'Well, there's one good thing,' Jake said, after he had examined it carefully. 'It's a clean break. I reckon a bit of cement will sort that out. You'll still see the crack, I'm afraid, but that'll maybe weather in time.' He glanced up at Fleur. 'Do you think she'll know yet?'

'Only if someone's told her while I've been away. Ruth won't, but Harry might if he finds out.'

'Right then, we'll see what we can do.' He straightened up and began to move back towards the car. 'Give us a hand, Kenny, will you?'

They carried all the paraphernalia that Jake had brought with him in the boot of the car through the gateway and set it all on the grass beside the grave.

234

'See if you can find us some water, Fleur. There's usually a tap somewhere in a churchyard.'

Fleur picked up a bucket and set off in search of water. She'd walked all the way around the church and arrived back at the main door when the vicar appeared from inside the church.

'Oh, hello, Vicar. Where can I find some water?'

'For flowers?' Revd Cunningham asked.

Fleur shook her head. 'We're trying to repair Mr Jackson's headstone. It got broken the other night and I know it'll upset poor Mrs Jackson if she finds out about it. I've just been home on a couple of days' leave so my father's brought me back and come to see what he can do.'

The man, who had led the most difficult funeral service only a few days earlier, beamed at Fleur. 'How very kind of him – and of you to think of it. The tap's over there, my dear, near the wall a little way along from the gate. I'll go and have a word with your father.'

Fleur followed the line of his pointing finger and saw the tap. 'Thanks, Vicar.'

When she returned, it was to find the three men talking and laughing together as if they had known each other for years.

'What a great bloke,' Kenny said when Revd Cunningham had excused himself and left them to their repairs. 'I thought all vicars were stuffy and superior. But he's a smashing chap.'

'He gave a lovely service last week,' Fleur said. 'At the funerals, I mean. It can't have been easy for him. But he seemed to know just what to say somehow. I can't remember a word he said now, but I know it was both moving and comforting at the same time.'

Jake had finished the mix of cement and had smeared it on top of the broken edge. 'Right, Kenny. Help me lift this up and when we've got it in place you can hold it whilst I put a couple of iron strips on the back of the headstone. Cement alone won't hold it. I don't know what it'll look like, but it's the best I can do.'

A little later they all stood back to assess Jake's handiwork. 'I'm afraid the crack still shows badly.'

'At least Arthur's got his headstone back,' Fleur said as they gathered everything up and reloaded the car.

'Now, do you think your Mrs Jackson could find us a cup of tea and one of those delicious scones she makes before we set off back?'

'Of course, she will. But not a word about what we've been doing.'

'Actually, love, I think we should tell her now. She's bound to hear about it and it'll soften the blow, perhaps, if we tell her what we've tried to do.'

Fleur sighed. 'Yes, I expect you're right.'

Mary Jackson not only made them a cup of tea, but also insisted that they should share the stew she had made.

'We can't take your precious rations,' Jake insisted at first, but then from the back seat of the car he carried in a box of a dozen eggs, half a pound of butter and a wedge of cheese.

'How very kind of you,' Mrs Jackson said. 'Now I insist you stay for your dinner. Besides, Harry would never forgive me if I let you go without him seeing you again. Ah, that'll be him now.

236

Come away in, Harry. We've got visitors.'

After the meal, whilst Fleur cleared the pots away and washed up in the scullery, Jake sat beside the old lady and, taking her hand in his, explained gently the reason for his visit.

'We've done the best we can, my dear. I'm afraid I can't say it's as good as new, though.'

Mrs Jackson dabbed her eyes with the corner of her apron, but she was smiling through her tears. 'How kind of you to come all this way to do that for me. You really shouldn't have, but I am glad you did. Thank you, Jake. Thank you very much.'

Twenty-Six

The next few weeks were a flurry of excitement, marred only by Betsy's obstinate mood. Meg, blithely ignorant of the depth of the trouble within Fleur's family, offered to make not only the bride's gown but also a bridesmaid's dress for Ruth. When the girls couldn't get to Nottingham for a fitting, Meg travelled by train and bus to the village where they were billeted, lugging a suitcase full of paper patterns and material samples with her.

Fleur hurried down the path to meet her. 'Oh, this is so good of you. Neither of us can get leave at the moment.'

'Don't mention it, love. It's nice to get away for a while.' She laughed gaily. 'Oh, don't get me wrong. I love Pops dearly, but with working at home as well I never seem to see anything but those same four walls.'

'I can guess what you mean. How is Pops? Is he better now?'

'As good as he'll ever be. He's got a bad chest and he's only to pick up a cold and it's bronchitis or even pneumonia. Hence the stay in hospital. Still, he's much better now the warmer weather's here. Edie, next door, is keeping an eye on him today. She'll fuss round him and he'll enjoy that.'

'Here, let me take that case for you... Goodness!' Fleur exclaimed. 'Whatever have you got in here? It weighs a ton.'

Meg chuckled. 'You'll see.'

'Come along in and meet Mrs Jackson. She's a sweet old dear and getting so excited about the wedding. Did Robbie tell you, we've booked the church here for Saturday, the sixth of September? And we've both applied for a week's leave.'

Following Fleur down the narrow path and round the side of the house, Meg asked quietly, 'Don't you want to be married in South Monkford?'

Fleur paused, her hand on the back doorknob, and turned to glance back at Meg. 'No,' she said quietly. 'It'll ... it'll be easier here. We're resident in this parish and ... and ... well, it'll be better all round. Dad and Kenny can get here and...'

Meg was staring at her. 'What d'you mean? Your dad and Kenny? What about your mother?'

Fleur kicked herself mentally. She hadn't meant to tell Robbie's mother yet. Of course, she'd find out eventually but... Anyway, she'd said it now. She sighed and said flatly, 'She won't

238

be coming.'

'Won't – be – coming?' Meg was scandalized. Then, after a moment's thought, she pursed her mouth. 'That's because of me, is it?' She sighed and shook her head in disbelief. 'I wouldn't have thought that Betsy's bitterness went quite so deep. So deep that she won't come to her own daughter's wedding.'

Fleur stared at Meg for a moment before she took a deep breath. 'I don't understand it at all. What *is* she so bitter about?'

Meg lifted her padded shoulders, but she was avoiding Fleur's candid eyes as she forced an offhandedness. 'My dear, I really have no idea.'

And there – for the moment – Fleur had to let the matter drop. She didn't want to risk upsetting Robbie's mother. She knew Meg was lying, or at least avoiding the truth, but she couldn't question her – not as much as Robbie would be able to do. And even he hadn't wanted to press matters any further than he already had done. He had his mother's reassurance that he and Fleur were not related and that was all he needed – or wanted – to know. As long as he could marry his lovely Fleur, that was all that mattered to him. So, Fleur took her lead from him, and instead of asking the awkward questions that still tumbled around her own mind, she smiled brightly and opened the back door. 'Come in. Mrs Jackson's so looking forward to meeting you. She's very fond of Robbie.' Fleur leant towards Meg to whisper. 'She gets all girlish when he's around.' She forbore to say that it was more that Mrs Jackson mothered him, perhaps remembering her own lost son.

Meg laughed. 'Well, he's a handsome boy, even if I say it myself.'

The awkwardness of a few moments ago was pushed aside, if not quite forgotten. At least, Fleur had not forgotten. Silently, she promised herself: one day I will find out what all the mystery is.

Very soon the old lady's kitchen table was spread with paper patterns and scraps of material.

'Now then,' came Harry's voice as he knocked on the back door, opened it and came in. 'What's going on here?'

'Harry,' Fleur called, winking at Mrs Jackson. She guessed the old man had seen Meg arrive and the sight of the pretty, smartly dressed stranger had aroused his lively curiosity. 'Come on in and meet my future mother-in-law.'

Harry stood just inside the doorway and stared at Meg. He stroked his white moustache and chuckled. 'You can't be young Robbie's mother. You're not old enough.'

Meg's eyes sparkled mischievously as she held out her hand. 'I assure you I am. And you must be Harry? I've heard a lot about you from Robbie – and from Fleur too. I'm very pleased to meet you.'

'Likewise, Mrs – er...'

'Meg.' Her eyes twinkled merrily at him. 'Please call me "Meg".'

Unbidden, her mother's words came into Fleur's mind. 'It'll be some poor old fool she's set her cap at.' Quickly, she pushed aside the unjust thought. She must not allow her mother's prejudice to influence her.

Bringing her thoughts back to the present, Fleur sighed as she fingered the pieces of silk and satin that Meg had brought. 'But how am I to raise enough coupons for any of these fabrics?' Fleur murmured. At the beginning of June clothing coupons had been introduced.

'Don't you worry about that,' Meg said. 'I've a trunk in the loft at home full of old dresses I've collected over the years. You know, when people have been getting rid of them. There are at least three silk dresses up there. I'm sure I can turn one of them into something for you if we can't raise enough coupons for new material. Only trouble is,' Meg said with disappointment, 'they're not white.'

'You can have my clothing coupons, dear,' said Mrs Jackson. 'I won't need them all.'

'And mine,' Harry put in. 'You can have all mine. Long as me good suit'll still fit me for the big day, I don't need no coupons for new clothes.'

Meg smiled at him archly. 'You'll have to try your suit on, Harry, and let me know if it needs any alteration.'

The old man chuckled, his eyes sparkling. 'Well now, I'm sure it'll need summat doing. It's a long time since I wore it.'

Fleur shuddered as once again her mother's words pushed their unwelcome way into her thoughts. Stop it! she told herself sharply. She's only being nice to the old boy. We all have fun with Harry. Even Mary Jackson teases him and Ruth positively flirts with him.

But now, Fleur could not help thinking, Ruth

might have a rival for Harry's affections.

'That's very generous of you,' Meg was saying, pulling Fleur's thoughts back to the moment. 'But it's not only the coupons, it's finding the right material too.'

'Er...' Mrs Jackson seemed suddenly hesitant. 'Er ... there is my wedding dress. It was white. You – you could have that, dear.'

Fleur stared at her. 'Oh, Mrs Jackson, no, I couldn't. It must hold such memories for you. I wouldn't want to...' Her voice faded away as Harry moved forward and put his arm around the old lady's ample waist. 'There now, Mary, that's a kind thought. A very kind action. And I'll match it. They can have my Doris's things, an' all. Time we stopped clinging to the past, eh, and let the young folks mek what they can of the present.' He wiped a tear from the corner of his eye. 'I reckon they're earning it, don't you? Besides' – he chuckled and winked at Fleur – 'Ruth'll be pleased to hear I'm getting rid of some more rubbish.' And they all laughed.

'You're right, Harry. My Arthur would agree and I know your Doris would have turfed all her old clothes out ages ago.'

The old man laughed again. 'She would that. I bet she's up there shaking her fist at me for letting the house get in such a mess. Anyway, thanks to young Ruth, it's bright as a new pin now. Doris'd've been pleased to help you, lass.' He nodded towards Fleur.

'And wouldn't Arthur be chuffed with his garden?' Mary Jackson was not quite finished with her reminiscing yet. 'And I owe that all to you, Fleur dear. So, yes, if Mrs Rodwell here...'

'Meg,' Meg interposed.

Mrs Jackson smiled. 'If Meg here can do anything with my wedding dress, you're very welcome to it.'

'And I'll get young Ruth to sort out all Doris's clothes and let you have them.'

Mrs Jackson was already moving stiffly towards the front room of the cottage that was now her bedroom. 'It's in here. In a trunk...'

But when they unearthed Mary's wedding dress, it was sadly yellowed and moth-eaten. The old lady fingered the material with tears in her eyes. 'What a shame. Such a happy day we had.'

Meg glanced at Fleur and at Ruth, who had now arrived home. Then she put her arm around the old lady's shoulders. 'It's a good job our memories last better than material, isn't it?' she said gently.

'But I thought it'd help Fleur...'

'Don't worry,' Meg reassured her. 'I know just what we can do. We'll scrape together enough coupons for Fleur to have a brand new dress.' She looked at Ruth. 'And I'm sure I can alter one of the dresses I've got, or one of Doris's, into a bridesmaid's dress for you. And some of the lace on this dress of yours, Mrs Jackson, is perfect. I can dye it to match whatever dress we decide on for Ruth.'

'Pink,' Fleur said.

'Blue,' Ruth insisted and fluffed her blonde curls. 'I look all wishy-washy in pink.' She made a moue with her mouth.

Meg regarded her thoughtfully. 'You know,

Fleur, I think blue would suit her better, if you don't mind me saying so.'

Fleur smiled. 'Of course I don't. To tell you the truth, I don't care what anybody wears as long as Robbie turns up.'

They all laughed now, but Meg said very seriously, 'Oh, he'll turn up all right, I promise you that.' Though it was not spoken aloud, the thought was in everyone's mind. *Just so long as he's able.*

Twenty-Seven

'I'm here again,' Meg trilled as she opened the back door of Mary Jackson's cottage.

'Come in, love, come in,' Mary said, struggling to her feet.

'Please don't get up, Mrs Jackson,' Meg said as she heaved the huge suitcase through the back door. As the old lady sank back thankfully into the armchair, Meg added, 'But I could do with a cuppa. Mind if I make one?'

'Of course not, love. Help yourself.'

'I don't like using your precious tea.'

'Don't worry. The girls bring supplies from the camp. They're allowed to,' she added hastily, 'seeing as they've had to be billeted off the camp.'

Meg nodded. 'How're they getting on with building the WAAFs' quarters?'

Mrs Jackson smiled. 'Slowly.'

Meg chuckled. 'But I can see you don't mind

244

about that.'

The old lady shook her head. 'Those two lasses have changed my life.' Her smile widened. 'And I'll be seeing a lot more of your boy too after they're married, I expect. He's a grand lad.'

Meg nodded. 'I think so,' she said earnestly, and then added with a smile, 'but then I could be biased.' She glanced out of the window overlooking the back garden.

It was the third week in June already and all Fleur's hard work was beginning to pay off. Lettuces and radishes were sprouting up on top of the Anderson shelter and rows of green ferny leaves had appeared where she'd planted carrots. In the front garden, runner beans were climbing their frames, as too, unbeknown to Mrs Jackson, were the sweet peas at the end of the cottage.

'She's working so hard,' Mrs Jackson told Meg. 'Every spare minute she's out there dressed in her old clothes and her woolly hat when it's windy. And your boy, too, he comes whenever he can. They both helped me yesterday to bottle some gooseberries and make some strawberry jam. Harry's got a strawberry bed and he gave us some of the fruit. Don't forget – before you go – I'll give you a jar.'

'Oh, how lovely! Home-made jam. That will be a treat. Didn't you find it tiring? You mustn't overdo it,' Meg added with concern.

Mrs Jackson laughed. 'Oh, they did it all.'

Meg's eyes widened. 'My Robbie? Jam making?'

'Well, under Fleur's instruction. I didn't have to do much. I just sat here and topped and tailed the gooseberries. Her mother must have trained her well. She knew just what to do.'

Meg's eyes darkened as she said, 'Yes, I expect she did.' Her tone – though unnoticed by Mrs Jackson – hardened a little as she added, 'I expect her mother is the perfect farmer's wife.'

'Fleur's even saying,' Mrs Jackson went on, 'that she can't be away too long on honeymoon because a lot of the fruit and vegetables will be ready in September.'

Meg laughed. 'Well, I think Robbie might have something to say about that, don't you? But I can understand what she means. She doesn't want all her hard work – and the produce – to go to waste.'

'Oh, I think we can manage for a week. Harry will come round and do what he can and even Ruth's promised to help.'

Meg's voice was dreamy as she murmured, 'Perhaps Jake would come over.'

'I expect he's got enough to cope with on the farm,' Mrs Jackson said, knowing nothing of Meg's inner thoughts. 'But Kenny will cycle over, I don't doubt. We – Harry and me – think he's got his eye on Ruth.'

'So,' Meg said, turning away from the window. 'When will the girls be home?'

Mrs Jackson's face sobered. 'I don't know. There's some sort of flap on at the camp. I ... I...' She hesitated to worry the young airman's mother, but she couldn't lie. 'I think there's a big raid on tonight. We're not supposed to know, but because so many of the personnel are living in the village at the moment, we ... we sort of get the feel that something's going on. They don't say anything, of course. Not a word. But we've got to know how to read the signs.'

'I see,' Meg said quietly. 'So ... so you think the girls might not be back today at all?'

Mrs Jackson shook her head.

Meg bit her lip. 'Well, I can't stay. I have to get back because of my father.' How she would love to have stayed – to have been here when the girls got home whatever time it was. To know at once that Robbie was safely back. But she couldn't impose on Mrs Jackson and, more importantly, she couldn't leave her father for all that time. Since his spell in hospital, he was even frailer and needed a helping hand to climb the stairs to his bed. 'But I'll leave the dresses here. They can try them on and help each other with the fitting. Tell them I'll come back a week today and if they still can't be here, then they must pin them carefully and leave me instructions. We've still over two months to the big day, so there's plenty of time.'

Mrs Jackson nodded. 'You'll be surprised how fast the weeks go and with the girls working different shifts it's difficult for you to meet up with them. But I'll be sure to tell them what you've said. The big day will soon be here.'

Meg nodded, unable to speak. She was too busy praying that Robbie would be there.

She kissed the old lady's wrinkled cheek and let herself out of the back door. As she walked down the narrow path between the two cottages, she heard Harry's voice.

'Now then, lass. All right?'

She glanced up, and despite her sober

thoughts, couldn't help smiling. To hear the old man call her, a woman of over forty, 'lass' always made her laugh. But, she supposed, to him she was 'no' but a lass'.

'Mustn't grumble,' she answered.

'Doesn't do any good if you do,' Harry chuckled. 'Nobody listens.'

He moved closer and leant on the fence running between the two pathways. 'I saw you arrive. I was just coming round. Are you off again?'

Meg nodded. 'Mrs Jackson doesn't think the girls are going to be home today.'

'Ah,' Harry nodded knowingly. 'So she said when I popped round this morning...' The idea of old Harry 'popping' anywhere, made Meg smile again. 'I'm very fond of them lasses, y' know. They're like me own.'

'Have you any family, Harry?' Meg asked, trying desperately to get her thoughts away from her own son and, for a few moments, to concentrate on some one else.

'Aye. Not now, lass,' his face clouded. 'Me an' Doris only had the one son and he were killed in the last war.'

'I'm sorry,' Meg murmured.

'What happened to Robbie's father then?' Harry asked, with the bluntness that old age seemed to believe it had a right to.

Meg gave a start and stared at him for a moment, then swallowed nervously. It was an innocent question. Of course, Harry couldn't know anything. This wasn't South Monkford...

'My husband,' Meg said carefully, 'was quite a few years older than me. He was too old for the last war, but he died in the influenza epidemic just after.'

Harry nodded sympathetically. 'Aye, I remember that. Took a few from this village. It were a bugger, weren't it? All them lads surviving the trenches to be hit by the flu when they got home. Bad business. Bad business.' He eyed her keenly. 'And you've brought that lad up on yar own?'

Meg smiled. 'It wasn't difficult. He's a good boy. And then my father came back – came to live with us. He worked a little at first. Here and there – just odd jobs, you know. And I've always been kept busy with my dressmaking.'

''Spect you're in demand now with all the shortages,' Harry nodded.

'Well, yes, I am. And I expect it will get worse – or better' – she smiled – 'depending on your point of view. Now they've brought in rationing, women want the clothes they've got altering to be a little more fashionable. Keeps their spirits up, you know.'

Harry looked her up and down. 'You always look so pretty and smart. Now I know why.' He paused, then cleared his throat and stroked his moustache with a quick nervous movement. 'Did you find anything useful amongst Doris's things?'

'Oh yes.' Meg was enthusiastic. 'There was a lovely long silk gown I've been able to make into a bridesmaid's dress. And it was blue – just the colour Ruth wanted.'

Harry nodded. 'Aye, I remember that.' His eyes misted over briefly. 'Doris looked a picture in that.' Then he chuckled. 'You might not think looking at me now, but I used to be quite a good

249

dancer. Loved dancing, did the wife, and she always liked to dress up if we went to a proper dance.' He cleared his throat. 'Well, I'm real pleased if her things were some use to you. Ruth sorted 'em all out for me. She was real good, didn't make me part with anything I didn't want to, but she's right, it's high time I let go. Doesn't mean I'm going to forget my Doris just because I let her old clothes go, does it?'

'Of course not,' Meg agreed gently. 'And I've been able to make use of those two nice suits of your wife's. It was such good material. I've altered one to fit Mrs Jackson for the wedding. They must have been almost the same size. I hope you don't mind. I mean, it won't upset you, will it, seeing her wearing it?'

'I'll not let it,' Harry said stoutly. 'I'll just remember that my Doris would have liked that. They were big pals, y'know. 'Er and Mary Jackson. Big pals. Allus in and out of each other's kitchens. Borrowing sugar and a bit of flour. And swapping recipes. No, lass, she'd have been thrilled. And so will I be.'

Twenty-Eight

Life at Wickerton Wood had been fairly mundane for several weeks, if being involved with bombing raids could ever be described as mundane, but on the day that Meg came to visit a bigger mission than usual had been planned for that night

250

and everyone on the airfield was tense.

Take-off, with more than the normal number of aircraft taking part, went smoothly and everyone in the watch office heaved a sigh of relief as the last bomber lumbered into the air and disappeared into the deepening dusk. The airfield was strangely silent after the drumming of dozens of engines. Yet for some reason the staff were unable to relax into their usual diversions for the waiting hours. Peggy made copious cups of tea until Fleur said, 'Do you know, when this war's over, I don't think I'll ever drink tea again.' She was trying to lighten the atmosphere, but failing. 'It's my landlady's cure-all and we seem to drink gallons of it here too.' Fleur, more than anyone, was feeling jittery. When she'd pricked her finger twice sewing a button on her blouse, she gave up and tried to read. But the words on the page blurred before her eyes and the light romantic novel seemed out of place when she was in the middle of a real-life drama.

The aircraft were late – all of them – and Bob began his restless pacing as he always did. At last, the first call sign came over the airwaves and one by one the planes limped home. And many of them had some damage. Several were landing on almost empty tanks. One plane had a damaged undercarriage and slithered off the runway to land on its belly on the perimeter track, the crash crews and fire tenders screaming out to it at once.

Then there were only three left to return, but the airwaves were silent. Fleur glanced up at the blackboard. Her heart missed a beat and then began to thump wildly.

Beside Tommy Laughton's name, the space was blank.

The minutes seemed to turn into hours whilst they all waited. The wireless crackled and a voice requested permission to land. But it wasn't Tommy and Robbie's aircraft. Kay snapped her answer. It was the first time Fleur had ever seen her colleague show any sign of stress whilst on duty.

The aircraft landed safely and then – there was silence once more. The tension in the watch office mounted. No one spoke as the minutes ticked by.

At last, when they were almost ready to give up hope, the radio crackled into life once more, and Fleur almost fainted with relief as she heard, 'Hello, Woody, this is D-Doggo calling...'

Fleur flew into his arms, not caring who saw them, not caring if she was reprimanded.

'I thought you weren't coming back. I thought we'd never get married. I thought...'

Though exhausted, with heavy dark rings under his eyes, Robbie could still raise a smile. 'Hey, what do you take me for?' He put his arm about her as they continued walking towards the debriefing centre. 'I'm not the sort of chap who leaves his girl standing at the altar. Not even Adolf is going to stop that.'

'Oh, Robbie...' She was crying openly now.

He paused a moment and turned to face her, taking her face between his hands. 'I have to go now, darling. You know that. But I'll see you to-morrow.'

She nodded. 'Get some sleep. You look all in.'

His eyes clouded. 'It was a bad one, Fleur. Our plane is badly damaged. But the one good thing is we won't be flying tomorrow. So I'll see you tomorrow night and you can tell me how all the plans are going. Love you...' He kissed her soundly on the mouth and turned to follow his weary crew into debriefing.

Suddenly, the tiredness washed over Fleur. Anxiety for Robbie had kept her going, but now that he was safe, the sleepless hours finally caught up with her. By the time she had walked to the cottage – it would be a while before Ruth could come home – Fleur had scarcely the strength to climb the stairs and fall into bed. So it wasn't until the following morning that Fleur heard from Mrs Jackson that Meg had visited.

'I told her I didn't think you'd be home yesterday, so she didn't wait, but she left the dresses for you to try on...' Mary Jackson repeated Meg's instructions about the fitting. Then she added anxiously, 'Fleur, I'm sorry, but I told her I thought there was something big going on at the airfield. I hope I didn't worry her.'

Fleur stared at her. She opened her mouth to say, *Of course you'll have worried her. You shouldn't have said anything. You shouldn't have said a word...* But seeing the troubled look on the old lady's face, her swift anger melted and instead she said, 'Robbie's back safely. I'll let her know somehow.'

'Don't send her a telegram,' Ruth said, her mouth full of porridge. 'That'll scare the living daylights out of her.'

Fleur bit her lip. 'But how can I let her know

then? I can't go in person, we're on duty again tonight, aren't we?'

Ruth nodded. 'But Robbie probably won't be flying. His plane won't be ready for tonight.' She glanced up at Fleur. 'Did you see it?'

Fleur shook her head.

'Badly shot up, it was. One engine out of action and holes all down the fuselage. It was a miracle they got back at all, and even more miraculous not one of them was hurt.'

Fleur shuddered and sent up a silent prayer of thanks.

'I'll ring Mr Tomkins at the shop on the corner. He's the only one with a telephone in our street, but he doesn't mind taking messages for folks. 'Specially not now. And his little lad positively longs for the phone to ring.' Robbie laughed. 'The little tyke gets a few coppers from anyone he delivers a message to. More, if it's good news he brings.'

'I hadn't the heart to tell Mrs Jackson off, but she really shouldn't have said anything.'

Robbie pulled a face. 'Ma knows the score, I doubt she's any more worried than usual. But I will ring. There might be something on the wireless about it being a bad raid. Then she will worry.'

'Let's walk down to the phone box and do it now,' Fleur insisted. Although it wasn't her fault, she felt guilty that Meg had been burdened with extra anxiety. Though the worry would always be present, miles away in Nottingham she was usually unaware of exactly what was happening.

But not this time.

As they walked down the lane, arm in arm, Robbie said, 'At least I've a bit of good news. My leave for the whole week after the wedding has been granted.'

Fleur grinned up at him. 'Mine too. I heard yesterday.' She hugged his arm. 'So where are you taking me on honeymoon?'

'Ah – now I haven't quite decided. But I'll tell you one thing. One of the chaps is lending me his sports car for the week, so as long as I can scrounge enough petrol we can go anywhere you like.'

'I don't care. Just as long as we're together.'

They reached the phone box and Robbie got through to Mr Tomkins. 'Just get your Micky to nip down the street and tell Ma and Pops I'm OK.'

'Right you are, lad...' Fleur, squashed into the box alongside him, heard the shopkeeper's voice faintly. 'Glad to hear you're OK. All ready for the big day, a' yer? All the best from me and the missis.'

'Thank you, Mr Tomkins,' Robbie said and turned to Fleur. 'Did you hear that?'

Fleur nodded as Robbie bent his head to kiss her. 'Oh, I'm ready for the big day all right.' Only the sharp rapping of someone on the glass window, anxious to use the telephone, finally disturbed them.

On a warm day towards the end of June, Fleur was at the end of the cottage tending the growing row of sweet peas. She sprayed the plants with

255

water and then pinched out the side shoots. Pulling up one of the plants where the leaves had turned yellow, she said, 'You're not going to give Mrs Jackson any pretty flowers, are you, poor thing?'

'Fleur, Fleur – where are you?' She heard Mrs Jackson calling from the back door. Not wanting to give away what she was growing in secret along the wall, Fleur quickly moved into the front garden, paused a moment to inspect the row of runner beans and then went around the house by the pathway.

'Did you call?' she asked innocently as she rounded the corner.

'Oh, there you are, dear. Come in and listen to this on the wireless. We can't believe it!'

'What is it? What's happened?'

Mrs Jackson beckoned. 'Come and listen – you'll never believe it.' The old lady turned and hurried as fast as her legs would take her back to her seat beside the wireless. Harry was sitting in the chair on the other side and, as Fleur took off her boots and stepped into the kitchen, she saw the old couple, one on each side of the wireless, leaning towards it, straining to hear every word the news announcer was saying.

'What's happened?' Fleur asked again, to be answered with a 'Shh' from both of them.

Fleur listened but could make no sense of the final words of the bulletin and, as Mrs Jackson switched off the wireless, Fleur glanced at them in turn, the question on her face.

'Old Adolf's invaded Russia.'

'Russia?' Fleur was shocked. 'Whatever for? I

thought he'd signed a non-aggression pact with Stalin?'

'He did. But he's broken it.'

Fleur sank down into a chair. 'But why? Russia's a massive country with an army of millions. How can he hope to beat Russia?'

''Cos he's a madman, that's why. Mind you, it'll probably be his downfall and while he's busy fighting that lot he won't be bothering us so much, now will he?'

Fleur wrinkled her brow thoughtfully. 'Maybe not.'

'If he tries to keep all his fronts going, he'll be spread too thin, see.' Harry stroked his moustache and beamed. 'What we want is for the Yanks to come in. Then we'd really see the end of Hitler.'

'I don't think they will. It's not their war, is it? You can't really expect them to do any more than they're doing,' Fleur said reasonably. 'I mean, I know we weren't exactly being attacked when war was declared, but we were certainly on his agenda, weren't we?'

'Aye, aye, I see what you mean, lass. It's just that – to my mind – with the might of America behind us, we couldn't lose.'

Fleur grinned at him. 'We can't anyway.'

Harry smile was tinged with poignancy. 'No, lass,' he said and his voice was husky with emotion. 'No, not whilst there's youngsters like you about, we can't lose.'

'Well, this won't get the hoeing done,' she said getting up. 'We're all going to a dance in Lincoln tonight, so I'll need a bit of time to get my glad rags on.'

As they climbed aboard the 'Liberty Bus' to take them into the city that evening, the chatter was all about the invasion of Russia and how it might affect Britain.

'It's got to take the heat off us, surely.'

'Well, I don't mind a bit of a breather, 'specially in September,' Robbie remarked, putting his arm around Fleur's shoulder. His statement was greeted with whistles and catcalls until Fleur blushed.

'Where are we all going?' she said, trying to divert attention from herself. 'It's too nice to sit in a cinema or a smoky dance hall, isn't it?'

'How about,' Robbie suggested, 'a row on the Brayford?'

'That's a good idea,' Tommy agreed. 'We could have a race.'

'Well, I'm popping home to see my folks,' Ruth said. 'But only for an hour or so. I'll meet you down there later.'

'Aw, come on, Ruth. Your folks won't mind for once, will they?' Robbie tried to persuade her.

'I won't be long, I promise.'

Robbie seemed disappointed. 'Where do you want the bus to drop you, then?'

'Monks Road near the school. I'll walk down to the Brayford from there. I'll only be about an hour.'

'My goodness,' Fleur exclaimed as they arrived beside the Brayford Pool. She shaded her eyes against the sun setting over the smooth expanse of water, the tall warehouses silhouetted against the golden glow. Sitting on a wall, three young boys dangled homemade fishing rods in the water. 'I've never been down here before. Oh, and look at all the barges. It's lovely.'

Boats were hired and soon everyone was out on the wide pool and heading towards where the Pool narrowed into the Fossdyke.

There was much shouting to one another and laughter and banter. A race of sorts developed until the airmen rowing decided the competition wasn't worth the risk of aching muscles the next day and they all rowed leisurely towards a pub set a little way back from the bank.

'We should have waited for Ruth,' Fleur said regretfully. 'She won't bring a boat out on her own.'

'Don't expect she'll be on her own,' Robbie said cheerfully.

'Really? Why? Do you know something I don't?' Fleur felt a little miffed. Ruth was her friend. Her best friend. Surely...?

'You'll see,' was all Robbie would say.

Fleur lay back in the prow of the boat and trailed her hand in the water that shimmered with a myriad of colours in the setting sun. Through half-closed eyes she could see the fields on either side of the water and the cathedral standing proudly on the hill bathed in golden light.

The war and all its turmoil seemed miles away.

'There's a boat behind us.' Fleur shaded her eyes but couldn't make out just who was in the craft.

'That'll be Ruth,' Robbie said. He stopped rowing and rested on the oars. 'We'll wait for them to

259

catch up.'

'Them?' Fleur teased. 'So you do know something.'

As the boat drew nearer, Fleur let out a gasp of surprise. 'Kenny! It's Kenny.'

Robbie's grin broadened. 'I know. I fixed all this up with him last time he was over to help you with the garden. He was to keep out of sight and meet us at the Brayford. And then Ruth had to throw a spanner in the works by going home to see her parents.'

Fleur laughed. 'I wondered why you were trying to persuade her not to go. You rogue! Trying your hand at a bit of match-making, are you?'

'Something like that.'

'Well, it won't work. Not with Ruth.'

'Oh, I don't know,' Robbie said, glancing across at the other boat where Ruth was waving excitedly and Kenny, though rowing hard to catch up with them, had a huge grin on his face.

The evening was a merry one, the landlord of the pub friendly and the regulars welcoming, and it was with reluctance that the party rowed back to the Pool as dusk settled over the waterway.

'Did you see?' Robbie was triumphant. 'Ruth sat with Kenny all night and he had his arm round her. And look at them now – laughing and talking as he rows her home. And I heard him insisting there was no room for anyone else in their boat when we all set off.'

'Mmm.' Fleur watched her brother and her best friend. She would've liked nothing more than to see them happy together, but soon Kenny would join one of the services, and the way he was talking these days, it sounded as if he was determined to become a fighter pilot.

And Ruth did not get close to fliers.

For a few hours they had been able to get right away from the war and all its anxieties, but now it was back with Fleur with a vengeance.

Twenty-Nine

Through July the bombing raids went on from Wickerton Wood, but now their targets were the docks and ports on the coast of France. These were being used by the enemy's shipping which was patrolling the seas around Britain in an effort to sink the convoys bringing vital food supplies to the country.

At the beginning of August the day came that Fleur had looked forward to: the day she could pick a huge bunch of sweet peas and present the bouquet to Mrs Jackson.

The old lady was dozing in her armchair, her cheeks red from the heat of the day, little beads of sweat on her forehead. Fleur crept into the room and stood on the hearthrug. As if feeling her presence, Mrs Jackson opened her eyes. For a moment, she blinked rapidly as if she couldn't believe the sight before her, and then tears flooded down her face.

'Oh, Fleur! How beautiful! They're just like Arthur used to grow for me. Wherever did you get them?'

Fleur chuckled. 'From the end of your cottage.'

'Eh?' Mrs Jackson was puzzled until Fleur explained what she had been doing. 'I didn't think you ever went round that end and it wasn't suitable for growing much else. Runner beans, perhaps, but I've got those in the front garden. So – I thought I would grow you your favourite flowers. I'm sure the authorities won't clap me in irons for it.'

Mary Jackson clasped her hands together. 'Oh, I hope not, dear. I do hope not. You don't know what pleasure you've given me. They'll remind me so much of Arthur.' She started to struggle to her feet, but Fleur said quickly, 'Don't you get up. Just tell me where I can find a vase and I'll stand them on the table where you can see them.'

Minutes later, as she went back into the garden, Fleur left the old lady smiling gently at the delicate blooms and reliving her happy memories.

'Mum? You didn't really mean it about not going to Fleur's wedding, did you?' Kenny asked as he sat down to supper in the farmhouse, three weeks before the date in early September that had been set. Jake was in the scullery washing his hands before coming to the table.

'Oh yes, I did. And if you and your father really care about me, you won't go either.'

'But why? What on earth have you got against Robbie?'

Betsy was silent, struggling against blurting out the truth. 'I've got my reasons,' she said tartly at last.

'What?'

'You're too young to understand...' She glanced towards the door leading into the kitchen from the scullery and lowered her voice. 'Maybe I'll tell you one day. Oh yes, maybe when you're a bit older I'll tell you it all. But...'

At that moment Jake stepped into the kitchen and Betsy fell silent. Jake looked from one to the other, sensing that something had been said. He sighed. 'Now what's going on?'

Kenny avoided meeting his father's eyes, picked up his knife and fork and attacked the plate of food in front of him.

'Nothing,' Betsy said, but her tight lips and the angry sparkle in her eyes told Jake far more than a thousand words.

'I see,' he said as he sat down heavily. 'Like that is it? Getting in practice for three weeks on Saturday, when you won't be speaking to either of us forever more.'

Betsy slammed down Jake's plate in front of him, spilling gravy onto the pristine white tablecloth.

'You think it's a joke, don't you, Jake? Well, let me tell you–'

But Jake cut her short, raising his hand. 'No, Betsy. I don't want to hear whatever it is you've got to say. I've heard enough. More than enough. And if you think your attitude is going to stop either of us going to Fleur's wedding, then you'd better think again. Because it won't. Now, sit down and eat your supper and let's see if we can hold a civil, pleasant conversation for once.'

Betsy stared down at him for a moment. Then she gave a little cry, pressed her hand to her mouth, turned and rushed from the room.

'Obviously not,' Jake muttered as he took his first mouthful.

Kenny said nothing and they continued the meal in silence.

The evening before the wedding, Ruth tugged the tin bath from Mrs Jackson's shed into the kitchen and set it on the hearth, as she had done every Friday night since coming to live in the cottage.

'Like me to fill it with water for you, Mrs Jackson?'

'No, no, I can manage now.'

The hot water came from a tap at the side of the range, and the old lady was used to filling the bath with a jug before undressing in front of the warm fire and stepping into the water. She had done it all her life. The only thing she couldn't manage any more was bringing the bath from the garden shed into the house.

'Do you know,' Fleur said. 'I quite fancy a soak in there myself tonight. It'd ... it'd remind me of home. It's what we did every Friday night. There's something very comforting about sitting in hot water in front of the fire. Would you mind, Mrs Jackson? After you, of course.'

'That's all right, dear. There's plenty of water. You can empty it after me and have some fresh.'

'What about you, Ruth?'

'Oh, I had a bath up at camp as usual. No, actually...' Ruth paused and a wicked gleam came into her eye. 'I was thinking of going next door. I've got the perfect excuse now.'

Mrs Jackson and Fleur exchanged a puzzled

glance. 'An excuse? What for?'

Ruth's smile widened mischievously. 'To get Harry in a bath.'

Mrs Jackson and Fleur stared at her for a moment and then they both burst out laughing.

'I'll believe that when I see it,' Fleur spluttered.

'Oh, I don't think he'd let you watch!' Ruth chuckled. 'But, you see, I've promised to trim his hair for him. Make him smart for tomorrow. His clean clothes are all ready for the morning. All laid out in his bedroom. Now all he needs is a bath.'

'You are good to him, dear.' Mrs Jackson was still laughing. 'But I don't think you'll get him to bath. Doris used to have a job. He's a "stand at the sink and wash up and down" sort of chap is Harry.'

'He'll love it – once he's in.'

'Ah – but that's the point,' Fleur laughed. 'It'll be *getting* him in!'

'Right then.' Ruth was determined. 'I'm going to give it a go. Wish me luck.'

'You're going to need it,' Fleur said.

They left the back door open. In the warm stillness of the September evening, they heard Ruth dragging the bath across the yard into the cottage. There was a moment's silence before they heard Harry come out of his back door as if a swarm of hornets was after him.

'Nah, lass. I dorn't need a bath. Only dirty folks need baths. You tellin' me I'm a mucky beggar.'

Fleur and Mrs Jackson stood together, peeping out of the scullery window. They could see Harry standing in the neighbouring back yard, his hair

265

ruffled in panic. Mrs Jackson chortled.

'Eh, this is just like the old days. The times I've seen poor old Doris chasing him round the back yard on a Friday night to get him in the bath.'

Ruth appeared in the doorway of Harry's cottage, her arms akimbo. 'Harry, it's a special day tomorrow. A big day...'

'I knows that. Don't you think I knows that but–'

'But nothing, Harry. You said you'd let me cut your hair–'

'Me hair – yes. I dorn't mind that, but–'

'Well, when I've cut it, it'll look nicer if it's washed.'

'Aye – well – mebbe,' Harry agreed reluctantly, then added, with a gleam of hope, 'But old Bemmy never said to wash it after.'

'Old Bemmy? Who's old Bemmy?'

'Feller who used to cut me hair. Lived in the village, he did. Used to cut all the fellers' hair.'

'So do you want him to do it for you? But you've left it a bit late now.'

Despite his agitation, Harry laughed. 'Much too late. He's been dead nigh on six years.'

'Ah!' Ruth paused a moment and then said, 'Aw, come on, Harry. All that lovely hot water in front of a blazing fire. Height of luxury, I call that.'

'Well, you're welcome to use it. I don't mind, duck.' Harry's eyes were twinkling now. 'I'll scrub ya back for ya.'

Ruth laughed. 'I bet you would.' Then her eyes glinted. 'Right, you're on. You can scrub my back if you let me scrub yours.'

'Eh!' Now Harry looked positively frightened. 'I was only kidding. I didn't mean...'

Ruth fell against the door frame, laughing helplessly, whilst Mrs Jackson and Fleur, still watching from the scullery, stifled their laughter as they heard Ruth say, 'I'm only teasing you, Harry, you old dear. But I am serious about you having a dip. I'll fill it with lovely hot water and then make myself scarce. I'll cut your hair first and then you can wash it.'

Harry made one last plea. 'Can't I just have me hair washed? At the sink in the scullery?'

Ruth shook her head firmly. 'No, Harry, it's all or nothing.'

Suddenly, Harry capitulated disarmingly. He smiled and his eyes twinkled. 'D'you know, lass. It's just like having my Doris back.'

Ruth crossed the space between them and linked her arm through the old man's. 'That's the nicest thing anyone's ever said to me, Harry,' Fleur heard her say as they disappeared into the house.

She turned back from the kitchen window to say in surprise. 'Do you know, Mrs Jackson, I really think she's managed it.'

'Wonders never cease,' the old lady murmured, smiling as she began to ready herself for her own bath.

By the time Ruth returned from next door, Mrs Jackson was tucked up warmly in her bed and Fleur was sitting in the bath in front of the glowing fire.

As Ruth flopped into Mrs Jackson's empty chair, Fleur, soaping herself, asked, 'And did he let you scrub his back?'

'Yes, and wash his neck. It was just like dealing with a grubby little boy. He chuntered and grumbled the whole time. But I think he enjoyed it really – once he got in. He even let me cut his toenails for him.'

Fleur blinked. 'You're kidding me.'

'Nope. I had to go out into the scullery whilst he got undressed but once he was in, he shouted me in. Do you know, Fleur, it was a lovely cosy time we had together. He told me all about his family. He was born in that little cottage, y'know. He was one of ten kids. Where the heck they put 'em all, I can't think.'

'So, has he got a lot of family left?'

'No. Sadly. He was one of the youngest and there's only a sister left and she's in Canada.'

'And then he and Doris lost their only son, didn't they? How sad.'

There was silence in the kitchen, the only sound the ticking of the little clock on the mantelpiece and the coals settling in the fire. Ruth stirred and moved to kneel beside the bath. 'Here,' she said gently, 'let me soap your back for you.' Fleur leant forward whilst Ruth gently smoothed soap over her back.

'You've got a lovely skin, Fleur,' she said. 'I'm quite envious. My back's all spotty.'

It was warm and cosy and the two girls were feeling drowsy. 'Oh well, I suppose I'd better get out and empty this bath...'

'Well, you can get out and get yourself dry and up to bed, but I'll see to the bath.'

'Oh, but...'

'No "buts". I'm your bridesmaid. Remember? I'm supposed to look after you. And if I want to pamper you a bit, then I've every right.'

'Yes, ma'am.' Fleur grinned and gave a mock salute. As she stood up carefully, Ruth wrapped a warm fluffy towel that had been warming on the fireguard around her. As she did so, she held Fleur close and whispered, 'You do know I wish you every happiness, don't you?'

Fleur rested her head against the other girl's shoulder. 'Course I do.'

'I didn't mean to be hard on you when ... when you first told me you'd got a boyfriend and when you said you were getting married. It's just...' She bit her lip, unable to continue for the lump in her throat.

'I know, I know,' Fleur sympathized. 'I didn't understand then, but I do now. You'd just been through it, hadn't you?'

'I let myself get very fond of Billy. I vowed I wouldn't. Right from coming into the WAAFs, I promised myself I wouldn't let myself get fond of anyone, but then I had to meet Billy.'

There was another long silence before Fleur, pulling back a little, looked into her friend's face glowing in the dancing light from the fire and asked gently, 'Tell me honestly, do you wish you'd never met him?'

Ruth blinked and then slowly, with sudden understanding, shook her head. 'No,' she said huskily. 'No, I don't. "Better to have loved and lost" and all that, you mean?'

'Well, I didn't want to get all poetic on you, but, yes, I suppose that's what I do mean.'

'You're right.' Ruth sighed heavily. 'But – oh, Fleur, it hurt so much. So much. I just didn't want – you know.'

'Yes, I know.'

'But seeing you with Robbie – well, I suppose I've changed my mind a bit. Whatever happens, you'll have such happy memories. No one can ever take them away from you and ... and despite everything – the war and even the trouble it's caused in your family – oh, everything, I still bet you don't wish you'd never met Robbie, do you?'

'No, I don't,' Fleur said emphatically.

Thirty

Fleur woke up on the morning of her wedding with a strange fluttering in her stomach. She lay a moment, trying to quell the unaccustomed nerves, and then she smiled and mentally castigated herself. What on earth am I nervous about? I've no doubts about marrying Robbie. So why? But she knew why. Today might mean the end of any sort of relationship with her mother. If Betsy did not attend the wedding, as she had threatened, then Fleur knew that her mother would carry out her threat to the letter. She would never speak to her daughter again. As she rolled out of bed, Fleur sighed. She just hoped her mother would not carry out the threat that extended to her father and brother.

For herself, she could cope with it. The relationship between herself and her mother had always been a strained one. Kenny had always been their mother's favourite; Betsy had never even tried to hide it. Luckily, it had not affected the love Fleur had for her brother, nor his for her. And Jake had always made up for Betsy's lack of demonstrative affection towards her daughter. Fleur just hoped that today was not going to cause a rift between herself and her father and brother. If they bowed to Betsy's demands and stayed away from the church today, then Fleur's day would be spoilt.

That – and only that – fear was what was causing her to feel nervous.

The service was set for midday, but Fleur was dressed and ready and standing nervously in Mrs Jackson's kitchen by eleven-thirty.

'My word,' Ruth teased. 'You don't intend letting him get away, do you?'

Fleur smiled nervously.

'You look fantastic,' Ruth said, standing back to take a final check on the bride's appearance. Mrs Jackson too nodded her approval.

'You look wonderful, my dear.' She stepped nearer and reached up to kiss Fleur's cheek and then dabbed a tear from her eyes. But the old lady's tears were tears of happiness. 'Now, I'll leave you. I'll go round to Harry's. He's borrowed a bath chair to take me to church.' She hesitated and then said, a little nervously, 'You – er – don't mind if he comes round? I know he ... he wants to see you before you leave for the church.'

'Of course I don't,' Fleur said and almost added, I might have to ask him to give me away if Dad doesn't turn up. When the old lady had closed the back door behind her, Fleur burst out, 'Oh, Ruth, they're not coming, are they? They promised to be here by now.'

'Aren't they meeting you at the church?'

Fleur, pressing her lips together to try to stop the tears flowing, shook her head. Her voice was shaking as she said, 'No. Dad said he'd come here to take me to church.'

'He'll be here, don't worry.' Ruth tried to make her tone reassuring, but even she had begun to have doubts. 'And Kenny,' she added, hoping that Fleur's handsome brother, young though he was, would have the guts to stand up to his mother.

They heard a sound in the back yard and Fleur's heart leapt, but it was Harry who passed the window and opened the back door. He stood in the doorway. 'Eh, lass, you look a picture.'

Fleur raised a smile. 'Thanks, Harry.'

'But where's your bouquet, lass? You can't get married without a bouquet.'

'Well, flowers are so hard to come by. I thought I'd just carry a prayer book. You know...?'

With a flourish as dramatic as any seasoned actor, Harry produced a bouquet of red roses from behind his back. 'I made it mesen,' he said proudly. 'Cut all the thorns off, lass, so's you don't prick yasen, and I begged a bit of fern from Mester Clegg to finish it off.'

'Oh, Harry. It's beautiful! I don't know what to say. Thank you – oh, thank you.'

Tears threatened again but Ruth was quick to rush forward and dab her eyes. 'Oh, Harry, you old dear. They're lovely, but if you make her ruin her make-up I'll chase you round the yard again.'

Laughing wheezily, Harry backed out of the door. 'In that case, I'll be off to get Mary to the church. See you there, girls.'

They heard his footsteps go round the end of the cottage and down the cinder path and then there was silence. The minutes ticked by and slowly the colour drained from Fleur's face until it was almost as white as her dress.

'What about Robbie's mum? Is she coming here?' Ruth asked, trying to turn Fleur's thoughts away, even if only for a few moments, but failing.

'No – she's going straight to the church. She ... she said she ... she didn't want to make matters worse by bumping into my family here.' Fleur's eyes filled with tears now. 'Looks like it wouldn't have mattered.'

'Look, love...' Ruth began, but at that moment they heard the sound of a noisy engine spluttering to a halt outside the cottage. The two girls stared at each other for a moment before Fleur's eyes shone. 'That's them. That's Bertha.'

'Bertha! Who the hell's Bertha?'

Fleur laughed. 'Our car. It's an old banger of a car. Now I know why they're late. Bertha's been playing up.'

'Mebbe your mother jinxed it?' Ruth laughed as she opened the back door and Jake, flustered and red faced, rushed in followed by a grinning Kenny.

'Fleur – I'm so sorry–' Jake began, but then he stopped short and his mouth fell open as he stared at his daughter in her wedding finery. 'Oh, Fleur,' he whispered. 'You look – beautiful.'

273

Now her tears spilled over and Ruth rushed to dab her cheeks with a clean handkerchief. 'Stop that – you'll wreck your make-up.'

Kenny grinned. 'Who is it, Dad? Surely it's not our Fleur? Where's her trousers and her woolly hat?' His teasing broke the poignant moment and they all laughed. Then Kenny held out his arm to Ruth.

'Come on, pretty lady. We'd better go ahead and see if the groom's been daft enough to turn up.' For a moment his glance lingered fondly on Fleur. 'You look great, Sis,' he said softly. 'We'll see you in church.'

As Kenny and Ruth left the cottage to walk the three hundred yards down the lane to the little church, Jake stood once more just staring at his daughter, drinking in the sight of her.

'You look lovely, Fleur.'

'Oh, Dad,' Fleur said, now a little more in control of her emotions. 'Don't set me off again.'

'I just wish–' Jake began and shook his head sadly. 'I just wish your mother could see you. Maybe...' His voice trailed away.

'She ... she's not come then?'

'No, love. I'm sorry. Nothing we could say made any difference.'

Fleur put her arm through his. 'But you and Kenny are here. Thank you for that and I'm so sorry if it's made things difficult at home. But I'm not going to apologize for marrying Robbie.'

Jake looked deep into her eyes. 'As long as you love him, Fleur, and you're sure he loves you...'

'I am.'

'Then that's all I need to know. And now, if

274

Bertha can manage to carry us another few yards, we'd best be going.'

Bertha spluttered and coughed her way down the lane, pulling up to a thankful halt outside the gate of the old stone church, with its gently leaning square tower and arched porch. The path was so narrow that they had to walk in single file until they reached the door where Ruth awaited them. Adjusting Fleur's headdress and veil and straightening her gown, Ruth then fell into step behind the bride and her father.

'Ready, love?' Jake asked, huskily.

Fleur's eyes glowed as she turned to smile at him with unmistakable joy. Her love for Robbie shone out of her, and as Jake led her into the church and they turned together to walk down the aisle, he saw Robbie standing tall and handsome and proud at the altar steps.

Beside the groom stood Tommy Laughton, resplendent in his uniform, and behind them both, in the second pew back, were the other crewmembers from D-Doggo. And to Jake's surprise, the church was almost full. There were a few other RAF and WAAF personnel, but then all the spare seats were taken up by villagers. They'd come to see a pretty wedding, to try to forget the war, just for a few hours, as they turned their backs on the gaping hole in the roof at the back of the church and watched the beautiful bride and her handsome groom.

Jake's attention came back to the young man who was about to become his son-in-law. He saw the love in the young man's eyes as he watched his bride coming towards him and Jake was left

275

in no doubt now. Fleur was doing the right thing. Whatever Betsy's feelings were, there was no mistaking this couple's love for each other. As they neared the steps, Fleur had eyes for no one but Robbie, but Jake could not stop his gaze roaming over the few guests in the front pews.

And then he saw her. For the first time after half a lifetime apart he saw Meg again.

Thirty-One

The service was over and Fleur and Robbie had stood just outside the porch as all the guests and villagers had filed past them, shaking Robbie's hand and kissing Fleur. Then the pictures had been taken with a great deal of laughter and amusement at the elderly photographer, who kept disappearing beneath the black cloth covering the square box camera which teetered precariously on a spindly tripod.

'Just look at him!' Kenny spluttered with mirth. 'Trampling all over the graves to get his antiquated camera in the right place. Is he allowed to do that?'

Robbie and Fleur were almost helpless with laughter.

'Well, I don't think the folks he's walking over are going to say much,' Robbie chuckled.

'I just hope there's none of their relatives watching though,' Fleur said, ever sensitive to the feelings of others. 'They might feel it's a bit ... a bit – oh, what's the word?'

'Sacrilegious?'

'Something like that.'

'Well, I don't think there's anyone left much to notice.'

Fleur glanced around her. Most of the villagers who'd been in the church had gone, and only a few were left peering over the church wall to watch the goings on.

'Now I wonder where they've all rushed off to?' Kenny mused. 'You'd've thought they'd have stayed to watch the comedy. Mind you,' he added, nodding towards the little man waving his arms about to position his subjects and looking as if he were directing traffic, 'I reckon he's done it before. He seems to know just where he wants us to be.'

'You sure about that?' Robbie murmured.

'Smile please,' trilled the photographer and they all tried to straighten their faces into sensible smiles rather than wide, toothy grins and fits of giggles.

As the photographer declared, 'That's it, folks,' Robbie turned to Fleur. 'And now, Mrs Rodwell, we're off on our honeymoon. Your carriage awaits, m'lady.'

'I'll just have to go back to the cottage and get changed. I can hardly travel in this...'

'Why ever not?' Robbie pretended surprise as he bent to kiss her. 'I want the world to see my beautiful wife.'

'Now then, plenty of time for that later, you two lovebirds.' Harry hobbled up to them and held out his arms. 'I haven't kissed the bride yet.'

There were tears in the old man's eyes as Fleur leant forward so that he could kiss her on both cheeks. 'Eh, lass, but you're bonny an' no mistake. You're a lucky young feller...' he added, holding out his hand to shake Robbie's.

'Thank you, Harry.'

'Right then, we're all off to the pub. You will let me buy you both a drink before you go, now won't you?'

Fleur and Robbie exchanged a glance. They couldn't wait to be alone together, yet they didn't want to appear ungrateful to Robbie's mother, who had worked so hard on Fleur's gown and Ruth's dress, nor to Jake and Kenny, who had defied Betsy to be here. They owed it to their guests, to Harry and Mrs Jackson too, to spend a little time with them.

'Of course we will,' Robbie said. 'That's very kind of you, Harry.'

The old man beamed. 'Right.' Harry raised his voice. 'Everyone across to the Mucky Duck.'

There was a ripple of laughter.

'The what?' Kenny blinked.

Ruth hooked her arm through his. 'It's the White Swan, really, but all the locals call it the Mucky Duck. Come on, you can escort me. I'm supposed to walk with the best man – handsome devil, isn't he, in that uniform – but his girl-friend's here and I don't want to spoil the little bit of time they've got to spend together.'

'It's my pleasure,' Kenny said gallantly and the faint flush on his face told her that indeed it was.

The crew of Robbie's aircraft and six WAAFs, Kay and Peggy amongst them, formed a guard of honour down the pathway. Handsome young men in their smart blue uniforms that not only set the hearts of the young women in the village aflutter, but caused several of the older women to smile fondly and wish themselves forty years younger.

Then Harry led the way from the church across the road, pushing Mrs Jackson in the borrowed bath chair. 'Come on, folks, follow me,' he called, his excitement bubbling over as the wedding party fell into step behind them, with the vicar bringing up the rear.

'Dear old Harry,' Ruth murmured. 'He's loving this, isn't he?'

Kenny was thoughtful. 'D'you know, I reckon he's up to summat.'

'Eh?' Ruth's eyes widened. 'What d'you mean?'

'I dunno. Maybe he's got them a special present that he can't wait to give them. But there's something going on behind those twinkling eyes. And there's something else funny too.'

'What?'

'Well, I'd've thought there'd've been crowds to watch my beautiful sister come out of church, but there's hardly anyone about now. In South Monkford, I know it's a town and we've got a big church, but the street's usually lined with folk when there's a wedding going off. Anybody's wedding – it doesn't matter whose. They just like to have a nosy.'

'Mm,' Ruth mused. 'Funny that. Mind you, most of them were in church. Maybe they've seen all they wanted to.'

Harry was rushing on ahead as fast as his bent old legs would carry him and wheezing a little as he pushed the bath chair in front of him. Arriving at the main entrance of the pub, he parked the chair outside and helped Mary Jackson to stand up and walk inside. But instead of disappearing, he threw open the double doors and stood just inside, beaming at the bride and groom walking towards him.

As they approached, Bill Moore, dressed smartly in a black suit, white shirt and black bow tie, came to stand beside Harry to usher the wedding party inside.

As Fleur and Robbie stepped into the dark interior of the public bar, a huge cheer threatened to shake the rafters. It seemed as if the whole village was crammed into the room.

Fleur gasped and gazed around, stunned by the applause that greeted them and the cries of 'Congratulations' and 'Good Luck' on every side.

'So that's where they all disappeared to.' Kenny laughed.

'Come through, come through,' Harry said, leading the way into a large room just beyond the bar. He stood to one side and waved his arm to show them a table at the far end, laden with food. In the centre stood a magnificent wedding cake, complete with bride and groom figurines on the top.

'Everyone in the village has contributed. The women have been baking all week and...'

'Oh, Harry!' Now the tears flooded down Fleur's face. The kindness of all the villagers, some of whom she hardly knew, was overwhelming. Even Robbie had tears in his eyes. He held out his hand and shook Harry's hard. 'Thank you,

Harry. This is wonderful. I really don't know how to thank everyone.'

'It's us who wanted to say "thank you", lad. To you and your lass here. To all of you really...' He nodded his head to include the best man in his RAF uniform and Ruth in her bridesmaid's dress. 'That's fighting this war for us. It's our way of showing our gratitude. But 'specially to you two and Ruth for all you've done for me an' Mary. You're ... you're like family to us. No disrespect to your own families, like.'

'None taken,' Jake, standing just behind Fleur, murmured. He was touched by the villagers' obvious fondness for his daughter and for Meg's boy, as he still called Robbie in his own mind. He only wished Betsy was here to see all this and hear what was being said. Perhaps it would melt even her hard heart.

But he doubted it.

Robbie was nodding his thanks, but unable to speak for the lump in his throat and Fleur was still trying to stem her tears. But they were tears of happiness.

Just for a few short hours they could all forget the war and its tragedies and celebrate a happy occasion. A very happy occasion.

Of course the moment had to come. The moment when Jake and Meg came face to face for the first time in twenty-two years.

As the guests milled around, helping themselves to the food, chattering and laughing, Meg made her way through the throng to stand behind him.

'Hello, Jake. How are you?'

He heard her voice and, slowly, he turned to face her. The breath caught in his throat. She was even more beautiful than he remembered. He didn't see the tiny lines around her eyes; to him the years fell away and there before him was his flame-haired Meg with her heartbreaking smile.

He cleared his throat but his voice was still a little husky as he answered, 'Fine, Meg. And you? You ... you look – wonderful.' He couldn't stop the compliment escaping his lips, even though he felt disloyal to the absent Betsy the moment the words were said. But Meg was smiling up at him, her green eyes gently teasing him. 'So do you.'

Jake pulled a face. 'I don't know about that. I've a lot more wrinkles and grey hairs.'

Meg's gaze never left his face. 'No,' she said softly. 'You haven't changed. You're still my – still Jake.'

There was an awkward pause before she went on, making her tone deliberately light. 'Who'd've thought it, eh? Your girl and my boy. Must be fate taking a hand, Jake.'

Jake sighed. 'That's one way of putting it, I suppose. But is it a kind fate or a cruel one?'

Meg glanced across at Robbie and Fleur, who were touring the room, making sure they spoke to each and every person there to give their thanks.

'He's not like me, Jake. Just in case you're worried. He's got none of my badness. He loves Fleur dearly. He won't hurt her like I...' Her voice trailed away and Jake saw the tears shimmer in her eyes.

'Oh, don't cry, Meggie, I couldn't bear it,' he whispered and fished out the spotless white handkerchief from his top pocket. 'Here.' His use of the pet name he'd always had for her all those years ago was almost her undoing. For a moment the tears threatened to spill over.

'Thanks.' Meg dabbed carefully at her eyes. Then she handed him the handkerchief, which he stuffed back into his pocket.

'You weren't bad,' he told her softly. 'Just … just very young and you'd been so hurt by – well – by life. I said some very harsh things to you then, Meggie. I'm sorry.'

'I deserved them, Jake,' she said simply. 'But I want you to know, I've changed. Ever since that day when I nearly lost Robbie, when that dreadful woman tried to snatch him away from me, I've tried to make up for all the terrible things I did. I know I can't change the past, but I've tried to be a better person. Truly, I have.'

'Don't be so hard on yourself, Meggie. We … we all make mistakes. We've all done things we maybe shouldn't have.' She looked at him keenly, but he was avoiding her gaze now. 'Can I ask you something, Meg? Don't answer, if you don't want to.'

She knew a moment's panic, but then remembered. This was Jake she was talking to: Jake, who knew everything there was to know about her. She had no secrets from him. Nor did she want any. If there was one person in the whole wide world whom Meg could trust, it was Jake.

'Is it true that you have your father living with you?'

Meg laughed with relief. 'Yes, but I can see why you're surprised.' She smiled impishly now. 'That's all part of my reformed character, Jake. How could I continue to bear a grudge against him when I did things that were just as bad, if not worse?'

Jake pursed his lips. 'Well, it was because of what *he* did that made you like that. You were only searching for security. For someone to take care of you. You couldn't wait for...' His voice trailed away.

Meg shook her head. 'Don't try to excuse me, Jake. I ... I should have had more faith.' Her voice was almost an inaudible whisper as she added, 'More faith in you.'

'How did he come back into your life?'

'Just turned up at my door one day. He'd been living rough. He was in a terrible state. How could I turn him away?'

'What happened to Alice Smallwood? The girl he ran off with?'

Meg shrugged. 'She'd found a bigger fish. Ran off with someone with money. Pops has never talked about her much, but I gather he tried to follow her, and the feller she'd taken up with got some of his cronies to beat Pops up. Nearly killed him. He'd still got a lot of the bruises by the time he found me.' She paused and then added softly, 'He's spent every day since trying to make it up to me and he's been wonderful for Robbie.' She glanced across fondly at her son. 'That's one thing I'm never going to apologize for, Jake. Having Robbie. Though I could have wished that his father–'

'Don't, Meggie, don't say it.' He reached out and took her hand. 'It shouldn't be spoken of. Not today of all days.'

'No, you're right.' She smiled up at him, her tears dried now. 'Today's a happy day. Let's just enjoy it. Let's just enjoy seeing each other again because I gather' – she looked around the room – 'that this might be the only chance we'll ever get.'

'Yes,' Jake said sadly. 'I'm afraid it probably is, Meggie.'

Thirty-Two

'Fleur,' Robbie whispered close to her ear so that no one else could hear. 'Don't look now, but your dad is holding my mum's hand.'

'Eh?' Startled, Fleur looked round quickly, her gaze seeking out Jake and Meg.

'No, no, don't look. Don't – spoil it. In a minute or two as we move round the room, take a look though. There's something between them. You can see it in their faces. Just look.'

Fleur tried to concentrate on what the woman in front of her was saying. 'My dear, you look lovely,' the little woman who helped her husband run the village bakery gushed. 'It's done us so much good to have such a pretty wedding in the midst of these dark times. Everyone in the village has loved planning this little surprise for you both. Of course, it was Harry's idea, but we've all chipped in. I made the cake. I'm so sorry it's covered with a cardboard decoration instead of real icing.'

'You've all been wonderful. You've made our day even more special. And the cake looks wonderful. You'd never know until you get right near it that it's not real. But the real cake underneath tastes delicious,' Fleur said and, impulsively, she leant forward and kissed the woman's cheek.

'Lots of people gave me fruit for it,' the little woman went on, blushing a little. 'And Mr Clegg gave me the eggs.'

'How very kind everyone has been.'

Then, at last, Fleur was able to move away and take a surreptitious look across the crowded room towards her father and Meg. What she saw made her catch her breath in a gasp of surprise.

Close beside her, Robbie murmured, 'See what I mean?'

'Yes.' Fleur nodded slowly. 'Yes, I do.' Jake and Meg were standing close together looking into each other's faces as if there was no one else in the room. They were oblivious to the chatter and laughter around them, completely lost in their own little world.

Fleur made an involuntary movement towards them, but Robbie touched her arm and said softly, 'Don't spoil it, Fleur. What harm can it do? Just this once. This may be the only time they'll ever have.'

Fleur bit her lip. Even from the other side of the room, she could see the raw emotion on her father's face, could see Robbie's mother's eyes shimmering with tears, and her tremulous smile.

'Yes, but what about my mum? What about her?'

'She was the one who chose not to come today.'

'Yes – and now we can see why, can't we?'

Robbie sighed. 'But if she had come, darling, that' – he nodded towards the couple – 'wouldn't be happening, now would it?'

'I suppose not,' Fleur agreed.

'I don't expect they'll ever meet up again. Let them just have these few moments, eh?'

Fleur nodded, a lump in her throat. She felt torn by divided loyalties: loyalty to her mother and yet now she understood a little more the reason behind the faraway look she had so often seen in her father's eyes.

'Kenny'll put a stop to it, though, if he sees.'

Robbie laughed softly. 'He's got eyes for no one but Ruth, darling. I don't think he'll even notice. Now, come along, I think we can be on our way without it looking too rude to all these kind people.'

They made another circuit of the room, saying goodbye to everyone and repeating their thanks.

Kenny pumped Robbie's hand. 'Look after my big sister, else I'll be after you.'

Robbie laughed. 'I will and thanks, Kenny, for today. I know it hasn't been easy for you.'

Kenny pulled a face. There was no need to pretend he didn't know what Robbie meant. 'It's Dad I feel sorry for. It's not long before I can join up and, believe me, I'm off the moment I can. But Dad'll be left there on his own with her.' He shook his head. 'I really don't know what's got into her. She never used to be like this. But maybe once this is all over, she'll settle down a bit. Come to terms with it, you know.'

'I hope so,' Robbie said, but as he turned away to go towards where Jake and his mother were still standing engrossed in each other, he thought, *but I doubt it.*

Meg and Jake broke apart, almost guiltily, as Robbie and Fleur arrived beside them at the same moment.

'You off now?' Jake said heartily. He held out his hand to Robbie. There had been no official speeches by the father of the bride or the best man. Only Robbie had stood up and thanked everyone present for the marvellous surprise reception. So now was the moment for Jake to say, 'I'm proud to have you as my son-in-law. Take care of each other...' He seemed about to say more, but his voice cracked and he swallowed as if having difficulty in holding back the tears.

Meg broke the moment by kissing Fleur on both cheeks and saying, 'And I already love you, my darling daughter-in-law. And I can't wait for you to make me into a granny.'

The tension was broken by Robbie saying, 'Hey, steady on, Mum.' But he enveloped Meg into his arms, giving her a bear hug. 'Look after Pops and we'll see you as soon as we get back.'

'Where are you going?'

'Now that's a secret. Even Fleur doesn't know. But I'll ring Mr Tomkins when we get there. I promise.'

After a lot more handshaking and hugs, Fleur and Robbie finally made their escape, running hand in hand down the lane, laughing together.

'I thought we'd never get away,' Robbie said.

'I know, but wasn't it a lovely surprise? How sweet of everyone.'

'It was. The perfect send off.'

Back at the cottage, Fleur changed quickly into her best outfit and Robbie loosened his tie and flung his cap into the back of the borrowed sports car as he stowed Fleur's battered suitcase in the boot space. He opened the passenger door for her to climb in and then he vaulted over the door on the driver's side.

'Ready?' He grinned at her and Fleur giggled, deliciously anticipating the week ahead. A whole seven days alone and away from the war.

As they passed the pub, a shower of confetti cascaded over them, thrown by the villagers who lined the lane. With shouts of 'Good Luck' ringing in their ears, they roared out of the village.

It was strangely quiet after the sound of their car had faded away, an anti-climax after all the frivolity. The villagers began to drift away back to their own homes, carefully carrying some of the food that had been left. It was too precious to waste. Jake and Meg stood awkwardly together, knowing the moment of parting had come. As Kenny came bounding towards them, Meg held out her hand.

'Goodbye, Jake. It's been lovely to see you, and Robbie will look after her, I can promise you that.'

Jake nodded. 'I know,' he said huskily. 'And ... and you take care of yourself, Meggie.'

'Ruth's had to rush off. She's on duty later.

So–' Kenny glanced from one to the other. 'Are you ready, Dad?'

'Just coming, just coming, lad,' Jake replied, yet he made no move.

It was Meg who turned to Kenny, held out her hand and said, 'It's been good to meet you, Kenny. Take care.'

'Can we give you a lift anywhere, Mrs Rodwell?' the young man asked.

'That's very kind of you.' Meg smiled. 'But I'll be fine.'

Then, before either of them could stop her, she turned and walked away from them without looking back. Jake stood a moment watching her until Kenny touched his arm and said gently, 'Come on, Dad. Time we were going home.'

'What's this, I'd like to know?'

Betsy thrust Jake's large white handkerchief towards him, shaking it under his nose. Even before he could look at it properly, she shrieked, 'Make-up, that's what it is. A woman's make-up. Whose is it, might I ask? As if I didn't know.'

Jake blinked and stared at the smear of pink on the white cotton. Keeping his face expressionless, he said mildly, 'It's Fleur's. Whose do you think it is?' He stared her straight in the eyes. 'She had a few tears, the lass did. And why do you think that was, eh?'

For a moment, Betsy was disconcerted. 'Over me, you mean?'

'Of course over you, Betsy. Doesn't every girl want her mother with her on her wedding day?'

'How would *I* know?' Betsy said bitterly. 'I

never had a mother. At least, not one I can remember very well.'

'Then all the more reason why you should've swallowed your own resentment and thought of her – for once. But you'll just have to live with it now, Betsy, won't you? That you didn't go to your only daughter's wedding.'

Jake turned on his heel and slammed out of the house, leaving Betsy – for the first time – feeling a twinge of guilt.

Thirty-Three

They drove to the east coast, to Skegness, where they walked along the sea front and viewed with sadness the lovely scene scarred with rolls of barbed wire. Areas of the wide expanse of sandy beach were mined. Even there, the war could not be forgotten entirely.

'There's a lot of RAF chaps about. I wonder why?' Robbie mused. In the bar of the guest-house where they were staying, they found out.

'It's a training centre,' the landlord, Jim Spriggs, explained and winked. 'Good place for square bashing, ain't it? All that drill along Grand Parade and Tower Esplanade. They're even using some of the quieter streets, an' all. It's a sight to see.'

'We saw them this morning,' Robbie said. 'We were trying to get on the pier, but couldn't. I wanted to see it from the ground.' He smiled. 'We often come over this way when we're setting off across the North Sea and Johnny – that's our navigator – uses your pier as a guide. Reckons he knows what course to set then.'

'Aye, I've heard that said afore,' Jim nodded. 'They've built an assault course near the pier and another in an overgrown area at the end of North Parade that the locals have always called "The Jungle". The RAF lads are billeted in the empty hotels on the sea front and their officers' mess is in one of the bigger hotels, the NAAFI in another.' He pulled a face. 'But I reckon a lot of the hotels are closed for the duration – to holidaymakers that is. Oh, we get a few, like yourselves, but not like we used to afore the war. The kiddies can't play on a mined beach, can they? There's even a gun position in the Fairy Dell.' His mouth tightened. The fact seemed to hurt him personally. 'But it's not the RAF being here we mind,' he said, as if fearful he might have given offence to his guests. 'We like having 'em, and, of course, we've got the Royal Navy just up the road. Taken over Billy Butlin's holiday camp. HMS Royal Arthur, they call it. Oh, there's a lot going on in Skeggy, I can tell you, but it's just this bloody war's altered everyone's lives, hasn't it?' He eyed them curiously. 'What about you two...?' Then, guessing correctly, a broad smile spread across his face. 'Ah, honeymooners, eh? A wartime wedding?'

Robbie grinned back at him. 'That's right.'

'Oi, missis,' the man raised his voice. 'We've got a couple of honeymooners here, love.'

His wife appeared from the kitchen, drying her hands on a towel. 'Oh, how lovely. I'll cook you something special tonight, my dears...' And with a smile and a nod, his 'missis' disappeared back into her kitchen.

'Now, mebbe I shouldn't be telling you this,' Jim said with a teasing smile, 'seeing as you're honeymooners, but there is a very good show on this week at the local theatre.' He reached under the bar and pulled out the local paper. Opening it up, he jabbed his finger. 'Aye, here it is. "All Clear" they call it. Some clever acts, so I've been told. And then there's two very good cinemas in the town.' He sniffed with annoyance. 'Used to have three we did until the Luftwaffe decided to bomb one of 'em last January. The Central and then there's the Parade on the sea front.'

'We saw it this morning. It was advertising a Henry Fonda film, I think.'

'That's right. *Chad Hanna*. It's got Dorothy Lamour in, an' all. I like her. Bit of all right, she is.' He glanced archly at Robbie. 'Mind you, you'll not be noticing, will ya, lad?'

'Of course not,' Robbie said gallantly.

Fleur grinned saucily and said, 'Well, I don't mind you looking, as long as you don't touch.' To which remark the two men laughed heartily.

'Then there's *Pygmalion* on at the Central with Leslie Howard and Wendy Hiller...' Jim went on.

'I've seen that,' Fleur said.

'So' – Robbie grinned – 'Dorothy Lamour it is, then.'

The variety show they saw at the Arcadia Theatre later in the week was slick and professional, with a silent comedy routine, a witty comedian, and a clever dancing act. To top it all, the female singer, Elsie, each night picked a serviceman from the audience to assist her in her song 'Arm in Arm Together'.

Robbie, sitting three rows back, in his smart RAF uniform, the silver buttons sparkling in the lights, was a sitting duck. He cast a rueful grin at Fleur, who dissolved into helpless laughter to see him taken up on stage to be greeted by rapturous applause from the audience. At the end of the song, Elsie brought him back to his seat and planted a kiss on his cheek, leaving a perfect impression of her mouth in lipstick.

'I thought I told you you couldn't touch,' Fleur spluttered and Robbie spread his hands in mock helplessness.

They had a blissful week before they had to return and be plunged once more into the middle of the war.

'I've missed you so much.' Ruth hugged her the moment she walked through the door. 'The girl they brought in to work in the watch office whilst you've been away is thick as pig whatsit. Kay's never stopped grumbling about her and can't wait for you to get back.' She pulled a comical face. 'Eh, hark at me getting all countrified. And you'll never guess what?'

Laughing, Fleur shook her head. 'Go on, tell me.'

'Harry's even had me gardening out there.' She nodded towards the back garden. 'Said I'd got to keep it in shape for you and that stuff needed gathering and it'd go to waste otherwise and then all your hard work'd be wasted.' She held out her hands, palms upward, fingers spread. 'Just *look* at my hands.'

'I just hope you've not pulled out all the plants and left the weeds.'

'Oh no. Harry was there, leaning over the fence, telling me what was what. Actually,' she added, self-consciously, as if she was quite surprised at herself, 'I've quite enjoyed it.' For a moment her eyes were haunted. 'It ... it gets your mind off this bloody war for an hour or two.'

'Has ... has it been bad?'

Ruth bit her lower lip as she nodded. 'Mm. We've lost eight planes during the last week.'

Fleur gasped. 'And the crews?'

Ruth lifted her shoulders in a helpless shrug.

And suddenly, the war with all its catastrophes was back with a vengeance.

Ruth linked her arm through Fleur's. 'Now, come and see what else I've been up to – with Mrs Jackson's permission of course.'

Fleur stared at her. 'What ... what do you mean?'

'Come upstairs. I'll show you.'

Mystified, Fleur followed her up the narrow stairs.

Instead of turning to the small back bedroom where Fleur normally slept, Ruth flung open the door of the large front room that had once been Mrs Jackson's and her husband's but was now Ruth's room.

'This is your room from now on. Yours and Robbie's, when he can get away from camp.'

'But ... but it's your room.'

'Not any more, it isn't. I've moved into your room at the back. I' – she let out a wistful little sigh – 'have no need of a double bed.'

'But you might. You might meet someone and–'

Now Ruth pursed her mouth and shook her head vehemently. 'No, I've told you. I made the mistake once of getting fond of someone and he got killed. I'm not putting myself through that pain again.' She glanced ruefully at Fleur. 'Sorry, love, I don't mean to put a damper on things for you. It's ... it's just how I feel for myself, that's all. Maybe it's me that's being stupid.'

'No,' Fleur said gently and touched her friend's arm. 'I can only guess how you must have felt, but I do know that if anything happened to Robbie, I wouldn't want to take up with anyone else. So, if you'd really fallen for this chap, then ... then ... I do understand.'

'Oh, it was only early days with Billy. Nothing serious. We weren't engaged or anything. Hadn't even got as far as discussing marriage before he – before he...'

'But you had the feeling that that's where it might have led?'

Again Ruth bit her lip as tears filled her eyes and she nodded. But then she wiped her eyes and smiled. 'Come on in and see what I've done.'

They stepped into the bedroom and Fleur gazed around her. 'I don't remember it being like this.'

'It wasn't.' Ruth laughed now. 'I've painted it. Or rather, Kenny did.'

Fleur's eyes widened as she stared at Ruth. 'Kenny? Kenny's been here?'

'Oh yes. Cycled over three times, bless him.

296

He's been great. He did all the painting and your mother-in-law has made the curtains and bed-spread. Aren't they pretty?' She grinned widely. 'It's the best we could do in the time to create a bridal suite for you both.'

'Oh, Ruth, it's wonderful.' Slowly Fleur turned and took in every detail. Then she glanced at Ruth again. 'Did Kenny say – how things are at home?'

'Not as bad as they'd expected. It's a bit frosty, but at least she's speaking to them both.'

'And ... and me?'

'He's not said. Sorry.'

Fleur sighed and turned her thoughts away from her mother and back to the present. 'I don't know how to thank you for all this. I don't know how you've managed it and keeping up with the garden an' all.'

'Think nothing of it. It's been fun doing it. We've had a lot of laughs, me an' your little brother.'

'I think a great deal of it, Ruth,' Fleur told her. 'And I can't wait to tell Robbie.'

For a few idyllic weeks, the front bedroom in Mary Jackson's tiny cottage became their little hideaway from the war even though it was still going on so close to them. But then Ruth came home with news that threatened their love nest.

'The WAAF quarters are finished. We've to move onto camp.'

Fleur stared at her in horror. 'Oh no! Really?'

Ruth nodded.

'What about–?' she began but, not wanting to sound selfish, went on, 'What about Mrs Jackson's garden and old Harry? He'll never manage to keep his house straight without you, Ruth.'

Ruth bit her lip. 'We'll just have to come whenever we can. We'll go and talk to ma'am. She's a good sort. I'm sure she'll let us come down here on our time off duty. Especially if we tell her about your garden. After all, that's part of the war effort, isn't it? As long as we don't take advantage of it.'

'Could we get hold of a couple of bikes, d'you think? It'd only be a few minutes on a bike.'

'We could try, but bicycles are in short supply just now. Everybody's riding them to get about camp.'

'I've got one at home. Maybe I could get it here somehow.'

'Perhaps Kenny would ride it over and hitch back.'

Fleur laughed. 'I'm sure he would – if *you* asked him.'

'Mission accomplished, then.' Her face sobered. 'But what about you and Robbie? It'll put paid to...'

She pointed upwards to the floor above and the bedroom that they had made their own.

Fleur nodded but could not speak.

But Mary Jackson, it seemed, had other ideas. 'You can come here whenever you can. As long as you look after the rooms – wash the sheets, an' that.'

'But won't you want the rooms for other lodgers. Evacuees maybe?'

Mary Jackson laughed softly and shook her head sadly. 'I'd've liked nothing better, my dears, than to have a couple of youngsters here, but I couldn't look after them, now could I?'

'They might want the accommodation for a mother with a baby or a young child,' Fleur said, still unable to believe that nothing stood in the way. 'They send the mothers too sometimes. They did at the beginning of the war.'

'They might,' Mary agreed. 'But I think it unlikely now. The evacuation seems to have slowed down. In fact, a lot of children are going back to the cities.'

'That's true,' Ruth said. 'Though I think the parents are daft. Old Hitler might choose any big city to have a go at. Look what he did to Coventry. Why Coventry, for heaven's sake?' She paused and then clapped her hands. 'That's settled then. As long as we can get permission, we'll come here every spare minute. Stay the night whenever we can. Fleur and Robbie can do your garden and I can still help old Harry.' She beamed. It all seemed so easy. 'Now all we've got to do is persuade ma'am.'

Squadron Officer Caroline Davidson was, as Ruth had put it, 'a good sort'. When the two girls asked to see her, she welcomed them into her office and heard what they had to say without interruption. She was thoughtful for a few moments whilst Fleur and Ruth waited anxiously. Then she smiled. 'I don't see why not. Just so long as you're very careful never to be late back on duty, otherwise it would have to stop immediately.'

Both girls nodded at once. 'Yes, ma'am. We'll make sure of that.'

As they saluted smartly and turned to leave, she added, 'And I'll have a word with Flight Sergeant Rodwell's commanding officer. Just to make sure he's aware of the situation. How very valuable Robbie's help is for the old lady's garden on his time off. We're very anxious to help in the local community whenever we can, you know.'

Fleur turned back to stare at her and was rewarded with a broad wink.

'Thank you, ma'am,' Fleur breathed.

Thirty-Four

The last weeks of September passed in a haze of busy hours on duty and, in a way, even busier off-duty time. Kenny brought Fleur's bicycle over and the following week he came again, pedalling one that Jake had unearthed from the barn for Ruth.

'It's a bit of a bone-shaker,' Kenny said, 'but I've cleaned it and oiled it.'

'As long as it gets me from A to B, I don't mind. Thanks, Kenny. I'll give you a kiss at Christmas.'

Though a flush crept up the young man's face, he was at ease enough with Ruth now to say, 'I'll keep you to that! And now, are you going to help me pick those apples down the bottom of the garden? That poor tree is so laden down, you can hardly see the bench underneath it.'

Ruth chuckled. 'Fleur often sits there for a bit of a rest. Her and Robbie.' For a moment, Ruth's eyes misted over. So often, just lately she had seen them sitting there under the apple tree, talking or just holding hands and watching yet another glorious Lincolnshire sunset. It always brought a lump to her throat. Half of her envied her friend, but deep in her heart she feared for her too.

But now she smiled brightly at Kenny as she added, 'But I haven't seen them sitting there lately. I reckon they're afraid of getting clouted on the head with falling apples.'

'Well, we can soon put that right. The fruit are well ready for picking – I had a look at them last week. It's a shame to let them fall off and get bruised; they don't store so well then. And then they can have their love seat back. Where are they, by the way?'

'Having dinner in the NAAFI. They'll be here in a bit.'

Kenny had only just reared the ladder up amongst the branches, when Fleur and Robbie rounded the corner of the cottage.

'Need any help?'

'Hi, Sis. Well, I suppose if you can find another ladder, we'd be done in half the time. I could do this side of the tree and Robbie the other.'

'Harry's got one in his shed.'

'I'll fetch it.'

Robbie was back in a few minutes with Harry following in his wake.

'Now mind how you handle them apples. They bruise easy.' The old man stood looking up into the tree and stroking his moustache. 'Fine crop you've got there. How're you going to store them?'

'Lay them out on newspaper under the beds,'

Fleur said.

'Aye, mind they're not touching an' you'll be all right. Just unmarked ones, mind. Any fallers, Mary can use straight away or dry them.'

'I'm going to help her bottle some this year,' Fleur put in. 'She can sit down to peel them and I can do everything else.'

'Mum's busy doing it at the moment. I picked all ours earlier in the week.'

For a moment, Fleur felt a pang of longing to visit her home again. To see her dad and – yes – her mother too.

'Harry – Harry!' Mrs Jackson was calling him from the back door. 'Come away in and leave them youngsters to it. They know what they're doing...'

With a comical smile, Harry shambled back up the pathway and disappeared into the house.

'They'll be sat either side of the wireless now,' Ruth smiled. 'Listening to–'

'The news!' the other three chorused and they all laughed.

'It'll be *Workers' Playtime* in a bit.'

'Well, we've no time to be playing. Let's get cracking...'

With the beginning of October, summer was over.

'By heck, it's nippy this morning,' Ruth shivered as they hurried towards the NAAFI. 'We ought to see if we can get Mrs Jackson any more coal. This weather won't do her arthritis any good.'

'I know. Have you seen her poor knuckles? They're so swollen. I didn't want her to peel all those apples when we were bottling last week, but she insisted.'

'Mind you she's that proud of her shelf of bottled fruit, I think it was worth it for her. Made her feel useful again.'

'Oh, she's doing her bit, all right. She's still knitting for the troops and it must be painful for her hands.'

As they walked into the dining room for breakfast, the air was thick with chatter, more animated than usual.

'Hello,' Ruth remarked, glancing round. 'Summat's up. Let's find Kay. She'll know. I reckon she sleeps with the wireless on all night so she doesn't miss the news.'

They took their places at one of the new tables that had recently been delivered – a table for four that they shared with Kay and Peggy. They were already there, eating breakfast, but talking rapidly too.

'What's up, Corp?' Ruth demanded, sitting down opposite with her loaded plate and reaching for the sauce.

'He's advancing on Moscow. That'll be the end of him. Fancy trying now! In October! Doesn't he know what the Russian winter is like?' Kay was excited by the thought. 'If Napoleon couldn't do it, I doubt Adolf can.'

'Well, if he's got other things on his mind, maybe he'll leave us alone for a bit.'

It did seem a little quieter at Wickerton Wood, but whether that was because the Germans were busy elsewhere or because of the atrocious winter weather that lay over the whole country, no one

303

could be certain. But everyone was thankful for a little respite, whatever the reason. Life settled into something of a routine, with off-duty times for Ruth, Fleur and Robbie spent at Mrs Jackson's little cottage. Kenny still cycled over at weekends whenever he could, but now Jake never came and Fleur missed her father more than she ever admitted to anyone.

The weather worsened, the temperature dropped and a cold winter was forecast.

November fog caused disruption to flying. No one minded too much if raids were cancelled, but the worst situation was if, after take-off, a swirling mist shrouded the airfield by the time the aircraft were due back.

'I hate it when they're all diverted,' Fleur muttered quietly to Kay on one such night as they waited in the watch office, the runway only a few yards in front of them completely blotted out. 'I like to know that D-Doggo is back – that they're all back safely,' she added hurriedly, in case she'd sounded selfish.

For once, Kay did not respond with a tart retort. Instead, she sighed. 'I know just what you mean. It's daft, but I feel just the same.'

'Do you?' Fleur couldn't stop the surprised question escaping her lips.

Kay smiled wryly as she glanced behind her to make sure that Bob Watson was out of earshot. 'Oh, I know I sound as if I don't give a damn most of the time, but inside – I do care.' Her voice was suddenly husky. 'I care very much. A lot of my ... my attitude is just an act, Fleur.

Bravado, if you like...' Her voice trailed away and then, suddenly, she was brisk and efficient and razor sharp as ever, 'But if you ever tell a soul I've said this, I shall deny it hotly. OK?'

'Naturally, Corp,' Fleur said and, though she gave a playful salute, her tone was sincere. The two girls, bound by their concern for the safety of the same aircraft, exchanged a look of complete understanding.

'Now, we'd better get ready for telling these boys that they can't come home tonight...'

Later, as they clattered down the steps from Control, they were met by the eerily silent fog-bound station. They stood a moment, listening, but there was absolutely nothing to hear. Fleur shuddered. 'Come on, let's get to bed. I hate it like this. It's ... it's ghostly.'

'Mm,' Kay, in a strangely pensive mood, pondered. 'Makes you think, doesn't it? I wonder if the ghosts of all the boys we've lost come back here? To their station?'

'Oh, don't! I don't even want to think about it. Come on, Kay, let's see if we can find the WAAF quarters in this lot. I tend to lose my sense of direction in fog.'

After taking a couple of wrong turns and ending up near the main guardhouse, they found their quarters and fell into bed. Fleur was exhausted, but sleep eluded her for over an hour. She knew D-Doggo had landed safely at another airfield, but it wasn't the same as knowing he was sleeping only a few hundred yards away in the airmen's quarters. If only they'd hurry up and get the married quarters built, it'd be even better.

The squadron had been forced to go on to land at an airfield in Yorkshire, many of them dangerously low on fuel. Only one didn't make it and had to crash land in a field. Luckily, the crew only suffered cuts and bruises and came back to Wickerton Wood the following day indignantly travelling in the back of a RAF lorry. The rest of the aircraft flew in throughout the morning. Other than the unwelcome diversion, it had been a successful mission and all the crews were safe.

'Talk about brass-monkey weather,' Fleur shivered as she joined the other three at breakfast. 'D'you know there were icicles on the *inside* of the window this morning? I wish I was back at Mrs Jackson's in her nice feather bed.'

'It'll be even colder in Russia. It's the first of December tomorrow,' Kay remarked, wagging her fork towards Fleur. 'If Hitler doesn't take Moscow in the next few days, his troops'll never survive the winter.' Her interest in the news never waned. 'And I'll tell you something else I've heard on the grapevine. All single women between the ages of twenty and thirty are to be called up. So – we'd all have been in the services soon even if we hadn't volunteered.'

For a moment Fleur felt a rush of relief. Her voluntary entry into the WAAFs had been vindicated, but at Kay's next words she felt a shudder of apprehension.

'And they're lowering the call-up age for men to eighteen and a half and raising it to men aged fifty.'

So in roughly a year's time, Kenny – he would

be eighteen next March – would have to go anyway. And what about her dad? He was still under fifty – just. Would he be called up? She had a sudden picture of her mother sitting at the table filling out numerous forms to stop her menfolk being sent to war.

Then Fleur remembered. Her dad still limped from an injury in the last war. He wouldn't be classed as fit enough now.

But Kenny would. Oh yes, Kenny would be A1 fit.

'We don't need a bloody wireless when you're around, Corp,' Ruth was saying, dragging Fleur's thoughts back to the conversation around the table. 'But could you give us a little light entertainment too, d'you think? Can you imitate Tommy Handley or sing like Vera Lynn?'

Kay enjoyed the banter. Both Fleur and Ruth gave her back as good as she gave out, but Kay never 'pulled rank' though, as a corporal, she could have done. Only Peggy was the quiet one of the four and just listened to the sharp exchanges with a placid smile.

But a few days later everyone was appalled by the news that was going round.

'Oh, they've done it now.' Kay was jubilant. 'That's America in the war for certain now.'

'But it's Japan that's attacked them. They'll concentrate on them, won't they?'

'It's a world war now. They'll just fight every-body.' Kay grinned as she added, ''Cept us. Good to have a mighty friend on our side, isn't it?'

Fleur shook her head. 'But why? Why have Japan attacked Pearl Harbor? They must know they'd reap the whirlwind.'

'Don't ask me. I'm just glad we're on the right side of the whirlwind.'

A few days later, the news guru said, 'I told you so. I told you didn't I?'

'You tell us a lot of things, Corp,' Ruth remarked dryly. 'To which particular piece of your undoubted wisdom are you referring?'

'Oh well, if you don't want to know, then...' Kay retorted but then she caught Ruth's wink. 'Oh, you...!'

'Tell us, then,' Fleur said.

The three of them were sitting at their usual table in the dining room for dinner. Peggy was away on leave.

'The Russians are chasing Adolf out. They've recaptured some of the places that the Germans had taken and now Adolf's boys are on the run. I told you the Russian winter would defeat him – his troops can't withstand the cold. Can't get supplies through either, I shouldn't wonder. But the Russians know how to cope, don't they? They're used to it.'

'Do you think he'll try again? Next spring?' Fleur, too, was caught up with the staggering news of the last few days.

Kay shrugged. 'Not if he's any sense.'

'But he hasn't, has he?' Ruth put in, her mouth full of stew and dumplings.

'What?'

'Any sense.'

They were silent, each concentrating on their meal, until Ruth asked, 'So? What are we all doing for Christmas, then?'

'Oh, crumbs, I haven't got as far as that yet,' Fleur said.

'You still haven't come down off cloud nine since your wedding,' Kay teased, and gave an exaggerated sigh. 'Ordinary life has to go on for the rest of us. Like planning Christmas.'

'Have we got leave?'

Ruth pulled a face. 'Shouldn't think so for a minute. I think – though I don't know – that leave will be granted to those whose homes are a long way off. After all – to be fair – we do get home a lot because our families live relatively near. I mean, we can get home and back on just a twenty-four, can't we?'

Fleur nodded. 'I see what you mean.' She was silent for a moment. 'I wonder if they'd let us do something on camp to celebrate? Those of us who don't go home?'

'Oh, I'm sure there'll be a dance in the sergeants' mess and–'

'No, I meant something a bit more than that.' She leant forward across the table towards the other two. 'I tell you what I'd really like to do.'

'What?'

'Throw a Christmas party for all the evacuee kids in the village – and the village kids an' all, of course.'

Ruth stared at her for a moment and then her face lit up. 'Fleur – that's a brilliant idea. Who do we have to ask?'

'Er – well, we could start with ma'am...'

Fleur's idea was taken up enthusiastically by everyone on camp and the date was fixed for the afternoon of Christmas Eve. A few days beforehand, willing hands – even those who would not be there on the day because they'd be on leave – helped to decorate the sergeants' mess.

'There's a bloke at the main gate asking for Fleur,' Johnny called from the doorway.

'Oho, Robbie,' Tommy shouted from the top of the ladder, where he was hanging paper chains across the ceiling. 'Got a rival already, old boy. Have to watch her.'

Johnny, grinning in the doorway, said, 'Well, he's a nice-looking bloke, I'll give you that, but he is old enough to be her father...'

Fleur gasped and her eyes widened. 'Dad? Here? Oh – I wonder what's wrong?' Before Johnny could say any more, Fleur had gone out of the mess and was running along the road towards the main gate, her hair flying loose, her jacket undone. She was lucky she didn't encounter any WAAF officers in her headlong flight, or she might have been on a charge and missed the children's party for which she'd worked so hard.

Jake was standing talking amiably to the guard commander as Fleur dashed up.

'What's wrong, Dad?'

'Oh, sorry, love, I didn't mean to worry you. Nothing's wrong. I've just brought you a Christmas tree. Kenny said you're throwing a party for all the kids in the village and I thought–'

'Oh, Dad, that's wonderful. We've only got a pathetic-looking thing made out of wire and green paper.' She turned to the guard commander. 'May he drive round to the sergeants' mess?'

Permission granted, Jake was greeted at the mess with open arms, quite literally, for Ruth ran towards him as he struggled through the door with the Christmas tree. 'Mr Bosley, you darling! We've got all these lovely tree decorations from Mrs Jackson, Harry and Bill Moore at the pub and no tree to put them on. Oh, that's perfect.' She clapped her hands. 'Now, where shall we put it?'

Already, Robbie, Tommy and Johnny were moving forward to help. 'How about over here in the corner? And then we can put all the presents for the kids under the tree.'

'Presents? My word, you have been busy,' Jake said.

'We've collected round the camp and we've managed to buy one present for each child.'

'And the CO has promised to dress up as Father Christmas.'

'Fleur,' Jake said softly, 'I tried to get your mam to make some extra puddings and a cake, but...'

'Don't worry, Dad,' she said, slipping her arm through his and hugging it to her side. 'This is absolutely great – you couldn't have brought anything better. And ... and it's lovely to see you. I ... I've missed you.'

His dark brown eyes regarded her soulfully. 'Why don't you come home any more? Surely you must have had a couple of days' leave some time since your wedding?'

Fleur ran her tongue round her lips. 'I ... I wanted to. At least, if I'm honest, *part* of me wanted to. The other part – well – I didn't want to make matters worse than they already are.'

Jake sighed heavily. 'Well, they're not going to get any better unless you do come home from time to time and try to heal the breach.'

311

'All right, Dad. I will come. I promise.'

His face was bleak for a moment. 'Kenny's going in March, don't forget. He'll be eighteen then and he still seems determined to go even before he really has to.'

'I know,' Fleur whispered. She was hardly likely to forget that. It blighted her waking hours and some of her sleeping ones too.

'Have you heard?' Robbie's face was ecstatic.

'Tommy's just told the crew.'

'Father Christmas has landed on the runway?' Ruth volunteered.

'Better than that!'

'The war's over?'

'It soon will be now. We're getting the new Lancasters and they're arriving on Christmas Eve.'

All eyes turned to look at Robbie and then the excited questions began. 'How many?' 'Will we get a chance to train on them?' 'How many crew do they need?' 'What bombs can they carry?'

'Whoa, whoa there!' Laughing, Robbie held out his hands, palms outwards, fending off the volley of questions. 'We'll find out soon enough.'

The arrival of the new aircraft was amazing. Every vantage point was lined with station personnel and Fleur and Kay, on duty in the watch office, held their breaths as the first of the magnificent planes approached the airfield and landed smoothly.

'My word, what a beauty!' Kay said, her mouth open in wonder as she stared at the lines of the aircraft, strangely elegant in such a powerful machine.

'What a Christmas present!' Fleur laughed as another approached the airfield and she heard the wireless burst into life. 'Hello, Woody, this is J-Janie calling...'

And in they all came, one after another until they were all safely landed.

'And now we're going to party,' Kay said as they clattered down the steps from the watch office and headed towards the sergeants' mess.

The party was a great success, even though one or two children over-indulged at the sight of so much food and promptly threw up. 'Father Christmas' played his part and earned a new respect from those under his command.

'D'you know,' Johnny said later, 'I always thought the CO was a miserable old devil, but he was really good with those kids. Did you see? And he was great on Christmas Day too, wasn't he?'

The station had followed the usual tradition of all the officers serving the lower ranks with their Christmas dinner. They had entered into the spirit of the occasion with great aplomb and accepted the ribbing with equanimity.

'No, he's a good bloke,' Robbie said. 'But, y'know, I think I'd be a miserable old devil in his position. I don't envy his responsibilities one bit. Sending crews off night after night, not knowing how many are going to come back. And just think of the dreadful letters he has to write when they don't.' Robbie gave a shudder. 'God – it must be a nightmare.'

Johnny's usual cheerful face sobered suddenly.

313

'Yeah, you're right, mate. I hadn't looked at it like that.' Then, his face crinkling once more into its usual grin, he punched Robbie's shoulder. 'Come on, let's go and play with our new Lanc.'

There would be no operations for a while from Wickerton Wood.

'We've to go on a course at a heavy conversion unit,' Robbie told Fleur. 'It'll be for about six weeks.'

'Six weeks! D'you mean I won't see you for six weeks?' She was staring at him in horror, but Robbie was grinning.

'It's only near Newark.'

Fleur let out a sigh of relief. 'That's all right then. You think you'll get leave now and then?'

Robbie shook his head. 'Probably not, but you should. There'll not be much going on here until we come back, I shouldn't think.'

Fleur pulled a face. 'I wouldn't bank on it. They'll find something for us to do, I've no doubt.'

The six weeks passed surprisingly quickly whilst the newly formed crews of seven instead of four underwent their training on the new aircraft: take-offs, circuits, landings and even flying across country at different heights to familiarize them-selves with how the aircraft, heavier than they had been used to with its four mighty Merlin engines, performed. Whenever they met up, Robbie talked of nothing else.

When they all returned to Wickerton Wood, Robbie was enthusiastic about his new instru-ments.

'It's all right for you, you jammy devil,' Alan, the rear gunner, complained. 'You've got the hottest seat in the house.'

Robbie laughed, but Fleur was anxious. 'What's he mean?'

'He means it's the warmest place in the aircraft.'

'Oh, I ... I thought he meant it was the most dangerous.'

'No. Actually, it's probably one of the safest places to be. I'm right behind the skipper and the back of his seat is armour-plated.'

'Really?'

'Yes, really.' He kissed her on the end of her nose. 'So stop worrying. It's a great aircraft.'

'It's the best Christmas present ever. Now we can get at 'em,' was the opinion of everyone.

Thirty-Five

'You know, you really ought to go home, Fleur. For a visit. Try to make it up with your mother,' Robbie murmured as they lay in each other's arms in the pale light of dawn after a blissful night of love. He kissed her hair. 'I don't like being the cause of a rift between you.'

It was February already and neither of them had been able to get home over Christmas or at New Year or since. Robbie because of the training course and Fleur because heavy falls of snow had given her the perfect excuse to stay at Wickerton. It was surprising that the crews had managed to complete enough flying hours on the course, but somehow they had.

Despite her father's plea, Fleur was still putting off the moment. 'I suppose you're right.' She sighed. 'But I don't want to miss any time with you.'

'Well, we're not always off duty at the same time,' Robbie pointed out reasonably.

'Mostly we are. Because ... because when you're flying, I'm usually in the watch office.' There was a pause before Fleur suggested, 'We could go together.'

'No, I don't think that's a good idea. Rather fuelling the flame, don't you think?'

'I suppose so.'

'Tell you what, next time we get a decent leave I'll go and see Ma and Pops and you go to Middleditch Farm.'

'All right.' Fleur sighed again, knowing he was right, but feeling she would much rather visit the tiny terraced house in Nottingham with him. She would receive a warmer welcome from Robbie's mother than she ever would from her own.

'Good,' he said as he began kissing her. 'And now, Mrs Rodwell, before we have to get up and face the day...'

'Hello, Dad,' Fleur said softly, leaning on the top of the bottom half of the cowshed door. 'I thought I'd find you here.'

Jake straightened up from the milking stool. 'Fleur, love.' His smile was warm and loving. He picked up the bucket of milk and came towards her. 'Good to see you.' He looked into her eyes. 'I don't need to ask if everything's all right. I can see it is.'

'Oh, Dad, if only it wasn't for this wretched war, then life would be perfect.'

'Aye,' Jake's face clouded. 'Aye, it would.'

'But then, if it hadn't been for the war, I might not have met Robbie.'

'True, true,' Jake murmured absently.

Fleur glanced behind him into the shadows of the cowshed. 'Where's Kenny? Isn't he here? Helping you with the milking?'

Jake shook his head. Fleur searched his face. 'What is it, Dad? What's wrong?'

'He's gone. Kenny's gone.'

'Gone? Gone where?'

'Into the RAF. Seems he volunteered a while back and he got his papers the day before yesterday and off he went.'

'But ... but ... he's not old enough. He's not even eighteen yet.'

Jake shrugged. 'He is next month. Seems it doesn't matter. He's in and that's all he cares about.'

There was a pause before Fleur said, 'He'd've been better in the army. Maybe they wouldn't send him abroad straight away, but the RAF. I mean once he's done his training he – they...'

'I thought it was the army he wanted too. It was – at first. But it seems ... it seems as if he was influenced by – by...' His voice fell away as if he couldn't bring himself to say any more.

'By Robbie, you mean,' Fleur whispered.

Her father nodded. They stood awkwardly for a moment, neither knowing what to say. At last Jake said haltingly, 'You'd best go in. See yer mother.'

'No, no, I'll help you finish here.'

'You'll get yerself mucky,' he said, glancing at her uniform.

She pulled in a deep breath. 'Then I'll go in and find some old clothes. Unless, of course, Mum's thrown them all out.'

'No, no.' Jake sighed. 'Your room's just as you left it.'

'I won't be a mo, then.'

'Fleur–' Jake began but she was gone, running across the yard towards the back door. As she stepped into the scullery, her mother looked up from the sink.

'Oh, it's you. Well, I hope you're satisfied. He's gone. Joined the wonderful RAF.'

'Mum – I'm sorry. But it's not all my fault. He was determined to join up somehow.'

'It's your fault he's joined the RAF, though. Yours and – and *his*.'

Stung to retort, Fleur snapped. 'His name's Robbie.'

'Oh yes, I know what his name is all right. And his bloody mother's. Oh, I know *her* name all right. As if I could ever forget it. I wish to God I could.' Betsy slammed down the plate she was washing onto the wooden draining board with such force that it cracked in two. 'Now look what you've made me do. I've broken one of me best plates.'

'Mum,' Fleur said tiredly. 'Won't you tell me what all this is about? Don't you think we have a right to know? What has Robbie done for you to hate him so? You don't even know him.'

Betsy didn't answer but picked up the shattered

pieces and dropped them into a bin at the side of the sink. 'It's not him. It's his mother.'

'Then why take it out on Robbie if it's not his fault?'

Betsy glared at her and avoided answering. Instead, she asked another question. 'Were they together at the wedding?'

Fleur frowned. 'Who? Robbie and his mother?'

Betsy gave a tut of exasperation. 'Your dad and her?'

Fleur blinked. 'Well – yes – they talked.'

Betsy held Fleur's gaze, as if daring her to look away. Fleur stared back boldly but her heart was thumping madly. She didn't want to lie to her mother, but neither did she want to admit that her father and Robbie's mother had stood close together holding hands and gazing into each other's eyes.

'Did they – did they go off together?'

Her heart rate slowed a little. 'Go off together? Of course not.'

'Hm.' Betsy sounded doubtful. She folded her arms in front of her and stepped closer to Fleur. 'Tell me – and I want the truth mind – did your father wipe your face with his handkerchief?'

Fleur gaped. 'Wipe my face? I don't know what you mean.'

'There was a woman's make-up on his handkerchief. He said it was yours. That ... that you'd shed a few tears and he'd mopped your face. Is that true?'

Fleur's gaze didn't flicker, but she felt her heart begin to pound again. Slowly, she nodded. 'Yes, yes, he did. When he first got to the house. He

319

was late and I thought he wasn't coming...' Her voice trailed away and she held her breath. Was her mother going to believe her? It was true she'd cried. It was true that someone had dabbed her face with a hanky. But that someone had been Ruth – not Jake.

After a moment, Betsy nodded. 'Very well then. But they did meet and they did talk?'

Fleur forced a laugh. 'Well, yes, of course they did. They could hardly avoid each other, now could they? But it was only at the pub afterwards and–'

'But you weren't there all the time, were you? You went off on your honeymoon. You don't know what happened after that, do you?'

'Well, no, but Kenny was still there.'

'Oh yes, Kenny. But he was so taken up with this ... this Ruth that he wouldn't see what was going on under his nose.'

'Ruth had to go back to camp straight after we left. Kenny wouldn't have wanted to stay on then.'

'Oh.' Betsy was thoughtful for a moment then she turned away. 'Anyway, what have you come for?'

'I came to see if I could put matters right between you and me, Mum.'

'Well, I'm sorry you've had a wasted journey. While you're married to that lad and seeing his mother, I don't want owt to do with you. And now Kenny's gone...' She left the accusation hanging in the air.

'Then I'm sorry, Mum, very sorry. But I love Robbie and he loves me and if no one will tell us what this ... this feud is all about, then there's nothing either of us can do. And I'm sorry about Kenny too. He would have gone somewhere – the army or somewhere – but yes, I agree, it is my fault he chose the RAF and I'm just going to have to live with that, aren't I?' Then she turned and fled upstairs, rushed into her old room and slammed the door behind her, leaning against it. She closed her eyes and groaned. Now she had two people she loved to worry about. Robbie – and Kenny too.

Ruth's reaction to Fleur's news that Kenny had joined the RAF was predictable.

'Stupid little bugger,' she railed. 'Why on earth didn't he stay out of it? He'd got the chance living on a farm and being in a reserved occupation. All quite above board. Why on earth does he want to play the hero?'

'Mum says it's all my fault. Because I joined up, he doesn't want to be left behind and have everyone thinking him a coward.'

Ruth let out a very unladylike snort. 'No one's going to think that. At least, not anyone with any sense.'

There was a pause before Fleur asked gently, 'Then why did you join the WAAF? You could have done your bit some other way – in a factory or something.'

''Cos I was just as stupid when it all began. Fighting for my country and all that tosh.'

'So you wouldn't mind if Hitler walked in then?' Fleur said with deceptive mildness.

Ruth sighed heavily, her anger dying. 'Yes, of

course I would. Oh, I know we've got to stop him. I know we've got to stop him coming here and we've got to help all these other poor folk he's already trampling over, but ... but – oh, Fleur – you should understand if anyone does – what with Robbie and now Kenny too in danger every day.'

'Oh, I do,' Fleur said grimly, thinking of the sleepless nights she was having even when she wasn't on duty. The only time she felt at peace was when Robbie was lying beside her. But even that was spoilt because now she had Kenny to worry about. She didn't even know where he was or what he was doing. She didn't know which was the worst: knowing – or not knowing.

'I'm sorry.' Ruth put her arms around Fleur. 'It must be awful for you. And with your mum making it worse by blaming you. How's your dad taking it?'

'He's worried. Naturally.'

'But – but does he blame you?'

'I don't know. He hasn't said except to say that Kenny had joined the RAF because of Robbie. He'd never say outright, but ... but maybe deep down...'

Ruth hugged her harder. 'Come on, girl. Chin up. Let's just pray they'll both stay safe, eh?'

Fleur rested her face against Ruth's shoulders and screwed up her eyes, trying to stem the tears.

She'd pray all right. Oh, how she would pray. But it was a lot to ask.

Thirty-Six

Towards the end of March, the RAF began a round-the-clock bombing campaign against the German arms' factories. Night after night the airmen at Wickerton Wood and their new Lancasters were involved, often escorted by Spitfires.

On a rare night off Fleur and Robbie spent the time at Mrs Jackson's cottage. Flying was still going on, so Ruth was on duty.

Robbie lay back on the bed, still in his uniform, his tie loosened, his hair ruffled. He closed his eyes with a weary sigh. 'Oh, Fleur, when is it all going to end and we can find our own little cottage with roses round the door and an apple tree we can sit under to watch the sunsets?'

She sat on the bed beside him, took his hand and kissed each finger. 'I don't know, but we're all doing our best to end it quickly. You especially.'

'But the end's nowhere in sight. At least, it doesn't seem to be. Two and a half years and we don't seem any nearer. In fact, it just seems to have got worse. What with Japan and America in it too now. Oh, darling, I just feel so ... so tired. I...'

Fleur leant forward to kiss him, but then she hesitated. Robbie was asleep. She put the eiderdown over him and then undressed quietly and slipped into the bed beside him. But sleep evaded her.

She was worried. She had never heard Robbie talk like that. With a defeated air. He was always so positive with a 'get up and get at 'em' attitude. But tonight he'd seemed – well – beaten.

He's just so tired, she thought. He'll be all right tomorrow. And tomorrow, she reminded herself, is his very last mission. The four men from the original crew would have completed a full tour of duty and deserved a well-earned break. But one worry ate away at her. With the newly formed crews, would they want to break them up? Would they make Tommy and the other three carry on? She wasn't sure of regulations and Robbie refused to discuss it. It was as if he was superstitious about discussing the elusive thirtieth op. Only very few aircrews survived to even reach it and to mention it seemed like tempting fate...

The following morning, they rose late and ate a leisurely breakfast, which Fleur had gone downstairs in her dressing gown to bring up to their room.

They set the tray aside and Fleur climbed back into the bed.

'Feel better this morning?' she whispered.

'Yes. I'm sorry about last night. I don't know what got into me.'

She stroked his hair. 'You're tired. You're all tired. But only one more mission tonight and then...'

'I know. Maybe that's what's getting to me. What'll happen then, d'you think? D'you think we might get split up? Posted, even?'

'Oh, I hope not!'

Robbie grinned wickedly and took her in his

arms, 'But we'd better make the most of this morning, just in case...'

'Fleur? Fleur, dear, are you there?' It was Mary Jackson calling from the foot of the stairs.

Robbie let out a groan and Fleur stifled her giggles against him, before she was able to lift her head and shout, 'Yes, Mrs Jackson. What is it?'

'Kenny's here, dear.'

'Kenny! How lovely! Oh–' She turned back to Robbie. 'I'm sorry, darling.'

Robbie smiled and kissed her. 'It's all right. Let's go down and see him.'

They dressed quickly and hurried downstairs. Fleur flung her arms round her brother, tall and resplendent in his RAF uniform.

'I've just got a spot of leave,' he said excitedly. 'Basic training'll soon be finished. Then it'll be passing out parade and I'm volunteering for fighter training... So, in the meantime...' He saluted smartly. 'Aircraftman Bosley reporting for duty, ma'am. Digging fatigues, is it?'

Fleur hugged him. 'We'll have a lovely day together, but we're on duty tonight. It's Robbie's last mission for a while.'

Kenny grinned and slapped his brother-in-law on the back. 'And there I was hoping to be escorting you in my Spitfire one of these days.'

'Oh, you'll get the chance. I've no doubt we'll be called on to do another tour before long.'

Fleur felt her heart plummet. Naively, she thought that Robbie's flying days would be over, that he'd be given a nice, safe desk job somewhere. In her wilder moments she'd even imagined him being in charge of the watch office, that they would be working together. But of course that would never happen. He was a trained wireless operator. Of course he would have to fly again...

But for today, she had both of them safely with her. They would make the most of today. 'So,' she said, forcing a bright smile onto her face. 'What are we going to do?'

'Well, I thought I'd help you in the garden a bit this morning – if you want me to, that is – and then this afternoon, I thought we'd go into Lincoln,' Kenny said. 'I'll treat you to a slap-up tea in Boots cafe. How about that?'

'You're on. A celebration tea.' She glanced at Robbie. 'Do you know what day it is?'

Robbie blinked. 'Er – Wednesday?'

Fleur smiled. 'Well, yes it is, but I meant the date. It's exactly a year ago today since we met.'

'Is it really? Fancy me forgetting.'

She reached up and kissed him lightly. 'You're forgiven. You've rather had other things on your mind just lately.'

'I'll make a stew for all of us for dinner and an apple pie,' Mrs Jackson said, struggling to her feet.

'We don't want to put you to any trouble, Mrs Jackson.' Robbie turned to her.

'No trouble, love.' The old lady patted his arm and chuckled. 'It'll make me feel useful.'

'Oh, I almost forgot, Mrs Jackson,' Kenny said. 'Dad's sent you some eggs and butter. I'll get them.'

As he opened the door, Ruth was coming round the corner of the cottage. Kenny's eyes lit up. 'Just the person I'd hoped to see. We're going into Lincoln this afternoon for tea.' He gave an exaggerated bow. 'Would madam care to join us?'

'Hi, Kenny. Fancy seeing you here. Got your wings yet?'

'Not quite, but I start training soon. Can't tell you where, of course.' He tapped the side of his nose. 'Careless talk, and all that, but it's somewhere down south.'

Fleur giggled. 'Oh, I think we're allowed to know where, Kenny. Else how will Mum know where to address all those food parcels she's bound to want to send you?'

He blinked and his young face wore a comical expression. 'Oh yes. I suppose so. I'm just not used to all this sort of secrecy. They dinned it into us so much that we mustn't say this and mustn't say that, that I'm not exactly sure what I can say and what I can't.' He grinned. 'So I thought it best just to say nothing.'

They all laughed, but Fleur said, 'I know what you mean. I felt that way too at first, but you soon find out what it's safe to say. You can tell your family where you're stationed but not the details about missions and so on.'

'But I'm going to train as a fighter pilot. That's a bit different, isn't it? We get scrambled when enemy aircraft are approaching, don't we?'

'I expect so.'

'And I suppose that's why I'm being sent down south. That's where the Battle of Britain went on, isn't it?'

Fleur felt a cold shudder of apprehension run through her as she imagined her baby brother up there above the clouds chasing after enemy bombers as they thundered towards England to rain death from the skies. She quelled the feeling swiftly and smiled up at him. 'Let's hope there's not so much going on now. Old Hitler seems to have other things on his mind.'

'Good job he has,' Kenny said with feeling. 'We were lucky he didn't invade in 'forty, y'know.'

'I do know. If he had done...' She said no more, but the same thought was in all their minds. If Hitler had pressed home his invasion plans in September 1940, what would life be like right now in Britain? It didn't bear thinking about.

'I wish Mum would see it like that,' Kenny murmured.

'How is she?'

Kenny pulled a face. 'Cross and then weepy. Hardly speaking to me one minute and then crying all over me the next.'

'Poor Mum,' Fleur said. 'It's not easy for her, Kenny.' She punched his arm gently. 'And for heaven's sake, take care of yourself. And, now,' she added briskly, 'this garden isn't going to dig itself.'

Ruth yawned. 'I'll just grab a couple of hours on my lovely soft feather bed upstairs and then I'll nip round to Harry's.'

The day passed all too quickly and then they were waving Kenny goodbye on the train back home. 'Well, I'll be off back tomorrow and then I'll soon be up in the clouds alongside you, Robbie. Wish me luck.'

The two men shook hands and Fleur hugged

her brother hard. 'Oh, we do, we do. Good luck, darling bro.'

And then Kenny turned to Ruth. 'Goodbye, Ruth,' he said and suddenly he was boyishly shy.

'Good luck, Kenny,' Ruth said, giving him a bear hug. As she drew back, she touched his cheek tenderly and looked into his eyes as she added earnestly, 'And take care of yourself.'

'I will. I'll ... I'll see you soon.'

Then, with a last wink to Fleur, he boarded the train and leant out of the window waving until they could no longer see him. For several minutes, Fleur stood watching the receding train until Robbie put his arm around her shoulders and said softly, 'Come on, love, time we were all getting back. Last trip for a while – I can't wait for tonight to be over.'

Fleur shuddered. It was the first time she'd ever heard Robbie talk like that. He must be wearier than even she had realized.

In the control tower, Fleur stood alone staring at the blackboard with the names of the aircraft chalked up as they returned. There was one blank space left. One plane had not returned from the operation.

Robbie Rodwell's bomber.

Fleur lost track of the time she stood there, just staring at the blackboard, willing the radio to crackle into life, praying to hear the call sign. 'Hello, Woody, this is Lindum T-Tommy calling...'

But the radio was silent, the space left blank. She couldn't even have Ruth with her. She was already on duty at the debriefing. But she knew that T-Tommy had not come home. Maybe, at this very moment, Ruth was hearing what had happened to Robbie and the others. It had seemed a good omen at the time, that the call sign given to the new Lancaster they were now flying had, by coincidence, the same name as its skipper. Now, Fleur wasn't so sure.

Kay, too, had remained in the control room, hunched over her radio but unable to meet Fleur's eyes. Bob Watson carried on with all the necessary duties he had at the end of a mission, his face grim. He was studiously avoiding looking at either of the girls.

The room was silent, the airfield outside the window silent too in the early morning light. Though she strained her ears, there was no welcome sound of a damaged aircraft limping home.

She heard the door open behind her and for a moment her heart leapt. She spun round, her face suddenly alight with hope. There'd been a mistake! T-Tommy had landed and they'd missed it. Robbie had been safely home all the time...

It was her heart speaking, not her head. Control never missed a plane landing. It simply didn't happen. They were all too professional, too thorough. But terror and hope are strange bedfellows and forced the mind to play strange tricks.

Of course it wasn't Robbie who had stepped into the room, but Squadron Leader Tony Harris, whose aircraft had been the last to land. His face was sombre and her heart plummeted as she saw the sympathy in his eyes.

'I'm sorry, Fleur. One of the other pilots has reported at the debriefing that he saw a bomber with two of its engines on fire going down just off the coast. It looks like it could have been T-Tommy. It's the only one that hasn't come back this time.'

It was a good night's work. Even Fleur had to acknowledge that. Only one bomber missing. But why, oh why, did it have to be Robbie's?

The lump in her throat threatened to choke her, but she managed to ask, 'Did they see any parachutes?'

'It was too dark to see.'

'Thank you for letting me know, sir,' she said, shakily.

'There's still a chance, Fleur. We don't give up hope until we know for definite, do we?' Like her, the squadron leader was forcing an optimism he didn't really feel deep inside. He was not relishing the thought of the difficult letters that he would have to write to all the families of the missing crew, should the worst be confirmed. Fleur nodded, now not trusting herself to speak.

'I'll see Caroline – your commanding officer.'

If she hadn't been so distressed, Fleur might have smiled at the squadron leader's use of ma'am's Christian name. Rumour on camp had it that they were seeing each other on the QT. As it was, Fleur was quite lost in a flood of grief that she scarcely noticed. She couldn't allow herself false hope. She'd already seen too much of it. 'I'll see if she can arrange a spot of leave for you,' he went on. 'I expect you'd like to go home. See your own folks. And ... and his mother. She's in Nottingham, I understand.'

Fleur nodded and managed to whisper huskily,

331

'Thank you.'

He moved across the room to have a word or two with Kay, who was still sitting in front of her microphone. He put his hand on her shoulder and bent down towards her, but Kay didn't speak, didn't even respond to his kindly gesture.

After he'd left the office, Fleur stood for a few moments longer just staring at the blank space on the blackboard. A space that would never now be filled in.

'Fleur...' She heard the scrape of a chair on the floor and heard Kay's voice, but she held out her hand, palm outwards. She closed her eyes for a moment and shook her head. She couldn't cope with sympathy – however well meant – at this moment. She was about to turn away, to run away as far as she could go, to deal with her anguish on her own, but then, even through her own pain, she remembered.

Tommy – Kay's Tommy! Of course! He was missing too. How could she have been so thoughtless, so selfishly wrapped up in her own grief that she had not given a thought to Kay?

'Oh, Kay – Kay...' She held out her arms and the two girls flew to each other, holding their friend tightly and crying against each other's shoulder. Quietly, his work finished, Bob Watson left the room.

The man felt guilty. There was nothing he could say. It would sound hypocritical. He'd never hidden his disapproval of wartime romances, let alone a wartime wedding. And now his fears had been realized and there was nothing he could say – or do. Not for the first time he silently cursed this blasted war!

After a few moments, Kay pulled herself free of Fleur's clinging arms. 'Right. This won't do any good. It's not what they would have wanted. Come on, get a grip, girl.'

Fleur was still hiccuping, overwhelmed by her grief, wallowing in a deluge of loss, despairing as to how she was ever going to cope with tomorrow and tomorrow and tomorrow. A lifetime of loneliness stretched bleakly before her. She raised her head and stared through her tears at Kay. She couldn't believe that the other girl was already being so callous.

With a sob she tore herself free and rushed from the control room. Once outside the building, she began to run and run until she felt as if her lungs would burst. Only when she could run no more did she sink down near the perimeter fence and lie, face down in the long, cold grass and weep.

'Oh, please, let him be alive,' she prayed wildly. 'I'll do anything, give anything – everything – if only you'll let him be alive.'

His poor mother, she was thinking. How is she going to take it? And his grandfather? News like that might...

I must go and see them, Fleur told herself. Once there's been time for the authorities to have informed them, I'll go.

She shivered; the damp coldness of the ground was beginning to seep through. She sat up and dried her eyes, but fresh tears trickled down her face. She couldn't stem the flow.

'Fleur? Fleur – where are you?'

Distantly across the open ground, she heard Ruth's anxious voice. She scrambled to her feet and through the pale morning light she could see her friend running up and down, calling her name. She waved and called weakly, 'Here. Over here.'

At once, Ruth was running towards her, 'Oh, Fleur – Fleur. I've just heard at the debriefing. I so hoped they'd just be late... But... I came as soon as I could...' She almost threw herself against Fleur and wrapped her arms around her, holding her tightly. 'It's my fault. It's all my fault,' Ruth was babbling against her shoulder. 'I didn't wave them off like I always do. After final briefing, Serg wanted me to deal with some paperwork. I lost track of time and, by the time I got down to the edge of the runway, most of them had taken off. Oh, Fleur – I'm sorry. I'm so sorry...'

Fleur clung to her, unable to give her friend any comfort, unable to exonerate her. She was drained, trembling with shock and weak with anguish. Deep in her heart, she knew it would have made no difference if Ruth had waved them off. It was just another superstition, but at this moment she was incapable of voicing it.

Against her, she felt Ruth draw in a deep breath. Somehow, the other girl found the strength to say, 'Come on, Fleur. You can't stay out here in the cold. Let's get you to the NAAFI...'

'I can't – I can't face anyone.'

'Don't be daft, Fleur,' Ruth said with brusque kindness. 'Everyone knows. Everyone under-stands. Most of us have been there at one time or another. You need to be with people who understand.' Ruth was saying almost the same as Kay, but somehow the words were not so harsh. She felt badly about Kay now. It was just her way. She must be hurting inside every bit as much as Fleur. For a moment, Fleur despised herself for her weakness. She wished she could be as strong as...

'Kay? Have you seen Kay?'

Ruth nodded. 'She came to find me. To tell me that you'd run off.'

'I'm sorry. She was only trying to help...'

'She understands. She was concerned for you, that's all.'

'She's so strong,' Fleur murmured. 'Look at me. I've gone to pieces. I'm a wreck. I'm – weak!'

'No, you're not. And Kay's not as tough underneath as she likes to make out. She'll be sobbing her socks off in bed tonight, you mark my words.' There was a pause before Ruth added shakily, 'And she won't be the only one. I feel so guilty. But we shouldn't give up hope. Not just yet.'

Sadly, Fleur shook her head. 'But someone saw a plane go down. It must have been them. And they didn't see any parachutes...'

Now Ruth had no answer.

Fleur sniffed. 'I ... I want to go home. I want to see my dad.'

'Course you do. Let's go and see ma'am. I'm sure she...'

'Squadron Leader Harris came into the control room. He said he'd see her. Ask her if I could have some leave.'

'That's OK then. Let's go.'

'I can't. Looking like this.' She brushed

335

ineffectually at the front of her uniform, blotched with wet grass stains.

'I'm sure she'll overlook it for once. You're usually the smartest of the lot of us.' Ruth took Fleur's arm firmly and urged her towards the buildings. 'You can't stop out here. You'll catch your death.'

With a laugh that was bordering on hysteria, Fleur said, 'You sound like my mum.' And at the thought of her mother, Fleur's tears flowed even harder.

Thirty-Seven

'Dad! *Dad!*'

Two days later, Fleur went home. Despite his disapproval of wartime marriages and romances, Bob Watson had quietly rearranged the rotas so that both Fleur and Kay were not on duty for four days following T-Tommy's failure to return. Kay went to her home down south, adding on a couple of days' ordinary leave that she was entitled to, and Fleur travelled to Middleditch Farm. She could not yet face Robbie's mother.

Dumping her bag near the back door, she ran round the yard, peering into the shadows of the cowshed then running into the barn, calling, 'Dad, where are you?' She didn't want to see her own mother, either. Not yet. She had to find her father. Fleur wanted her dad.

But it was Betsy who appeared at the back

door, drying her hands on a tea towel. 'What-ever's the matter? Fleur? Is that you?'

Fleur stood a moment amidst the straw on the floor of the barn, summoning up the courage to answer her mother. She moved slowly to the doorway but she did not cross the yard. The two women stared at each other across the space between them and then Fleur saw her mother's hand flutter to her face to cover her mouth. Slowly, Fleur began to walk towards her.

'Well, Mum,' she said harshly as she neared her. 'You got your wish. He's gone. Robbie's–' She bit hard down on her lip to stop the tears. 'Robbie's missing, presumed killed.'

'Oh, Fleur, how can you think that of me? I didn't want you married to him. To have any-thing to do with him. But I wouldn't have wished him any harm.'

Fleur's eyes filled with the tears that were never far away. 'I don't know what to think. How can I when you won't tell me anything? What on earth can possibly have happened in the past to make you so – so – vitriolic against him? You didn't even know him.'

The bitterness of years was in Betsy's eyes again. Then she sighed deeply and gave a little shake of her head. Flatly, she said, 'Like I said before, it wasn't against him personally. Just his mother.'

'Why? What happened?'

Betsy's mouth tightened. 'She was a wicked woman. Devious, manipulating and utterly – utterly – selfish.'

'How? What on earth did she do?'

Betsy turned away. 'I don't want to talk about

337

it. I *won't* talk about it.'

'You really hate her, don't you? Well, if you wanted some kind of ... kind of revenge on her, then you've certainly got it now. She's lost her son. Her only son.'

Betsy just stared at her, her face expressionless, saying nothing.

'You really won't tell me?' Fleur tried again.

Betsy shook her head.

'Then I'll ask Dad. I'll ask him this very minute.'

'Perhaps it is time you knew,' her mother murmured and nodded, as if answering an unspoken question she was asking herself. At last she dragged out the words reluctantly. 'He's ... away up the ... fields with ... the sheep. You ... you'll find him in Buttercup Meadow.'

Fleur gave a brief nod and moved towards the back door. She picked up her bag and made to step into the house, but her mother didn't move aside. It was as if she was almost barring Fleur's way.

Fleur stared at her. 'I'll just change my clothes.' Her uniform was still a mess from her spasm of weeping in the wet grass the night she had heard that Robbie was missing. It would need sponging and pressing before she went on parade again. She would change into her old clothes before she went tramping through the fields to find her dad.

Betsy blinked. 'Can't you go as you are?'

'No, I can't. I need to change.'

'Well, you can't. I mean – you can't come in. There's ... there's someone here that ... that I don't want you to see. That you didn't ought to see.'

'What on earth are you talking about, Mum? What's going on?'

'Nothing. Nothing. I just don't want you to see her. Not just now. It'll be – awkward.'

'Who? Who is it you don't want me to see?'

Betsy bit her lip. 'You don't understand. I mean – I don't want *her* to see *you*. Not just this minute.'

'Who?'

Fleur was getting angry now. What was all the mystery and why – when Fleur was suffering the worst moment in the whole of her young life – was her mother acting so strangely? 'Mum – just tell me who it is you don't want me to see?'

Betsy sighed. 'Louisa. Your Aunt Louisa.'

'Aunt Louisa? Why on earth shouldn't I see her?'

'It's ... it's complicated. It's all to do with ... with Robbie and his mother. You don't understand,' she finished lamely.

'No, I don't.' Now, Fleur pushed her mother aside. 'But I'm jolly well going to find out.'

'No, Fleur. Please don't. You don't understand – Fleur...!' Betsy tried to grab her daughter's arm, but Fleur shook her off and marched into the kitchen where Louisa was sitting at the table drinking tea.

'Fleur, my dear, how lovely...' Louisa began as she rose and held out her arms to hug Fleur, who submitted a little stiffly to the embrace. Then she stood back. 'My dear girl. What is it? What's wrong?'

Fleur stared into the older woman's eyes for what seemed a long time but was in fact only seconds.

'It's Robbie,' Fleur whispered at last. But before she could say more, Louisa took a step back. Her hand fluttered to cover her mouth and her eyes widened in horror. 'Oh, no!' she breathed. 'Don't say it – oh, don't say it!'

Fleur was puzzled. Despite the sorrow that anyone might feel to hear of a young airman's death and the sympathy Louisa, as a friend of the family, would naturally feel for the young bride so cruelly widowed, the woman's reaction was extreme.

'Aunt Louisa,' Fleur began, reaching out to take Louisa's hands. 'What is it? Whatever's the matter?' But Louisa snatched her hands away.

'No, no, don't. I must go. I can't stay...' She cast a beseeching, almost frantic look at Betsy who had followed her daughter inside. Then she snatched up her handbag and scarf and fled from the room. As the back door slammed behind her, there was silence in the room until Fleur moved woodenly and sank down into her father's chair by the range.

'What is it, Mum? What's it all about?'

Betsy sighed heavily and flopped down into the chair on the opposite side of the hearth, as if suddenly all the energy had drained out of her.

'Go and find your father,' she said flatly. 'Ask him,' was all she would say.

With sudden renewed vigour, determined to get to the bottom of the mystery, Fleur sprang to her feet. 'Then I will. I'll go now. This very minute.' She stood a moment, staring down at her mother, willing her to say something – anything. But Betsy was silent, just staring into the fire. She didn't move as Fleur hurried upstairs to change her clothes. When she returned, her mother had not moved. She was sitting just as Fleur had left her, staring silently and sadly into the flames.

'Mum?' Fleur said tentatively, but Betsy made no move, no sign that she had even heard her.

Fleur left the house and stood a moment outside the back door. She pulled in a deep breath. It helped to calm her, but nothing could assuage her terrible grief. She felt as if she would never smile or laugh ever again. The sun had gone out of her life. She thrust her hands deep into the pockets of her old coat and trudged across the yard, out of the gate and down the lane towards the field where she knew her father would be.

Even before Jake saw her, Bess, the black and white sheepdog, barked and came scampering across the field towards her.

'Bess!' Jake roared angrily, as the sheep scattered in fright. Then he saw Fleur and he grinned and began to walk towards her. But as he neared her, his smile faded. 'Aw lass, don't tell me. Is it Robbie?'

Tears choked her and all she could do was nod as he limped towards her and put his arms around her, holding her close. 'Aw love,' he said huskily.

They stood for a long time until he said gently, 'Come on, let's go back to the house. Let's–'

'No, Dad. No. I want to talk to you. I *need* to talk to you.' She drew back, her eyes brimming with tears.

For a moment, he studied her face. Then he gave a deep sigh and nodded. 'All right. But first, tell me what's happened.'

'He ... he didn't come back from a mission the night before last. It's so ironic – so cruel. It was their thirtieth mission. A full tour, Dad. They'd done a full tour. At least, the four of them had.'

'Those lovely boys at your wedding? They're all missing?'

Fleur nodded. 'They – some of the other pilots – told Ruth at debriefing that they'd seen a plane go down with two of its engines on fire just off the coast. Tommy's a wonderful pilot, but...'

'Was that the one who was the best man?'

'Yes. But ... but even he wouldn't be able to do much if ... if it was on fire.'

'Was it near our coast?'

She nodded.

'Then–' Jake began, with a tiny hope, but Fleur shook her head sadly.

'No one saw any parachutes. And there's been no word. We'd've heard by now if they'd been picked up.'

'Are you sure? There's been some dreadful bombing down south again. They reckon it's in retaliation for this round-the-clock bombing we've been doing.'

'It's no good having false hope, Dad. I've worked in the control room long enough, seen enough missions, to know that, nine times out of ten, when they don't come back that night then – then they don't come back at all. Oh, sometimes they do. The lucky ones. Their plane limps home late or lands at another airfield or they've parachuted out of the plane and been picked up. Even become prisoners of war, if it was over enemy territory. But ... but this wasn't. It was over the sea.' She pulled in a deep breath. 'I've got to face it, Dad. He's gone. I've lost him.'

Jake shook his head, as if unable to believe the dreadful news, and yet it shouldn't really have come as a shock. Every day young men were dying for their country. Young men just like Robbie, young men just like Kenny.

'Have you ... have you seen his mother yet? Have you seen Meggie?'

Fleur shook her head. Even now, she noticed he used the pet name for Robbie's mother that she'd never heard anyone else use apart from Pops. Meg's father called her that too. Maybe that's what she'd been called as a girl...

'But you will?' Jake was pulling her thoughts back to the present. 'You ... you'll be going to see her?'

'Of course.'

'Then ... then tell her I'm so sorry, won't you?'

Fleur raised her head and stared into his face. For a moment a shudder ran through her. The haunted look was back in her father's eyes and now it was ten-fold in its despair.

'Of course I will, Dad,' she said softly. There was a moment's silence before she added, 'Dad, will you please tell me what all the mystery is? Don't you think I have a right to know?'

Jake closed his eyes, sighed and shook his head. 'They're not my secrets to tell, Fleur love. If they were, then of course I would tell you. But...'

'But Robbie's gone. It ... it can't hurt him now, can it?'

'No,' Jake said sadly. 'It can't and I can't tell

343

you how sorry I am that that's the case. Poor Meggie. To lose her boy...' He wiped the back of his hand across his eyes and coughed to clear the emotion catching his throat. He sighed. 'Well, if I do tell you, you must promise me one thing first, Fleur.'

'Anything, Dad. I just want to know. I want to understand.'

He sighed heavily. 'You might not understand even when I've told you it all.'

'I'd like the chance to try. Mum and I have always clashed – you know that – but I don't want us to carry on like this – like we are now. It ... it's tearing our family apart.'

Jake sighed. 'To be perfectly honest, I don't think your knowing about the past will help that. It's more this business with Kenny that's coming between you and your mum now.'

'What about you, Dad? Do you blame me for Kenny joining up?'

His answer was swift and certain. 'No, love, not for a minute. Like I've said before, I'm proud of him – and of you – even though I'm worried sick about you both. But your mother just wants to keep you safe. She doesn't even want to see the wider picture.' He gave a wry smile. 'I think she'd even rather Hitler marched in unhindered than lose either of you.'

Fleur shuddered. 'Well, I don't think any of us would last long if he did, do you? Can you imagine his jackbooted cohorts tramping through Britain?'

Jake shook his head. 'No, I can't and I don't even want to try. It doesn't bear thinking about.'

344

He glanced at her, their faces almost on a level and so close. 'We can't let that happen, Fleur, and it's up to you and Kenny and all those wonderful young people just like you to stop it. Whatever it costs.'

'Yes,' she whispered. 'Whatever it costs.' Already it had cost her everything. It had taken away her future. There was no future for her now that Robbie was gone. Yet she had to summon up the courage to continue the fight Robbie had believed in so passionately. What would happen after the war was over, she dared not think. She couldn't face the thought of the empty years stretching ahead without Robbie.

Jake was speaking again, pulling her thoughts back to the present. 'I want your promise that even if you go on seeing his mother now and again – as I'm sure you will – you'll never breathe a word to her about what I'm going to tell you. It's not something she'll want to talk about or even like to think you know about. I don't want to hurt Meg any more than she's going to be hurt now. This is going to devastate her, Fleur. Oh, love–' He touched her arm. 'I don't mean to minimize your grief. But you're young. You've a whole life ahead of you–'

Fleur closed her eyes and groaned. 'But it means nothing without Robbie, Dad. Don't you see?'

'I know it feels like that now, but ... but in time–'

'No, Dad. You're wrong. Eternity wouldn't be long enough. I'll never get over this. He was all I ever wanted. The only man I'll ever love.' She lifted her head and stared him straight in the eyes. 'And now I want you to tell me about the past. I swear I won't breathe a word to his mother. But I have to know. I have to try to understand what it is that makes Mum so bitter that she can hardly bring herself to say she's sorry he's dead.'

Jake blinked as if that shocked even him. Then he sighed again as he said heavily, 'All right, then. I'll tell you. But you must promise me not to say anything to Meggie. Not a word. Not ever.'

'I promise, Dad,' Fleur said solemnly.

'I'm being dreadfully disloyal to her.' His eyes were full of pain at the thought, though Fleur wasn't sure if her father was referring to his wife or to Meg Rodwell.

There was a long silence before Jake, haltingly at first, began to speak.

'I'll go right back to the beginning. It's time you knew a few other things besides matters that concern Robbie. It's high time you knew about your mum and me too.'

He paused again and pulled in a deep breath as if he was about to launch himself over a precipice. Perhaps that's how it did feel for Jake to talk about things that had not been spoken of for years.

Thirty-Eight

They leant on the gate, watching the sheep, whilst Bess lay panting beside them, as Jake began to speak. 'You know the big building on the outskirts of South Monkford?'

'The one that used to be a workhouse? It's some kind of convalescent place for the forces now, isn't it?'

Jake nodded. 'That's where I was born. And your mum came into the workhouse as a young girl when her mother died.'

'You were both in the workhouse?' Fleur was shocked. She would never have imagined that the successful farmer owning Middleditch Farm and all its acres, the man who was well liked and respected in the neighbourhood, could have been born into such lowly circumstances. Then another thought struck her. 'But ... but you had a mother. Gran.' She spoke of the woman who had lived with them for the last few years of her life.

'Yes.' Jake's voice was husky. 'But I didn't know I had until ... until – well, all the bother happened.'

'All the bother?'

'Mm.' He was silent again.

Though she was impatient for him to continue, Fleur held her tongue. Quite literally, for she had to hold it between her teeth to stop all her questions tumbling out.

'All I knew as a lad was that I'd been born in the workhouse,' Jake went on as he gazed out across the rolling fields that were all his now. But he was seeing, Fleur knew, pictures and events from the past. 'I thought I was an orphan. A feller called Isaac Pendleton ran the place. He was what they called the master of the workhouse and the matron was his sister, Letitia Pendleton. *Miss* Letitia Pendleton.'

'But that was Gran's name. Except – well – I always thought it was *Mrs* Pendleton. I never knew that she was a ... a "Miss". She was always just "Gran". I'm sorry, Dad. Go on.'

'As a young girl she'd fallen in love with Theobald Finch.'

Now Fleur gasped and before she could stop herself she interrupted his tale again. It was impossible not to show surprise or ask questions, so she gave up trying. 'The Finch family who live at the Hall?'

'Aye, but there's only Miss Clara Finch left there now. Mr Theobald' – he paused over the name, still unable to refer to the man in any way other than the name by which he'd always known him – 'died a while ago.'

'I do vaguely remember seeing him in the town. I think Mum pointed him out to me once.' She glanced sideways at her father but his gaze was still far away.

'Dad, was he – Mr Finch – your father?'

Slowly, he nodded. 'My mother loved him,' he said simply, 'but his family didn't think her good enough for him. At the time, Isaac – her brother – was running the workhouse with his wife. But

348

she left him – so the rumour went. Isaac took me in as an orphan and Letitia became matron.' He smiled wistfully. 'She took the job so that she could be near me, yet she was not allowed to acknowledge me openly.' Now his smile broadened. 'As a lad I always wondered why she favoured me. She saved me many a beating from Isaac.' Now he chuckled. 'Though I still got plenty.'

'Oh, Dad!' Fleur rested her cheek against his shoulder, tears filling her eyes. Jake put his arm about her shoulders and held her close.

'Don't cry, love. It's all a long time ago now.'

'I know, but I can't bear to think of you as a poor little boy, believing yourself an orphan and being beaten and growing up in a *workhouse*. I mean, I know it's a magnificent building, but it was still a workhouse. Why, even now the old folk in the town fear it, don't they?'

'Oh yes. We all still live in the shadow of the workhouse. Those of us who grew up there.' He smiled gently. 'And even some of those who didn't. It's still a threat hanging over us all even if it isn't a workhouse any more.'

Fleur wound her arms tightly around his waist and nestled her head against his shoulder. She said nothing. The lump in her throat wouldn't let her, but her actions implied: you'll never go back in the workhouse, Dad. Not while I'm around.

'There, there,' Jake murmured, feeling her compassion. 'I was a tough little tyke. And then' – he smiled fondly – 'Meggie arrived at the workhouse. And she changed my life.'

He didn't need to elaborate. By the tone of his

voice, Fleur could tell he remembered that time as very special. That Meg was very special.

'She was so – so *alive*,' he went on. 'So spirited and … and full of daring. D'you know, Fleur, I'd lived in that place all my life and I was– Let's see, I'd be about fifteen by the time she came and in all that time I'd never ventured out. Never asked to go out to seek work, never really gone out of my own accord. Oh, I knew *how* to get out. Several of the others did. There was a hole in the wall. And once or twice I went through the gates, but I never went more than a few yards.' He laughed aloud now. 'Not until she came and took me out with her one day. She went looking for her dad.'

'The old man? Pops?'

'Well, he wasn't old then, love. He was a young man and a bit of a rascal, by all accounts.' He gave her shoulder a squeeze. 'We were all young once, lass. Even me and Meg.'

'Oh, I think she still looks young, Dad. She looks years younger than Mum.' The words were out before she could stop herself. 'I'm sorry. I didn't mean...'

''S all right, love. There's only you an' me here.' He glanced down at the dog, dozing at their feet. 'And Bess won't say owt, now will she? But just think a minute. Your poor mam's a busy farmer's wife. She can't dress like Meg and wear those flimsy shoes, now can she?'

'No, of course not,' Fleur said hurriedly. Privately, she was thinking that her mother could still make a little more effort even if it was only now and again. 'But I don't think Robbie's mum's had it that easy. The front room at their house is her sewing room. She's worked to keep them all. Herself, Robbie and the old man.'

Again, Jake had a faraway look in his eyes as he continued with his tale. 'Her father, Reuben Kirkland – the old man as you call him – worked for the Smallwoods and so did Meg. She worked in the dairy. And then, Meg's father had an affair with the Smallwoods' daughter, Alice.'

Fleur was shocked. 'Pops did?'

'Yes. Pops.' Jake was adamant. 'Of course, they dismissed him and his daughter, Meg, and then turned the whole family out of their tied cottage – the one old Ron lives in now. Reuben took his family – his pregnant wife Sarah, Meg and her little brother Bobbie – to the workhouse, promising to return to get them out when he'd found other work.'

Fleur was ahead of her father, guessing what had happened. 'And he never came back for them? He ran away with Alice?' She paused, taking in all the startling revelations. Then she asked, 'Did Meg know?'

'Not then. Not when she first came into the workhouse. She believed him, trusted him. She told everyone that they wouldn't be there long. That he'd come back for them. She didn't know why they'd been dismissed. For a while I think she blamed herself.' He smiled fondly again. 'She was a cheeky little tyke and she thought the missis – Mrs Smallwood – didn't like her friendship with her daughter.'

'*Her* friendship? Meg was friendly with Alice too?'

351

'Yes. Complicated, isn't it? So, you see, when she did find out about their affair, she felt doubly betrayed. By her father *and* by her best friend.'

'So how did Meg find out?'

'Her mam gave birth to a stillborn child in the workhouse and Meg went in search of her father to tell him. Of course, she didn't know about her dad and Alice then. She just went to try and find him to tell him about her mam. And she took me with her. We went to the racecourse. She thought her father might be trying to find work there. He was good with horses.'

Fleur nodded. South Monkford racecourse was famous, though sadly neglected since the war had begun.

'Did you find him?'

'Oh yes.' Jake's face was grim. 'He was with her. With Alice. Bold as yer like, walking round the racecourse with his arm around her.'

Fleur gasped. 'Oh, poor Meg!'

'Yes,' Jake said thoughtfully. 'D'you know, as far as I can remember, it was the only time I ever saw Meggie cry.' Again, he used the pet name as he spoke of her fondly. 'She was heartbroken and vowed never to forgive her father. Said she'd cut him out of her life for ever.'

'Well, she can't have done because he lives with her now.'

'She's changed. But back then, she swore that she'd never forget and never forgive.'

'Did she?' Now Fleur was surprised. 'She doesn't strike me as being like that.'

'No. Like I say, she's changed since then. Life changed her. I know now that she's sorry for everything she's done. I could see that when I met her at your wedding. I asked her about her father and she said, "How could I turn him away, when I'd been just as bad?"'

'But she hadn't done anything, Dad. It was her father's fault,' Fleur said, mystified. She still couldn't reconcile the picture of the sweet old man sitting by the fire in the little house in Nottingham with the heartless womanizer who'd dumped his family in the workhouse and run away with his mistress.

'I'm coming to that, love. But I want you to see the whole picture. And to do that, you have to hear what led up to – well – what Meg did.' Even now, though he had promised to tell her everything and had begun the tale, there was reluctance in his tone. He still didn't want to speak ill of Meg. Not even after all these years.

'Whatever did she do, Dad, that was so bad?'

He was silent for a moment, lost in memories in which Fleur had no part. Now, in short staccato sentences, he answered her question, explaining everything. 'After she found out about her father and Alice she became very bitter. The tragedies didn't end there. Her little brother, Bobbie, died. Then Isaac Pendleton – he was a one for the ladies, an' all – he took up with her mother. And that was the last straw for Meg. She never forgave her mother – called her some wicked names. And Meg herself became hard and calculating. There was only one person she cared about then. Herself. She left the workhouse and got a job working for Percy Rodwell.' Now Jake's mouth suddenly became a hard line.

'She wound him round her little finger and he fell for it. Poor sod!'

Fleur twisted to look up into her father's face. She saw his pain and, yes, now there was anger and disgust there too. 'Were you in love with her, Dad? Were you in love with Meg all those years ago?'

Jake stared down into his daughter's eyes. 'Oh yes. I loved her then and–'

There was a breathless silence until Fleur whispered, 'And you love her now, don't you, Dad? You've always loved her.'

'Fleur, love.' He squeezed her shoulders again. 'I know you feel now that you'll never love again. That Robbie was the love of your life – and maybe he is. Who's to say? But you may well meet someone one day, fall in love, get married–'

'Never! I could never love anyone the way I love Robbie.'

'Listen to me, love.' Her father gave her a gentle shake. 'No, not in the same way, maybe you won't, no. I can understand that. He was your first love and that's very special. But you might love someone else differently. There are all kinds of love, Fleur. Passionate, overwhelming and for life. Then there's infatuation that seems like love, but isn't and dies as quickly as it flared. And then...' He paused again and took a deep breath before he said, 'And then there's the way I love your mother. After Meg went, I left the work-house and I came to work for the Smallwoods here. Their daughter had gone, of course, and they never heard from her again as far as I know. A year or two later, Betsy came to work at the farm too. In fact, I sort of got her the job there. She'd spent several years in the workhouse. She was a shy little thing and I always felt protective towards her. The Smallwoods treated us both as their own and Betsy grew and blossomed. She was a pretty lass and – well – that's how it happened. I married her before I went to the war, and when I came back you were born and then Kenny.'

There was a long silence whilst Fleur digested all that he had told her.

'There's a bit more you ought to know,' Jake said at last.

'More!' Fleur forced a smile.

'When Meg went to work for Percy he was engaged to Miss Clara Finch – had been for years – and when he married Meg Clara sued him for breach of promise.'

Fleur gasped. 'Never!'

'Oh yes. There was a big court case and it was the talk of South Monkford for weeks.' His mouth twitched. 'You see, the judge found in Miss Finch's favour, but he awarded her damages of one farthing.'

Fleur stared at him for a moment and then burst out laughing, but Jake's face had sobered now. 'Clara was a bitter, dried-up old spinster, and after Percy Rodwell died, she tried to force Meg to hand over her baby – Robbie – because she believed in her twisted mind that the child should have been hers. Hers and Percy's. When Meg refused, Clara had her turned out of the shop and her home – the Finches owned both properties – and she tried to kidnap Robbie and have Meg thrown back in the workhouse. With the power the Finches wielded in South Monkford then, I doubt Meg would ever have seen the light of day again if...' He stopped and was silent.

Intuitively, Fleur whispered. 'You helped her, didn't you, Dad? You helped her get out.'

'She was locked in the punishment room and her boy was missing. We found him – Robbie – in the dead room in a coffin. Clara, in her twisted mind, had had him hidden there until she could take him home. Just think.' Jake tried to inject a note of lightness into their conversation. 'Your Robbie might have been a toff and brought up at South Monkford Hall.'

The dead room. The punishment room. Fleur shuddered. It all sounded like another world from the safe and happy childhood she had known.

'It was then I found out about my own mother – just who she was. Maybe if all that hadn't happened, I might never have known.' For a long moment, Jake was silent, then he came back to finish his telling of the story. 'That was when Meg changed from her hard and calculating ways. Almost losing her son had jolted her because there was never any doubt about her love for him. After that...' Jake sighed softly. 'She left the district and I ... I never saw her again. Not until your wedding day, Fleur.'

'I suppose poor old Clara Finch wanted something of her sweetheart's,' Fleur said with understanding. 'She wanted Percy's son.'

'Ah,' Jake said, 'but that's the irony of it all. You see, love, Robbie wasn't Percy's child.'

Her eyes wide, Fleur stared at him wordlessly. Surely, after all, her father wasn't about to tell her that he was, in truth, Robbie's father too?

'Pei..... you can't see it like I can, because you wouldn't remember his father as a young man.'

Her voice was husky as she asked hesitantly, 'Dad, just tell me. Who was Robbie's father?'

'The man you call Uncle Philip. Dr Philip Collins.'

'I can't believe it. I mean, how–?'

Despite the seriousness of their talk and all the long-held secrets he had just revealed, Jake laughed. 'Now surely I don't need to be explaining the facts of life to you, lass, do I?'

Fleur smiled briefly and shook her head. 'I mean, when did it happen? Before *he* married Aunt Louisa?'

Sadly, Jake shook his head. 'No, love, nothing so above board as that, I'm sorry to say. They had an affair.' His mouth hardened again. 'While Percy was ill with the influenza that killed him. Of course, Meg was able to make out the child was his, but there's no hiding it now. Not for anyone who remembered Philip in his younger days and then ... saw your Robbie.'

'Oh, Dad.' Fleur clutched his arm. 'Auntie Louisa saw him. I introduced them. In a cafe in South Monkford. Just after I'd met him. You know – the day I invited them out to the farm and–' She bit her lip. 'Aunt Louisa seemed – well – odd. Now I know why. She ... she must have guessed.'

Slowly, Jake nodded. 'I wondered at the time if she suspected. Poor Louisa, specially as she's never had any family herself.'

'Did Uncle Philip know he had a son?'

'I've no idea. But knowing Meg as she was then, I've no doubt she told him. Maybe–' He began to say something and then stopped himself. 'No, that's not fair to speculate. I shouldn't judge her.'

'No, none of us should. I certainly won't. She's Robbie's mum and she's been kind to me and ... and she's suffering now. Whatever she did in the past, Dad, she's paying for it now.'

'Aye, love,' Jake said sadly. 'I know she is.'

And once more the haunted faraway look that Fleur had so often seen on her father's face was there again. But now, she understood exactly what caused it.

Thirty-Nine

'Oh, Philip – I'm so sorry. I shouldn't have ... I mean ... I wish–'

'Now, now, my dear. What's the matter?'

Philip took her arm calmly and led her into the front sitting room. The huge room was cold; no welcoming fire burned in the grate. They were trying to economize on coal and only lit the fire when the room was to be used for a lengthy period. Otherwise, they now sat in the two easy chairs in the corner of the kitchen, close to the wireless on which Philip loved to hear the latest war news.

Louisa clung to him. 'Forgive me, Philip, oh, say you forgive me.'

'I'm sure I shall, darling, if only I knew what it is I'm supposed to be forgiving. Here, sit down. Let me make us both some tea.'

'No, no, I should do that. That's my job.'

'Not just at this moment. I can see you're upset. Sit down whilst I make it and then we'll talk about it. Whatever it is.'

'But ... but you've got surgery, haven't you?'

'There's no one out there at the moment. My patients are remarkably healthy today, it seems.' He smiled at her archly, trying to lighten her mood. 'I must be a better doctor than I thought.'

'Oh, Philip, you're a wonderful doctor.' Her eyes filled with tears. 'A wonderful man. I don't deserve you. I...'

'There, there, my dear. Please, don't upset yourself. We'll sort it all out – whatever it is.'

Philip was becoming increasingly worried about his wife. From being a calm, serene, perfect doctor's wife, she had in recent weeks become nervy and irritable and weepy. Had she been one of his patients, he would by now have diagnosed a nervous breakdown. And whilst he could scarcely believe – didn't want to believe – that that was what might be happening to his wife, ethics aside, it would be better for her to be treated by someone else. He was no expert in psychiatric cases.

He shuddered at the thought, but if that was the case, then it would have to be faced. She was such a tender-hearted person and even though they weren't experiencing particular hardship themselves, nor the loss of a close relative, still the community as a whole was being badly hit.

And Louisa felt it, he knew. As he set her cup of tea on a small table beside her, he sat down opposite, leant forward and took her hands in his. 'Now,' he said in the kindly but firm tone he adopted when speaking to a distraught patient, 'tell me what is troubling you.'

Fresh tears spilled down her cheeks.

'Oh, Philip – he's dead.'

'Who's dead, my love?'

She raised her red-rimmed eyes to look into his face as she whispered, 'Meg's boy. He's – he's missing, believed killed.'

She felt his hands holding hers twitch involuntarily and saw the colour drain from his face. They stared at each other for long moments before, haltingly, Louisa broke the silence. 'You ... you do know who he really is, don't you, Philip? Who ... who his father is?'

The colour flooded into his face and she had her answer without him saying a word. Before he could speak, she rushed on. 'I wish you'd told me. I wish you'd had enough faith in my love for you to have told me the truth at the time. I presume you've always known?'

Wordlessly, Philip nodded.

'I know – I know you wanted to spare me the hurt.' Now it was she who was giving comfort. 'The fact that you'd been unfaithful to me – and with Meg of all people. But don't you see, if only you'd confided in me, perhaps, all those years ago, we could have adopted him? Brought him up as *our* son. Oh, Philip, I wish you'd told me then.'

He shook his head as he said heavily, 'No, my

dear, it would never have worked. You ... you say you'd have forgiven me, but you're speaking now with the benefit of hindsight. Back then, you didn't know that we'd never have children of our own. You didn't know that someone else's son could have filled the void in our lives–'

'But he was *your* son, Philip. I could have loved him, I could have–'

'Could you really, Louisa, have loved *Meg's* son? Be honest now, since we're talking honestly. Let's be absolutely straight with each other.'

When she didn't answer, he added softly, 'No, I thought not.' He smiled wryly. 'Besides, Meg wouldn't let Clara Finch have him, would she?'

'Of course she wouldn't,' Louisa cried now. 'Meg knew – though Clara Finch didn't – that he wasn't Percy's son. But if *you'd* wanted him, she'd've let him go.' Her lip curled. 'Remember how selfish she was, how self-centred? Oh, she'd've let you have him like a shot. Been glad to be rid of him, I dare say.'

'I think you're wrong, my dear. Whatever Meg may have been – and yes, I admit, she did some reprehensible things–'

'Reprehensible? Reprehensible, you call it. Unforgivable, I'd call it. Seducing poor Percy. Yes – yes – she seduced him, Philip. Poor, bumbling Percy Rodwell didn't know what had hit him when she batted her eyelashes at him and smiled so winningly.'

'My dear,' he said softly. 'We've all made mistakes. Especially me.'

Louisa held his gaze as she asked, 'Do you regret it, Philip?'

His answer was swift and he hoped that it sounded sincere. 'Of course I do. I wouldn't have hurt you for the world. Louisa, I've always loved you and I always will. You must believe that. Meg was just – was just a stupid, stupid mistake. An aberration. Please – please say you forgive me?'

'Oh, Philip!' Tearfully, she threw her arms around his neck. 'Of course I do. It's a long time ago. And ... and you haven't seen her since. Have you?'

'No, no. I swear it.' That part, at least, was true. As for the rest, deep in his heart he couldn't be sure. He buried his face against his wife's neck and hugged her tightly, trying to block out the memory of that vibrant red-haired girl who had brought such passion into his life. Even though the affair had been brief, he'd never been able to put her completely out of his mind. And never a day had gone by through all the years since that he had not thought about the son she had borne him and wondered what he looked like.

And now he would never know.

'So now you know, do you?' Betsy asked, her mouth tight, as Fleur came back into the house. 'Heard the whole sorry story?'

Fleur sighed and said flatly, 'Yes. If that's what you like to call it. Yes, I think I've heard it all.'

'Well – it is a sorry tale. Your father loved her. I expect you've guessed that now, haven't you? Even if he hasn't admitted it.'

'He did admit it, Mum,' Fleur said simply. 'He loved her *then*. Not now. Not since he fell in love with *you* and married *you*.'

362

'Oh well, if that's what you like to think.'

'Look, Mum. Let's have all this out – once and for all. Just what is it that upsets you so much? Do you think Dad had an affair with her? Maybe you think it's been going on all these years. I mean, with all your insinuations you had us – me and Robbie, I mean – thinking that we were half-brother and sister.'

'*Wha-at!*'

'Oh, you can sound surprised, but look at it from our point of view. That first day you were screaming at Dad that he was in love with her and that he's loved her all these years. And you were so ... so vitriolic towards Robbie's mother. And him. It was something terrible. It was all we could think of.'

Betsy wriggled her shoulders. 'Well, I don't know, do I? Maybe they did have an affair. Maybe it has been going on all these years. He's had plenty of chances. All those supposed trips to market. How do I know where he *really* went?'

Fleur shook her head. It saddened her to think that, perhaps for the whole of her married life, Betsy had lived with the torment of imagining her husband was being unfaithful to her. For the first time, Fleur pitied her mother.

'Do you want to know what I think?'

'Does it make any difference?' Betsy snapped, recovering some of her spirit. 'I'm no doubt going to hear it anyway.'

'Dad was in love with Meg, yes, when they were kids in the workhouse.' She saw her mother flinch at the word that obviously brought back dark, unhappy memories. 'He owed her a lot. She

363

had spirit. She gave him the courage to get himself out of there. To seek work here.' She pointed down at the ground, indicating their home, the farm, everything he now owned. Fleur paused a moment, letting her words sink in. And driving her point home she added, 'Just think, Mum, if he hadn't done that he – and you – wouldn't have everything you have now. Where would you have been, eh? Still in the workhouse?'

'It closed in 'twenty-nine,' Betsy murmured, but her protests now were without substance.

'But you wouldn't be here, would you? You wouldn't have been taken in and treated like the Smallwoods' son and daughter and left their farm because their own daughter had run away.'

A spark of sudden interest ignited in Betsy's eyes. 'Is it really her dad that lives with her?'

Fleur sighed inwardly. Still, her mother could not bring herself to speak Meg's name. 'Yes, it is. Evidently the girl he ran off with – Alice, was it?'

Betsy nodded.

'She left him and went off with someone else. He tried to follow her, but this chap got his cronies to beat him up.'

Betsy sniffed and her mouth hardened. 'Serves him right. And her? What happened to Alice Smallwood?'

Fleur shrugged. 'No one knows.'

'She was a bad 'un.'

'As bad as Meg?' Fleur put in slyly.

''Bout the same,' Betsy answered, refusing to give any quarter. 'Made a good pair, they did.'

There was a long silence before Fleur said softly, 'Meg's changed, Mum. She's not the girl you remember any more. Not, by all accounts, since she had Robbie. Having a baby changed her. She made some mistakes, did some terrible things. I see that now and I do understand how it must have hurt you to think that Dad loved her. But he chose *you*. He married *you* and he's stayed with *you*.'

'And that's supposed to comfort me, is it? When all the time I think he's been hankering after her.'

Fleur took in a deep breath. Although she knew that what Betsy said was perhaps true, she had to try to get her mother to get over it and move on. 'I think "hankering" is perhaps the wrong word. I think he remembers her with fondness. I ... I suppose you never forget your first love.' Her voice broke a little, but she carried on bravely. 'But it was a love between children, Mum. What he has with you is different. Very different.'

Betsy gave a sad smile. For once she knew her daughter was trying to help her, trying to get her to let go of the bitterness and resentment she'd held all through the years. But it was impossible. She couldn't expect the young girl who'd only loved and known the love of one man to understand. To understand the heart-wrenching pain of knowing that the man you love and live with is, every day, thinking of someone else. Living your whole life believing yourself to be second best. It was a pain that Betsy had lived with all of her adult life – an anguish that Fleur would never understand unless she experienced it for herself. There was only one person who might understand.

She wondered if Louisa Collins had suffered the same wretchedness.

But Fleur was living her own agony. A sharp, intense pain that would never quite go away, but would, Betsy believed, lessen in time even if Fleur could not believe it now.

With a supreme effort Betsy said, 'I'm sorry about Robbie. Truly. I can't help how I feel about his mother, but I wouldn't wish that on anyone. Not ... not even on her.'

Fleur sighed deeply. It was no use. She couldn't get through to her mother. Betsy would never change.

Forty

Fleur had to face Robbie's mother, but she didn't know how she was going to do it. She almost wished now that she had not bullied her father into telling her the secrets of the past. Perhaps they would, as both Jake and Betsy had tried to tell her, have been better left buried. It had changed her view of Meg; she couldn't help but look at her differently now. It was difficult to imagine the pretty, smiling woman as a scheming temptress who had seduced two men and ignored the man who had always loved her. What puzzled her, though, was why her parents hadn't told her the truth from the outset when she had first met Robbie. If they had maybe–? No, Fleur was honest enough to answer her own question.

No. Nothing they could ever have said would have stopped her. She had fallen in love with Robbie at that very first meeting on the station platform in the blackout and from that moment she'd known – they'd both known – that they had to be together.

The next morning, Fleur packed and came downstairs, ready to leave. She had sponged and pressed her uniform and washed her underwear the previous evening. Now she was ready to go back and get on with fighting the war. The war that had taken away everything she had ever wanted and yet, if it hadn't been for the war, it was unlikely she'd ever have met Robbie.

But she knew that to get back into the thick of it would help. It would help her to feel close to him still.

But, first, there was something else she had to do. She must go to Nottingham. She couldn't avoid it any longer.

'So, you're going back are you?' Betsy said to her as they sat at breakfast.

'I'll take you, love,' Jake began, but Fleur shook her head.

'I'm going to Nottingham first. I'm not due back at camp until tomorrow, but I don't know when I'll get any more leave. Ma'am has been very good, but ... but I'm not the only one...' Her voice cracked and she stopped.

Jake cleared his throat and glanced briefly at his wife before saying, 'Then I'll take you there.'

Betsy opened her mouth as if to protest, but then thought better of it. She got up, clattered the breakfast dishes together and moved away into the scullery, but her shoulders were tense with disapproval.

'It's all right, Dad,' Fleur said gently. 'The trains fit up quite nicely, but if you could just run me to the station in town so I can catch the Paddy to the Junction...'

When Meg opened the door to her, the two women stood staring at each other for a long moment. At first sight, neither looked any different. Meg was still prettily dressed, with her face cream and powder carefully applied. There was even a pale tinge of lipstick on her generous mouth. And Fleur was smartly turned out in her WAAF uniform.

It wasn't until they each looked closely into the other's eyes that they could see the undeniable grief they shared.

'Oh, Fleur!' Meg opened her arms and Fleur fell into them, hugging the older woman.

'Oh, Ma!' was all she could say, poignantly using Robbie's pet name for his mother that brought tears to their eyes.

'Now, now.' Meg, dabbing at her eyes, tried to smile. 'He wouldn't want us to be doing this. Come in, come in...' she urged as she drew Fleur into the warm kitchen.

'Where's ... where's Pops?' she asked at once as she saw the empty chair by the range.

'In bed. He's taken it very hard and, of course, at his age...'

She said no more, but Fleur understood. For someone of his age grief was a strange thing. Some old folk took bad news in their stride. Not that they didn't feel it, but life had conditioned them to deal with tragedies and, if not exactly immune to them, at least they had learnt resilience. But for others, such news was the last straw as if they had no strength left to field another blow. Fleur understood. With each morning, when she awoke, the full horror hit her afresh and she wondered how she would get through the day.

'I suppose,' Meg said as she handed Fleur a cup of tea and sat down in the old man's empty chair opposite, 'that we shouldn't hope.'

Fleur bit her lip. How could she answer? How could she say that every moment of every day she prayed that a miracle would happen? I'll give anything, she kept promising, if only he's alive. 'They – they say not,' she said at last.

Meg sat down opposite her. 'I've had such a nice letter from Wing Commander Jones already. I was surprised. I ... I thought Robbie would have put you down as his next of kin now.'

Fleur smiled wanly. 'I think he must have forgotten to get it changed. Besides, the CO's like that. I think he'd have written to you anyway.'

'And he sent me the names and addresses of the next of kin of all the other members of the crew in case I wanted to write to them. Do you think I should, Fleur?'

'Yes, I've got that list too. Maybe ... maybe we could both write in ... in a week or so.'

Meg nodded. 'Yes – yes, that's what I thought too. Let a bit of time elapse. But ... but I thought I'd like to write to Tommy's family and Johnny's too. All of them really. They helped to make your wedding day so special, didn't they? Such lovely boys...' Her voice trailed away.

Fleur was staring at Meg – she couldn't help it. All the things that her father had told her about this woman were whirling around her brain. And Meg was staring back.

Softly, she said, 'You know, don't you? Jake's told you.'

Fleur blinked and said quickly – too quickly. 'Told me? Told me what?'

'Don't deny it, Fleur. Lying doesn't suit you.'

Fleur felt her cheeks grow hot. How could she have been so foolish as to let her feelings show so openly on her face? It had always been her downfall and now she had let her father down. He'd never forgive her. She tried to salvage the situation by saying, 'I don't know what you mean.'

'Dear Fleur.' Meg shook her head, smiling gently. 'You've got such an open, honest face. You really shouldn't be trusted with secrets.'

Fleur closed her eyes and groaned. 'Please – don't be angry with my dad. It ... it wasn't his fault. I ... I bullied him into telling me.' She sighed. 'And now I wish I hadn't. He swore me to secrecy. Made me promise that I'd never say a word to anyone – especially to you. And now–' Tears sprang into her eyes. 'You've guessed and he'll be so angry with me.'

Meg reached across and, though there was a wistful note in her voice, she said, 'It doesn't matter now, Fleur. Nothing matters now.' There was a long pause before Meg added softly, 'Do you hate me?'

Fleur's eyes widened as she stared at her. 'Hate you? Heavens, no!' and was touched as she saw

Meg's tremulous, grateful smile.

'I couldn't bear it if ... if I never saw you again,' she said. 'You're ... you're all I have left of Robbie. I don't suppose–' Suddenly, her eyes were filled with a fresh hope. 'I don't suppose there's any chance you could be carrying his child?'

Fleur pressed her lips together and shook her head. 'No,' she whispered. 'I only wish I was.'

A week later Meg opened the door, half expecting to see Fleur standing there again. She had promised to visit as often as she could and had said that her commanding officer was being very understanding. The girl had already written twice to her during the week, trying to give comfort even though her own heart was breaking. Meg loved her for that.

But instead of her daughter-in-law standing there, there was someone she had expected never to see again. She felt as if she had been dealt a blow just below her ribs and the breath had been knocked from her body. She clutched at the door for support. 'Philip! Oh my God!'

'Hello, Meg.'

He, of course, had prepared himself for the sight of her, but she'd had no such warning. 'May I come in?'

'Yes – well – yes, of course. But – but–' She stepped back to let him into the house. 'Why are you here? Why have you come? Now, of all times. Why have you come now?'

'I should have come years ago, Meg. I shouldn't have abandoned you and ... and our son so callously.'

371

Meg gasped at his open admission, but he wasn't finished yet.

'If I'd been more of a man, I'd've acknowledged him. Been a part of his life. And now – I've left it too late, haven't I?'

'Oh, Philip,' she said. 'We both made a mistake but ... but you know, I won't ever say I'm sorry for having Robbie. He's been the light of my life. He–' Tears filled her eyes and spilled down her cheeks as Philip clasped her hands. 'He was a wonderful young man. You ... you'd've been proud of him.'

'So Louisa has told me.'

'Louisa? She ... she's talked to you about it?'

Philip nodded soberly. 'Yes. Come – let's sit down and I'll explain. Is there – is there somewhere we can talk alone? I understand you have your father living with you?'

'Yes, I do, but he's still in bed. He – since Robbie – he doesn't get up until the afternoon. It ... it's hit him hard.'

'And you, Meg. I can see you're putting a brave face on it, but you're devastated, aren't you?'

And now the tears that she had tried so hard to keep in check ever since she'd had the telegram flooded down her face and she let out a howl of anguish like a wounded animal. She'd held herself together for her father's sake, for Fleur's sake, but Philip's kind and understanding words had opened the floodgates of her grief.

'Oh, Philip ... how ... am I to ... bear it?'

He put his arms around her and held her close as she sobbed against his shoulder. Even in this dreadful moment, he felt again the stirring of the

372

feelings he'd had for her all those years ago. And though he knew that for her all the passion that had once been between them was gone, he was honest enough to admit that if she had at that moment led him up the stairs to her bedroom, he would have gone willingly, like a lamb to the slaughter. He felt a surge of shame that after his lovely wife's generous forgiveness, he could even think of being unfaithful again. Was it really possible to love two women at the same time? Once upon a time he would have dismissed such a notion as ridiculous, branding it as a man's excuse for philandering. Yet now, he was not so sure. If it was love he felt for Meg, then, yes, it was entirely possible, for he knew he loved Louisa. He always had done. But theirs was the love that deepened and grew through their years together, based on true affection for each other and caring for each other.

Yet Meg had wielded such a seductive power over him. He'd been helpless against the consuming passion he'd felt for her all those years ago that had made him embark on a dangerous affair with her. He had believed, when it ended, that no one but the two of them had been hurt. He knew that she had kept her counsel, that she had told no one, not even her own son, who his father was. But it seemed that fate had had other ideas. In making their boy the spitting image of his father, there was no hiding the truth from those who'd known Philip in his younger days and had, more recently, seen Robbie.

There had been no hiding it – not even from his wife.

He let out a deep sigh and, above her head, he closed his eyes in anguish. He felt her pain and, even though he had never known Robbie, his own grief was for the lost years, the lost chances.

He felt ashamed of the flare of passion he was feeling for this woman, but now, all she wanted from him was comfort in her grief for the loss of her son. Their son. He held her tightly and stroked her hair and his heart was full of regret.

If only, all those years ago, he had been braver.

'Come, Meg. Sit down.' He urged her gently towards a chair. 'Have you any brandy in the house?'

Meg gave a hysterical laugh as she dried her tears. 'You, a doctor? Prescribing brandy.'

'Very medicinal on occasions,' Philip remarked dryly.

'Under the sink in the scullery,' Meg instructed.

As she sipped the amber liquid a moment later, she asked, 'Why have you come?'

'Louisa was at Middleditch Farm visiting Betsy when Fleur came home with the news that Robbie had been posted missing–'

'Presumed killed,' Meg ended flatly.

'They haven't said for sure though, have they?'

Meg shook her head and nipped her lower lip between her teeth.

'Then – then he might be all right. He might have–'

'Fleur doesn't think so,' Meg burst out. 'She's amongst it every day. She should know.'

'Well, yes, but even if his plane was shot down, maybe he baled out, maybe–'

'There were no parachutes.' She looked up at

him, her eyes brimming with tears. 'And it was over the sea. I'm sorry – I know you're trying to be kind. But we have to face it, Philip.'

'Oh, Meg,' he said softly. 'Still as brave as ever.'

She smiled wryly. 'That's not a word I've heard used to describe me very often. Scheming, devious, wicked, a temptress. Oh yes.' She put up her hand as he made as if to argue. 'Yes, I was all those things, Philip. Once. But not any more. Not since the day that Clara Finch tried to kidnap my baby. I saw that as my punishment and if ... if it hadn't been for Jake, I might really have lost him. It was Jake who found him.'

Philip stared at her. 'And it's Jake you've always loved, isn't it? I can see it in your eyes when you speak his name. You love him still, don't you?'

'Yes,' she said simply, too weary to hide the truth any longer. 'Oh, Philip, I was so wrong, so bad. To seduce poor Percy into marrying me just so that I had security...'

'Now, Meg, I won't have you blaming yourself for everything. Percy adored you and in the short time you were married to him, you made him very, very happy. You were loyal and...'

She raised her head and met his gaze. 'But not faithful, eh, Philip?'

'Well, no, but he never knew.'

She shook her head slowly. 'That doesn't excuse it.'

'Of course not, but – but what I mean is – you didn't hurt him.'

'But I hurt Louisa.'

'That was my responsibility. I betrayed my wife, not you. Meg, we share the blame for what we did. You don't carry the burden of guilt alone, you know. And, like I said, I should have behaved in a more gentlemanly way. I should have admitted everything at the time and stood beside you.'

Meg shook her head. 'No, no. You had everything to lose. Your career, your good name – and Louisa.'

'I might not have lost Louisa,' he murmured, as if thinking aloud. 'She says now that if I had told her at the time, she might have been willing to have adopted Robbie. It's been a great sadness to her that we have never had children.'

'But she didn't know that then, did she?'

'No – that's what I told her. It's how she feels now, but I very much doubt she would have felt that way back then.' He paused and then added, 'She told me she came to see you a little while back.'

'It ... it was after she'd seen Robbie for the first time. In a cafe in South Monkford. It ... it must have been a dreadful shock for her.'

'I wonder why she never said anything then?' Philip pondered.

Meg shrugged. 'I wouldn't admit that he was your son. I told her that my father had had fair hair and blue eyes, but I don't think she believed me. I think she had seen the truth only too clearly with her own eyes when she saw Robbie.'

There was a long silence between them before Philip said softly, 'And now she's regretting that she didn't give me the chance to meet my own son.' He caught and held Meg's gaze. 'Would you have let me see him, Meg?'

She was silent a moment more before saying slowly, 'Probably not. You see – I never told him the truth. Perhaps I should have done...' And she went on to tell Philip how Robbie, after meeting Fleur, had begun to ask questions. 'All he wanted was to know that Jake wasn't his father. And, of course, I was able to answer him honestly about that.'

'And he didn't probe any further?'

She shook her head.

'Yet someone or something must have put a doubt in his mind,' Philip said. 'About Percy not being his father, I mean.'

'It was Betsy. She became hysterical when she knew that Fleur had met Robbie and that they wanted to go on seeing each other. Wouldn't have him in the house and wouldn't say why. Naturally, the young ones wanted to know.'

'And so he asked you?'

'Mmm.'

'But you didn't tell him.'

'No. But Fleur knows now. Jake told her recently. Since ... since Robbie was killed.'

'Why on earth has he told her now?'

Meg gave a small smile, thinking of her feisty daughter-in-law and admiring her spirit. 'She said she bullied him into telling her the truth. She told him it couldn't hurt Robbie now and that she wanted to understand why her mother had behaved as she had.' Meg sighed. 'I don't blame her for wanting to know. I would have done in her shoes.'

Philip gave a wry laugh. 'You'd've found out months ago.'

And even Meg had to smile. 'I felt so sorry for her. She didn't mean to let it out that Jake had told her. He'd sworn her to secrecy. But I could see it in her eyes when she looked at me. Not disgust or anger or anything like that, but just ... just something different. Just that – she knew.'

They sat together for several moments until Philip said, 'So – what now, Meg?'

'I don't understand. What do you mean "What now?"'

'What will you do?'

'Do?' She shrugged her shoulders helplessly. 'What can I do but carry on as best I can? Care for my father, hope that Fleur will still visit us now and again.'

'And Jake?'

'What about Jake?'

'Shall you – will you see him?'

'I very much doubt that I shall ever see Jake again. Betsy will see to that.' There was no bitterness or resentment in her tone, merely a calm acceptance of the inevitable, yet Philip could hear the desolation in her tone. She had lost her beloved son and the one man she had ever truly loved was also as good as lost to her.

As if seeing the sympathy written in his eyes, she reached out and touched his hand. 'I'm not the only one to lose my boy. There are so many of us – too many of us – all over the world grieving for the waste of young lives.'

'I know, I know,' he said gripping her hand. 'I'm just so sorry I never met him. But I'll tell you this, Meg, if by some miracle he is still alive, then by God I will see him. I will meet him and I will acknowledge him as my son. I promise you that. If I'm given a second chance, I will try to behave as a father to him.'

Forty-One

Fleur threw herself into her work. When she wasn't on duty she cycled down to the little cottage and attacked the garden as if it was personally responsible for Robbie's death. It was the only way she could think of to stop herself sinking into a dark abyss of grief and regret. Ruth was a tower of strength and even Mrs Jackson and old Harry played their part in helping her to cope.

'Time to plant carrots, love,' Harry told her, leaning on the fence between the two back gardens and jabbing the stem of his pipe towards the freshly dug ground. 'Fancy, it's a year since you came and started all this, lass. Least you haven't got all that grass and rubbish to get rid of this time, eh?'

'No, but I could do to go and see Mr Clegg again. See if his pigs are still producing what I need.'

Ruth came to the cottage too, as often as she could. She still helped keep Harry's house clean, his clothes washed and ironed. 'And he'll not have a bath from one month's end to the next if I don't personally drag the tin bath into that kitchen and push him into it,' she said as they were cycling down one afternoon.

The picture of Ruth pushing Harry into the steaming bath, probably fully clothed, made Fleur smile. She chuckled – the first time she had really laughed since Robbie had been posted missing. 'It's only because he wants you to scrub his back for him.'

Ruth glanced at her friend, relieved to see a brief smile on her face. 'Well, at least now his hair's cut regularly. And his toenails. You should have seen them that first time I did them, Fleur.' She screwed up her face. 'Disgusting, they were. Almost curling round the ends of his toes!'

'No thanks,' Fleur said with feeling. 'I'll stick to my gardening.'

'Actually, if I'm honest, that sort of thing – Harry's mucky feet, I mean – doesn't bother me. My old grandad lived with us when I was a kid and the things my mam had to do for him – well, you don't want to know.' She shrugged. 'But she just accepted it and got on with it. Like ya do. And it was the norm for us kids.'

'You should've been a nurse,' Fleur remarked. 'You'd've been a good one.'

'Mm. Maybe you're right. Well, here we are again,' she said, squeezing the brakes on her bicycle to bring it to a squealing halt. 'You go and tackle Mrs J's garden and I'll tackle old Harry's toenails.'

Fleur laughed again. 'I call that a fair deal.'

Fleur had been working for a couple of hours under the warm sun. She straightened up, mopped her forehead, wet with sweat, and decided to take a breather. She dropped her fork and went to sit on the seat under the apple tree. Leaning her back against the trunk of the tree, she gazed out across the flat expanse of the airfield. It was silent today and she hoped it would stay that way. There hadn't been an air raid for a while now. They'd been lucky but there was an ominous kind of tension in the air as if any day they expected to see the Luftwaffe in the skies overhead again.

In the cottage, Ruth saw Fleur sitting beneath the tree. 'Breaks ya heart, doesn't it? To see her sitting there looking so lost and lonely.'

'It does,' Mrs Jackson agreed. 'And there's nothing any of us can do, is there?'

Sadly, Ruth shook her head. 'Not a thing. I'd go out and join her, but I think she'd rather be alone.'

'There are times when you just want to be by yourself,' the older woman said softly. 'Just to let go for a little while.'

'I know,' Ruth said, remembering only too well how she'd felt at Billy's loss and she hadn't even been married to him. She ached for the pain her friend must be feeling, yet she was helpless to comfort her. There was nothing she could say or do that would bring Robbie back and, right now, that was the only thing that would put a permanent smile back on Fleur's face. The only thing.

The days dragged interminably. Fleur couldn't believe that it was only just over a week since she had had news that Robbie was missing. And there was Kenny to worry about too. Now, he would be up there in the clouds, doing his training, hoping

381

to be good enough to become a fighter pilot. Fleur sighed as she clattered down the steps from the control tower after another shift on duty.

I ought to go home again as soon as I can, she thought, but she shuddered at the thought of facing her mother. Betsy would be worried sick about Kenny and would turn her anger on her daughter. Yet Fleur knew her father would be feeling it keenly too. And she knew too that Jake would be sorrowful for Meg – a feeling he could never talk about with his wife. And I ought to go and see Robbie's mother again. See how the old man is too. It's what Robbie would have wanted me to do. But she shied away from the thought. Seeing Meg's grief only heightened her own.

As she was walking away from the control tower, she heard the dreaded sound of an air raid warning. Automatically, she turned to run to the nearest shelter, but then she remembered. She'd left Kay in the control room finishing off. She glanced back, hoping to see the girl emerging from the tower and running across the grass towards her. But there was no sign of the slim, dark-haired figure.

Fleur bit her lip. She was anxious about Kay. Since the loss of Tommy's plane, Kay had changed. She'd seemed very strong at first, but since she'd come back from leave, she'd been the one to sink into an abyss of misery. Fleur was constantly having to watch her at work to make sure she didn't make any mistakes, for Bob Watson had eyes like a hawk now and his disapproval of wartime romances was still evident every day.

Fleur turned and began to run back towards the watch office. She reached the foot of the steps as the first aircraft came swooping in, dropping incendiaries on the runway only a few feet from the control room.

'Kay! Kay!' Fleur shouted, but knew the girl wouldn't hear her above the noise. She almost fell into the room and then stopped in shock. Kay was standing in front of the long window overlooking the airfield, her arms outstretched, her head thrown back. She was laughing and crying hysterically and shouting, 'Come on. Get me! Get *me!* You've got him, now get me. Here I am...'

At that moment another plane screamed by, so low that Fleur fancied she saw the pilot sitting in the cockpit, could fancy she saw him press the button and pepper the ground with gunshot.

'Kay,' she screamed. 'For God's sake! Get down!' And she launched at the girl, bringing her to the floor and pushing her beneath the desk just as another aircraft dived towards them. The bomb landed just outside the tower, rocking its foundations, blowing all the windows into the room and showering the whole room with deadly shards of glass.

'Where's Fullerton and Bosley – I mean, Rodwell? Have you seen them?'

The raid was over, the all-clear wailing out and staff were emerging from their bolt holes. Bob Watson was first out, demanding of anyone nearby if they had seen 'his girls'. Bluff and disapproving though he might be of their private lives, nevertheless he secretly held them in high regard. Both were excellent in their work, and even though Fullerton had been a little preoccupied these last few days he'd found it in his heart to overlook it. Besides, he assuaged his duty-bound conscience, the other girl – Rodwell, as he must remember to call her – was emerging as the stronger of the two. He had noticed her keeping a keen eye on her colleague and leaping in to avert what could – in the hectic, tense atmosphere of Control – have been a disaster. Twice, to his certain knowledge, Fleur had prevented two aircraft being told to land at the same moment. Strange, Bob Watson couldn't help thinking to himself, how things turned out the way you didn't expect. He'd've laid money on it that the Rodwell girl would have cracked first, been a weeping wreck, whilst the outspoken Fullerton would have shrugged her shoulders, muttered, 'Well, that's war for you,' and moved on to the next handsome airman.

But it seemed, Bob was man enough to admit if only to himself, he'd been wrong.

Now, he was on the verge of panic himself as he realized suddenly just how fond he had become of those two girls, however much he tried to keep himself their aloof superior.

Ruth came running across the grass, shaking her fist in the direction the aircraft had disappeared.

'Bastards! Bastards! We'll get you. You wait till our fighter boys catch up with you...'

'Morrison,' Bob roared at the outraged girl. 'Have you seen Fullerton and Rodwell? Are they with you?'

Ruth stopped at once, her arm still in the air,

her fist clenched. Slowly she let it fall to her side and turned to face him.

'Flight?' she asked stupidly and Bob repeated his question, watching her eyes widen in fear.

'No. I was in the shelter near debriefing. I thought – I mean – aren't they with you?'

'No.' Grimly, his glance went towards the tower. 'I left them in the watch office.'

The tower itself was still standing, but even from here they could both see that not a window was left whole in the building.

'Oh no!' Ruth began to run towards the tower, Bob Watson pounding close behind her. She flew up the steps and thrust open the door, the broken glass crunching beneath her feet, bracing herself for what she might find.

'Fleur! Kay!'

'Here. We're here – under the desk. Can you help me, Ruth? Kay's...'

She said no more but as Ruth bent down and offered her hand, she saw that Kay was as white as a sheet and shaking from head to foot. Tears were running down her face. Ruth's mouth dropped open. 'Kay?' she said in disbelief and again, 'Kay?'

'It's all right now, Kay,' Fleur was saying soothingly as Bob too arrived, panting heavily.

'Are they all right? Oh, good thinking,' he added as he saw they had taken shelter beneath the sturdy desk. 'Out you both come then. They've gone. Can't you hear the "all-clear"? But mind the glass, it's all over the bloody place.' He glanced round at the debris around him. Not only had the windows been damaged but radios and telephones. The blackboards hung drunkenly off the wall and papers had been scattered everywhere. 'Bloody 'ell,' he muttered. 'It'll take a month of Sundays to clear this lot up. And the runway's damaged. I reckon there won't be flying from here for a few days. Come on, you two, what are you mucking about at?'

'It ... it's Kay. I think she's badly shocked,' Fleur said, crawling carefully out from under the desk. 'I can't get her to move.'

Kay was crouched beneath the desk, rocking backwards and forwards. 'Saved my life. She saved my life. Fleur saved my life,' she was muttering.

'Yes, yes, I'm sure she did, but come on out now,' Bob snapped. Now he'd found they were safe, his patience was soon wearing thin.

'We'll sort her out, Flight,' Ruth suggested, standing up. 'Leave it with us. And we'll start and clear up here, if you like.'

'Ah well, yes. I ought to – er – yes, well. I'll leave you to it then.'

He left the room, and when they heard his footsteps clattering down the steps, Ruth breathed more easily. 'Right. Now he's out the way, we can sort her out.' She squatted down again and her tone softened, became cajoling, as she said, 'Come on, love. All over now. Give me your hand. Take her other hand, Fleur. Don't let her kneel else she'll cut her legs. God, what a mess!'

Whether Ruth was referring to the state of the control room or the state of their friend, Fleur could not have said.

'We'd best get her across to the doc's pronto,' Ruth muttered to Fleur and then again turned to

Kay. 'Come on, love, that's it. There you go. Safe and sound.'

'Saved my life, she did.'

Kay emerged slowly from the makeshift shelter but she was still shaking visibly.

'It's the doc for you, Corp,' Ruth said, taking control. 'And you'd better come too, Fleur. You've had a shock an' all.'

'I'm fine. Honestly, but I'll help you take her across and then come back here.'

'Right-o. I'll come back and help you.'

The doctor – as they'd feared – was in great demand, but thankfully only for cuts and bruises. No one, it seemed, had been killed or even seriously injured. The worst casualty seemed to be Kay and that was shock more than physical harm. She hadn't even a scratch though Fleur had cut the palm of her hand on some glass and had bumped her head as she'd dived for cover pushing Kay in front of her.

At last Kay was admitted to the sick quarters for observation. Ruth and Fleur, the cut on her hand bathed and dressed, returned to the control room to help tidy up. Already, there were plenty of willing hands sweeping up the glass, picking up pieces of paper and testing the radios. It would not take as long as Bob had feared to have the control room operational once more.

Fleur was very much afraid that it would take far longer for Kay to heal.

With the airfield out of action for a day or two, Fleur grabbed the chance of a couple of days' leave whilst repairs were carried out. Enough time to go home and to Nottingham.

For some reason she couldn't explain, this second visit to both places seemed more difficult than the first, but she couldn't put the moment off any longer. She ought to go to see Meg again and then she would have to go home. It was easier to get back to camp from her home than from Nottingham because if, for some reason, there was no train running at the time she needed one, her father would always bring her back.

But first she cycled down the road to make sure Mrs Jackson and old Harry were safe and unharmed. A few stray bombs had fallen in the village and she was anxious about the old couple.

But the two cottages looked unscathed and to her relief Harry was sitting drinking tea in Mary Jackson's kitchen.

'Now then, lass. All right?'

Although Harry's greeting was casual, Fleur could see her own relief mirrored in his eyes and Mrs Jackson said outright, 'Oh, love, I'm so glad to see you. We've been that worried. And Ruth? Is she all right?'

'She's fine. She'll be down to see you later, but I've got a forty-eight, so I'm ... I'm going to see Robbie's mother and then going home.'

The old couple exchanged a glance and nodded. There was a pause before Harry, deliberately changing the subject, said, 'That there shelter in the garden you built for us came in handy.' He jabbed his finger towards Mary, teasing. 'And I got her in it, an' all. First time I've managed it on me own. But they was coming a bit too close for comfort yesterday. Don't mind admitting it.'

'We heard one or two had landed in the village. Was anybody hurt?'

Now Harry's face sobered and again he glanced at Mary Jackson. 'A couple of young lads playing down near the stream were killed. Fishing, I expect they were. Always been a favourite place for youngsters. Too busy to think of taking shelter, I dare say. Thought it would be just the airfield being targeted. Y'know?'

Fleur nodded. 'I'm so sorry,' she said.

'Three of Mr Clegg's cows were killed an' all. But that's nothing compared to the loss of a human life...' Old Harry's voice trailed away.

'No, of course it isn't,' Fleur agreed sadly. There was a pause and then she said, 'Well, if you're sure you're both all right, I'll be off. I'll come again as soon as I can.'

'Aye well, there's plenty to do in yon garden.' He jabbed towards the window with his pipe. 'There's a lot of planting to do and there's always hoeing needed. Weeds grow as fast as the plants, ya know.'

'Faster, if you ask me.' Fleur managed to raise a smile. 'But I'll be here.' Already she was looking forward to the peace and quiet of working alone in the garden. Of sitting under the apple tree – her quiet time to think about Robbie.

Forty-Two

Fleur hesitated outside the door, not really wanting to come face to face with Robbie's mother. Meg had seemed so strong when she'd seen her immediately after it had happened. But she'd seen now at first hand how easy it was for a seemingly strong person to crack. Who'd have thought Kay would be the one to end up a quivering wreck? Thankfully, she was already beginning to recover and, much to Fleur's embarrassment, was telling everyone how Fleur had saved her life.

Fleur took a deep breath and raised her hand, but before she could knock the door flew open and Meg was standing there, her face wreathed in smiles.

'Fleur! How lovely to see you. Come in, come in.' Meg reached out, grasped her arm and almost hauled her inside.

Fleur stared at her, anger welling up inside her. Well, she thought, it hasn't taken you long to get over your son's death. How can you be so cheerful? How can you be carrying on with your life as though nothing has happened?

'You got my message then?' Meg said as Fleur stepped into the cluttered front room and followed Meg's trim figure through to the back.

'Message? What message? No, I didn't get any message. All the lines have been down. We had an air raid the day before yesterday. No, I just came because...'

But Meg didn't seem to be listening. She was flinging open the door leading from the front room into the kitchen and announcing Fleur's arrival with a flourish and a beaming smile. 'Just look who's here...'

Perhaps she thinks I'm going to help raise the old man's spirits, Fleur thought. That's what all her cheerfulness is for. To try and buoy the old man up. Fleur tried to force a tremulous smile onto her mouth as she took a step forward past Meg and into the room.

The old man was indeed sitting in his usual chair, but there was someone else sitting in the chair on the opposite side of the hearth. Suddenly, the whole room seemed to spin. She swayed and clutched at the doorjamb. She felt the colour drain from her face and her legs felt as if they would no longer support her.

'Catch her, Ma. She's going to pass out. Damn this bloody leg...'

Fleur felt Meg's strong arms about her as she helped her to a chair near the fire. 'I'll get her some water...' were the last words Fleur heard Meg saying before everything went black.

Someone was bending over her and holding a glass to her lips. She opened her eyes and tried to focus on the beloved face close to her.

'She's coming round.'

Fleur felt clammy and cold and still dizzy, but she murmured, 'I'm all right now. It was just such a shock. I thought ... I thought–' She reached up and touched Robbie's face, still unable to believe that he was really here. Her prayers had been answered. Robbie was alive and smiling down at her. 'I mean, I was told your plane went down in the sea.'

'It did.' Robbie was grinning at her. 'Hence this.' He tapped the plaster cast on his right leg.

'But no one saw a parachute.'

'No time. We were too near the water. But thanks to a brilliant bit of flying by our skipper, who managed some sort of belly flop with the plane – God knows how he did it – we all got out. We were picked up by the local lifeboat and here I am.'

'Yes,' Fleur said, grinning stupidly up at him. 'Here you are.'

Then she promptly burst into tears and clung to him, burying her face against him.

The rest of the afternoon was spent with laughter and tears, hugs and kisses. Tactfully, Meg left them alone with the excuse that she had a dress hem to finish.

'Now, come along, Dad. You can sit in the front room with me for a while. Let's leave these two young ones alone.'

Fleur watched as Meg helped her father to his feet and steadied him as he shuffled into the next room. 'Don't go without saying ta-ta to me, will you, lass?' he said in a quavering voice.

'I won't,' Fleur promised, a lump in her throat as she watched Meg's patient tenderness with the frail old man. Then she turned back to Robbie, still unable to believe the miracle that had really happened. 'Are you really all safe? Tommy too?'

'Yes, all of us. But, like I said, without Tommy's

brilliant flying, we probably wouldn't be.'

'Oh, I can't wait to tell Kay.' Then she told him all about the air raid and Kay, and then for the rest of the afternoon they thought about no one else but themselves...

At five o'clock Fleur said reluctantly, 'I must go.'

'Darling, I wish I could come with you.' He grinned. 'But I really can't hop as far as the station and back – even on my crutches.'

'I'll be all right.'

'Just so long' – he tapped her playfully on the nose – 'as you don't let any strange young RAF types pick you up. Just remember, you're a married woman now.'

She wrapped her arms around him and held him close. 'I won't. I've got the only RAF type I want. And I'll come as often as I can. Are you staying here until your leg's healed?'

'I think so. They couldn't wait to ship me out of hospital as soon as they could. They needed the bed. Oh, darling.' His face sobered. 'I'm so sorry you've been worried. I can't understand why word didn't get through from Bournemouth.'

'Is that where you were? Bournemouth? Isn't that odd?' she murmured. 'Kenny's down south somewhere now.'

'Is he? Is he all right?'

'I hope so. He'll have started his flying training by now. He was so excited. Couldn't wait to start flying. Can't wait to get into the thick of it.'

'I hope he'll be all right,' Robbie said.

'I don't expect it's so bad for the fighter boys, is it? Not now? I mean – they did their bit in the

Battle of Britain.'

Robbie smiled thinly and nodded. He couldn't bring himself to disillusion her. That every day the fighter boys were in the air attacking incoming enemy bombers, trying to stop them reaching their targets.

Maybe Fleur hadn't heard the latest news and he didn't want to be the one to tell her. Hitler had issued orders for his air force to begin a series of attacks upon British cities. Exeter, Bath, Norwich and York had been targeted already and Robbie feared the German leader would turn his attention to the industrial cities of the Midlands next. But he said nothing of this to Fleur. Instead he said, 'I still can't understand why word didn't get through to you that we were all safe. I mean, I wrote to you from there myself, let alone the fact that the War Office should have let them know at Wickerton that all the crew were safe. I can't understand it at all. I think it must be something to do with the telephone lines being down. I tried to phone Mr Tomkins at the shop to let Ma know as soon as I could hop around again.' He tapped his leg again. 'And I tried ringing camp. But I couldn't get through to either of you.'

'Well, the lines are certainly all down now – since the raid. That is a fact.'

'And there I was thinking you were safe and sound.' He held her close. 'Oh, darling, do be careful.'

'I will,' she promised as she kissed him again and again, loathe to leave him. 'But I must go. I must go to Middleditch Farm. Dad will be so pleased to hear you're safe. And I must get back to camp first thing tomorrow morning.'

'Oh, I don't want to let you go,' he said, hugging her tightly to him as they stood at the front door saying their goodbyes. She laughed as she prised herself free and, planting a last kiss on his nose, began to run up the street, turning to wave once more before she turned the corner

The house at Middleditch Farm was strangely quiet as she entered by the back door. The scullery was deserted, but as she stepped into the kitchen she saw her mother sitting motionless in the chair by the range, her head resting on her hand.

'Mum?'

Slowly, Betsy raised her head and stared for a moment at her daughter. Then with a low sound in her throat that sounded almost like a growl, she said, 'Get out! Get out of this house and don't ever come back.' Then she grasped the arms of the chair and pushed herself up. 'Don't ever show your face here again.'

'Mum—'

'Don't "Mum" me. You're no daughter of mine. I have no daughter. It's all your fault. He's gone because of you. My Kenny's gone. And it's your fault. All your fault.'

'Mum – I know he's gone. But he'll be all right. It's not like before when the fighter boys—'

'What d'you mean "He'll be all right"? He's gone, I tell you. Dead. Killed. His plane crashed when he was training. In *training!* He didn't even get to fly a Spitfire like he wanted.' Betsy shook her fist in Fleur's face. 'He's dead – and all because of you.'

For the second time that day, Fleur felt her legs give way beneath her. She felt as if the breath had been knocked from her body. The room swirled around her and she staggered forward towards her father's chair. She sank down weakly, blinking and taking short, panting breaths, trying desperately not to pass out again.

'Oh no – no, you can't mean it. Not Kenny. Not my ... little ... brother.' The heartrending sobs came then, flooding out of her. She was shaking, feeling cold, so very cold.

Yes, her mother was right. It was all her fault. Kenny had only joined the forces because she had done so. He hadn't wanted to be outdone by his sister. But there was worse than that. Much worse than even her mother knew. Fleur had tried to bargain with God. What was it she had said? 'I'll give anything, if only You'll let him be alive.' So now, Kenny had been taken in his place.

Fleur was beside herself with anguish. From the heights of joy that Robbie was alive, she was plunged once more into the depths of despair. Her grief was a physical pain. She wrapped her arms around herself and rocked to and fro in the chair, sobbing in agony.

'Oh aye, you can shed tears now, can't you? Why didn't you think of that before? Why didn't you stop him going? Why did you ever–?'

'I did. I tried. I begged him not to go,' Fleur screamed. 'He'd've gone anyway, whatever I'd said or done.'

Neither of them heard the back door open and

396

close, but suddenly Jake was in the room and hurrying towards Fleur. He knelt beside her chair and put his arms about her. Fleur hid her face against his shoulder, the sobs still racking her body.

'That's right. You comfort her. You comfort each other. But who's going to comfort me?'

Jake looked up at his wife, his own eyes bleak with suffering, his face ravaged with loss. 'Fleur's had a double loss, Betsy love,' he said gently. 'First Robbie and now this. Can't you – just for once – feel for her?'

Betsy stared at them both for a moment, but instead of turning and running up the stairs as she usually did, she sank back wearily into her chair as if utterly defeated, without the will or the strength to argue any more.

Fleur raised her head slowly and whispered, 'No, Dad. That's ... that's what I came home to tell you. Robbie's turned up. He's alive. The pilot managed to ditch the plane in the sea, just off our coast and ... and they all got out. He's got a broken leg but–'

Betsy lay back in her chair and began to laugh and cry hysterically. 'Oh, that's good, that is. Her son is saved. It'd have to be *her* son that was saved, wouldn't it?'

Jake and Fleur stared at her, helpless to do or say anything.

Forty-Three

Early the following morning, before either of her parents were up, Fleur slipped away from Middleditch Farm. She hitched a lift into the town with an early milk lorry, but before going to the station Fleur slipped into the church in South Monkford. She sat down in a pew near the front and laid her cap, gas mask and bag on the seat beside her. She sat for a long time, just staring ahead at the altar. The tears ran silently down her face and she didn't even bother to wipe them away. She didn't pray. She didn't know how to now. She couldn't even bring herself to give thanks for Robbie's safe return. She didn't know what to say. Not now.

A man came out of the vestry. He crossed to the centre of the chancel, bowed to the altar and then turned and came down the steps towards her. He was dressed in a lounge suit, but in place of a shirt and tie he was wearing the collar of a clergyman. He wasn't the vicar she'd known since childhood: this man was a stranger. Old Revd Pennyfeather must have retired, she thought vaguely, but her mind was too numbed to even want to ask. The man hovered for a moment at the end of the pew where she was sitting. Then he sat down beside her, following the line of her gaze for a moment and staring, too, at the brass cross on the altar.

'You know it's a terrible thing to admit, but I really don't know what to say to people any more.'

Fleur said nothing.

He turned his head slightly to glance at her. 'But the good Lord will–'

Fleur held up her hand to silence him, but still she did not speak.

'Would you ... like to tell me what's troubling you?'

She let her hand sink back down to rest on her lap, but she just continued to stare at the cross on the altar. Still she did not answer him.

'Would you like us to pray together?'

Still, there was silence until, haltingly, Fleur spoke in a hoarse whisper. 'I have no right to pray.'

She held her breath, expecting him to come out with some trite remark. To her surprise, he just said, 'Why?'

Another long silence before she dragged out the words. 'Because ... I tried ... to bargain with God. And lost.'

'Ah.' The sound held a wealth of understanding and sympathy. Fleur turned her head slowly and looked at the man for the first time.

He was small and white haired with a kind face. She could imagine that normally his face would be wreathed in smiles, that he would have a lively, almost saucy sense of humour, but at the moment, the lines on his face drooped with sadness. 'Would you like to tell me about it, my dear? Perhaps I can help.'

'No offence, Vicar, but I doubt it.'

'Try me anyway.'

Several minutes passed before Fleur could bring herself to speak. At first the words came slowly and then faster and finally in a flood as she poured out her anguish.

'My husband – we'd only been married a few months – was posted missing, presumed killed.'

'Oh, my dear, I'm sorry–'

'No – no – he's come back. That's the trouble, you see.'

The man was naturally puzzled. Fleur rushed on trying to explain in short, staccato phrases. 'I'm sorry. I'm not explaining this very well. We met by accident. On a railway station. In the blackout. We didn't know it then, but our parents – well, my parents and his mother – had known each other years ago. There were – well – complications, and when my mother found out who he was she refused to meet him. Refused to let him come to our home. She ... she didn't even come to our wedding. And then ... and then there was my brother, Kenny.'

Fresh tears welled in her eyes. 'He was younger than me. When I joined the WAAFs, he made up his mind he was going to volunteer too. As soon as he was old enough. And ... and he did.'

'Why do you say "volunteer"? He'd've been called up sooner or later.'

Fleur shook her head. 'We live on a farm.'

'Ah,' the vicar said, understanding at once. There was no need for her to say more.

For a moment, Fleur covered her face with her hands. Then she straightened up, brushed away her tears, sniffed and went on. 'When my husband was posted missing, I prayed. Oh, how I prayed. And ... and that's where I made my mistake. You see, I said, "I'll give anything if only You'll let him be alive." And now ... now He's given Robbie back to me but ... but He ... He's taken my brother in Robbie's place. Kenny's plane crashed while he was training. He never even got to fight the enemy. And that was what he wanted to do most of all. He wanted to help save his country.'

The older man laid his hand gently on her shoulder and said softly, 'That's not how the good Lord works, my dear. We've all, in our time, been guilty of doing exactly what you've done. Promising anything so that we get what we want. God hears, He listens – but do you really think He's going to take a scrap of notice of our – well, as you put it – "bargaining" with Him? I think not.'

'I feel as if I'm being punished.'

'No, no, you shouldn't feel that. You really shouldn't. God has His reasons.'

'What reasons? How can there be a God when all this is happening? How can He let it happen? All these young men – a whole generation – being wiped out. Again. Just like the last terrible war. Why?'

'Don't you think we all ask that? But I see it as a test. A test of our faith.'

'Huh! Some test!'

'I know, I know. That's why it's called "faith". We have to believe without question, without being given answers or reasons why things happen. We just have to put our trust in God. And you see, to God, your brother isn't dead. None of these brave young men are. They're in a far better place than we are right now. In the arms of Jesus.' He paused a moment, before asking quietly, 'Do you believe that?'

'I ... I'd like to, but it's hard.'

'Oh yes.' The vicar gave a wry laugh. 'It's hard. I'll grant you that. I have to admit, I sometimes feel weighed down with all the suffering and heartache I see every day. I've railed against Him, but somehow He keeps sending me the strength to carry on giving comfort where I can.'

'My mother blames me for Kenny joining up,' Fleur burst out. 'She'll never forgive me. She ... she says she doesn't want to see me ever again.'

'I'm sorry to hear that,' he said and Fleur marvelled that, yet again, he didn't make any kind of trite remark, saying that given time she would come round. Slowly, Fleur turned to face him. 'You've been very kind and understanding,' she said and added simply, 'thank you.'

'Would you like to pray with me now?'

Fleur nodded and together they slipped to their knees. The vicar began to speak in a soft, deep tone, making up the words of a prayer to suit. He asked for forgiveness and understanding for Fleur in her sorrow and for reassurance that she bore no blame. He prayed, too, for Fleur's parents in their grief and especially for her mother who found her loss so hard to bear. He ended by inviting Fleur to join him in saying the Lord's prayer.

As she left the church a little later, Fleur was surprised to find she felt a great sense of calm settle on her. It would be some time before she would be able to forgive herself, but with the help of the kindly clergyman she had made a start.

'Come back and see me any time, my dear. I'm always here.'

'Thank you,' she said and, as she walked away from him down the path, she was already giving thanks in her mind that she had met him.

As she entered the main gate, Ruth came rushing towards her. 'I've been watching out for you. We've only just heard. Isn't it wonderful? Everyone's so delighted for you. And Kay. You must go and see her. She's almost back to her old self. I think they'll be letting her out of the hospital tomorrow. Have you seen him? How is he?' Her face was wreathed in smiles, but then she became aware that Fleur's face was not so joyous. 'What is it? Is he badly hurt?'

Fleur shook her head. Flatly, with no hint of the turmoil of emotion inside her that she was trying, desperately, to hold in, she said, 'No. Only a broken leg. Once that's mended, he – he'll be back.'

Ruth blinked, staring at her friend's face. Then, slowly, thinking she understood, she nodded. 'Oh, I see. Once he's well, he'll be flying again. Is that it?'

Fleur lifted her shoulders in a helpless shrug. 'Partly, I suppose.'

Ruth stepped closer and put her arm around Fleur's shoulder. 'It's more than that. I can see it is. Fleur, tell me what's wrong?'

Slowly, Fleur looked up into her friend's eyes. Hesitantly, she dragged out the words she had prayed never to have to speak. 'It ... it's Kenny.'

Close to her, she heard Ruth's sharp intake of breath, saw her eyes widen in shock and fear. 'Kenny? Oh no!' She shook her head, refusing to believe it. 'Oh no! Not Kenny.'

'He crashed while training. In *training*, Ruth. How unfair is that?'

'Silly bugger!' Ruth muttered, but her eyes filled with tears. 'The stupid, stupid bugger.'

Her arm dropped from around Fleur. Her head lowered and she covered her face with her hands, her shoulders shaking. Now it was Fleur who comforted Ruth.

'I knew I shouldn't do it,' Ruth wailed.

'Do what?' Fleur asked gently.

'Let myself like him. I put a jinx on people.' She let her hands fall away and raised her head. Her face was wet with tears. 'Oh, Fleur,' she whispered. 'I'm so sorry. It ... it's all my fault.'

Despite her misery, Fleur smiled a little. 'Darling Ruth, if anyone's to blame, it's me. He joined up because I had. That's what my mother thinks. And, of course, I blame myself too.'

Ruth wiped her face with a quick, fierce action. 'It's this bloody war that's to blame. Nothing – and no one – else. Not you, not me. Just the war.'

'You're right. It's not our fault.' Fleur sighed and murmured, 'But I can't help feeling so guilty.'

Ruth, a little more in control of herself, said, 'You ought to ask for compassionate leave. You ought to go home to be with your mam and dad.'

Fleur shook her head sadly. 'I've been. Mum's more or less told me not to bother going home again. Besides, I reckon I've used up all my leave on compassionate grounds. Ma'am's been very good, but just about everyone on camp has a good reason for asking for leave. I can't expect any more for a while now.'

'But what about Robbie? Won't they let you go and see him?'

'I doubt it. But d'you know something, Ruth? I don't mind going weeks without seeing him, if it means keeping him out of this war for a while longer.'

Ruth pursed her lips and nodded. 'Well, I'm with you there.'

They walked slowly towards the WAAF quarters. 'Tell me what happened to Robbie,' Ruth asked. 'All we know is that they were picked up by the lifeboat and all the crew are safe, though there are a few injuries between them.'

Swiftly, Fleur told her all that Robbie knew. 'He said it was all down to the skill of their skipper. But for Tommy, none of them would be here.'

Ruth smiled. 'Yeah. Tommy's a great bloke. All of them are. I'm so glad they're all safe.' Her voice petered out and they were silent, both with their own thoughts of Kenny, the one they had both cared for. The one who hadn't come back.

Forty-Four

Fleur was wrong about having used up her entitlement to compassionate leave. Two days after her return to camp, she was summoned to see the WAAF commanding officer.

'I'm glad to hear your husband is alive, but I understand you have suffered the loss of a near relative. Your brother?'

'Yes, ma'am,' Fleur answered quietly.

'I'm surprised you haven't requested leave to go home.'

'I–' Fleur began and then faltered. She was about to admit that she believed she wasn't wanted at home. She bit her lip and then altered what she had been about to say. 'I thought – I mean – I didn't think I'd be entitled to any more. Not for a while, ma'am.'

Caroline Davidson looked down at the papers on her desk, appearing to consult them. 'Your friend, Morrison, has offered to cover your duties. She was trained in R/T work before remustering to become an intelligence officer. She feels – though she has not betrayed your confidence – that there are special circumstances in your case why a further period of compassionate leave should be granted to you.' She looked up again, her clear blue eyes boring into Fleur's. 'I expect your parents would welcome your support at this time?'

Fleur licked her lips. Her heart was beating painfully. She didn't like telling lies, yet if she agreed with her superior and was granted extra leave, she could go to see Robbie. Even if she was found out and punished, it would be worth it for a few extra precious hours with him.

Concentrating on her father's feelings rather than her mother's, Fleur was able to say truthfully, 'Yes, ma'am, I'm sure they would.'

Caroline leant back in her chair and smiled, her

blue eyes twinkling with a sudden mischief. 'And, of course, if your transport arrangements should have to take you via Nottingham...'

Fleur stared at her for a moment, speechless. Really, she was thinking, sometimes their superior officers were capable of showing their human side.

Caroline straightened up and shuffled the papers on her desk with a brisk, businesslike movement. 'I can't let you go for a couple of weeks, I'm afraid. The forecasters think we're in for a spell of good weather and you know what that means.'

'Yes, ma'am.'

'So – we'll see in a couple of weeks' time. Come and see me then.'

'Thank you, ma'am.' Fleur saluted smartly and left the office, still unable to believe her luck. But, she realized, it wasn't so much down to luck as to her friend, Ruth. She went to find her to tell her what had transpired. Ruth listened with a wide grin on her face, particularly when Fleur reached the part about the transport arrangements.

'She's a nice old stick, really, though she can be a tartar if you kick over the traces.'

'Old stick!' Fleur laughed. 'She can't be much older than us.'

Ruth wrinkled her brow. 'No, I suppose not when you think about it. I expect it's just her rank that makes you think she must be as old as the hills.'

They laughed together and then Ruth's smile faded. She eyed her friend keenly as she said, 'Er, we're not on duty until six. I – um – reckon we ought to cycle out to Mrs Jackson's...'

Before she had finished speaking, Fleur was shaking her head. 'Oh no, I can't face her. Not yet. She was ever so fond of Kenny...'

'I know,' Ruth said softly and touched Fleur's arm. 'All the more reason why we should go and see her. And old Harry. If they've heard, they'll wonder why we haven't been to see them. And if they haven't been told, then ... then it's us that ought to tell them.'

Fleur sighed deeply. 'You're right. I know you're right. It's just – just...'

'I know, I know,' Ruth said softly. 'But we'll go together. I'll be with you.'

Fleur was touched by her friend's thoughtfulness. Despite her adamant declarations that she would not allow herself to get seriously involved with anyone whilst the war was on, Ruth had allowed herself to become fond of Fleur's brother. And whilst she was strong, the same sadness that was in Fleur's heart was mirrored in Ruth's. Yet she was still sensitive to the feelings of others who had known – and liked – Kenny.

'You're right,' Fleur said firmly, summoning up her own strength. 'We ought to go. In fact, we'll go right now before I chicken out.'

Ruth smiled. 'Oh, you're not one to do that.' She linked her arm through Fleur's as they went in search of their bicycles.

'Oh, my dears,' Mrs Jackson held out her arms, trying to embrace them both as they let themselves in through her back door and stepped into the kitchen. Tears ran down her wrinkled cheeks. 'Harry only heard yesterday. He told me last night. We're so very sorry. Your poor mother...' She patted Fleur's arm. 'Sit down, dear. I'll make a cup of tea.'

'I'll do it,' Ruth said. 'Then I'll nip round to Harry's. And you' – she wagged her forefinger in Fleur's face – 'can get down to a bit of digging when you've drunk your tea. Do you good.'

As they sipped their tea, Fleur asked tentatively, 'You ... you had heard about Robbie? That he's safe?'

The old lady nodded and smiled. 'Yes. Harry heard that at the same time.' She sighed. 'Dearie me, what terrible times we're living in. We were thrilled to hear that, but then the awful news about that lovely boy...' She wiped the tears from her eyes with the corner of her apron. 'It doesn't bear thinking about.'

Ruth returned a few minutes later with Harry in tow. The old man patted Fleur on the shoulder and just said, 'Now then, lass,' but the tone of his voice and his action spoke volumes. His sympathy and understanding, though not put into words, were very real. 'Plenty of work in the garden, lass. Need any help?'

Fleur smiled tremulously. Robbie was out of action for some time and Kenny... Poor Kenny. She'd never hear his cheerful whistle and see his broad grin again. Oh, how she would miss him and not just for his help in the garden.

'I'd better get on. I – we – can't stay long today.'

'I'll bring your tea out to you then.'

Minutes later Fleur was digging in the garden. So many times Kenny had been here beside her, helping her. She had thought that the memory, the poignancy, would be upsetting, but in fact she found it comforted her. She kept glancing up, half expecting to see him a few feet away digging alongside her. Involuntarily, her ears strained for his merry whistle. But there was only the sound of the wind rustling in the apple tree and the sound of bird song.

When Ruth brought out their tea, the two girls sat together on the bench beneath the tree.

'Robbie'll soon be back here with you, sitting under the apple tree.' They smiled at each other.

Fleur nodded, though just at this moment she could not share her thoughts with Ruth. There was another thought that had just crept its way into her mind. I wonder, she was thinking, if Dr Collins has heard that his son is still alive.

Louisa was waiting at the front door when her husband drew his car to a halt in front of the house and climbed wearily out of it.

Oh, he looks so tired, Louisa thought. This war's almost as bad for him as the last one. She had been waiting on tenterhooks for hours, ever since she had heard the two pieces of news. One would bring him further sadness. And the other? Well, of course he would be glad that Robbie was safe. But with that piece of news would come further complications. Louisa knew he had visited Meg. He had told her on his return from the city.

'There are to be no more secrets between us, Louisa,' he had said, taking her hands in his. 'You have been a dear, dear girl in being so understanding and – and forgiving – and the last thing

410

I want to do is to cause you any more pain, but–'
Here he'd paused, not knowing quite how to
continue, so Louisa had squeezed his hands and
said softly, 'Philip – I do trust you. As long as you
promise to tell me everything, we can deal with
whatever happens – together.'

'Oh, my dear,' he had said, taking her in his
arms and holding her close. 'I don't deserve you.'

Then she had laughed, trying to lighten the
emotion of the moment, and teasing him had
said, 'No, you don't.'

And then they had sat down together, the glow
from the fire in the grate giving them the only
light in the room, whilst he had told her of his
visit to Meg. He ended by saying, 'I shan't see her
again, Louisa, I promise you that unless ... unless
by some miracle Robbie comes back. Because ...
because I told her that if he did then ... then–'
Again, he had faltered not wanting to hurt her.

But Louisa was not only forgiving, she was compassionate and she finished the sentence for him.
'You'd want to meet him and get to know him.'

He nodded, but he had such a hangdog expression on his face, like a naughty boy that had been
caught scrumping apples, that Louisa had
laughed aloud and touched his cheek. 'Oh, my
dear, of course you would. He's your son.'

'You – you wouldn't mind?'

She had shaken her head. 'Not now, no. Once I
would've done. Once I would have minded
dreadfully. You were right when you said that my
idea that we could perhaps have adopted him was
foolish. I was, as you so rightly said, only speaking
with the benefit of hindsight. I've thought about

411

what you said a lot since we talked and I've admitted to myself that, no, at the time I would have been far too upset to have even thought such a thing. But ... but not now. I'm older and I hope a lot wiser. What happened in the past cannot be changed. He's your son. There's no denying that. I saw it for myself. Of course, if we'd had children of our own then it might have taken a little more thinking about, for their sake. It would have been a shock for them to discover they had a half-brother, but since we haven't...' Her voice trailed away.

Philip had squeezed her hand. 'I ... I don't think Meg would let us see him very often. I mean I don't think she would want him to become – well – part of our family.'

Louisa had smiled softly. 'If the Lord is good to us and he comes back, then I don't think she will have any say in the matter. He's a grown man and he will make his own decision.'

Philip had sighed heavily. 'Only if she agrees to tell him that I am his natural father.'

Louisa's eyes had widened. 'You ... you mean he didn't know? She never told him?'

Philip shook his head.

'Oh,' was all Louisa had said then and silence had fallen between them. They'd not spoken of the matter again but now, as she waited at the door to greet him, she knew they had a great deal to discuss. The miracle – and all that it entailed – had happened.

He was coming up the path towards her now, smiling as he approached. 'Hello, my dear.' Then, as he became aware of her anxious face, he added, 'Is something wrong?'

'No – yes, well – oh, come in, Philip. Your supper's all ready. We'll talk later.'

He glanced at her, seeing she was on edge, but he said mildly, 'Whatever you say, my dear,' as she helped him out of his coat and took his medical bag out of his hand.

Louisa picked at the food on her plate, eating so little that at last Philip leant towards her across the table and said, 'I think, my dear, you'd better tell me now, else you're going to waste all this lovely food you've spent hours preparing. And' – he smiled – 'you're making me so nervous that my appetite's disappearing by the minute. Now, tell me. What has happened?'

Louisa laid down her knife and fork and looked up at him. 'Firstly, I must tell you that poor Kenny has been killed. In training, would you believe? Isn't that cruel? I've been to see Betsy today and she's in a dreadful state. Poor Jake too. He's like a zombie. Just going through the motions of work but ... but they're both devastated.'

Philip's face fell into lines of sadness and he let out a long, deep sigh. 'Oh dear. I'm so very sorry to hear that.'

There was silence between them whilst they each spared a thought for the boy whose life had been so cruelly snatched away before Louisa added, 'But there is good news.'

Philip smiled bleakly as if nothing could be counted as 'good news' after what she had just told him.

Watching his face, she said softly, 'Robbie is alive.'

His head jerked up and she saw the spark in his eyes and knew that, whatever it cost her, she had to let him get to know his son.

'Alive? How – I mean – what happened? Do you know?'

'Jake told me. He didn't mention it in front of Betsy, but he followed me out into the yard to tell me. Robbie's plane came down in the sea only just off the coast and the local lifeboat rescued all the crew. He has a broken leg, but apart from that, he's fine.'

Philip let out the breath he'd been holding in a huge sigh of relief whilst Louisa went on. 'It seems that Fleur didn't know until she arrived at Meg's house in Nottingham. She'd been granted compassionate leave to go to see his mother only to walk in and find him sitting there. It seems they didn't even know on the station until just before she got back. There'd been an air raid and all the telephone lines were down. And then, when she was so happy, she went to Middleditch Farm on her way back to camp only to hear that Kenny had been killed.'

'Good news one minute and bad the next, eh?' Philip said. 'Poor Fleur.'

'Betsy's turned totally against her. She's blaming Fleur for it happening.'

'For Kenny volunteering, you mean?'

Louisa nodded.

He sighed. 'I'll have to go and see her. Betsy, I mean. See if I can talk to her. I might be able to help.'

'Philip – there's something else.'

He glanced at her, waiting.

414

'Jake told me that after Robbie was posted missing, presumed killed, Fleur pressed her father to tell her about ... about the past.' She ran her tongue nervously around her lips but Philip finished her sentence for her.

'And he did. He told her just who Robbie's father is?'

'Yes,' Louisa whispered.

'And you think she'll tell Robbie?'

'Well – yes.'

'D'you think Meg realizes Fleur knows?'

Louisa shrugged. 'Jake says he swore her to secrecy. Made her promise never to say a word to Meg, but, I mean, now he's come back...'

'Who's to know what will happen?' he murmured and, whilst his wife picked up her knife and fork to finish her meal, Philip sat lost in thought.

Forty-Five

Two weeks later, having been granted special leave, the thoughts that now occupied Philip's waking hours also slipped into Fleur's mind. She didn't like having secrets from Robbie, but as her father had once said to her they weren't their secrets to tell.

She went straight to Middleditch Farm, but her mother would not speak to her, would not even acknowledge her presence and deliberately turned her back on her. Fleur stayed only an hour, talking with her father in the yard and then begging a lift to the station to catch the train to the Junction and then on to Nottingham, arriving late in the afternoon at the terraced house. She had, of course, written every other day to Robbie, so he knew about Kenny, but she had not mentioned anything about what Jake had told her. Nor did she intend to. She had made up her mind. It was Meg's place to tell her son, not Fleur's. She wondered if she had already done so. Though Fleur knew nothing of Philip's visit and the quandary Meg now found herself in, she did believe that Robbie should know the truth. But it wasn't her place to tell him.

'Well, if it's not Long John Silver.' She grinned as the door opened and Robbie stood there.

'Darling! How wonderful,' he said, pulling her inside, shutting the door and enfolding her in a bear-like hug all in one movement. 'However did you wangle more leave?'

'Ma'am's been very good. She actually called me to her office. This is supposed to be compassionate leave for Kenny, but I'm not really wanted at home...' And then she could say no more, because he was kissing her hungrily.

Some time later, they emerged into the light of the kitchen. 'Look who's here,' Robbie said, limping into the room.

'As if I hadn't guessed.' Smiling, Meg got to her feet and hugged Fleur. 'Darling girl, we're so sorry to hear about Kenny. How are your mother and father?'

Fleur pressed her lips together. 'Not good.'

'Here, come and sit by the fire. I'll make some tea.'

'I've been to the farm today, but Mum won't even speak to me. She blames me, you see.'

'Yes, you said before. I'm sorry. I wish I could help, but...' She left the sentence unfinished but they all understood.

Fleur glanced towards the old man's empty chair beside the range. 'Where's Pops? Is he all right?'

'He is now Robbie's safe. He's in bed, but he always goes early. He's fine. Better than he was.'

Fleur smiled with relief and sat down in his chair.

'There, love, drink that.' As Meg handed her a cup of tea, Fleur looked up and met the older woman's gaze. There was no mistaking the look of pleading in her eyes. Don't tell him, she was asking silently. Don't say anything. Unseen by Robbie, who had hopped out of the kitchen into the scullery in search of something to eat, Fleur smiled and gave a little nod.

Meg bent closer and whispered, 'I shall tell him, Fleur. I just ... just haven't had the right moment.'

'It's all right. I promise I won't say–'

'And what are you two whispering about?'

'I was just asking your mother if you've been behaving yourself.'

Robbie laughed and pulled a face. 'I'm bored out of my skull.'

Meg, straightening up, laughed. 'We're not very exciting company, I'm afraid. Just me and the old man.'

'I didn't mean that, Ma. I love being with you. It's just that it's all going on without me.'

'Just be thankful it is for a while,' Fleur replied tartly. 'It's giving us all a bit of a rest knowing you're safe. Think about us for once instead of being the hero.'

There was silence until Fleur covered her face and said contritely, 'Oh, I'm sorry – I'm so sorry. That sounded awful. It came out all wrong. I just ... I just – what with you going missing and we all thought you were dead and then Kenny...'

'Darling, it's all right.' Robbie hopped towards her, rescued the cup of tea that was in danger of slipping out of her grasp and then sat down close to her and took her hands. 'I understand. I know it's worse for you and Ma and Pops when I'm up there. You see, we've all too much to think about when we're in the thick of it, but you're just all waiting – and fearing the worst. It must've been dreadful for you the night we didn't come back.'

Fleur sniffed. 'It was. I stood for ages just watching the blank space on the board.'

'It's worse for Fleur than for us in a way,' Meg said gently. 'She's on the spot seeing what's happening.'

'Do you think you should apply for a transfer?' Robbie suggested, but before he had finished speaking Fleur shot back, 'No! I want to be there. I want to be near you. I *have* to be near you, even if it is tearing me apart. I'm not the only one: there are several girls on camp with boyfriends or fiancés – even one or two more are married like us. It's the same for them.' She pulled in a deep breath and forced a tremulous smile. 'No, I've just got to keep going but – just for a while – whilst you're laid up, I've got a bit of a respite.

And, now you've done a full tour, you...'

Her voice faded away at the rather sheepish look on his face. Her heart sank. Without him saying a word, she knew that Robbie would get back on operations as soon as he could. But she said nothing more. She didn't want to worry his mother. At least she could let Meg stay in blissful ignorance if only for a while. She forced a smile as she added, 'Now you're grounded, we can all relax.'

She looked up at him and he smoothed her hair back from her forehead. 'Except that you've lost Kenny,' he murmured.

'Yes,' she said heavily. 'I've lost Kenny.' She closed her eyes and leant against him. Perhaps one day she would tell him about the heavy guilt that lay on her. How she had bargained for Robbie's life. But not just now. She couldn't speak of it just now. It was all too raw.

The hours of her short leave were over all too quickly. Her goodbyes said, she left the house as the air raid warning sounded. Fleur hurried along the street. I hope Robbie and his mother and Pops go to the shelter. Robbie can hobble that far on his crutches, she thought. And if I can make it to the railway station, I'll be safe there... She could hear the drone of enemy aircraft yet no bombs seemed to be falling on this part of the city. As she hurried along she was sure she heard thuds in the distance, and saw the night sky to the north of the city illuminated by exploding bombs.

Some poor devils are taking a hammering, she

419

thought, but at least it's not us tonight. Reaching the station, she found that the trains had been delayed.

'Air raid Newark way,' the waiting passengers were informed. 'No trains running until it's over.'

And even when it was and the all-clear sounded, the announcement came that the line had been damaged and no trains would be running that night.

'Oh Lor',' Fleur muttered. 'I'm going to be in trouble. I'll be late back at camp. And I'm not even supposed to be in Nottingham. Oh heck!'

'You stranded like us, love?' a merry voice called out and Fleur turned to see three young men in RAF uniforms standing together.

'Seems like it.' She smiled and moved closer. 'Where are you heading?'

'A place called Wickerton Wood.'

Fleur's smile widened. 'Me too. I'm stationed there.' She held out her hand and the four of them exchanged first names. Then Fleur suggested, 'Shall we share a taxi?'

'A taxi? That'll be awfully expensive, won't it?'

'Not if the four of us chip in.'

'Righto – I'll see if there are any outside the station, though they might all have gone by now...' The youngest-looking one of the three men dropped his kitbag and loped off in search of transport.

The others stood together, feeling awkward, smiling in that embarrassed way that strangers meeting for the first time do. In only a few minutes the airman returned. 'There's just one left,' he panted. 'Says he'll take the four of us.' His grin widened. 'And he'll only charge us for the petrol. He's got a lad in the RAF down south. A fighter pilot. He's glad to help, he says. Hopes someone'll do the same for his lad if he's stranded anywhere.'

'Righto. Come on, love. Need any help?'

'I'm fine.' Fleur smiled. 'As long as he gets us back to camp, I'll ride on the running board.'

They laughed but they all squeezed into the car, three squashed in the back and the airman with the longest legs taking the front seat beside the driver.

'Now then, mi duck, what are you doing out with these young rascals?'

Fleur laughed. 'I've only just met them on the platform whilst we were waiting for the train. I've just been home to see my *husband*.'

There was a unanimous groan and one of the airmen said, 'Just my luck! And there I was thinking I'd met the girl of my dreams.'

In the darkness, Fleur smiled to think that that was just how she had met Robbie.

There was laughter before another asked, 'Your husband? What does he do?'

'He's a wireless operator on bombers, but he's on sick leave. A broken leg.' She stopped herself saying more. These boys looked incredibly young. They were probably just out of training. Maybe this was their first posting. It wouldn't do to talk to them about crash-landings.

'How did that happen?'

Fleur chuckled. 'You seem to be asking an awful lot of questions. I'm not sure I should be telling you.' And again, the car was filled with laughter.

They chugged along, going at a steady pace

421

through the blackout with only the pencil-thin beams from the partially blacked-out headlights to illuminate their way. It wasn't until the early hours that they reached the gates of the camp.

'Now for trouble,' Fleur muttered as she clambered out. 'I'm about four hours late.'

'So are we,' one of the airmen said cheerfully. 'But it's hardly our fault Jerry decided to drop a few bombs – just to make us feel welcome.'

'Right, tip up, chaps. Let's pay this kind feller for bringing us. At least we've got here. If we'd waited for the train it could have been a week on Tuesday!'

Fleur fished in her bag to find her money but the airman said, 'No, love. We'll sort it. It'll be nice for us to have a friendly face about the camp. This is our treat. All right, lads?'

'Yeah, course it is. Where is it you work, Fleur? Canteen, is it?'

Fleur smiled to herself. Why did all men take it that the only job women could do was to serve them their meals?

'No. I'm in Control. I'm an R/T operator.'

'Really? That's great. It'll be good to know we've got you watching out for us when we're up there.'

Did she imagine it, or was there a tiny note of apprehension in the young man's voice?

Fleur was allowed straight into the camp, but she had to bid the others farewell whilst they waited for their identities to be checked and all the formalities for new arrivals to be gone through. Thankfully, Fleur slipped away into the darkness towards the WAAF quarters and crept into the room she shared with Ruth.

'Oh, thank goodness!' Ruth sat up in bed at once. 'I've been that worried. Are you all right? I've been ringing your home, but it seems the lines are down.'

'I'm not surprised,' Fleur whispered. 'There's been an air raid in the Newark area, but I was in Nottingham.'

Ruth's chuckle came out of the darkness. 'Now why doesn't that surprise me? Good job you've got back when you have, else you'd've been for it. How did you get back? Are the trains running?'

'No. I met three RAF lads coming here, would you believe, and we shared a taxi.'

'A taxi? Heavens! Have you come into a fortune?'

'No,' Fleur giggled softly as she climbed into her single bed. 'They paid. But the driver was very generous. Didn't charge us the going rate as we're RAF. His lad's serving down south.'

Ruth sighed and lay down. 'There's still some nice people about.'

They lay in silence for a few minutes and Fleur was just about to fall asleep when Ruth asked tentatively, 'D'you think your folks are all right? I mean, you said the air raid was in the Newark area, didn't you?'

'Mmm,' Fleur said sleepily. 'They'd be after the airfield there, I expect. But we live several miles from Newark. Right out in the country. There's nothing there worth bombing.'

'But the telephone lines are down.'

Fleur yawned. 'Well, they will be, won't they? But they'll be all right. Our farm's miles from anywhere. Right out in the wilds. Dad didn't even build a shelter...' And with that, she fell asleep.

But for some reason she couldn't explain, Ruth was left wide awake staring into the darkness.

Forty-Six

Meg read the news in the paper the next morning and her blood ran cold.

The bombing raid last night in the Newark area caused loss of life and severe damage to properties. Several of the bombs fell outside their target and a remote farmhouse some distance to the west of the town, which should have been considered relatively safe, received a direct hit. The farmer received extensive burns whilst trying to rescue his wife from the building, which was destroyed by fire. Sadly, his efforts were in vain and his wife perished. The man is in hospital and is thought to be in a critical condition. The names of the casualties have not yet been released as next of kin have yet to be informed.

'Robbie, oh, Robbie...' Meg was hurrying up the stairs to his bedroom, breathless as she pushed open the door. 'Oh, Robbie, it's Jake – it's Fleur's folks. I know it is.'

'What?' The young man sat up in bed and snatched the paper from her trembling hands. He scanned the newsprint whilst she sank down on the end of the bed, clasping and unclasping her hands in agitation.

He looked up at her. 'It doesn't mention South Monkford. It could be anyone. It doesn't even give the name of the farm. What makes you think it's them?'

Meg stared at him and pressed her hands to her bosom. 'But South Monkford is west of Newark. And I just know, Robbie. I feel it. In here. I know it sounds daft to you, but I just know.'

'Well, there's one way to find out,' Robbie said, swinging his legs out of the bed and hoisting himself upright. 'We'll ring the hospitals.'

'Oh, Robbie, can we do that?'

He looked down at her and tenderly touched her cheek. 'Anything, Ma, to take that devastated look off your face.'

Robbie spent half the morning in the phone box at the end of the street, feeding in coins one after another and hopping on his crutches between it and the corner shop for more change. After several calls – he lost count how many – he replaced the receiver slowly and pushed open the door of the box. As it swung to he leant against it briefly and his glance went to the front door of his home.

She was standing on the step, her hands clasped together, looking up the street towards him, but as he pushed himself away from the phone box and began to limp towards her, he saw her fingers flutter to her mouth. Then she turned and disappeared inside the house.

She knew already, from the droop of his shoulders, that he was about to bring her bad news.

The news was broken to Fleur by Caroline Davidson. How many more tragedies is this poor girl going to face? she was thinking as she said gently, 'My dear, we have just received information that your home was hit in last night's air raid.'

Fleur swayed momentarily, but remarkably she remained standing at attention. Silently, she was thinking, I was glad that it wasn't the city getting it last night and all the time... But aloud, all she said was, 'Are they dead, ma'am?'

'Your mother – I'm sorry – yes, but your father is in hospital. Evidently, he wasn't in the house when it was hit, but he tried to get into the burning building to save her. He's ... he's very badly hurt, my dear, but he is still alive.' There was a pause and her unspoken words seemed to hang in the air. At the moment. 'He's in hospital in Nottingham. I need hardly say you are released from your duties immediately. I am issuing you with a seventy-two-hour pass on compassionate grounds...'

The journey back to Nottingham by public transport was impossible, but Caroline had pulled strings and arranged a lift for Fleur with an RAF vehicle due to go to the city that day. The journey seemed to take three times as long as normal. All the way, Fleur repeated the same prayer. 'Don't let him die. Oh, please don't let him die.'

This time she made no rash bargain with God, but just prayed simply and directly.

She reached the hospital late at night, and though their resources were already stretched the nurses found her a bed in an unoccupied side ward for the night.

'If we need it, we'll have to turf you out,' they told her cheerfully. 'Now, come along to the staff room and we'll get you something to eat.'

'How is he? Can I see him?' was all Fleur wanted to know.

'Best not tonight, love, he's sleeping now.'

'Can't I just see him? I promise not to disturb him.'

'I should wait until the morning, love.' The sister was gentle and understanding but there was a note of authority in her tone. 'You'll feel better able to cope after a night's rest.'

'Is he ... is he ... that bad?'

The woman's face sobered. 'He's not good, my dear. I can't lie to you, but the doctor will talk to you tomorrow.'

'Does he – my father, I mean – know about my mother?'

Sadly, the sister nodded. 'Yes.' More briskly, she went on, 'Now, a bite to eat, a sleeping pill and into bed with you, my girl.'

Exhausted by the journey, grieving for her mother and worried sick about her father, Fleur did not expect to sleep a wink. But the sister's pill knocked her out for a full ten hours and she might have slept even longer if a merry little trainee nurse hadn't bounced into the room, pulled open the curtains and woken her up.

'I've brought you some breakfast, miss,' she

beamed. 'We don't do this for everyone, but your dad's a bit special.'

Fleur heaved herself up in the bed and rubbed her eyes. 'Oh?'

'Oh, yes. We've all been vying to be the nurse who looks after him.'

'Has he come round then?'

'He comes round for a bit and keeps apologizing for being such a trouble. But he isn't, miss, I promise you. Then he drifts off again. But he's a duck, ain't he?'

Despite her anxiety, Fleur smiled. She looked down at the tray, not expecting to be able to eat a thing. To her surprise, she suddenly found she was very hungry.

'How is he?'

The little nurse's face clouded. She moved closer to the bed. 'It ain't my place to say, miss. You must ask the doctor or Sister, but' – she leant closer – 'he's still very poorly but I heard 'em say he's going in the right direction, if you know what I mean. But – please – don't tell 'em I said owt, will yer. I could get the sack.'

'Of course I won't. And thank you.'

'That's all right. See yer later.'

Fleur finished her breakfast, washed and dressed and stripped the bed. She knew it would have to be changed, and anything she could do to help the busy nurses she would do.

Now, she thought, taking a deep breath, I wonder if they'll let me see Dad.

He was in a small ward with three other seriously ill patients, each with their own nurse. Though

428

she had tried to prepare herself, Fleur gasped when she saw her father swathed in bandages. She wouldn't have recognized him.

'He was badly burned,' the sister told her. 'But the medical profession are making huge strides in the treatment of burns. It's because of the war, you know. So many pilots, poor boys, get burned when they're shot down.'

Fleur shuddered. It could so easily have been Robbie she was coming to visit. Robbie lying in the bed...

She moved closer. 'Dad? It's me. How ... how are you feeling?' It was a stupid question, but she didn't know what else to say.

He didn't answer her and she glanced up at the sister, a question in her eyes.

'Keep talking to him. We want to try to get him to regain consciousness fully. And you're the best person to get him to do that, Meg.'

Fleur stared at the sister. 'Why did you call me "Meg"?'

The sister blinked. 'Er – I'm sorry. I thought that was your name.' Obviously embarrassed, she looked first at her patient and then back to the girl.

'No, it isn't, but just tell me why you thought it was?'

'Er – it's the only name he's said when he's drifted in and out of consciousness.' The sister's face cleared. 'Oh, it was your mother's name, was it?'

Slowly, Fleur shook her head. 'No, as a matter of fact, it wasn't.'

'Oh dear, I am sorry. I shouldn't have said anything.' The sister was obviously upset and worried. 'I have put my foot in it, haven't I?'

The sister was only young for the post she held, little older than she was, Fleur thought. In all the forces, promotion came earlier and earlier and the nursing profession was every bit a fighting force as any of the others. They were all working round the clock for the same thing: the end of this war.

'It's all right.' Fleur touched her arm. 'Honestly. The thing is – I know who Meg is. And if he's calling for her then–?'

The sister nodded. 'Yes, if you could find her. It really might help him.'

'Oh yes,' Fleur whispered. 'I can find her.'

Forty-Seven

'Sit down, dear. There's something I have to tell you.'

'Oh no, it's not Fleur's dad, is it? You haven't heard something, have you, Ma?'

'No, no. Just – sit down, Robbie. Please.'

Robbie lowered himself into the old man's chair and waited whilst his mother settled herself on the opposite side of the fireplace. For a long moment, she stared into the fire, the flames dancing on her beautiful face. Robbie stared at her, marvelling at her smooth skin, at how young she still looked. It never ceased to amaze him that there wasn't a line of men beating a path to their door.

Slowly, she raised her head to meet his gaze. 'There's something I have to tell you. Something that – maybe – I should have told you years ago, but ... but I couldn't bring myself to do it. I was so frightened of ... of losing you.'

'Losing me!' Robbie leant forward, a little awkwardly because of the thick plaster on his leg still hampering his movements. Then he moved to sit on the hearthrug at her feet, taking her hands and holding them tightly. Earnestly, he said, 'Darling Ma, whatever it is, you couldn't lose me. Not ever. Not ... not the way you're meaning.'

They stared at each other for a moment, each knowing just how close they had come to Robbie being lost, but a different kind of 'lost'.

'When ... when you were missing, Jake told Fleur and ... and it's not fair of me to expect her to keep such a secret from you – from her husband.'

Robbie was silent, giving his mother time to tell her story. A story that was obviously difficult, maybe painful, for her to tell.

He stroked her hands tenderly. Those clever hands that had earned them a living all these years. Hands that had caressed him and nurtured him. Hands that lovingly nursed the old man now asleep upstairs.

Then slowly, haltingly at first, Meg began to tell Robbie about her past. Her shameful past. How she had once been a wilful, selfish girl, who had cared nothing for the feelings of others in her desire for security.

'You'll have to be patient with me, because I want to tell you everything. Right from the very

431

beginning. I'll miss nothing out and then you can ... can judge for yourself just what sort of a woman you have for a mother.'

He squeezed her hands encouragingly. 'I'm not going to judge you, Ma. Whatever it is.'

Meg lifted her shoulders in a tiny shrug. 'Well, we'll see,' she murmured.

Another silence before she took a deep breath and began. 'We were such a happy little family, Dad, Mam, Bobbie and me.'

'Bobbie? Who's Bobbie?'

Meg nodded and smiled a little. She was perhaps the one who was going to have to be patient with his interruptions. 'My little brother. You're named after him.'

'Your brother? I didn't know you had a brother.'

Meg nodded and her voice was husky as she went on. 'We lived in a small cottage on Middle-ditch Farm...'

Again Robbie could not keep silent. 'Middle-ditch Farm? But – but that's Fleur's home...' He stopped, realizing that the farmhouse now lay in ruins.

'Pops worked as a waggoner for the Small-woods who owned the farm then. And I worked as a dairy maid for Mrs Smallwood.' A small smile twitched at her mouth as she added wryly, 'She was a tartar to work for. I was always in trouble with her. "You'll come to a bad end," she used to say to me.' Again she paused. 'Maybe she was right.'

'Oh, Ma, don't say that. You call this "a bad end"?'

'No, of course not. I'm content. At least...' She

sighed inwardly. Was she about to jeopardize her contented life with her son when he heard the truth about her? Bravely, she pushed on. 'I was a bit cheeky and ... and a bit of a flirt with the village lads. I was friendly with Alice Smallwood, their daughter. She was older than me and – if anything – it was her that was the flirt, but her mother thought *I* was the bad influence on *her*. Anyway, we jogged along quite happily, I thought, until one night my dad came home and said we'd both been dismissed without a reference and we were being turned out of our home too. It was a tied cottage, you see. It went with the job.' Meg bit her lip as if reliving the moment. 'I thought it was my fault. I thought I'd been cheeky to the missis once too often.'

'And was it?' Robbie asked softly.

Meg shook her head. 'No. It ... it was Pops. He – well, I'll come to that in a minute. We had to leave the very next day and the only place we could go was the workhouse.'

'The workhouse?' Robbie was shocked. 'That big building on the outskirts of South Monkford?'

'You've seen it?'

He nodded. 'Oh, Ma,' he breathed sadly. 'You've lived in the workhouse?'

She smiled thinly. 'Dad took us there.' Talking of the times past, Meg referred to him by the name she had called him then, not 'Pops' as he was now known. 'Mam – she was expecting another baby – Bobbie and me. He left us there. Said he was going to look for work and that he'd come back for us...' Her voice trailed away for a moment, but then she took another deep breath

433

and continued. 'But the weeks went by and he didn't come back. We had to work of course – in that place. Mam wasn't very well but they let her do mending and easy work. And they put me to work with the school marm. And for a while, I thought she was my friend. She was very kind to me. She was in charge of all the children and had to look after them all the time. One night, there was a little girl who was ill.' Meg glanced at Robbie. 'Actually, it was Betsy, Fleur's mum.'

Now Robbie was truly horrified. 'Fleur's mum was in the workhouse?'

Meg nodded. 'And so was Jake. He'd been born in there. So that's where I met them. Jake and I were friends even though we were segregated. Girls and boys, men and women. Poor Jake got a beating once for being seen with me.'

'And Fleur's mum? Were you friends with her?'

Meg ran her tongue round her dry lips. 'Not … not exactly. She was younger than us. Jake and me, I mean. Anyway, this night she was ill, the school marm left me in charge of Betsy when Isaac Pendleton sent for her. He was the master of the workhouse – a lecherous old devil...' She paused and then put her head on one side thoughtfully. 'No, actually, that's not quite fair. And I am trying to tell you this very truthfully. He was a ladies' man, but he could be very kind.' She sighed. 'I didn't see it that way then, but now I have to admit that he was. In his own way. Well, at that time he had his eye on Louisa, the school marm–'

Again, Robbie could not help interrupting. 'That's not the woman Fleur calls Aunt Louisa, is it? Mrs Dr Collins?'

'Yes. She was working as the schoolmistress at the workhouse. I believe she had an elderly mother she was supporting. She was engaged to Philip Collins then, and was trying to avoid old Isaac as much as she could. So, this particular night, she left her watch with me and told me that after a certain time, I was to go and knock on his door and say that she was needed – that Betsy was worse. I did just as she said, but when we got back the watch was missing and she accused me of having stolen it. I hadn't, of course. Whatever else I may be, I'm not a thief. Anyway, it turned out that Betsy had it. She'd wanted to hear it ticking. It reminded her of her daddy, she said. Louisa apologized but I was impulsive and fiery in those days–'

'Must be the red hair,' Robbie teased and they both smiled.

'And I was unforgiving. Oh, Robbie, how unforgiving I was. I suppose, looking back, that was what caused all the trouble. If only I had been more willing to forgive and forget then maybe–'

'Go on, Ma,' he prompted gently as Meg seemed to get side-tracked. 'What happened?'

'I refused to work with Louisa any more. I couldn't forgive her for having accused me. And – quite wrongly – I bore Betsy a grudge too. I said I'd rather scrub floors than work with Louisa. And I did,' she added wryly. She sighed again and went on. 'Anyway, I'm getting a bit ahead of myself. Earlier that same day, my mother had gone into labour and the baby was stillborn.'

She saw Robbie wince but he said nothing.

'So a couple of weeks later I decided I should

try to find my dad and tell him what had happened to Mam and the baby. And ... and I just wanted to see him anyway. I got permission from the master to go in search of him, and Jake came with me.' Now she smiled. '*Without* permission.'

'Ooh-er,' Robbie said imagining the severe punishment he might have incurred.

'He didn't care. He wanted to be with me.'

'Did you find your dad? Pops?'

'Oh yes, we found him all right.' Meg's voice was suddenly hard as she relived that dreadful day. 'We went to the racecourse. He was so good with horses that Farmer Smallwood sometimes took Dad with him when he went to the races. And then we saw him, walking along, bold as you like, with his arm around Alice Smallwood.'

Robbie blinked. 'His arm? Alice Smallwood?'

Meg nodded and now there was no hiding the bitterness in her tone. 'My father had been having an affair with the daughter of his – of our – employers. They had found out and turned him and all his family out because of it. So, it wasn't my fault as I had feared. It was his.'

'Pops? I can't believe it.'

Meg raised a smile. 'Oh, Pops wasn't always the frail old man you see now.'

'Well, no. When he first came to live with us he was still – well – quite sprightly.'

'When he was younger, he was a fine figure of a man, I have to admit.'

There was a long silence before Robbie asked gently, 'So – what happened then?'

'I went back to the workhouse, but from that moment on I cut him out of my life and vowed

436

I'd never forgive him. It was up to me to take care of my mother. I went out into the town to seek work and I found it. With poor Percy Rodwell in his tailor's shop.'

'Why do you say "poor" Percy Rodwell?'

Meg sighed. 'He was a lovely man. A kind and generous man and I ... I seduced him.'

'Oh, Ma! Whatever next?' Robbie began to laugh, but seeing his mother's serious face, he stopped. 'Mind you,' he added. 'You're still a stunner, so I expect the poor bloke hadn't got a chance.'

For a brief moment Meg's eyes sparkled with mischief. 'He hadn't.'

She explained about his long-standing engagement with the sour-faced Miss Finch and how, when Percy jilted her to marry Meg, he found himself in court on a charge of breach of promise. 'Poor Percy,' she murmured. 'He really didn't deserve all the trouble I brought to his door.'

'What happened to your mother and to your little brother?'

'Bobbie fell ill soon after I'd found out about my father.'

Robbie was intrigued by the way Meg kept referring to the man he knew affectionately as 'Pops' as 'my father'. It was as if she, too, couldn't think of them now as one and the same person.

'And he died. D'you know?' she said, the sadness still in her tone even after all the years. 'We buried little Bobbie on my sixteenth birthday.'

'And ... and your mother?'

Meg's mouth hardened even more. 'She became Isaac Pendleton's mistress. I disapproved and refused to see her ever again. Jake tried to persuade me to go to see her. In the end I did, but I was told she had no wish to see me. I think it was a lie – in fact, I know it was now. I did go, truly I did.' She met his gaze, pleading with him to believe her. He gave her hands another little squeeze. 'But she fell ill and died before ... before I could make it up with her.'

'So why did you think all this was so very dreadful, Ma? I mean, I know it's a shame you didn't make it up with your mother, but you were young and...'

'I haven't finished yet.'

'Ah.'

'I married Percy and the following year Louisa and Philip were married. Then the war came. Jake volunteered in 1916 and he married Betsy before he went. Then Philip went too. They were lucky – they both came back, but then we got that dreadful epidemic of influenza. Percy caught it.' She bit her lip. 'And I called Philip – Dr Collins. I ... I'd always known he ... he was attracted to me and ... and I was lonely. Percy was ill – dying – and I... I mean we–'

'You had an affair with Dr Collins?' Robbie said gently, without any note of censure in his tone.

Meg nodded and tears filled her eyes. 'It was wicked of me. I ... I still felt resentment against Louisa for believing I could have stolen her watch. You see? I never forgave anyone. And yet I did worse things myself than ever they'd done. Far worse.'

'How long did the affair go on?'

'Not long. When Percy died, Philip had an attack of conscience. It finished, but by then, of course, you'd been conceived.'

Robbie raised her hands to his lips and kissed them gently. 'So – Dr Philip Collins is my natural father?'

'Yes,' Meg whispered. 'But I want you to believe me, Robbie, that whilst I do regret so many of the things I did, I do not regret having you. Not for one moment. And if I hadn't had the affair, I wouldn't have had you. But it wasn't really until after you were born that I changed.'

Swiftly she recounted what Jake had already told Fleur about Miss Finch and her twisted belief that she had a right to Meg's baby boy. 'Angry and disgusted though Jake was with me – oh, he knew all about me. There was no hiding the truth from Jake – he still came to my rescue when I needed him. I suppose,' she ended reflectively, 'that's why Betsy has hated me all these years. From what Fleur says, Betsy believed that Jake still loves me.'

'Maybe he does, Ma,' Robbie said softly. There was a long silence between them until Robbie said at last, 'And what about – my father? Does he know that I'm his son? Has he always known?'

Meg nodded. 'He came to see me when he heard you'd been posted missing. He ... he said that if ... if a miracle happened and you came back that he wanted to meet you. Get to know you.'

'Did he indeed? And what would his wife say to that? Does *she* know, d'you think?'

'Yes. She does now. Perhaps – perhaps she's

always suspected, but now she knows for certain. You you're so like he used to be as a young man. Anyone knowing him then and seeing you now...'

'So *that's* why she looked so startled that day I met her in the cafe with Fleur. I thought she was going to pass out.'

'It must have been a shock for her. Specially when she found out just who you were.'

Again there was a long silence between them, before she asked tentatively, 'Do ... do you want to meet him?'

'What do you want me to do?'

'Oh, it's not up to me. Not any more.'

'But will it cause you pain? I wouldn't want that, darling Ma.'

She looked down into his upturned face, his handsome, open, loving face, and tears filled her eyes. 'You ... you don't hate me, then?'

'Oh, Ma!' Again he kissed her fingers. 'How could you even think such a thing?'

'I ... I thought you might be disgusted. I ... I wasn't a very nice person back then, Robbie.'

'You had a tough time.' He laughed gently. 'Because of that old rogue up there. Who'd have thought old Pops could do such a thing? The old rascal, him.'

Suddenly, Meg was frightened. She clung to Robbie. 'Oh, you won't say anything to him. Oh, please, Robbie, don't–'

'Of course I won't. If you can forgive him, then I certainly can.'

'And ... and you forgive me?'

'There's nothing for me to forgive where you're concerned. I'm still me, whoever my father is.'

He paused and cocked his head on one side. 'Did you love him very much, Ma?'

Meg bit her lip. 'That ... that's the worst part. I don't think I loved him at all. I was just lonely and ... and he was handsome and besotted with me.' She looked him straight in the eyes then, meeting his gaze as she said solemnly, 'There's only one man I've ever truly loved, but I was too blind, too ambitious and too selfish to see it. And I've spent the rest of my life regretting that – through my own stupidity – I lost him.'

Slowly, Robbie nodded. 'You're talking about Fleur's dad, aren't you?'

Meg nodded and whispered, 'Yes. Jake was the only man I've ever really loved. And – once upon a time – I know he did love me. But I lost him. I lost my beloved Jake.'

Forty-Eight

Fleur knocked on the door of the terraced house and then waited for what seemed an age. At last, thinking they must be out, she turned away, disappointed. But she had only taken a few steps when the door opened and Robbie stood there.

'Sorry, it takes me a while to get to the door. Fleur, darling, how is he?'

'Oh, Robbie!' She rushed to him and was enfolded in his strong arms. He held her tightly, believing the worst had happened.

'Darling, I'm so sorry,' he murmured against

441

her hair.

'No, no, it's not that,' she said, her voice muffled against him. She pulled back a little to say, 'He's all right. Well, he isn't – what I mean is, he's still alive.'

There was puzzlement in Robbie's eyes and she knew exactly what he must be thinking: then why aren't you with him?

'I've come for your mother,' Fleur was babbling in her anxiety. 'He's asking for her.'

'Asking for my mother?' Robbie was startled.

'Yes – yes. She will come, won't she? Is she here?'

'Oh yes, she's here, but as for coming to the hospital–'

Fleur's eyes widened. 'She won't refuse to come, will she? Oh, she can't. She must come. It might help him. It *will* help him. I know it will.'

'It's not that, Fleur. But she ... she's not well herself. Come in and see for yourself. She's just sat by the fire, not moving. She's been like that ever since yesterday.'

He drew her into the front room and closed the door. They did not move further into the house, but stood just inside the door whilst Robbie whispered, 'We had a long talk the night before last. She told me everything. All about what your dad told you.'

Fleur nodded. 'I'm glad you know. It wasn't my place to tell you but I hated having a secret from you. You do understand that, don't you, Robbie?'

'Of course.' He ran his hand distractedly through his hair as if, at this precise moment, that was the least of his worries. 'But ever since

442

then, she's just sat there. She's not even been to bed for two nights. She's not eating or even drinking. I'm at my wits' end...'

'Let me see her.' Fleur pushed past him and almost ran through the front room and into the back part of the house.

Just as Robbie had said, Meg was sitting by the fire, her hands lying limply in her lap. She was just staring into space, oblivious to everything around her. Across the hearth, the old man sat huddled in his chair, staring helplessly at his daughter. He didn't speak, merely nodded at Fleur and then wiped away a tear running down his wrinkled cheek.

Fleur knelt in front of Meg and touched her hand. It felt cold, almost lifeless. 'Mrs Rodwell,' she began gently, 'I've come to ask you a big favour.'

There was no response from the woman. She seemed unaware of Fleur's presence.

'See?' Robbie said as he limped into the room. 'I told you. I can't get her to do anything. She won't even speak to me. I can't get through to her.'

Taking both Meg's hands in hers, she said firmly, 'Mrs Rodwell, listen to me. My dad needs you. *Jake* needs you.'

Meg blinked and seemed to be trying to focus her eyes on Fleur. It was the name 'Jake' that had prompted a tiny response. Fleur latched on to it. 'Jake wants to see you. He's asking for you. Please, will you come and see him? Come and see Jake.'

Meg's lips moved stiffly and her voice was husky. 'Jake?'

'Yes – Jake. He's in hospital. He's drifting in and out of consciousness. I can't reach him. I've tried. I've been there all morning and he won't wake up. Not for me. And the only name the nurses have heard him say is "Meg". Oh, please.' She gripped the woman's hand even tighter and her voice was full of tears. 'Oh, please, say you'll come.'

Meg stirred as if she was awaking from a trance. 'Me? He ... he's asking for me?'

'Yes.'

But Meg was shaking her head. 'I can't.'

'Why ever not?' Fleur cried passionately. 'Don't you want to help him? Surely – whatever happened in the past – you can put it aside to ... to save his *life*, can't you?'

'You don't understand. It's not *me* who doesn't want to see *him*...' Her voice trailed away and tears trembled on her eyelashes.

'But he's asking for you.'

Meg shook her head. 'He doesn't know what he's saying. He must be delirious. He – he won't want to see me. Besides, it wouldn't be right. With poor Betsy only just – only just...'

'It can't hurt my mother now,' Fleur insisted. 'She's gone. If she was still alive, then I wouldn't be asking you, but she isn't. Dad is and he needs you.'

'What will people say...?' Meg asked. 'Folks have long memories.'

'Look,' Fleur cried passionately, 'I don't give a damn about what anyone might say. I don't care about what happened years ago. I don't even care that my mother hated the very sound of your name...' She saw Meg flinch and was sorry she

444

had been so blunt, but she pressed on now. 'I don't care about any of that. All I care about is my dad and trying to keep him alive. I – I can't bear to lose him.' The final words ended on a sob and she buried her face in Meg's lap.

She felt the older woman's gentle touch on her hair and heard her say, 'Neither can I, Fleur. Oh, neither can I.'

The ward was quiet and peaceful in the middle of the afternoon. The morning flurry of doctors' visits had passed and the daily routine of work finished.

'It's not really visiting time,' the sister greeted them, 'but you, I take it, are Meg?'

Meg, still looking anxious as if she didn't feel she had the right to be there, nodded.

The sister turned to Fleur. 'There's no change, I'm afraid, since this morning. But maybe now...' She did not finish her sentence, but glanced hopefully back at Meg. 'Come this way.'

They followed the sister and, as she led them towards Jake's bed, Fleur heard Meg pull in a sharp breath at the sight of him, but she controlled her feelings and sat down in the chair beside him.

His hands and arms were bandaged and most of his face was covered with dressings. There was nothing she could touch. She couldn't hold his hand, couldn't kiss his face. All she could do was say, 'Jake, it's me. It's Meg. I'm here.'

Fleur and Robbie stood at the end of the bed, their arms around one another. They all saw Jake's eyes flicker open and he tried to turn his head towards the sound of her voice. Meg stood up and leant over him.

His eyes focused slowly and he saw her face as he remembered her. Her red flying hair, her smooth skin, her smile. Oh, her smile! That heartbreaking smile of hers. To him she was still the young girl he had met all those years ago. The girl whose strong spirit had lifted him out of the workhouse. The girl he'd loved and lost and who, despite his contented life with Betsy and his children, he'd never been able to forget.

'Meg, oh, Meggie. You came.' The words were faint and slightly slurred but understandable.

At the end of the bed, Fleur buried her face into Robbie's jacket and wept tears of thankfulness. He was going to be all right. Her dad was going to be all right.

'Yes, Jake,' Meg was saying simply. 'I came. I'm here to stay and I shan't leave you. Not unless you tell me to.'

He tried to lift his hand to touch her face, but winced with the pain. 'I won't do that, Meggie. Not ever.'

'Then just rest, Jake, and get well. I'll be right here. Always...'

If the past was not entirely forgotten, at least now it was all forgiven.

The publishers hope that this book has given you enjoyable reading. Large Print Books are especially designed to be as easy to see and hold as possible. If you wish a complete list of our books please ask at your local library or write directly to:

Magna Large Print Books
Magna House, Long Preston,
Skipton, North Yorkshire.
BD23 4ND

This Large Print Book for the partially sighted, who cannot read normal print, is published under the auspices of

THE ULVERSCROFT FOUNDATION

M D